FRANCINE'S
SPECTACULAR
CRASH AND BURN

FRANCINE'S SPECTACULAR CRASH AND BURN

✦ a novel ✦

Renee Swindle

Tiny
Reparations
Books

An imprint of Penguin Random House LLC
1745 Broadway, New York, NY 10019
penguinrandomhouse.com

LIBRARY OF CONGRESS CATALOGING-IN-PUBLICATION DATA

Names: Swindle, Renée, author.
Title: Francine's spectacular crash and burn: a novel / Renee Swindle.
Description: First edition. | New York: Tiny Reparations Books, 2025.
Identifiers: LCCN 2024031115 | ISBN 9780593475584 (trade paperback) |
ISBN 9780593475607 (ebook)
Subjects: LCGFT: Novels.
Classification: LCC PS3569.W537 F73 2025 |
DDC 813/.54—dc23/eng/20240705
LC record available at https://lccn.loc.gov/2024031115

Printed in the United States of America
1st Printing

BOOK DESIGN BY LAURA K. CORLESS

The authorized representative in the EU for product safety and compliance is
Penguin Random House Ireland, Morrison Chambers, 32 Nassau Street,
Dublin D02 YH68, Ireland, https://eu-contact.penguin.ie

For my mother

FRANCINE'S SPECTACULAR CRASH AND BURN

CHAPTER ONE

'm not going to spend too much time telling you about my mother's death. I have to tell you about it because it's what started everything, but her passing isn't the point. I mean, it's not the focus. Not really. I will say that even after all the therapy in the world I still sometimes blame myself for what happened, or I'll blame Aunt Liane, even though neither is true; no one was to blame. Prior to her death there was nothing going on in my life—just the days sort of bleeding into each other. I was twenty-five years old, living at home, and I spent most of my time with my mother. And yes, it was as pathetic as it sounds.

Mom gave astrological readings and motivational talks. I was in charge of filming her YouTube channel. She was corny as hell, but her followers liked her videos and trusted her readings. At the time she had over a hundred thousand subscribers.

Anyway, Sunday, two days before she died, she sat behind her desk wearing a bright yellow raincoat and hat like a meteorologist stuck in a storm. She used all kinds of props and costumes in her videos; the garage was filled with her stuff.

I fixed the lens so that it held tightly on her face. "Ready?"

She did one of her warm-up exercises—closing her eyes and blowing through her lips, making them vibrate like a rudder. She gave a nod and I counted off like a director on a movie set.

"Good morning, love doves. Corrina Stevenson here with today's astrological weather sighting. Jupiter enters Aquarius, so take hold; it's going to get stormy!"

She picked up the umbrella next to her desk and gave it a twirl. Like I said, corny as hell.

"My Leos, it's time to start that project you've had on the back burner; the winds of Venus will be growing stronger, which will create problems if you're not prepared."

We made her videos on the weekends and posted them throughout the month, one or two per week. At the end of each reading, Mom shared advice—things she'd read in books or heard from the self-help gurus she followed. She'd put her own personal spin on the lesson and pass it on. It was all bullshit when you considered the lie she was living. She was like all the other charlatans out there, like those preachers damning you from the pulpit, then you find out they're having an affair or molesting a kid. Well, she wasn't that bad. I guess you could say she was more like the celebrity you thought was living their best life, only to learn they'd checked themself into rehab.

Mom suffered from anxiety and bouts of agoraphobia that were so bad she wouldn't leave the house for weeks at a time, sometimes months if I let her get away with it. You'd never have known any of this based on the videos or if you met with her over Zoom for a reading, yet she ticked off every box for the most severe cases of agoraphobia. I asked her several times what started it, if something had happened, but she'd never tell me anything except BS like, "The past is the past for a reason, and I refuse to live there."

For the last video, Mom changed into a Viking princess costume with a Viking hat that had long blond ponytails attached to the inside.

Mom had soft features: big warm brown eyes, a small gap between her front teeth. I knew her heart was in the right place, but the blond wig clashed with her dark brown skin, and at five feet four inches, she was nearly three hundred pounds and the dress she wore tight and ill fitting.

I counted off. Pointed. She held up her plastic sword and shield, did her thing until I said cut.

"Are you sure that was okay?"

I was tired and ready to tell her whatever she needed to hear. "You were great."

"I don't know. I feel like my energy is off today. I think it's because you-know-who is coming."

You-know-who was my Aunt Liane, my mom's half sister. Those two couldn't stand each other.

She took off the silly Viking hat. "Go and get me a pill, would you?"

"You already had your pill."

She begged, and we went back and forth. Mom and I bickered like enemies at times, but she was my best friend, my only friend, really, and I knew how much Aunt Liane stressed her, so we compromised on her taking half a pill.

"Thanks, baby." She smiled her Corrina Stevenson smile, the smile she saved for her videos. I hated that smile.

Her pills were lined up on the kitchen counter under the windowsill. She'd stopped taking her regular medication about two years before, after one of her clients, Alfonse, became her direct supplier. We weren't sure how Alfonse—he didn't give his last name—a man from the Czech Republic of all places, had access to so many drugs. We assumed he was a chemist or pharmacist. Mom didn't ask and Alfonse never disclosed his secret. Through the tarot, she predicted his wife was cheating and guided him through his divorce. Eventually, they became friends and she told him about her anxiety and depression. One day, she read his chart and advised him not to go to work. Sure enough, the train he normally took jumped the rails, leaving two passengers dead and several others injured. He'd paid her back for saving his life by sending her pills. *You no longer go to doctor. I take care of you*, his note read.

And boy, did he take care of her. No matter how much I complained, she refused to go back to her regular meds. The prescriptions were printed in Czech, so Alfonse wrote on the labels with a black marker in scrawny script and poor English, instructions like TAKE THESE WHEN YOUR SAD ALWAYS or TAKE THESE FOR GOOD SLEEP.

I halved a pill from the bottle TAKE THESE FOR VERY GOOD COURAGE and poured a glass of orange juice.

Mom's anxiety had started several years earlier, around my freshman year of high school. She'd always had bouts of depression, but with my help—and this meant sometimes pleading with her to get out of bed—she was able to keep her job working in the human resources department at East Bay Utilities.

Over time, she stopped letting *anyone* into the house. But her YouTube business kept growing and she started selling bath potions and oils meant to help customers ward off bad juju and manifest the life of their dreams. By the time I'd graduated from high school, she was living solely off her astrology business and a telemarketing job she'd found that required no commute.

I had a shitload of resentment toward her during that time, which you'll have to forgive me for. I mean, I had no idea she was going to *die*. How was I supposed to know she was going to *die*? Which leads me to telling you right now, ask forgiveness, accept the apology, ask the burning questions, give the hugs, and say your I-love-yous, because it may be cheesy AF, but it's true: We are all on borrowed time. Every one of us.

CHAPTER TWO

Aunt Liane and Uncle CJ showed up a few hours after we'd wrapped up filming. It was a week before Christmas. Uncle CJ was a Jehovah's Witness, so out of respect, Mom and I decided not to put up a tree until he was out of sight. Neither of us was into the holiday anyway since there was no one to celebrate it with. Aunt Liane and Uncle CJ were our only remaining relatives, and the best thing about Aunt Liane was that she lived in Fresno, a two-and-a-half-hour drive from Oakland, which meant we didn't have to see her much. My dad, I should mention, died when I was nine years old. He was one of a handful of black foremen in the Bay Area and was struck by a beam on a construction site. He was the kind of man who liked to joke around. Like the time he gave me a plate of Oreo cookies but had secretly replaced the fillings with toothpaste—that kind of thing.

Aunt Liane and Mom lasted a good thirty minutes before the bickering started. Aunt Liane said something about Mom's weight, and Mom mentioned getting plenty of exercise from working in her garden.

Aunt Liane rolled her eyes. "Planting flowers is not exercise." Her latest weave featured maroon-colored strands that framed her face. She was always very matchy-matchy: her blouse was maroon, the heavy makeup she wore was maroon, and her nails, decorated with tiny gold studs at the tips and as long as mosquito legs, were also maroon. She and Mom were as opposite as characters in a Grimm fairy tale. Aunt Liane was toothpick thin and hadn't seen her real hair in decades, while Mom was big and kept her hair natural. The only resemblances their drunk father passed down to them were their dimpled chins, dark skin, and emotional trauma.

Aunt Liane pulled back the foil on the scalloped potatoes she'd brought. "Are you using the Fitbit I got you?" She turned to me before Mom had time to respond. "Has she been getting out at all? Has she been going on her walks?"

Mom tossed her head back and barked. Literally. "Ruff! Ruff!"—followed by a burst of laughter. That's when I noticed her pupils pirouetting about in her eyes like ballerinas on steroids. *Shit.* "I'm not a dog, Liane."

Aunt Liane frowned. "No one said you were a dog, Corrina."

She turned to put the potatoes in the oven, giving me a second to join Mom at the sink. "How many?" I whispered.

She raised two fingers.

Two?! I mouthed. I looked over my shoulder to see if Aunt Liane was paying attention, but she was busy checking the pot roast. "You've been taking too many pills lately," I whispered.

"Don't be mad. She drives me crazy." Mom twirled her finger near her ear and crossed her eyes.

I shook my head. We were never going to get anywhere at this point.

Aunt Liane opened the drawer for silverware and said to Mom, "We all know the more you stay inside, the worse you get. How long has it been?" She directed her question at me.

Usually I helped defend Mom, but I was pissed she'd taken extra pills behind my back. "Tell her, go on."

Mom pursed her lips. "Almost two months, but I'm perfectly fine."

"That is not fine. What in the hell does it take for a person to open the front door and walk the fuck out? I don't understand." She began one of her never-ending lectures on Mom's weight and her phobias.

There's a reason for Aunt Liane's bitchiness. Isn't there always a reason? Aunt Liane's mother died from cancer when she was ten years old, and not six months later, her rolling-stone drunk of a father knocked up an out-of-work waitress, and out popped Mom nine months later. Drunk Grandpa moved Mom and her mother into his house, and soon after, my mom's mother, the former waitress, decided motherhood wasn't her thing and took off, leaving three-year-old Mom in the care of her big sister, Liane, who was barely fourteen by then. My grandpa stayed wasted, so in a real sense Aunt Liane raised Mom. Who knows what went down in that house? I can only imagine what it was like for Mom to lose her mother and to be raised by her pissed-off teen sister and drunk father.

I took the plates and silverware to the dining table. The kitchen, den, and dining room were a shared space. Uncle CJ sat in a recliner in the den with his cane nearby. He was born in the Stone Age and had suffered a stroke two years before. But Uncle CJ was the sweetest man, before and after the stroke.

I asked if he needed anything. He pointed his good hand toward the TV, and I changed the channel until he gave a thumbs-up to a basketball game. For all Aunt Liane's bitchy attitude, she loved Uncle CJ, and even though they shared a twenty-year age gap, as far as I could tell, the only downside to their relationship, besides his stroke, was that he'd wanted to move from San Leandro to Fresno after he retired so he could be close to his family. And Aunt Liane hated Fresno.

To be honest, Aunt Liane and Uncle CJ were always there for me, especially before their move. Uncle CJ taught me to drive and play chess, and he and Aunt Liane helped me move into my dorm when I went to college and Mom's agoraphobia was acting up—things like that.

◆ ◆ ◆

Later, over dinner, Aunt Liane decided it was my turn to be berated.

"Uncle CJ and I worry about you, you know."

"I'm fine."

She cut into her roast beef, studying me. "You'll be thirty soon."

"I'm twenty-five, give me a minute."

"Time is ticking right on by and you're still living at home and working as a maid."

"I'm not a maid." I don't know how many times I had to tell her this.

"You pick up that white woman's laundry and you babysit her child. Sounds like a maid to me."

"I only had to babysit twice, and both times were emergencies."

Mom returned from wherever Alfonse's pills had taken her. "Oh, Liane. We all know you mean well."

"The child has a degree from UC Berkeley but what is she doing with it?"

"Li," warned Uncle CJ. "Calm."

Aunt Liane looked at him defensively, then said to me: "I own my own salon in country-ass Fresno after starting from scratch and now every black woman in that backward-ass city knows about me. You need to have a goal."

Mom stared at the green bean on the end of her fork as if it had magical powers. "I'm getting better," she said to the green bean. "I've just had a setback."

"You're always having setbacks." Aunt Liane turned her attention to Mom while tucking a maroon-dyed strand of some Indian woman's hair behind her ear. She pointed at Mom with her mile-long nail. "I took care of you when you were a child and now"—she pointed at me—"your daughter is missing out on life because *she's* taking care of you, and I know *exactly* what that feels like."

Mom's expression grew increasingly pained. Even Alfonse's pills couldn't stand up to Aunt Liane's truth bombs. "I help people every day."

"You sure as hell aren't helping your daughter. You two living here like old maids in this weird-ass house."

"*Li,*" Uncle CJ said.

"No, CJ. She needs to hear this."

Mom's eye twitched. She took a breath, her shoulders trembling. *Shit.*

She crossed her fork and knife at the top of her plate as if ending a meal at a fine dining establishment. "I've had enough." And then she got up and left.

"Rina!" Uncle CJ cried. "Back!"

"She'll be okay," Aunt Liane said, shrugging. "She's just looking for attention."

I tossed my napkin on the table and stood up, feeling guilty for not defending Mom in the first place. "I don't know why you have to be so mean."

Aunt Liane pointed up at me. "Do not go after her. Sit down."

But I ignored her and headed straight for Mom's room, where I found her sitting on her bed, clutching one of her jasper crystals to her chest.

"Do you want me to tap?"

She nodded and closed her eyes.

I used the tips of my fingers, tapping lightly on the crown of her head while she repeated words like *safe* and *calm.*

"Better?" I asked.

"I know I'm failing you." Her voice was so quiet I could hardly hear her.

"You're not failing me."

"Yes, I am. Liane is right: I ruined her life, and now I'm ruining yours."

I sat down next to her. "Aunt Liane should learn to keep her mouth closed."

"It's the Scorpio in her. She can't help it. But she's right. I need to do better." She locked her eyes with mine. "I'm going to do better by you, Francine. I am."

We heard a thump followed by a slow dragging sound—Uncle CJ making his way down the hall. He stood in the doorway leaning on his cane. "O... kay?"

Mom said, "I'm fine, CJ. You ready for dessert?"

"Al... ways... ready for... p... pie." He fought the stubborn side of his mouth, motioning at me with his good hand. "We worry... about... Francine."

"I'm fine."

He gave a thumbs-up, trudged back down the hall.

Mom took my hand. "We'll walk together after you get off work."

"And not in the backyard. A real walk. Promise me."

"I promise. Tomorrow will be perfect for a restart; the asteroid Vesta is in Libra and opposes Virgo."

"Whatever, Mom. Just keep your promise."

She smiled and said, "I promise, baby."

And that was Sunday, which meant I had one day left with her.

Hindsight is such a bitch.

CHAPTER THREE

So yeah, about college and how I ended up at Peeps. For starters, we had no AP classes at MacDowell High—we barely had regular teachers who showed up and did their jobs—but I studied my ass off, and despite being... *highly unpopular*, shall we say, I graduated from high school as valedictorian. I was supposed to give a speech for graduation, but I lied and told Mom I was too sick to attend the ceremony. I knew someone would shout rude names in the auditorium as I gave my speech and everyone would laugh, or some other horrible *Carrie*-like incident would occur—pig's blood pouring down on me and all that; I'd spent four years with my classmates and knew what they were capable of. The salutatorian, a girl with a measly 3.2 grade point average, ended up giving the speech. Meanwhile, I hid under the covers in my bed playing sick, imagining I could somehow summon the courage to tell Mom I felt better, then walk across the stage in my cap and gown and give the entire senior class the finger, just span both my middle fingers across rows and rows of my classmates in a highly satisfying *Fuck you*.

UC Berkeley, or Cal, as it's known, was my new start. I loved it there. I liked that I could sit in my classes and actually learn something. I liked that no one knew me. I'd spend my time taking long walks around campus, and in true nerd fashion I even joined the chess club. Cal was also where I discovered my love for photography. I took an art appreciation class as an elective. The professor introduced us to photographers like Gordon Parks and Diane Arbus along with standard painters and sculptors. I started studying their work, then taking pictures with my phone. I even bought a camera and zoom lenses later on. Making the most mundane object or person interesting or beautiful is my personal way of saying I see you.

I lived in the dorms for three years, then moved into a sweet studio on Colby Street, walking distance from the shops and restaurants in Elmwood. I always had to check in on Mom—daily calls, sometimes two, three times a day—and I went by the house at least twice a week, but I was able to make a handful of friends, and I dated, too. Let me tell you, good times. Good times all around.

After graduation, I worked at a nonprofit for five minutes. They had a great mission, helping pregnant teens, but it was so poorly run I started sending out my résumé within a year. I was hired at Peeps, a social media company created to help people find others with the same interests—a kind of Reddit meets Facebook. There was also our dating service, PeepMe, which was so popular it was fast becoming the country's top-rated dating app. *At Peeps the world is your friend!*

Hayden, my boss, had heard of the nonprofit where I'd worked and hired me on the spot, casually mentioning Peeps had diversity issues and needed more people of color. They still had diversity issues, frankly. I mean, I was the only black person who worked there except for the janitor and the security guard. There was also the woman who managed the café, an Afro-Latina. I'm sure she counted as *two* people of color as far as the higher-ups were concerned.

Anyway, Mom and I survived dinner with my aunt and uncle. The following morning, Monday, Hayden greeted me with, "I'll need you to take a few items to the dry cleaners." No hello or good morning, which wasn't like her—just the dry cleaner command. She avoided eye contact, too, which was also kind of weird.

I'd just arrived. She stood in her office riffling through mail. The floor-to-ceiling windows served as backdrop; outside I could see more office buildings and gray skies. Hayden had wickedly straight posture due to years of yoga and Pilates. I was average in height and weight, but just looking at her made me feel like a lazy slob. Her hair was slicked back into a razor-sharp ponytail that landed at the top of her shoulder blades. She was Scandinavian pale, her hair so blond it bordered on white. Cheekbones painted Dior Pink. Lips: Armani Nude Glow #7 or Yves Saint Laurent Nude Beige. Height: five foot eight. Dress size: a paltry 4.

"Did Maddi have fun at Brooklyn's birthday party?" Madison was her six-year-old daughter. It was part of my job to pretend I cared about her kid.

"Pony rides and a mini waterslide. It was very cute. How was your weekend?"

I thought of Aunt Liane berating Mom and me, Mom high on pills. "Nice. Relaxing."

She kept her eyes on her mail. "I had a terrible migraine this morning. I'm better now, but there was an accident. I'd clean it, but I don't have time. Would you mind?" She glanced my way, then went straight back to her mail.

Shit. "There was an accident" was code for: *I didn't make it to the toilet and there's puke you need to clean up.* She had a migraine condition that caused her to erupt without warning if the migraine was bad enough. The janitors didn't arrive until the offices closed at night, which left either her or me. For the record, the other time she'd puked, she'd cleaned up after herself and had only asked me to get the cleaning supplies and take her vomit-stained jacket to the dry cleaners.

She ripped through an envelope with a mail opener. As COO she oversaw daily operations and reported to the founder, Brad Harlington, whose dad gave him and his brother a shitload of money, then told them to go outside and play. Brad used his portion to start Peeps, although he was rarely around. Except for when he showed up in gossip columns with the latest model or actress he was dating, you'd never think about him. It was Hayden who held the reins and kept the shareholders happy.

Her eyes scanned the letter she'd opened. "I know cleaning up after me is a lot to ask, but I have a conference call I need to get to."

I could hear Aunt Liane in my ear: *Don't you dare clean up after her. Bitch needs to clean up her own vomit!* But I thought of the bonus she'd given me the last time she puked, enough to purchase a wide-angle lens out of my price range. Plus, I knew she hated to ask. Hayden wasn't one to avoid eye contact. A part of me felt bad for her.

"I'll get to it right away."

She made an apologetic face. "Thanks, Francine. I don't know what I'd do without you."

You'd clean up your own puke, for starters, I thought.

She handed me the mail she'd been riffling through—"Toss these"— then sat at her desk and turned to her computer. "I need to send off a few numbers before my call."

I picked up her travel mug. The thing was temperature controlled and cost nearly two hundred dollars—I kid you not. Part of my job was rinsing out the mug and getting her a fresh cup of coffee from the café downstairs. "Espresso or cappuccino?"

"Cappuccino." Hayden typed into her computer, her fingers racing across the keyboard. "Did you have a nice weekend?"

I considered reminding her she'd already asked. "It was fine. Relaxing."

"Good. Let's go over my schedule after you've finished with... everything."

"Sure."

Okay, I'll admit it. Maybe I was maid-ish. The thing is, I liked my job. Did I want to clean up Hayden's vomit? Hell no. But I liked that the woman in front of me—a powerful, strong, highly intelligent woman—trusted me with her schedule and her secret migraines. I loved getting a front-row seat for the life of someone on *Forbes'* 100 Most Powerful Women list. Sure, I took care of Hayden at the office and Mom at home, but at least Hayden inspired me to work on my fledgling confidence. Despite the vomit, she really was a badass.

My workstation was separated from Hayden's by a glass partition with an etching of San Francisco's skyline that ran in a single line from one end of the glass to the other. Two bouquets of flowers arrived weekly: the smaller bouquet was placed on the top shelf of my desk and a larger bouquet on the coffee table in Hayden's office. Everything on our floor was tasteful; none of Mom's spiritual-offering gourds or amulets, or horseshoes for good luck above the doorways. I could turn from my desk and stare down at the people below or the sky above. I liked my role as Hayden's gatekeeper: everything came through me. And the sound of my block heels on the shiny hardwood floors made me feel accomplished.

I reminded myself of all these things as I placed her mug on my desk and went to the restroom to check the damage. The first of two stalls was clean, but the second—gross. *Gross!* Green-colored puke, her morning smoothie, was splattered in front of the toilet. It wasn't much, but, damn, if she'd taken just one more step—one tiny step—I would've been saved.

The janitor's supply room was located at the bottom level of the parking garage. I found everything I needed and had just turned off the light when I heard the distinct sound of voices reverberating throughout the lot.

"I say no. She's too much of a motormouth."

"I agree. Totally self-absorbed."

"Okay, that's a no for Helen and a no for Julia. That leaves Francine."

I froze, a rag in one hand, cleanser in the other. *What the fuck?* I peeked from behind the door of the supply room. Sure enough: the Jessicas and Bethany, Peeps' FUN Committee—*FUN* standing for "Finding Ultimate Nirvana." Feel free to roll your eyes.

They were only a few yards away, so I could hear every word. It was like Deep Throat except with mean girls. Jessica Ko was Korean American and worked in publicity, and Jessica Klein was white and in advertising. Because they had the same initials and same first name, Jessica Klein went by Jess, saving everyone from having to refer to them as White Jessica and Asian Jessica, although I referred to them that way in my head. The three had started the FUN Committee as a way to help the company remember to maintain our emotional health and to *have more fun!* They hosted all kinds of meet-ups throughout the city: rock climbing, eclectic dance parties, golf lessons—things I had zero interest in.

"She's just kind of hard to get to know. It's not like we haven't tried." This was Bethany: white, advertising, strange asymmetrical haircut.

Asian Jessica lit a cigarette, puffed, and passed it to White Jessica, who inhaled deeply. The Jessicas were health nuts, which was probably why they were hiding out in the bowels of the parking lot. I thought, *F-U-N: Finding Ultimate Nicotine.*

White Jessica blew out a stream of smoke. "Remember how she came to my birthday party, then turned around and left?" She pinched her face. "She's kind of weird."

"She was the only African American there," Asian Jessica said in my defense. "Besides, the retreat is supposed to help us connect."

"But she doesn't want to connect. And she wasn't the only African

American. If she had chosen to stay for more than five minutes I would've introduced her to Calvin and Denetria. It's not like I don't have black friends." White Jessica was a lesbian and should have known better. Why would she assume I'd naturally get along with Calvin and Denetria, whoever the hell they were, just because they were black? Idiot. "She drove all the way to Pacific Heights to stay five minutes. Who does that?"

Bethany chimed in, "She did the exact same thing at the anniversary party, remember? She drove all the way to Mountain View just to leave."

White Jessica: "I remember. That was weird."

Okay. The anniversary party. Brad, our CEO, who, along with dating models, liked to throw parties, rented a club to celebrate Peeps' five-year anniversary. I ended up standing off to the side pretending to enjoy the loud house music and my first gin and tonic—which was all I could think to order, but it tasted like poison with lime, not to mention a strobe light kept cutting across my face. I suddenly felt beyond stressed out. I just wanted to go home, where I could make hot chocolate and eat popcorn with my mom.

At one point, Bethany and the Jessicas came over and tried to make conversation. I tried to talk with them, but that damn strobe light! I swear, every fifteen seconds it swiped across my eyes.

I told them I didn't feel well and handed Asian Jessica my drink. "Would you mind holding this? I have to go to the restroom." I drove straight home, back to Mom, where I felt safe and comfortable.

White Jessica took a puff of cigarette. "If we invite her to the retreat, she'll either drive out and turn around and leave, or she won't speak to anyone. I know I'm being harsh, but we agreed: *expansive women only*."

She offered Bethany the cigarette, but Bethany shook her head no. "What if they find out they're not on the list, especially Francine? She could sue the company for racism."

"Maybe *she's* the racist," said White Jessica. "Maybe she left my party because she only wants to hang out with black people. It's a thing."

"This isn't about race." Asian Jessica took the cigarette from White Jessica. "And I should know." She puffed, gave back the cigarette. "I just don't want to be mean. Everyone should be invited."

Thank you, Jessica!

"We're not being mean," said Bethany. "We're all adults here, and we want a certain kind of energy at the retreat. It's nothing personal. I like Francine. She works under Hayden, for fuck's sake. I like Julia and Helen, but they can come next time. It's not like this is the last retreat we'll ever have."

White Jessica took a final puff of her cigarette and smashed it underfoot. "I'll send out the invites on Friday. With deposits due by the end of next month."

Bethany said, "I'm *so* looking forward to getting away, and it's going to be so empowering."

Asian Jessica started texting someone. "Oh my God, look at this." She showed Bethany and Jess her screen as they made their way toward the elevator.

"I'm going to give him so much shit for that," Bethany said, shaking her head at Jessica's phone.

"Right?" said White Jessica. "He's such a douche."

I closed the door to the supply room and waited in the pitch dark until the FUN Committee—newly rebranded Fuck U Narcissists—left the parking garage and it was safe to leave.

It had been three years since I was hired at Peeps, and I hadn't made any friends. I was around Hayden all the time for starters, and I wasn't all that great at introducing myself to people out of the blue. *Hi, my name is Francine, can I be your friend?* There was also my crippling impostor syndrome. Everyone at Peeps had gone to good schools and graduated from places like Yale and Stanford. Sure, I went to UC Berkeley, but I wasn't the traditional Cal student. The high school I graduated from in Oakland wasn't exactly rolling in resources, after all. So yeah, I had my guard up, always waiting for someone to call me out as ghetto or, like the FUN Committee bitches, "weird."

There was just something about me that repelled people. I was the antithesis of "black girl magic." In other words, confidence, glow, and charisma were foreign concepts. News flash: some of us black girls *lack* magic, some of us are shy and afraid and alone.

I was thinking about my depressing life while cleaning up Hayden's puke. What a great day I was having! I was fed up with everything. And damn it if Aunt Liane wasn't right: Mom and I *both* needed to make some serious changes. I didn't want to end up afraid of my own shadow and taking care of my mother for the rest of my life. I wanted to be normal and go on retreats with mean girls led by the Fucking Ultimate Narcissists Committee.

After cleaning the bathroom and scheduling Hayden's meetings, I sent Mom a text: Don't forget your promise. We're walking as soon as I get home. NO BACKING OUT!

I wanted to say, *I can't go on like this*, but instead I typed, Promise me.

Seconds later: I promise!

Of course, I had no idea that would be the last text she'd ever send me. See how shocking it is? Death, I mean. You think you have all the time in the world, you think you're going to go home and take a walk with your mom and everything is going to be all right, but no. So let me remind you again: Ask forgiveness, accept the apology. Do what you have to do, because you never know.

CHAPTER FOUR

My plan was to drive home and tell Mom she needed to start seeing her regular doctor again and I wouldn't take no for an answer. She'd also need someone else to help her with her videos, which meant she was going to have to let people inside the house. As for me, I was going to try harder to make friends and get over my insecurities.

I found Mom in her office wearing a pair of sweats and sitting at her desk. I could tell just from her body posture alone that she was ready to back down from her promise.

"We had an agreement."

"Can't you say hello?"

"No, I can't. You promised."

She let her head hang low. "I know, baby, but it's been a long day. I'm feeling beat."

I thought of telling her about *my* long day, cleaning up Hayden's puke, the FUN Committee, but telling her about my problems would only get us off track and stress her out. "I'm going to go change. When I come out, we're going for a walk."

"You don't want to relax first?"

"No, Mom. Let's get it over with. You were the one saying the stars are aligned today or whatever."

"I don't think I feel well." She stood, using the desk as support. *What an actress.* "I might be coming down with something. Let's go tomorrow."

I had no idea what it was like to fear leaving the house, taking a simple walk around the block, but I knew giving way to her anxiety was not helping. "You can do this, Mom. We can't let any more time pass or you'll get worse."

"I hate that I'm like this."

"I know. Do it for me."

She reluctantly started putting on her tennis shoes, a kid forced to go to soccer practice when all she wanted to do was stay home and play video games.

By the time I changed, she was standing in front of her altar, holding her favorite quartz, a purple amethyst cluster. "I'm going to bring this with me."

"No way. It's just a walk. You're not supposed to make it any bigger than that."

"It's not hurting anything. Stop being so bossy." She walked to the front door, pausing to check her face in the mirror as if she were about to meet someone and wanted to look cute. Once she gripped the doorknob, she stopped and dropped her hands at her sides. "I feel nauseous."

"It's your nerves. You can do this."

She raised her head, and after a deep inhale, she opened the front door. She walked down the first step of the porch, gripping her quartz and breathing through each step. She walked the pathway lined with rosebushes that led from our house to the sidewalk, her movements glacierlike. The street empty, no one around.

I cheered her on from the porch. "You're doing great."

When a plane flew overhead, she followed it with her eyes until it was nothing more than a white dot in the distance. Her attention shifted when a bird landed in our neighbor's tree. It was then that she clutched at her heart and her legs began to shake. In an instant she dropped to her knees, gasping for air.

"Mom?" I ran over.

She dropped her quartz, her eyes wild with fear as she tried to breathe.

And that's when it happened.

I guess I said her name, I guess I screamed. I remember watching the quartz roll down the sidewalk. I told her she would be okay, but when I stood to go back to the house to get my phone, she gasped and took her last breath.

She died like that. Her messy, anxiety-riddled, optimistic heart deciding *no more*; pumping for all those years and then without warning just... stopping.

CHAPTER FIVE

Months later, when I finally went into therapy, my therapist, Pamela, explained that I'd gone into shock after my mother's death. I was suffering from PTSD, which I suppose explains my strange behavior. It was like what everyone says, like I was inside a thick fog, and in my fog-induced, zombielike state, I walked around the house expecting Mom to show up at any moment. Or I'd sit and gaze vacantly off into space, watching her die again and again in front of the house.

I was left stunned, like someone in a near-death car accident or plane crash, standing in spirit form next to the wreckage, staring into my hands and wiggling my fingers, wondering if I was dead or alive. I couldn't even get myself to call Aunt Liane and Uncle CJ to tell them about Mom's death. Telling them would make it real.

I completed tasks without thought—signed her death certificate, closed her accounts. I hardly remember speaking with a funeral director, but somehow I'd made the decision to have her cremated, and when the UPS guy arrived with her remains—"Happy holidays!"—I had to remember what I'd done. I stared at the box he handed me. *My mom is inside a box.* I wanted to laugh. This could not be happening.

I threw a handful of her ashes around her garden but then changed my mind. It was too depressing knowing she'd never work in her garden again, so I headed back inside and tried to think of what to do. I looked around the den, then went to the kitchen. Her coffee mug was half-full with horrid, skinned-over coffee she'd started to drink on the day she died. Next to the mug was a doughnut she'd bitten into. I picked up the mug and pressed my lips to the blot of lipstick where she'd taken a sip. At the time it felt like her death was completely my fault—if I hadn't insisted she take a walk, she'd still be alive.

Not knowing what to do with the ashes, I gave up and grabbed the Aunt Jemima cookie jar at the end of the kitchen counter and replaced the peanut butter cookies with her remains. The cookie jar was racist as hell. It was advertised as original black memorabilia, but at the bottom of the skirt it was clearly marked *Made in China.* Mom, for whatever reason, loved that damn cookie jar.

Hayden told me to take the time I needed. I signed more papers, posted to all of her various platforms that she had passed. *My mother has died. Corrina Stevenson is dead. I'm sorry. Be well.* I even wrote Alfonse a note, using the address on the boxes of pills he'd sent. *Fuck you, you drug-peddling fucker. She's dead. Happy now?*

What I couldn't do was to bring myself to call Aunt Liane and Uncle CJ. I just couldn't. On the plus side, I guess, I didn't have to worry about Aunt Liane seeing the message about Mom's death since she'd blocked Mom from her social media years before. She and Mom had one of their falling-outs and the next day Mom posted a diatribe about Scorpios and how mean and vindictive they can be. To her credit, she added a few positive attributes. But none of it went over well with Aunt Liane, who immediately DMed Mom that she'd had enough of her new-agey bullshit, then promptly posted the hashtags #FuckYouVeryMuch and #BlockParty. They eventually made up, but Aunt Liane never unblocked her. #SisterlyLove #Family

Instead of contacting my aunt and uncle, I wrapped myself inside Mom's favorite afghan blanket, crocheted with green and yellow squares. The blanket smelled of her, her homemade body oils and incense. I sat in the den on the couch in the afghan, wearing one of her hats—the purple one—with the Aunt Jemima cookie jar in my lap, watching TV or her YouTube videos. I'd spent most of my life looking after my mother, hoping she'd get better. We were a dysfunctional, codependent mess, and I had absolutely no purpose without her. No wonder my thoughts began to go dark. *Why go on? What's the point?* After days of staring into space, I began thinking I should end it all. It made sense to my grief-wrecked brain. I had nothing to live for, so why not take her sleeping pills and say good night—like, forever.

I went to the kitchen and stood in front of the lineup of Alfonse's pills. But instead of taking TAKE THESE FOR GOOD SLEEP, I thought, *What the hell*, and reached for TAKE THESE WHEN YOUR FEELING LOST AND SCARRED. I was curious. And damn, if anyone felt lost and "scarred," it was me.

I tossed a couple back with orange juice, then returned to the couch with Aunt Jemima. It wasn't long before I started to hear a soft swishing sound. *Swoosh... swoosh...* like a broom brushing the floor.

I tried to see where the sound was coming from until I realized it was coming from ... *inside me*, a broom sweeping the insides of my brain. *Swoosh, swoosh.* A warm sensation fell over me as if I'd been transported from the couch to a sunlit beach. The walls pulsated a soft yellow; Mom's recliner vibrated cherry red.

Swoosh, swoosh. I stared at the Aunt Jemima cookie jar and watched Aunt Jemima's mouth begin to move: "Baby, yous is high." The Medusa bust on Mom's altar wiggled her tongue and laughed.

I would've been frightened if I hadn't felt so good. I mean, I felt *fucking good!*

I moved to the living room and turned on the large disco ball. It was daytime but the curtains were drawn, and the lights shimmered and circled the room. I turned on the stereo and had a good time dancing to the Bee Gees and Donna Summer, Chic and Sylvester. Sometimes Mom and I would dance under the disco ball or we'd sing using the karaoke machine. We really knew how to have a good time.

Don't ask me how long I kept that party train going. All I know is, I woke from my trance pouring sweat and downing a glass of water. After drinking a second glass, I opened the curtains in the den and saw the blue sky showing through the patio doors. I went outside and pulled a lemon from the lemon tree and brought it to my nose. A bird landed on my shoulder. I said hello and it smiled before flying away.

I imagined Mom alive and taking care of her garden, imagined her strong and healthy and traveling and doing whatever she wanted in life.

"Assholes! You can't have it! Leave me alone!"

I imagined Mom and me taking a walk together—in Paris!

"Leave me alone! *Assholes!*"

I tilted my head toward the street. Someone was yelling. Or was I hearing things? It was a great mystery.

"Give it here, you little bitch."

"Stop it! No, you can't. It belongs to me!"

Nope. The voices were real, as real as the lemon tree I was currently hugging.

I walked to the fence on the side of the yard and peeked over the edge. I saw a kid, no more than nine years old, standing in the middle of the street, clutching something to his chest. Books were scattered everywhere, their pages flapping in the wind; an open backpack lay at his feet. Two older boys—twice the kid's size—took a few steps toward him. He stepped back. In my altered state it looked like a strange tango. Moments later I was somehow back inside the house, peering from behind the living room curtains. One of the older boys, whose plaid underwear was on full display beneath his sagging pants, grabbed the kid by the arm and twisted it in a way that forced him to the ground. The kid screamed, but he held on to whatever he was clutching to his chest.

I heard someone yell, "Leave him alone! Stop right now!"

When the older boys turned in my direction, I realized I was poking my head out the front door. *I was the one yelling.*

I stared into the sky and quoted my mother: "Under the mud of our egos, we are all love. We need to be kind to each other."

The boys stared at me. Hell, I would've stared too. *What was I doing?*

Saggy Pants snickered, "She is high as a motherfucker."

The kid on the ground stood up and scrambled toward the house. I yanked him inside as soon as he was within reach and slammed the door.

The kid and I looked at each other, then went to the front window. Saggy Pants walked up and stared back at us. I saw that he was younger than I thought—only twelve or thirteen. I jumped when he banged on the window and raised his middle finger.

The kid, showing no fear, practically pressed his nose into the glass. "Asshole!"

Saggy Pants laughed and flipped him off again before he and his friend sauntered off.

The kid looked up at me, holding what I now saw was an iPad. "Thomas Jefferson believed slavery was a moral depravity. *Depravity* means he thought it was evil."

I stared. My skin felt tingly. I wondered if I was dreaming. After giving myself a moment to remember what had happened, I reached out to see if he was real. *How did he get in here again?*

He stepped back. "I do not like to be touched. People have germs and touching makes me uncomfortable." He took a small pause. "It's very uncomfortable."

"Am I dreaming?"

"Mmmmm…" He hummed. "Thomas Jefferson owned six hundred slaves."

"That's a lot."

He paused and looked me over, narrowing his small brown eyes. I looked down at what I was wearing—one of Mom's dresses, many sizes too large, over gray sweatpants, mismatched socks, the afghan, the purple fedora. "You look like a weirdo."

"My mother died."

"My mother died, too."

Was he serious? I waited for him to say more.

"Steve Jobs's mother gave him up for adoption."

"Yeah, but did your mother die?"

"Mmmmm," he hummed. "I read Steve Jobs's biography. It's called *Steve Jobs*. It's six hundred fifty-six pages long. I'm ten and I'm in seventh grade. I'm exceptionally smart." He looked around the room and pointed at the ceiling. "What's that?"

"It's a disco ball." I watched it spin and shimmer. "My mom loved it. We liked to turn off the lights and dance beneath the spinning ball to disco hits."

"What are disco hits?"

"Disco is a type of music."

He typed into his iPad. "Disco. The term is derived from the French word *discotheque*. That's very interesting."

I did a few moves—pumping my finger in the air, ceiling-to-floor, John Travolta style. I circled my fists and sang, "Ah, ah, ah, ah, stayin' alive, stayin' alive."

The kid stared up at me, doubtful, then looked around the room at the gourds placed in various corners, filled with things like crystals, snake tails, and bird feathers.

"This is a very interesting house. The second president was John Adams. He was interesting. He never owned slaves."

"*What?*"

"I should get my backpack."

Without warning, he left, closing the door behind him. No goodbye. No explanation.

I went to the window and watched him collect his things from the street, put them inside his backpack, and walk away. *This is a dream*, I thought.

Back in the den, I picked up the Aunt Jemima cookie jar and sat with it on the couch. My head was somewhere in outer space and I was loath to move. Mom would say that all the time. *Baby, I need to get up off this couch, but I am loath to move.*

CHAPTER SIX

rolled onto my back in the dark room and stared at the disco ball spinning above my head, its glowing dots circling the ceiling. I tasted the funk of my breath and tried to remember the last time I'd brushed my teeth or bathed. Gazing into the spinning orb, I counted the days I'd been absent from work. Ten or eleven, I guessed. I did remember the fireworks and gunshots going off New Year's Eve.

I had no idea what time it was, but I told myself I should either go to work or end my life. For whatever reason, it came down to those two choices. The holidays were officially over and staying at home was doing me no good.

I went into the den for my phone. It was almost four a.m. I sent Hayden a text telling her I'd be returning to work that day. It was then that I saw a message from Aunt Liane asking why Mom wasn't responding to her. *Shit.*

I quickly typed, She's fine. I'll tell her to get back to you.

After putting coffee on, I showered and dressed like any other adult. I read the texts Aunt Liane had sent to Mom's phone while eating a bowl of cereal. She'd sent two messages asking if Mom was getting out of the house.

Texting on Mom's behalf, I typed: Sorry for the delay. Venus square and Saturn moon occurring. I've been doing a phone cleanse. Been walking daily. Feeling blessed!

The quiet inside the house was startling. I found myself scrolling to the last text Mom had sent me: I promise!

Placing her phone next to mine, I prayed she would come from her bedroom or call for me. *Baby, come here a second.*

I stared at her altar, which was made from an antique dining room table and took up the length of the wall next to the patio doors. She'd decorated it with a bust of a bronzed Medusa, crystals, bowls filled with dried black-eyed peas and dried chicken feet, her numerology chart, and tarot cards, and covered the wall behind it with a blue-green African print and African masks.

I imagined her sitting there, helping a client on the phone or meditating. And then I was crying into my bowl of cereal. Why had I been so mean to her all the time?

Guilt-ridden, thoughts of suicide crept back in, zapping any forward momentum. But it had taken so much energy to get dressed, I figured I might as well go to work first and kill myself later. No, I'd kill myself if I had a bad day at work. For some odd reason, it seemed like a brilliant plan: Bad day? End everything.

I finished my coffee and picked up the Aunt Jemima cookie jar to say goodbye to Mom. Another onslaught of tears. Thinking the last thing I needed to do was lose it at the office, I put down Mom's ashes, opened NO MORE ANXIOUS, and took out a single pill, sealing it in a plastic baggie in case there was a need for pharmaceutical support.

Pulling out of the driveway, I noticed a composition book near the gutter. Snatches of my conversation with the kid came back to me like a dream. *So he was real*, I thought. *What do you know.*

At work, Hayden greeted me with a hug. Actually, I'm not sure if I should call it a hug per se. She sort of draped one arm around my shoulder while standing several inches away. "I'm so sorry." Hearing the compassion in her voice, I ran with the moment and pulled her into me. I was reminded, as I pressed my body into her bony frame, that I would never hug my mother again. My eyes grew teary and I tightened my arms, prepared to hang on as long as she'd let me, which was about three seconds. "All—all right," she stammered, peeling herself away. "Are you sure you're okay to come back?"

"I'm fine." I was embarrassed but also thinking, *Boss lady, it's either stay here and work or kill myself.*

She led me to the chair in front of her desk, told me about her own mother, who'd died nine years before, and her difficulty recovering from the loss. Blah blah blah. I stared into those blue eyes of hers only half listening. I mean, her life was so perfect. It was almost laughable how she was going on about her mother. What did she know about pain? She'd gone to ritzy private schools, worked at Yahoo in her twenties, then Google, then was snatched away from Google to work at Peeps. Later that night she'd go home to her husband, Dalton—yes, that was his name—who rock climbed and kite surfed—*eye roll*—and get this: Dalton had invested in Netflix before it was *the* Netflix, when it was no more than a little company peddling mail-order discs. Now Hayden and Dalton lived in Sea Cliff, one of the most expensive neighborhoods in San Francisco, an already overpriced city. The house itself was straight out of *Architectural Digest*. I'd been there while babysitting their daughter. After she fell asleep, I FacedTimed Mom and took her on a tour, ending the show outside by the front yard, where the view of the Golden Gate Bridge lit up the night sky. Throughout the tour Mom kept saying things like, "Oh my God," and "Hold up your phone so I can see better."

Hayden folded her hands on her desk. "Let me know if you need anything. I understand what it's like."

Sure you do.

Work kept me busy enough, but during my first break—I don't know why, it was a dumb move—I locked myself in a bathroom stall and pulled up a video of Mom on my phone. I'd always judged her for being corny and a fake in her videos, but I would've done anything to help her film again, to have her back. I watched her smiling into the camera. Poor Mom. Her own mother had abandoned her, leaving her alone with Drunk Grandpa and Aunt Liane. She was doing her best. For the millionth time I wished I hadn't suggested that damn walk.

Tears were running down my cheeks when I remembered the pill. I wiped my face and went back to my desk, fished out the baggie from my purse, and bit off a tiny amount of NO MORE ANXIOUS.

About thirty minutes in, I regretted the note I'd sent Alfonse. *God bless him!* NO MORE ANXIOUS kicked any sadness to the curb. I took calls with a smile and sped through my tasks. I practically skipped to the dry cleaners with Hayden's workout clothes and the suit she needed laundered.

I had so much energy! I felt I could do anything. I even flirted with a woman who was entering the dry cleaners as I was leaving—and I never flirted, like ever—which gave me the perfect idea: I needed to date! It had been *two years* since my last date. Two! And I needed to kiss someone. I needed sex! No wonder I was so sad and mopey. I would not kill myself! I would have sex. *Yes!* With NO MORE ANXIOUS surging, I pulled up Tinder on my walk back to the office. I certainly wasn't going to use PeepMe; there was no way I wanted the FUN Committee or any of my work colleagues to know I was looking for *loooove.*

I posted a photo and the necessary bullshit and started swiping away. Anyone who caught my eye—*swipe.* Pretty eyes? Swipe! Long legs? Swipe! Clean teeth? Swipe! Swipe! Swipe! Swipe!

NO MORE ANXIOUS cleared my brain of fear and worry. I soon realized Mom's death could be a chance for me to start over. I would date and travel without having to worry about her. Redecorate the house so I could invite people over and not be embarrassed by the dried snake tails in her offering gourds. I'd get rid of her weird-ass altar!

I told Hayden I was going to lunch and would return in thirty. Shoulders back, confidence pumping, I headed to the cafeteria to join the lackeys instead of eating at my desk or the café up the street per usual.

The cafeteria-slash-lounge had everything an employee could want, including a café, gourmet snacks, a boxing bag to work out frustrations, a Ping-Pong table, and an old-fashioned Pac-Man game. Employees sprawled on the futuristic furniture. I ordered a sandwich and an espresso. I was learning NO MORE ANXIOUS and caffeine were a dynamic duo. I smiled at my colleagues, not that any of them noticed since they were staring into their laptops or eating. I found a table and played several games of speed chess on my phone. I was on fire.

The problem with drugs, however, is they eventually wear off. Halfway through my sandwich, I was right back to visions of Mom dropping to her knees. My chewing slowed. Fighting back tears, I spit the last mouthful of my sandwich into my napkin. I needed to get out of there. But wouldn't you know? The fucking FUN Committee was stepping out of the elevator just as I was waiting to go inside. Asian Jessica said hello, but I couldn't look at her; I was too busy biting down on my lip and willing myself not to cry or freak out. "Are you okay?" Bethany asked.

No, I am not okay, bitch. Wait. Were they trying to be nice? I couldn't tell. I pushed past them into the elevator and pressed up up up! I started crying as soon as the doors closed.

So yeah, after the drugs wore off, my first day back at work pretty much imploded. I devised a plan to go home and eat as much pizza and ice cream as I wanted, then down an entire bottle of TAKE THESE FOR GOOD SLEEP and never wake up. I felt sorry for Aunt Liane and

Uncle CJ, though. They would have to find out about my death and Mom's passing all at once. Damn.

I drove home thinking of Mom's death, my death, my last meal—a deep-dish with everything from Zachary's Pizza and two pints of Ben & Jerry's ice cream: Chocolate Fudge Brownie and Triple Caramel Chunk.

I was pulling up to the house when I saw a kid pacing in front of the driveway. It took me a second—that's how out of it I was—but his backpack and tablet tipped me off. *The kid from the other day.* I parked and rolled down the window.

He read from his tablet: "The electric I-on weighs eighteen hundred pounds. It has a lithium-ion battery. Ion! I-on! Ha!"

He held up his iPad and showed me a picture of the car I drove. Mom and I were big believers in climate change and did everything we could to keep a low carbon footprint, which is why we shared a Prius. For my twenty-first birthday, she'd bought me the electric I-on, my dream car.

"What are you doing here?" I asked.

He wore an oversized T-shirt with a picture of Steve Jobs on the front. "The I-on is turbocharged! I-on. I on. It's one hundred six inches long and sixty-five inches wide." He had a narrow head planted on a small, thin body, so thin I wondered if he got enough to eat. His uncombed Afro rose and fell in several places; his hair and skin were more copper than brown.

"Have those kids been bothering you?" I asked, although I knew the answer. Some of us, like the kid and me, have a target on our back.

He rocked on his feet and hummed. "Mmmmm."

Watching him, I thought of my days in elementary school—the nine blissful years of normalcy before Dad died and then the disaster that was fourth grade. We had one of those Bring Your Parents to School days, and my mom, who was supposed to talk about her job, thought it would be fun to give tarot readings and predicted Craig would spend ten years in prison for armed robbery, and Brittany Williams would be hooked on drugs by the age of twenty. She tried to explain to Craig he'd eventually live a happy life after he was released, and Brittany was going to beat her addiction, but Brittany was already crying by then, and the entire class started calling me the witch's daughter, and later just "Witch."

Thankfully I met Gabby in fifth grade. She was obese and we became the Witch and the Whale, but at least I had someone to eat lunch with. She moved, though, and in sixth grade I was caught staring at Monique Woodson—whom everyone stared at, frankly, she was so pretty, but I was busted. So in addition to being called a witch, I got the occasional "lesbo witch." I was picked on relentlessly. Then a new girl enrolled in our school and the real nightmare started. *Anyway.*

I studied the kid closely as he hummed softly. He kept his gaze on the passenger seat as though someone were sitting next to me. "Mm-mmm," he hummed.

Mom and I had watched the series *Parenthood* and the kid reminded me of the young boy in the show who was neurodivergent. Yeah, he was definitely on the spectrum.

He read from his tablet. "Your car is so small you can fit it on a pool table."

He was obviously obsessed with the car, so I figured what the hell. "Do you want to sit inside and see what it's like?"

Avoiding eye contact, he stared near the side of my face. "Over eight hundred kids are reported missing every year and two hundred thousand are kidnapped. Counselor Hayes told me to scream if I ever thought someone was touching me inappropriately."

"I'm not going to touch you or kidnap you, the last thing I need is a kid. My name is Francine, by the way."

"I know, you already told me."

"When did I tell you my name?"

"The last time I was here. You're not very smart." He swiped on his tablet. "What's your last name?"

"Stevenson. Why?"

He typed into his tablet. "Are you on Facebook? I can't find you."

"No, and don't say Facebook around me."

"Snapchat?"

"Nope."

"TikTok?"

"Nope."

He frowned. *"Do you exist?"*

"I'm on Instagram sometimes, but I use a pseudonym. Go to Peeps' platform." I directed him to my work bio.

"You work at Peeps?" he said, studying my information. "That's very interesting. Give me your car keys so you won't be able to drive off with me."

"You were in my house the other day. If I wanted to kidnap you, I would've done it then."

"That's a very good point. I'll take the keys now."

"Fine." I unlocked the passenger-side door and handed over my keys.

He climbed inside and began inspecting the interior like a buyer in the mood for a purchase. When he turned, his nose practically touched the back window, that's how small the car was. "It's like sitting inside a shoe."

"What's your name, anyway?"

"David Mayes Jr., but everyone calls me Davie. I'm named after my father. My father died in a car accident when I was a baby." He opened the glove compartment, looked inside, then closed it. "My mom got on drugs and died when I was four."

"My mother's dead, too."

"I know. You already told me. And I already told you my mother's dead." He shot his gaze somewhere near my shoulder. "Mmmmm," he hummed. "You don't have a good memory, but you have an interesting house. You have a disco ball in your house. Disco is music with syncopated beats."

"So where do you live?"

"In an apartment. I'm in foster care where no one cares! Ha! Counselor Hayes says my life is Dickensian. *Dickensian* means my life is like something written by Charles Dickens. Charles Dickens wrote twenty-one novels. I already read *Oliver Twist*."

A kid who read books by Dickens? I looked at him curiously. "It's late. Do your foster parents know where you are?"

"The foster parents said I can go to the library after school. They have a program for kids. I go there sometimes, but I'm supposed to be home soon." He pulled down the visor, then pushed it back up. "When you move in with a new family, the number one best thing to do is make yourself invisible. *In-cog-nito!* I know what that means because I'm very smart. I'm ten and I'm in seventh grade."

"That's impressive." I meant it, although with his baggy clothes and small frame, I couldn't imagine him hanging out with other seventh graders.

"The new foster mother said as long as I don't bring trouble to the door, we'll get along just fine. Ha!"

I felt bad for feeling sorry for myself when this kid had already lost both his parents so young and was in foster care. "My dad died in an accident, too. On a construction site."

"That means you're an orphan like me. *Orphan* is spelled with a PH, not an F. If you spell it with an F it's like *fins*. Steve Jobs met Steve Wozniak when they were working at HP. I read his biography. It's called *Steve Jobs*. It's six hundred fifty-six pages long. I'm exceptionally smart."

"You are." I stared at the exact spot where Mom fell to her knees. *I am an orphan, spelled with a PH.*

He picked up his backpack and climbed out of the car. "I have to go now, but I think you're very interesting. I'll see you tomorrow."

I thought of the pizza and ice cream I was planning to eat. The sleeping pills. I was also going to leave a letter for Aunt Liane and Uncle CJ. I didn't want them blaming themselves for my suicide. They also needed to know about Mom. *What a depressing letter.*

I spoke in a whisper: "I won't be here tomorrow."

"Where are you going?"

"I'm moving."

"Where are you moving to? Where's your moving van?"

"Just don't come back, okay? Go home."

He did that thing again, humming in a low voice, rocking from side to side on his feet. "Mmmmm." He stared upward toward the sky, his lips pushed into his nose. "Mmmmm."

He was kind of freaking me out, to be honest. "Would you stop that?"

He aimed his eyes further skyward. "A lot of slave children were separated from their families, or their parents died. They were alone."

I wondered how far along he was on the spectrum. "What are you talking about?"

He heaved his backpack up over his shoulder. "I'm going to catch my bus now." And then he ran off. No goodbye, nothing.

I watched him stop at the corner, look both ways, then run across the street as if a car might strike him at any second, his backpack pounding against his spine. I then returned my gaze to the spot where Mom fell. "What the hell, Mom," I muttered, as if she had something to do with Davie showing up, as if she had anything to do with anything at all now. "What the hell." And then I got out of the car. I had a depressing letter to write to Aunt Liane and Uncle CJ and a pizza to order.

CHAPTER SEVEN

turned on the TV in order to drown out the silence of the house and changed out of my work clothes. It was when I took out my phone to order pizza that I saw I'd been messaged by two women on Tinder. *Whaaaaat?* I had to trek back through the day to remember NO MORE ANXIOUS. Apparently during my pill-induced elation, I'd swiped right on over fifty women. Fifty! I'd contacted women from Oakland to Alabama.

My mouth fell open as I scrolled through the catalog of women I'd messaged, who had nothing in common except gender. Initially I was excited about the two responses, until I realized the return was pathetic when you considered I'd swiped right on so many women and had only two replies.

I read my bio: *Good-time girl! Last chance for this, bitches!*

As soon as I opened my first Tinder message, I forgot about my low returns and embarrassing bio. I stared at a photo of a conventionally beautiful twenty-two-year-old college grad, the type of woman who normally wouldn't look my way.

Hi, I liked your profile. I was wondering if you'd like to get a drink tonight. Hit me up. —Jasmine

I refreshed the page, concerned there might be a glitch in the app and she'd messaged me by mistake, but there she was again. I swiped through her pictures. In the last photo she was in a bikini lying out on the beach, her hair in box braids, her eyes hidden behind sunglasses, her toes painted pink.

I glanced at the Aunt Jemima cookie jar next to me on the couch. "What the hell does this girl see in me?" I was average looking at best, with no discernible features except my dark skin and the same dimpled chin as Mom's, Aunt Liane's, and Drunk Grandpa's.

I looked at Jasmine in her bikini, my thoughts going back to Kelly Musa. I hadn't been in a relationship since I'd dated her back in college. We met junior year and fell hard for each other. Kelly was skinny and wore thick glasses, and was first-generation Nigerian and nearly as dark as me. We liked to link our hands and compare our skin tones—dark against darker. And we made out all the time. Like, *all the time.*

Kelly and I would stay up late and she'd tell me about her fairy-tale upbringing—only child of Olu and Grace Musa, all-girls Catholic school, annual trips abroad. I, on the other hand, never had the courage to tell her much about Mom, but they did meet once over brunch. We dined out since I didn't want Kelly to see the inside of our house—specifically Mom's new-agey voodoo stuff. But I was proud of Mom for showing up properly medicated—asking Kelly appropriate questions and telling us what a cute couple we were.

The only minor downside to our relationship—no, scratch that, it was more than some minor problem, it was huge—Kelly didn't want anyone to know she was gay! You would've thought it was the 1950s. She didn't want a single soul to know, especially not her Nigerian parents, so she told everyone we were best friends. Which was fine at first—I get it, no one should be forced to come out before they're ready—but after two years of dating, our secret relationship started to wear on me.

Things came to a head a few days before graduation when her parents were visiting. I happened to run into them as I was coming from Doe Library. I wasn't going to rush up to Kelly and tongue her in front of her parents or anything—I wasn't dumb—but I at least wanted to say hello, have her introduce me as a "friend." My smile brightened as they drew closer. Seeing me, though, Kelly began shaking her head as if she had a nervous tic—a tic that said, *Do not come near me! I do not know you!* Her parents smiled and gave a subtle nod, but I was too flustered to smile back. I was half tempted to say, *Your daughter was feeling on my titties last night!* Instead, I gave Kelly a final look and kept it moving.

She broke up with me a few days later with some bullshit story about "giving up on women." Now that we were graduating, she said she wanted to "try men again."

I couldn't believe it and quickly reminded her, "You don't like men! You specifically told me that sleeping with guys made you want to puke."

"Maybe I didn't try hard enough."

"Do you hear what you're even saying? And there's nothing wrong with being gay, just so you know."

"There is to my family," she quipped.

She was their "miracle child," she explained, and they expected a lot from her. She added, "It's not like we were going to stay together forever. You're too clingy, Francine. Breaking up would be good for you, too."

It was not news to me that she thought I was clingy, but I didn't expect we'd break up so soon—or ever.

To be fair, I had no right to blame Kelly for hiding her sexuality. I never told her how bad Mom's mental issues were. All of our secrets wormed their way into our relationship and took hold until it was destroyed.

I scrolled through Jasmine's pictures again, homing in on a photo of her wearing a minidress. I knew I was supposed to kill myself, but *damn*! She looked good. And I needed a win—I needed sex! I immediately sent her a note; she wrote back a few seconds later. And there you have it. I, Francine Stevenson, had a date with conventionally hot Jasmine for seven p.m. I could not believe my luck.

I remembered the second message and quickly opened it. Kenji was Asian American with a boyish face—short, cropped hair parted on the side and slicked down with pomade, 1950s style. In typical butch fashion she wore Doc Martens, jeans, and a white tee in one photo and a tailored suit in the next.

I read her skillfully crafted, poetic message:

Yo, dinner?

I thought, *What the hell. How often do I have two dates in one week?* Answer: never.

I responded yes, then looked at Aunt Jemima. *Can you believe this? Two dates!*

I quickly showered and changed, thinking suicide would have to wait.

Jasmine chose a trendy restaurant in downtown Oakland for our date. She sat at the bar staring into her phone, miraculously as good-looking in person as in her photos. I walked up and introduced myself. She wore a short dress that showed off her legs and strappy heels. I wore a casual suit jacket with jeans, a printed blouse, and a pair of Converse, which said, *Trying, not trying.*

Turned out I didn't have to worry about how I looked or even how I behaved. Jasmine was one of those extreme talkers. All you had to do was nod and ask an occasional question and she was off to the races. At one point she said, "Oh my God, I like talking to you like so much. This is, like, so nice."

I *think* she may have asked me where I grew up. I was fine with being a gigantic ear for most of the night, though. I mean she looked so beautiful and sexy under the low restaurant lighting. I still couldn't believe I was on a date with her.

As our meal progressed, she told me she'd recently lost her job and her beloved cat Moo was sick and the vet bills were "like hella expensive." We were touching hands from across the table by then, my thumb tracing the inside of her palm. "Sorry I've been talking so much," she said. "I've been so stressed."

I intertwined my fingers with hers. "I understand. I've been having a hard time, too."

"Have you? I want to hear about it. I want to know, like, everything about you. I keep meeting, like, so many fucking flakes. But you seem so nice. I'd like to see you again if you'd be into it." Her full, pillowy lips curled into a smile.

I swallowed. "That would be nice."

We arranged to meet again that Saturday. I couldn't believe my luck: from suicidal thoughts to love, all in a single day.

We shared a dessert and she ordered a cognac. "Oh my God, I'm, like, so obsessed with after-dinner drinks." She snapped a selfie, raising her phone in order to capture the drink and her face. I'd told her I was interested in photography, but it went over her head.

When the waiter arrived with the bill, she took my hand. "I'm really happy we're going to see each other again, Francine. Between Moo being sick and losing my job, I like really needed something nice. It's been a long time since I've felt so good." She blinked back her tears.

"I feel the same." I placed both my hands over hers. "I feel lucky to have met you."

She sniffled and reached for the bill. "How much is it?"

I looked at the amount. *Holy shit.* Two hundred fucking bucks!

I skimmed over the tab. Oysters. Artichoke tapenade with rosemary oil, salt cod fritters, two salads; four cocktails—*all hers*, I'd only had mineral water. Sea bass for me and a porterhouse steak for her. Fuck.

She tried to take the bill from my hand. "How much?"

"I've got it," I said coolly. Maybe she shouldn't have ordered so much, but I wasn't going to make her pay after hearing about Moo and her job.

"*Really?*"

"Yeah, I've got this."

"I can't." She ran her hand across her bangs. Did I mention she had bangs? She was *adorable*. "It's too much. I can't, like, let you pay for the whole meal."

"You'll pay next time."

She brought my hand to her lips and kissed it. "Deal."

We made out in front of the restaurant—her lips on mine, my lips on hers. I left thinking, *I wanna live!* Or at least I wanted to live long enough to kiss Jasmine all over her conventionally gorgeous body.

Okay, sure, my mother was dead. I would go home and wouldn't be able to tell her about my date. But watching Jasmine walk away? I felt hope. I felt all those things inside my body going haywire like they do when you have a major crush: butterflies floating and tiny ballerinas twirling and cartoon hearts pumping. I felt as if I'd taken TAKE THESE WHEN YOUR FEELING LOST AND SCARRED but without having to take the actual drug.

Of course I stalked her social media once at home. I was in Mom's bed, where I'd been sleeping since she'd passed. I knew Jasmine graduated from Sacramento State, so I used Peeps' alma mater feature to find her last name. It took about an hour, but after finding her surname I was able to open the portal to all things Jasmine. Based on her posts, she did have a cat named Moo. And she was so damn pretty. I had to wonder again what she saw in me. *I feel like I can tell you anything*, she'd said while sipping her expensive glass of cognac.

Kelly used to say the same thing about me. *Kelly.* I wondered what she was up to but talked myself down from the ledge of stalking her. The last time I'd checked her social media, she was dating some dude. I tortured myself by scrolling through photo after photo of Kelly living her best *lie*. I vowed never to look at her social media again.

I ended up texting Kenji, the second woman who'd contacted me. I asked her if she wanted to meet Thursday, the following night, which would give me something to do while I waited for my date with Jasmine. It didn't take Kenji long to respond with yet another deeply heartfelt message: *Yo, where?*

I wasn't all that excited about meeting her, to be honest, and chose a relatively cheap Japanese restaurant in Piedmont. This time I'd split the bill.

So yeah. Kenji.

I wished I'd suggested meeting for coffee instead of a meal. She annoyed me from the start. She ate too quickly and kept getting food on her face. And we argued about everything—even the weather. How do you argue about the weather?

"Ninety degrees isn't hot," she said when I mentioned the prolonged heat wave we'd had in the fall. I was stretching for things to talk about. "I know hot. I lived in Houston for a year. Yo, hot is ninety percent humidity at ten a.m."

Why was she always saying *yo*? Who said *yo* anymore?

The good thing was that she annoyed me so much, I didn't care about what she thought about me. Besides, my heart was already with Jasmine. I really just wanted the date to be over with. So when we fell into, I'll admit, a ridiculous argument over which was better, *Stars Wars* or *Star Trek*, I made the point that from its inception *Star Trek* was always more diverse than *Star Wars*.

She chewed quickly and spoke with her mouth full. "I don't think so."

"Are you kidding? There's Lieutenant Uhura, Captain Kathryn Janeway. What show had female commanders like that back in the day? There's Commander Deanna Troi, Whoopi Goldberg as Guinan. I could go on."

"I could go on about *Star Wars*. There's Princess Leia—"

"Oh please. Princess Leia and her stupid cinnamon-bun hairdo have nothing, and I mean nothing, on Lieutenant Uhura."

She proceeded to eat mouthfuls of rice until she emptied the bowl. I waited to see if she'd pick it up and lick it. "*Star Wars* is better. *Star Trek* is boring, yo."

I knew Mom was rolling over in her grave, or rather, rolling over in the Aunt Jemima cookie jar. Mom and I loved *Star Trek*. My father, too. One of my happiest memories was dressing up as *Star Trek* characters for Halloween. Dad was a Klingon, Mom went as Guinan, and I went as Geordi.

Kenji pointed to a sashimi roll on our plate with her chopsticks. "You gonna eat that?" She opened her mouth wide, but the roll was too big and she ended up half chewing it and half spitting it out.

I watched in disgust. It was time to drop our silly argument and move on to a more adult conversation, but I couldn't let it go. "The *Star Trek* universe has taken on race issues, war crimes, homophobia, all of it."

The waiter came to check on us. Kenji looked up at him. "Which is better, *Star Wars* or *Star Trek*?"

"*Star Wars*." He poured water and walked away.

"End of discussion," said Kenji.

"Because one person agrees with you?"

She peered around the restaurant, which was fairly empty with only ten or so patrons. Then she raised her voice over the din of conversation: "Excuse me, everyone. Excuse me!"

Diners paused, worried. I ducked in my seat.

"Quick question: *Star Wars* or *Star Trek*?"

Some people mumbled, some shouted: "*Star Wars!*" "*Star Wars.*" "Fuck yeah," said a guy in the back.

"Thank you, everyone!" Kenji took a large bite of her teriyaki chicken, her lips glistening with grease. "Told you."

I leaned back in my chair, dumbfounded. "Wow," I said, as in, *Really? Was that necessary?*

She continued stuffing her flat face. We barely spoke for the remainder of the meal, both of us just wanting the night to be over.

After we paid, Kenji broke our impasse. "Don't take this personally, but this will be our last date."

"As if I care," I blurted. "I'm seeing someone this Saturday and she's gorgeous." I sounded bratty and defensive, but I wanted her to know just how much I cared about not seeing her again, which was not at all.

Kenji had the gall to make a face like she didn't believe me. So I took out my phone right then and there and showed her a picture of Jasmine.

That's when she laughed in my face. She laughed and laughed and gave the table a hard slap. "I know that girl." She cupped one hand over her mouth, laughing like crazy, pointing. "Yo, that girl is a sneater!"

"A what?"

"A sneater. She's *sneating*—sneaking around and eating free food. She's a food ho."

"*What?*"

"I went out with that girl till I realized what she was up to. She's playing your ass. What's her name again?"

"Jasmine."

"That's right, Jasmine. Jasmine the sneater."

"She's *not* a sneater," I said, teeth clenched.

"You paid for the meal, didn't you." More statement than question.

"So what? I wanted to."

"Yeah, 'cause her dog has cancer."

"Cat."

"Dog, cat, whatever. And she's unemployed and she hasn't met anyone like you in a long time." She started playing an invisible violin. "Wa wa wa wa wa. They're all sob stories so some sucker will feed her. She's good in bed, though."

"You slept with her?"

"Didn't you?"

I fell silent.

"I'll take that as a no." She stood and put on her jacket. "Anyway, enjoy getting used." She gave a halfhearted salute. "It's been real, yo."

"It's been something," I muttered, grabbing my purse. "And she's *not* a sneater."

But of course Jasmine was a sneater.

We met Saturday at another expensive restaurant for brunch. Jasmine gave me a deep kiss when she arrived. Initially I thought, *My girl is* not *a sneater*. Matter of fact, she waved my hand away as though offended when the check came. *Take that, Kenji.*

But then she started searching inside her purse, growing increasingly frantic. "Shit. My wallet isn't here." Blah blah blah. "Oh my gosh!" she declared like a bad actress. "Where could it be?"

I waited for her at our table while she went to see if she'd left her wallet in her car. I knew good and well she was not going to find it. She was a sneater. Of course someone would use me for food—and there was no indication there'd be sex later either.

When she returned without her wallet, apologetic and embarrassed,

I told her not to worry and that I'd pay. I was too defeated to bother to call her on her bullshit. I was an idiot for thinking someone like Jasmine would want me in the first place.

Back at my car, I did the thing no one should do after a horrible date: I broke my personal vow and stalked my ex on social media. I almost threw my phone out of the car when I saw that Kelly was newly engaged. In one picture, she, the dude, and her parents were done up in Nigerian garb with the dude giving her a side hug and kissing her cheek. In another photo, she showed off her ring. *Unbelievable.*

"You're gay!" I yelled into my phone.

Tears springing to my eyes, I started my car thinking of how much I wanted to go home and see Mom, the one person who loved me no matter what.

I cried the entire drive back, my thoughts nose-diving. No one would ever love me like my mother, and there was absolutely no point in living. I was worthless and my life was shit.

CHAPTER EIGHT

'd sent only one other text on Mom's behalf to Aunt Liane: **Using the Fitbit and feeling good!** But once I was at home from my date with the sneaker, I found stationery so I could write her and Uncle CJ a proper letter goodbye. I didn't want them thinking they had anything to do with my suicide. I also needed to tell them Mom's remains were inside the Aunt Jemima cookie jar.

I went to the kitchen, poured soda, and grabbed the bottle of TAKE THESE FOR GOOD SLEEP. I played Nina Simone on the stereo and took the pills and soda to the den. With Aunt Jemima looking on from the coffee table, I began drafting a letter.

Dear Aunt Liane and Uncle CJ,

Please know that I love you both very much and I'm grateful for all you've done for me. I'm sorry to tell you this, but Mom has died. I'm sorry

The doorbell.

I waited for whoever it was to go away, half expecting Mom to yell from her office, *Sounds like my package is here. I'll get it.*

The bell rang again and again.

Dang, I thought, *can't a girl write a suicide note in peace?*

I tore down the hall wondering who it could be in the middle of the day. Was it the sneater? Had she followed me home prepared to tell me some sob story about how she needed money?

I shot open the door without looking through the peephole.

It was the kid, Davie, still pressing the doorbell with his skinny finger even though I was standing right in front of him.

"Okay. Enough!"

He pointed to my car. "Your electric I-on is in the driveway."

"And?"

"I thought you said you were moving. Where's the moving van?"

"It'll be here soon." I needed to keep my momentum going. If I thought too much about what I planned to do, I'd chicken out. "I'm busy right now, okay? Take care."

He shot out his hand, stopping me from closing the door. He kept his gaze straight forward, not once making eye contact. "What are you doing?"

"None of your business." I started to slam the door in his face so he'd get the point and never come back; it would be awful if he saw the cops removing my body. Thinking of Mom, I looked out toward the yard, where the EMT crew had put her limp body on a stretcher. "I'm packing, okay? I won't be here anymore so go away."

"Mmmmm. Ten million Africans were taken to Brazil."

I waited for him to say more, to make some kind of point. Then, frustrated, hand on hip: "Listen, you need to go away. Go play with your friends."

He rocked from foot to foot, staring straight ahead, before shouting at the top of his lungs, "I have no friends, asshole! You are an asshole!" He turned and stormed off.

I went back inside, making it as far as the den. Thing is, I knew what it was like to be his age and not have any friends. Feeling guilty as shit, I immediately rushed outside. No one was around except for a neighbor washing his car. I saw Davie up ahead, walking quickly, already at the end of the block, his backpack bouncing against his small frame like a bulky tortoise shell with every step.

I took after him. "Wait! I'm sorry!"

He continued to walk at a fast pace, eyes straight ahead, even after I caught up with him.

"I'm sorry, okay? I didn't mean it. I'm not moving. I'm not going anywhere."

"Mmmmm."

When I touched his shoulder to get his attention, he whirled—"I do not like to be touched! You need permission to touch me!"

I drew back, my hands in the air. "Okay, calm down. I'm sorry. I had a bad day. I shouldn't have taken it out on you."

"Plastics have been found in sixty percent of all seabirds and one hundred percent of all sea turtles. They mistake plastic for food! I know a lot about history and science."

"I know you do. I also know what it's like not to have any friends."

"That's not possible. You work at Peeps and you drive an electric I-on."

"I had a hard time when I was your age, though."

He gazed somewhere off to the side as if seeing something suspicious just beyond my shoulder. "They called me f-a-g at my old school and they called me the R-word when I was in Mrs. Jewell's class, but then I skipped two grades. Ha!" He had an odd one-note laugh.

"You showed them." I meant it, too. Good for him.

"Counselor Hayes told me to never ever say f-a-g or the R-word. I'm at the new school now so no one calls me names yet."

Yet landed hard. "Listen, Davie. I'm sorry, okay?"

"Mmmmm."

"Do you want to come back to the house?"

He looked somewhere near my neck or chin before sending his gaze skyward. "Ha!" he exclaimed, pointing a professorial finger in the air.

"Is that a yes or a no?"

"Can I have a snack?"

"Sure."

He ran ahead of me, straight up to the door. Once inside the house, he walked around the living room as if in a gallery. I opened the blinds to let in more light. The living room was fairly normal except for the offering gourds, and the disco ball, of course. Oh, and the horseshoes. Horseshoes were over most doorways. They were a gift from one of Mom's followers, supposedly for luck and protection from evil juju.

Davie bent over and inspected the gourd next to one of the potted plants. Mom put them in most corners of the house, except in my bedroom, where I wouldn't allow them. "What are these things?"

"They're offering gourds. They bring good energy."

He plucked a dried rattlesnake tail. "What's this?"

"A rattlesnake tail. It's to ward off spirits. The white crystals are for psychic energy."

He examined the rattlesnake tail from every angle then gave it a shake. "Ha!"

It was beyond strange having someone walking through the house, poking at this, staring at that. We never had company since Mom feared people bringing negative vibes into our home, and I feared being judged for her witchy décor. I mean, I guess the kids in elementary school had a point. But Davie was the perfect first guest. He didn't make judgments. Everything was "interesting," or he'd point a professorial finger in the air with a "Ha!" He made no reaction to the mess in the den and kitchen—the open pizza boxes, the snotty wads of balled-up tissues on the floor and everywhere else. The first thing he did when we entered the den was to run up to the taxidermied fox—a gift from one of Mom's clients. The woman who gave it to her said foxes were symbols of wisdom.

"I've never seen a fox up close. I've never seen a fox ever. Ha!" He knelt down and stared into its glass eyes. "Does he have a name?"

I blinked. "Not that I know of."

"I'm going to call it Hello Mr. Fox." He petted the top of the fox's dead fur. "Hello, Hello Mr. Fox. How are you today?"

He stood and took in the entire altar. I cringed when he picked up Mom's favorite amethyst crystal. "Be careful with that."

"Mmmmm."

"It's just—her things are special." We all knew Mom's altar was sacred. Even as much as Aunt Liane loathed her altar, she maintained a respectful distance from it, as though it could do her harm. "Would you mind putting that back, please?"

"Steve Jobs was adopted. He's very interesting." He returned the crystal, then leaned close to the bust of the Medusa, his nose almost touching her nose. "What's her name?"

"That's Medusa. She's... it's Greek mythology."

"I don't know much about Greek mythology. I know about the Civil War, the Revolutionary War, slavery, science, and Steve Jobs."

He turned from the altar. Spotting the Aunt Jemima cookie jar, he went to the coffee table and the next thing I knew—"Can I have a cookie?"—he'd grabbed the cookie jar, ready to help himself to Mom's remains.

"Put that down!"

He narrowed his already small eyes and glowered. "Mmmmm."

"Don't open that." I tried to sound as calm as possible. The last thing I needed was for him to dunk his hand into a jar filled with my mother's ashes.

"Is it because it looks like a slave?"

"If you give it to me I'll explain."

He handed it over.

"Do you know what *cremation* means?"

"Of course I do." He appeared annoyed that I should doubt his intelligence. "Do you know what *trothplight* means?"

He had me.

"It means 'engagement.' Ha!"

I held Aunt Jemima close. "My mother is inside this cookie jar. I had her cremated."

"Why'd you put her in a cookie jar that looks like a slave?"

"I don't know. I don't know what I'm doing. Like, with anything. I don't know who I am without my mom." I thought of Jasmine and how stupid I'd been, how my life wasn't worth living. I sat down on the couch feeling drained.

Davie sat at the opposite end, staring just above my head. "Mmmmm."

I was about to put Aunt Jemima on the coffee table but seeing the bottle of sleeping pills next to the letter I'd started to Aunt Liane and Uncle CJ, I kept "Mom" firmly in my lap. I wasn't sure what to do, how to divert Davie's attention away from the evidence of my soon-to-be suicide attempt.

I showed him the *Made in China* label on Aunt Jemima's skirt. "It's supposed to be memorabilia, but it's fake."

"That's very interesting. Can I have a snack now?"

Perfect. "Sure!" I quickly took the letter and pills to the kitchen and put everything on the counter near the stove. The fridge was filled with spoiling food I needed to toss. What the hell was I going to feed this kid?

Davie read from his tablet: "Aunt Jemima's real name was Nancy. She was a slave and spent all day making pancakes at a world exhibition in Kentucky."

"Racism is a bitch," I muttered.

I ended up making peanut butter and crackers. Davie said he wanted the crackers served open-faced with the peanut butter in the center of the cracker in a neat circle. He ate each cracker like a food critic, taking dainty, thoughtful bites as though mentally preparing a restaurant review. Then, as if I weren't there at all, he pulled up *Finding Dory* on his tablet and made himself a world—just him, his snack, and his movie.

"Do you want me to stream that on the TV so you don't have to watch it on your tablet?"

He shook his head and continued eating. I figured he'd want to talk when he was ready and was left with nothing to do except observe him watching the cartoon on the opposite end of the couch, the sounds of *Finding Dory* filling the house.

I knew nothing about Pixar or animation. Mom and I watched all kinds of TV shows and movies but were never interested in cartoons. Based on what I was hearing, though, *Finding Dory* was kind of good. I moved close enough so that I could see the screen. He squirmed, a warning not to get too close, but he didn't ask me to go back to my side of the couch either.

His attention on the movie, he said, "Me and my mom watched Pixar cartoons when I was little. I know everything about Pixar and everything about Steve Jobs."

"What was your mother like?"

"She liked to watch Pixar movies with me. I remember her. I don't remember my dad. And I will probably want to talk about something else in five seconds. One thousand one, one thousand two, one thousand three..."

I imagined him and his mother watching Pixar movies together. It was heartbreaking. I had a lot of nerve being so whiny about my life.

When he turned off the movie, I asked if I could see his tablet. He stared off into space, humming, his eyes darting back and forth.

"Please? I want to show you something. I promise it'll be worth it."

He hummed but gave in.

I went to Mom's YouTube channel. "Move closer." He leaned close enough to watch the video but kept enough distance so we wouldn't touch. "This is my mom."

In the video, Mom wore a red pantsuit with leopard-print heels and matching hat. "There's a full moon in theatrical Leo! Mercury retrograde starts Sunday, my darlings. Prepare for conflict and clarity." She began dancing to Donna Summer. "Are you keeping up with my challenge to replenish? Dance with yourself. Buy flowers for yourself!" She snapped her fingers and showed off her outfit. Now that I knew about the strength of her pills, I had to wonder how many she'd taken.

"Why is she dancing?" asked Davie.

She's as high as a fucking kite, that's why. "She's trying to make people happy."

"That'll never work," he grumbled.

I watched Mom dance. "I told her on the day she died that she needed to exercise and she had a heart attack. She might be here if I had listened to her, she said she wasn't feeling well." What was wrong with me? Why was I dumping my baggage on a ten-year-old kid who had problems of his own? Real problems.

"People have heart attacks because of clogged arteries; the arteries pump blood to the heart."

I came out of my fog momentarily and looked at him.

"The heart beats one hundred fifteen thousand times a day. I watch Mr. Science."

He clicked the thumbs-up icon beneath the video. There was something so sweet about his liking Mom's video. I brushed away the tears dotting my cheeks.

"Mmmmm." Davie stared just to the left of my face.

"Sorry."

He stood and stretched his T-shirt so I could see the man on the front: A tall, skinny white dude pointed to an old-fashioned chalkboard with chemistry formulas. *Science is FUnDaMEntal!*

"This is Mr. Science. I know everything about science because of him. The heart pumps two thousand gallons of blood every day. The Amazon is home to approximately ten percent of species on Earth. Mr. Science is exceptionally smart. I emailed him once and he emailed me back. He's my friend." He sat down and asked for the iPad, then pulled up a video of Mr. Science, who rapped a math formula with no sense of rhythm. "I watch Mr. Science all the time. They don't teach anything interesting at any of the schools I've been to. Not even this new one. All the teachers there are assholes. Counselor Hayes says I'm lucky I'm so smart and that Kevin and Michelle read to me all the time."

Kevin and Michelle? Counselor Hayes? "So is Counselor Hayes your... *therapist*?"

"Counselor Hayes says I have a photographic memory. I never forget certain factual things. President Bill Clinton's father died when he was a baby and his stepfather was an alcoholic who beat up his mother. Bill Clinton has a photographic memory, too."

I stared at him in wonder, struck by his smarts and idiosyncrasies. "Who are you?" I found myself asking.

"I already told you. I'm David Mayes Jr. Everyone calls me Davie. I'm in foster care where no one cares. Ha!"

"So what are your foster parents like, anyway?"

He shrugged.

"What are their names?"

"Asshole one and asshole two. Ha!"

I snickered, although I knew I shouldn't have. I asked if he wanted something to drink and he nodded.

I went to the kitchen and poured two glasses of water—there was nothing else. "Do your foster parents care where you are? It's the middle of a Saturday. Are they okay with you roaming the streets?"

"Ha!"

"How long have you been living with them?" I returned to the couch, gave him his water.

"Three months, eight days. As long as I don't bring trouble to the door we're fine."

"What the hell does that even mean?"

"I play games with their son. He's dumb but he's good at Fortnite. The foster father gambled their money away and now the foster mother isn't talking to him. Ha!"

Holy shit, he had a lot going on. "How many families have you lived with?"

"Seven."

"Seven?! You're only ten."

"Steve Jobs got fired after he created Apple, then he created NeXT and then he helped to create Pixar and then he went back to Apple. Steve Jobs was probably as smart as I am when he was my age. I'm exceptionally smart."

Pixar Animation Studios was in Emeryville, a ten-minute drive from the house. "Did you know Pixar is nearby?"

He took several gulps of water, looking off to the side as if I couldn't have been more stupid. "Of course I do. The one good thing about the new family is they live near Pixar. I've taken the bus to Pixar studios after school three times already, but they never let me inside. They don't give tours."

"All the money they make and they can't offer a single tour?"

"They should let me inside because I know everything about Pixar and Steve Jobs. *Finding Dory* is my favorite Pixar movie, but I've seen them all several times."

"Maybe if I went with you and spoke to someone we could figure out a way for you to get a tour."

"That's a very interesting idea." He turned off the tablet and lowered the flap. "Let's go."

"Wait. *Now?*"

He put his iPad inside his backpack, and next thing I knew he'd disappeared down the hall.

"Sure," I said into the empty room. "I'll drop everything and take you to Pixar. Let me just grab my car keys."

CHAPTER NINE

You would never know the nondescript buildings on the other side of the black iron fence had anything to do with making movies. It was the sign over the entrance that made the site impressive—*Pixar*, in huge black letters and that particular Pixar font.

We walked to the fence and pressed our faces between the bars. Since it was Saturday, the grounds were quiet. The Steve Jobs building was front and center behind gigantic sculptures of a painted lamp and ball. Oak trees lined a private trail and palm trees reached toward the sky near a sprawling green lawn. We could see Adirondack chairs and couches on the deck of the tallest building, which brought to mind lazy work breaks with glasses of lemonade. I envied the employees. Sure, they had their own share of pressures, but they worked with art, they drew and created stories. I wished I had the talent to take pictures for a living. What a dream.

I followed Davie to the parking lot entrance booth, thinking, *What a difference a couple of hours can make.* I mean, I'd gone from brunch with Sneater Jasmine to preparing my suicide to taking a kid to Pixar. Go figure.

The security guard stared down at Davie from his perch, while he rambled on about Steve Jobs.

"We'd like to take a tour, please," I said.

He smiled smugly like I'd told a solid joke. I gathered he was twenty-one or so. "That's good. Everyone would like a tour."

"No tours? Ever?" I asked. "Is there a special day for children or anything? This kid knows everything there is to know about Pixar and Steve Jobs. Tell him, Davie."

"Steve Jobs was born February twenty-four, 1955. He helped start Pixar in 1986. Pixar was started by four people and now it's worth billions."

The guy—his nametag read *Guillermo*—raised both hands as if begging Davie to stop. "That's impressive, shorty, but there's no way. They don't let anyone in here unless they have a pass. These people are serious. It's like they're making nuclear weapons in there or something. That's a joke, by the way. They aren't, but I'm just sayin'."

"Do they have any charity passes?" I asked. "Anything?"

He held up a small sign: *NO TOURS*. "Sorry, kid."

Davie narrowed his eyes at Guillermo. He hummed and paced, then threw his head back and let out a piercing scream: "AAAAEEEEEE!"

I had to raise my voice over the sound of his shrieking. "Davie, calm down. It's not his fault."

"AAAAEEEEEE!"

Guillermo covered his ears. "Can you make him stop?"

I looked at Davie, helpless. "No, I just met him."

"AAAAAEEEE!"

"Please, Davie," I begged. "Screaming isn't going to help."

"Counselor Hayes says I can yell if I need to! Everybody's an asshole!"

He marched up to the parking lot entrance, where there were two guardrails that kept cars from passing. He tried to shake one of the bars. When that didn't work, he walked back to the booth, then turned around and marched right back to the entrance gate, where he tried to shake the bar again. I wondered what meds he was on, and if his foster parents were making sure he was taking them.

He returned from the gate and started pacing in front of Guillermo and me. "Forty percent of white people in New York owned slaves."

Guillermo whispered, "What's he talking about?"

"He likes to talk about slavery when he's upset, I think."

Davie continued to pace while muttering slavery facts. Someone with clearance drove inside the main entrance. "Asshole!" he yelled. He watched the gates close, then ran to the curb, where he sat down, yanked off his jacket, and buried his head in his arms.

"Poor kid," said Guillermo. "I'd let him in if I could."

I thanked him, then joined Davie on the curb. I wasn't sure what to say, so I just let him be upset. At least he wasn't screaming.

He kept his face hidden inside his jacket. "Letting me inside Pixar would be the smart thing to do. People are idiots."

He glanced up, obviously angry, but there were no tears. When I reached over, he pulled away. "Do not touch me. I do not like to be touched." I noticed, then, a bruise on his upper arm, the size of a quarter.

"What's that?"

He sat up straight and put on his jacket.

"Too late. I already saw it. Who did that? Did those boys do that to you?"

"Sometimes when slaves ran away and then were caught they'd have a limb amputated. *Amputated* means—"

"I know what it means. What happened? Do your foster parents know you're getting bullied?"

He hummed for several seconds, as if seeing how long he could hold his breath in a single note: "Mmmmm."

"Davie, stop it."

"Mmmmm."

After a moment or so of listening to him hum, I said, "I used to get beat up at school, you know."

He turned toward me, keeping his gaze just to the side of my face. "That's not true. You didn't say you got beat up."

"I didn't tell you everything." I bit down on the corner of my lip, stopping myself from speaking any further. Now was not the time to say anything about what I'd put up with in school. It would never be a good time to say anything about all that.

"Mmmmm."

"If someone is hurting you, you have to tell an adult. Tell your foster parents. Tell your teachers. You have to make someone believe you." It was as if I were talking to my ten-year-old self. I knew what it was like to be his age and defenseless.

"Counselor Hayes says that when I feel stress I can talk about what I want."

"Have you told him about the bullying?"

"Counselor Hayes says I can talk about what I want."

"Are you listening to me? Did you hear anything I just said? You need to let the adults help you."

He began humming while playing with his jacket sleeve, wrapping the fabric around his finger, tighter and tighter. The side of his Afro shot up and fell like a ski slope.

I thought of my suicide note, my plan. There was no way I could leave him alone. I hated that someone had hurt him, bruised him even. I wanted to help if I could, at least until he felt better, until he met friends of his own age. I'd kill myself later.

"Is there anything I can do?"

"You can get me inside Pixar," he griped. He began rocking slightly side to side, his eyes tracing some invisible tennis match in the sky. "The human body replaces three hundred thirty billion cells a day. I watch Mr. Science all the time and I read." For no reason I could tell, except to avoid eye contact, he untied and retied his shoes.

"I'm sure there are other students who are interested in science at your school. Are you making any friends at all? It helps to have just one friend." I told him about Gabby, my friend in fifth grade, how nice it was to have someone to hang out with. Gabby knew how to play chess, too, and we'd play after school at her house.

I asked him if he knew how to play chess.

"It looks very interesting."

"I could teach you sometime. I have a feeling you'd be good at it."

"Steve Jobs and Steve Wozniak met at HP. They both liked playing pranks. Steve and Steve!"

"I want you to be safe, Davie. I want you to have friends."

"I have friends," he said, as though I were an idiot. He started counting off on his fingers. "Counselor Hayes. That's one. Even though he told me he was my counselor he can still be my friend." He held up a second finger. "Mr. Science. I sent him an email once and he wrote me back. I like the new foster brother. His name is Sterling, but I call him Ling Ling. Ling Ling. Ha! He's dumb, but he's good at video games." He pointed at me. "And you. That makes four. Ha!"

I could feel my eyes wanting to well up. He thought of me as a friend. Okay. Suicide was definitely going to have to wait. *Davie thinks of me as a friend.* I would not hurt him by offing myself. "I am your friend. I'm here for you, okay? I want you to contact me if you ever need anything. I'll give you my information and you can text or call whenever you want."

"I don't like cell phones. It's hard to understand people on phones."

"You can email me then. And come by whenever you need someone to talk to. Will you promise me?"

He nodded.

Relieved, I leaned back on my hands. Now that suicide was off the table, however, there was something I was definitely going to have to do—something I'd been putting off since Mom's death. "I have really screwed up big-time."

"Ha!" Davie barked.

I picked up a twig from the gutter. It was not lost on me that Davie and I were sitting on a curb again, although at least this time I wasn't high. "I still haven't told my aunt and uncle about my mom. They're our only remaining relatives and they don't know she died."

"Mmmmm."

"*Yeah.*" I snapped the twig in two. "I'm going to have to tell them, though. I should call them tonight, especially now that I'm not going to..."

"Not going to what?"

"Never mind." I demolished the twig and began tossing broken pieces into the street. "We should get going."

"Yeah," he said.

But I leaned back on my hands and crossed my legs, neither of us making any effort to move.

A car drove by and we watched as it entered Pixar.

"Asshole," I said, picking up a broken stick and throwing it toward the entrance.

"Ha!"

CHAPTER TEN

I called Aunt Liane and Uncle CJ after saying goodbye to Davie. What can I say about the phone call except it was as awful as you'd expect. Aunt Liane let out a wail like none I'd ever heard. After she calmed down, she kept saying, *"You should have told me,"* as if that was the issue.

She and Uncle CJ showed up later that night after driving straight from Fresno. Aunt Liane fell into me as we sat on the couch and sobbed into my lap. Uncle CJ looked on sadly while patting her back with his good hand.

We were a unit in our mourning. Aunt Liane would weep uncontrollably or I'd cry. At one point, Uncle CJ managed to perfectly form his words: "She was a bighearted woman. I'll miss her." He came from a large family; it was good to know Aunt Liane wouldn't be alone. I felt bad for her. For all the resentment she held against Mom, I knew she loved her.

I woke the next morning to the smell of bacon and eggs—someone must have gone to the store. I was groggy and stumbled down the hall. None of us got much sleep. I stopped at the edge of the den when I saw Aunt Liane taking apart Mom's altar. Her hair was up in a headwrap and she wore cleaning gloves. She held a large trash bag and picked up wads of tissues from the floor, then she straightened up and took one of Mom's votive candles from her altar and threw it into the bag.

Uncle CJ drank coffee at the dining room table; his plate was empty. "You slept... late."

"Yeah," I mumbled. I kept my eyes fixed on Aunt Liane. I couldn't fathom what she was doing, touching Mom's things like that. She'd never even gone near the altar before. Was I dreaming? I needed coffee. "What time is it?"

Aunt Liane went back to picking up tissues. "It's almost noon." By her tone and hardened face I could tell the woman who'd been crying for her dead sister was long gone and she was back to her mean, controlling self. She tossed an empty pizza carton into the trash bag, then a couple of empty soda bottles. "This place is a damn pigsty. You should be ashamed of yourself living like this."

Where was the woman who'd been crying in my arms?

She picked up the plate Davie had eaten from, brushed the crumbs into the trash bag, and stacked it on top of the other dirty dishes in the kitchen. She then went back to Mom's altar and in one swoop dumped a bowl filled with cowrie shells into the trash bag. The shells clinked against each other like tiny pebbles.

"What are you doing?"

"What does it look like I'm doing? Now that she's gone, I'm getting rid of all this weird-ass shit."

In went another candle. When she picked up Mom's rose quartz, I rushed over and snatched it from her hand. "No one asked you to come here and do this."

"Give me that."

I gripped the quartz. "No." I tried to take the trash bag, but she yanked it out of my reach. "Leave Mom's things alone. You can't come here and start throwing her stuff away. Tell her, Uncle CJ."

Uncle CJ looked up from his paper. "Best th… thing for you."

"But it's not."

Something in the sound of my voice must have softened her. She took my hand. Her eyes were bald without her fake eyelashes, small and bloodshot from crying and lack of sleep. "She's gone, Francine, and nothing is bringing her back. We have to move forward, and keeping all this creepy satanic shit around is helping no one, certainly not you."

"But I'm not ready to get rid of her things." I returned the crystal to the altar.

Aunt Liane picked it right back up. "You don't know what's best for you right now. Help yourself to some breakfast. I've got this."

She tossed the crystal into the trash bag, then tossed Mom's wooden statue of a Yoruba woman holding her child. It was like she was assaulting my mother. I caught the end of the trash bag, tried to take it away. "Stop it."

She looked at me, surprised, but held on tight, and we struggled like kids fighting over a toy. "Let go!" "You let go!"

"Stop it. Now!" cried Uncle CJ from the dining table.

"She was my mother and I don't want to get rid of her things yet!"

I tried to take the trash bag, but damn that woman was strong, and with one firm yank she pulled it out of reach. "You need my help whether you know it or not. This house is a mess, and you waited weeks before you told me she was gone." She pointed in my face, her voice rising. "And my sister is in a fucking cookie jar."

I'd had a feeling she'd bring that up sooner or later. I glanced at Aunt Jemima sitting on an end table. "She doesn't know the difference," I muttered, guilty as charged. "It's not like we can't toss her remains together. We can scatter them somewhere special."

"Don't try to change the subject. What you're saying does not take away from the fact that you put her in a cookie jar." She picked up a chicken foot from one of the offering bowls and made a face before tossing it into the trash bag. "A truck from Goodwill will be here Monday. We'll pack her clothes and anything else we need to get rid of. You should start looking to see if there's anything you want to keep."

Aunt Liane was difficult to stand up to. She was just so intimidating. I couldn't pinpoint if it was her authoritative way of speaking or her menacing expressions. It broke my heart to think of my mother under her control as a kid.

She ran her entire arm over the spread of Mom's tarot cards. When she reached for the Medusa, anger surged through my body and I pushed her hand away. "Get out of here!"

She shook her head as though I'd just proven her point and was losing it.

Uncle CJ said, "Francine, you calm... d... down."

"You want me to calm down? Hell no." I spoke directly to Aunt Liane. "I want you to leave."

She responded as if it were her job to keep me calm, a psychiatrist working with a patient in a mental hospital. "Go eat your breakfast. Relax."

I stared at the altar in its disarray. My mother was gone. Her altar was a mess. Maybe I was having a breakdown. For a second everything went black and I saw her dying again on the front lawn. I saw her staring into my eyes, begging for help. Thinking of Mom, I looked back at Aunt Liane. "Maybe you mean well, Aunty, but I'm not ready. I can't do this." I hadn't called her Aunty since I was a kid.

"We," started Uncle CJ, "helping you."

"I don't want your help," I said meekly.

Aunt Liane started picking up dirty napkins and more tissues from the coffee table. "I told her she needed to exercise. Didn't I tell her? I told her exactly what she needed to do. Been telling her what she needs to do her entire life, but she never listens to me. I spent my life watching her make mistake after mistake."

"You never respected her and that's all she wanted."

"You didn't respect her either."

"But she was my mother." It was all I could come up with. I didn't respect Mom half the time, but she was my mother and I loved her. Maybe Aunt Liane didn't understand the complexities of a mother-daughter relationship since her mother had died when she was so young. Still—"You were always putting her down. She was sensitive about how you treated her."

"*Please.*" She picked up the seat cushions from the couch as if she was checking for change. "She wasn't too sensitive to make her videos. She was an attention seeker. She was the same when she was younger. And you know what? You need to get your life together as much as she did. You are all I have left. I wish CJ and I could've raised you, to be honest. We should've taken you after your father died."

She shook her head at Hello Mr. Fox in disgust. "It's wrong to live like this. You can't see it because you've been living in it for so long, but I mean, look at this shit." She kicked Hello Mr. Fox and he fell onto his side.

His beady eyes stared up at me. Again, I saw Mom gasping for air, the terrified look on her face. I repeated under my breath, "I can't do this I can't do this I can't do this." I stood up Hello Mr. Fox. "I want you to leave."

"I'm not going anywhere. I'm going to do what your mother wouldn't do and *help you*; otherwise you're going to end up as messed up as she was."

"Don't you care that she's dead?"

"Of course I do. You saw me last night. I'll mourn and do all the crying I need to do later, but right now we have to clean up this house."

When she reached for the Medusa, I lost it. I grabbed the trash bag before she could fight me off and pointed toward the living room. I was like Davie at Pixar: I was prepared to throw my head back and scream and scream and let out all of my frustration—a life's worth of repressed anger. My aunt was like everyone else. No one ever listened to me. "Get the fuck out of my house!"

Uncle CJ: "Enough! Calm... down! B... b... both of you."

"It's fine, CJ," said Aunt Liane. But I could see fear creeping into her naked, lash-free eyes. She stared at me while taking off her cleaning gloves, tugging at them, one finger at time. "You win. Your uncle and I will leave. We'll give you some space."

I tried to sound calm even though I was shaking. "Thank you."

"We'll come back around dinner."

"Don't. You'll be wasting your time. I don't want you staying here. I want you and Uncle CJ to get your things and go. I'm sorry, but I can't do this." I dug inside the trash bag, took out a handful of tarot cards, and placed them on the altar.

She glanced over at Uncle CJ. "You hear your niece? She doesn't want us staying here. She's kicking us out."

Uncle CJ reached for his cane and stood. "Francine, you... not... th... thinking right."

"I can't deal," I mumbled. "Sorry."

Aunt Liane pointed a mile-long nail at me. "You didn't tell me she died. You need to think about that."

I crossed my arms and looked away. I wasn't going to think about anything except her getting out of my face.

We didn't say a single word to each other, not even after she packed and told Uncle CJ it was time for them to leave.

She called from the living room while Uncle CJ stood with me: "CJ, come on now. We don't want to be in her way."

Uncle CJ gave me a final look, but, worn out, he shook his head and left.

I picked up the cookie jar—Mom—and held it close to my chest until I heard the door close. When Aunt Liane called hours later, I didn't pick up. I didn't talk to my aunt for months.

CHAPTER ELEVEN

The altar was back together by the time Davie stopped by on Sunday. He'd been watching tutorials on how to play chess and reminded me I'd promised to teach him how to play. He was as good as I thought he'd be, and by our second game he had the hang of it.

After chess, he asked if we could watch a movie and chose the nine-part Ken Burns documentary *The Civil War*. What kid wants to watch a nine-part documentary series on the Civil War? I said nothing and found where it was streaming. Turned out it was as good as, if not better than, watching a regular movie. Actors read letters from the time period and there was interesting commentary. I learned more from the first one-hour segment than I had in all my history classes combined. Another plus: watching the documentary also helped to keep my mind off Aunt Liane and Uncle CJ.

I asked Davie how many times he'd watched the series as the credits rolled.

"Several. Counselor Hayes says I can watch what I want."

"Where's his office anyway? Maybe I should see him. I could use some therapy." I was only half kidding.

"He only sees kids."

We ate from a plate of peanut butter crackers while watching the second episode, Davie taking squirrel-like bites from his open-faced crackers, his feet up on the couch. His hair was combed that day, his expression dour, as though he was learning for the first time about slavery and the fate of the enslaved. He was so thin, yet unlike me at his age, something about him was solid and confident. I hated to think of how he got his bruise, though, and wondered what his foster parents thought about what was going on. Were they trying to protect him? They certainly didn't seem to care who he spent his time with—apparently he'd told them he was going to a friend's house, which was true, I guess, but still, I had a bad feeling about them.

"Don't forget to talk to an adult if someone is hurting you. Junior high can be a nightmare."

"Mmmmm."

"I just want you to feel safe."

He crossed his arms, dug his chin deep into his chest. "Mmmmm."

I decided to drop it, and we continued watching the documentary until he said he had to go home. When he asked if he could come back the following day, I told him sure. He took off in the way I was starting to expect, grabbing his backpack and leaving the house without a goodbye.

I dreamt I was in junior high that night and slept horribly. I was inside the girls' bathroom when this faceless figure, twice my size, walked inside and punched me in the eye. Aunt Liane materialized from out of nowhere and tried to give me a knife for protection, but this person—a teenager? An adult?—grabbed the knife and held it to my throat. Davie appeared next. When the person saw him, they let me go and lunged at Davie.

I woke up, freaked out and chasing my breath. I went to work, but the dream lingered—a fist flying toward my face, a knife at my throat.

"You okay?" Hayden sat at her desk.

I was inside her office with no idea of how long I had been staring into space.

"Yeah, I'm fine. I'll be right back." *Wait.* Where was I going? Oh right, laundry. Sleep deprived and out of it, I picked up the basket filled with her smelly workout clothes.

"Take the blouse in my closest, too. And when you get back set up dinner tomorrow night with Angela. Seven o'clock. She'll need a car."

I started to leave.

"Francine?"

"Yes?"

She gestured toward the closet. "My blouse?"

"*Right.*"

To be honest, I wished I had one of Alfonse's pills. I wasn't sure why I couldn't shake the dream. It had reminded me, though, how Aunt Liane had tried to give me a knife once after I admitted to being bullied. She told me to start carrying it with me for protection, but I feared someone taking it and using it against me. Besides, I just wasn't built for violence, and getting caught with a weapon at school would've meant suspension and a disaster on my record. I wanted out more than I wanted to hurt someone.

I took care of Hayden's laundry and appointments, wondering all the while if I should give Davie a knife. Was I going to stay on the sidelines like Mom had while kids beat him up? Was that the point of the dream?

I was still in my head later in the afternoon when Hayden approached my desk.

"Angela just told me we're having dinner tonight at Coi."

I waited. *And?*

"I wanted a reservation for *tomorrow* night. You've double-booked me?"

Shit.

"You've been off today."

I could tell she was irritated, but I thought, *Cut me some slack, will you? When was the last time I double-booked you? Uh... Never!*

Maybe she picked up on my mood because she shrugged and said, "Mistakes happen. Why don't you go home after you change the reservation? I'm going to wrap things up soon."

I checked the time. She was letting me leave a whopping ten minutes early. *Partay!* "Thanks," I said, watching her walk away in her designer suit. *Could our lives be any more different?*

Eager to get out of my work clothes and change into a pair of sweats, I drove home listening to Nina Simone's more upbeat songs—"I Want a Little Sugar in My Bowl," "Feeling Good."

Rounding the corner of my block, I saw Davie in the distance, wearing his backpack, his chin jutted forward, his gait determined. I smiled at the timing.

I slowed at a stop sign and gave my car horn a toot. Davie waved but showed no emotion. It was then Saggy Pants came from around the corner and pushed him from behind.

I sped up when Davie made a run for it. Saggy Pants continued the chase and Davie ran back and forth across the street, darting behind trees in hopes of dodging him.

I gripped the steering wheel. I refused to let anything happen to him. Last night's dream was all too prescient at this point, and I needed to protect him. I was so sick of bullies, including Aunt Liane, and their fucking bullshit.

I drove through the second stop sign just as Davie ran up to the porch of the house. Saggy Pants tried to follow, but I was on him in an instant. I aimed my electric car in his direction and barreled toward him. Before he reached the sidewalk, I stuck my head out of the window. "Leave him alone!"

Saggy Pants froze and gave me the finger. I wasn't going to do anything, but I liked the look of fear in his eyes and shot the car forward. He started to run but forgot to hold up his pants and tripped over himself. I hit my brakes.

He straightened up, frustrated. "Come on, man. Stop playin' like that!"

"Stay away from Davie." I pressed the pedal and my small, golf-cart-sized car lurched forward.

Saggy Pants jumped back. "You're crazy."

"Damn straight I am! Leave him alone. If you touch him again, I'm calling the police."

I lurched the car forward. He stepped back. I lurched forward. He stepped back. I—you get it.

He threw his hands up. "All right, crazy bitch."

"That's me," I said. "Stay away from him."

He glanced at Davie on the porch, then started to walk off, middle finger in the air.

"Asshole!" Davie yelled.

I waited to make sure Saggy Pants wasn't going to try anything before pulling into the driveway.

Davie walked up to the car and hummed. "Mmmmm."

"Are you okay? What's his name anyway? Where does he live? I want to talk to his parents."

"Mmmmm."

To be honest, I wasn't altogether sure I wanted to talk to the people who raised the kid who was bullying Davie, but I was going to have to do what Mom would not: be an adult and help her child who was being bullied and picked on and traumatized.

I told Davie to get inside the car.

"Why?"

"There is no way I'm letting you go through what I went through. I'm going to talk to your foster parents so we can get a plan together and make sure Mr. Saggy Pants doesn't bother you again."

"Who's Mr. Saggy Pants?"

"The asshole."

"Mmmmm." He looked up at the sky, rocked on his feet. "I think I will want another plan."

"Too bad. You already have a bruise on your arm. Enough is enough. Do your foster parents know he's bothering you?"

"Mmmmm…"

"I didn't think so. I'm going to talk to them. And if anyone ever hurts you again, call me or 911. Now get in the car."

"Mmmmm…"

Did I really want to meet his foster parents? Hell no. But he needed help. "Get in the car, Davie. Let's go."

He relented and got inside. "George Washington owned his first slave when he was eleven years old."

"That's too bad. Which way?"

I followed his directions while he spouted facts about slavery. The neighborhood where Mom and I lived was well maintained. Mom and Dad had bought the house in an area of Oakland that was working-class. After home prices began soaring in San Francisco, though, money-eyed white folks started cautiously trekking across the bay, bringing their native ways and staples with them. At the supermarket where Mom and I shopped we started seeing things like rows of kombucha, organic quinoa, and shaved jicama. The value of our house tripled.

Davie, however, lived a mere ten blocks east, a five-minute drive that led us to a section of Oakland with no real businesses and vacant houses. I knew the particular stretch of Oakland well since I'd walked through the area to get to school. I had begged Mom to let me go to private school, but there was no way she was paying an exorbitant amount of money for private education when I could go to school for free. So after Grover Junior High I followed my peers to MacDowell, which carried the same crap motto as Grover: "Give us your child and with our overworked and underpaid teachers, oversized classrooms, and lack of resources, we will put them on a track that will lead to a life in and out of prison, teen pregnancy, or a mediocre job." *Go Pythons!*

Davie pointed to the apartment complex where he lived. The sign above the entrance read *alms Apartments*; the P in Palms was missing. The complex was next to a vacant lot where a homeless encampment was set up with tents and an abandoned couch and love seat.

I tried to keep my reaction as neutral as possible as we walked through a security gate that hung off its hinges. The complex was two stories and U-shaped. A graffitied fountain filled with trash harkened to an era of well-paying factory jobs and kids frolicking about. Most apartment doors were barricaded behind security screens; a few residents used sheets for curtains. Someone still had their Christmas tree up, twinkling lights and all. Davie walked ahead, unflappable as ever.

Two women, laughing and talking together, stopped and stared. My resolve started to fade. Was it really necessary to speak to Davie's foster parents? What the hell was I going to say? *Your foster kid has been hanging out with me, not that you seem to care?*

I was considering turning around, but we'd reached the apartment, which was at the end of the balcony. Without any warning whatsoever, Davie opened the door with his house key and let himself inside, leaving me to wait alone.

I heard a woman's voice telling him to close the door. I thought, *Now is the time to make your escape. Run!* But then a woman appeared in the doorway, looking me over from head to toe, much like the women downstairs. I was still wearing my outfit from work, a skirt and blouse.

"Yes?" she asked.

"I live up the street. Davie has been stopping by and eating crackers and watching documentaries." Words vomited from my mouth. What was I saying?

"Stopping by?" she said. "Stopping by where?"

"My house."

"Your... *house*." She turned and admonished Davie. "You were supposed to be at the after-school program at the library. You are on punishment, you hear me?"

"It—it's not his fault," I stammered.

"Who are you?"

Davie spoke from somewhere inside the apartment. "That's Francine Stevenson."

The woman glared at me. She was roughly thirty, heavyset, and honey-skinned, with the prettiest hazel eyes, so bright they took me by surprise. Except... there was also something familiar about her eyes and face.

"What was he doing at your house?" she asked.

"Some kids were trying to steal his iPad when we met. I was trying to help."

"Okay, but what was he doing at your house. *Who are you?*"

"That's Francine Stevenson! She owns an electric I-on. I-on. It's battery charged."

The look on her face revealed just how much I'd blown it. I hadn't been thinking straight. I should have made Davie tell his foster parents about me right away. I should've asked for their contact information and introduced myself.

There was no running away at this point, though. All I could do was apologize and start over. "I'm sorry, my name is Francine. Davie is having trouble with some bullies. When I met him, he was running from a couple of boys who wanted to steal his iPad. Today, I saw one of the boys chasing him. And he has a bruise on his arm."

"If somebody is bothering him, he hasn't said anything about it."

I stared into her eyes. There was only one person I knew with such bright hazel eyes. *I knew her.*

She called Davie, opening the door wide enough that I was able to steal a peek inside the apartment. A kid, who I assumed was Davie's foster brother, was stretched out on the couch, staring at his phone. A man sat in a recliner watching TV.

Davie came to the door and his foster mother asked about the bruise.

"Mmmmm."

"Show her your arm, Davie."

"Some slaves were burned with a hot iron when they were disobedient."

His foster mother sighed. "All he does is talk about slavery. Did someone hurt you?"

"Some slaves had to wear a punishment collar around their necks. It had four long spikes sticking out."

"Show her, Davie. Please?"

His foster mother clicked her tongue. "You were allowed to go to the library. Not some stranger's house."

"I'm not allowed to bring trouble to the door."

"Exactly." She pointed in my direction. "So who the hell is this?"

"Francine Stevenson drives an electric car. It's battery charged!"

"Do you understand that you told a lie? You're on punishment now, you understand me?"

"It's my fault," I interjected. "There's no need to punish him."

She shot me a look that clearly signaled I needed to mind my damn business.

Davie's head moved from left to right as though he were tracking a fly. "Francine Stevenson works at Peeps where everyone is your friend. She taught me to play chess. I'm exceptionally smart. Her mother is dead. Her mother is in a racist cookie jar. Francine Stevenson tried to run over Mr. Saggy Pants today with her electric car! Turbocharged electric E!"

And with that, he headed straight back inside the apartment, leaving his foster mother staring at me wide-eyed while she waited for an explanation.

Mom was right about avoiding people. I wanted to go home where I was safe. What the hell was I doing? Except... Those hazel eyes. *I know her*... She was older and she'd put on weight and had cut off all that long hair. But it was her.

"I think I know you."

She looked me over, scrutinizing my shoes and purse, a designer handbag—a gift from Hayden. "I highly doubt we know each other."

"No," I said, "I *know* you."

Because I did. She'd been the prettiest girl in high school. She was older than me so I never had a class with her, but it was her—*Jeannette Tomlin*. I'd often see her sitting in the principal's office and would wonder how someone who was so beautiful could get into so much trouble. I mean, the girl was always in a fight. She got kicked out of MacDowell her senior year, which takes talent, to get kicked out of one of the worst schools in Oakland.

"You went to MacDowell."

A glint of interest.

"You used to date Kenny somebody."

"*Kobe.*"

"Yeah, you and Kobe. I went to high school with you."

She looked me over again—my shoes, my purse. My buttoned-up blouse. "*You* went to MacDowell?"

"I was a couple of years behind you. You wouldn't remember me." I fidgeted with my purse, thinking of the name she would know me by. But I certainly wasn't going to remind her. I met her gaze. "Your name's Jeannette, right?" As if I didn't know. I recalled her hair swinging down her back, her legendary fights. Davie's foster mother was Jeannette Tomlin from MacDowell. It was unreal. "You used to have long hair."

"A lifetime ago." She paused, softening now. "Look, I appreciate you coming by and trying to help. I do. But you don't have to worry about Davie, he's fine."

"But—" I realized the door was closing in my face. Our conversation was over.

"You have a good night. We appreciate it."

And she closed the door. I listened to the voices coming from inside the apartment.

I heard murmuring and then screaming. "AAAAAEEEEEEE!" *Davie.* My breath caught in my throat. I knocked lightly. "Hello?"

"AAAAAEEEE!"

I heard Jeannette: "Stop that yelling."

I stood listening, wondering what I should do. Call the cops? Break down the door?

"AAAAAEEEE!"

I started to knock but then covered my ears with both hands. I was worried about Davie, but my body was having its own reaction to the sound of his screaming. My heart was beating too quickly, my hands growing clammy. This was not good. The last thing I needed was an outbreak of Bell's palsy. I felt sick leaving him, but I was in no position to help a troubled kid on the spectrum. Hell, I could barely help myself. Besides . . . *Jeannette Tomlin was his foster mother.* It was crazy! I had no choice except to believe he was in good hands. I sure as hell hoped so. Because I was outta there.

CHAPTER TWELVE

Hurrying back to my car, I shut myself inside and covered my ears. It was as though I could still hear Davie screaming.

I took slow breaths to calm myself down. I was about to start the engine when I heard, "Hey! Wait up!"

It was Jeannette, walking toward my car with Davie in tow. I rolled down the window.

Winded, she rested her hands on her knees and took a breath. "He says he won't stop screaming unless you say goodbye. He means it, too."

On cue, Davie threw his head back and screamed: "AAAAAEEEEE!"

I quickly climbed out of my car.

"AAAAEEEE!" His hands were balled into fists; his chest reached for the sky. "AAAEEE!"

"Davie, it's okay. Calm down. I'm right here."

He began to pace back and forth with his arms wrapped tightly around his small chest. "Slave children were separated from their families without warning. They never saw their families again."

"None of that slavery talk," Jeannette snapped. Light strands of hair fell out of her ponytail. She looked as exasperated as she sounded. "You said you'd stop screaming if you could say goodbye to Francine. Well, here she is."

"Counselor Hayes says I can talk about what I want!"

"Counselor Hayes doesn't live with us. Now say goodbye."

"Maybe we'll see each other again soon," I told him. I gave Jeannette a hopeful look, but her focus was on Davie.

"Francine Stevenson taught me how to play chess. I'm almost as good as her and I just learned how to play. I'm exceptionally smart."

Jeannette kneaded the spot above her brows as if fighting off a headache. "I did not need this today. I have had such a shitty day. Can you do something about him?" she asked me. "Anything?"

Davie paced, muttering to himself. I saw him through Jeannette's eyes: hearing about slavery and Steve Jobs day in and day out. "Why don't you let me talk to Jeannette in private?" I said to him. "I'm sure we'll see each other again soon."

Davie stopped moving and stared above Jeannette's shoulder. "Steve Jobs was worth ten billion dollars when he died." And with that he turned on his heel and left.

Jeannette and I watched him stride through the broken security gate. As soon as he was out of sight, she let out a long breath. "That boy, that boy…" She pursed her lips, eyes still on the apartment complex.

"Is he your first foster child?" I asked.

"He's our third. We had a newborn, but he only stayed a week, and then we had this little girl. She was the sweetest thing. Then we got Davie. His case manager didn't tell us half of what she should have. He was wetting the bed all the time—"

"Wetting the bed?"

"Girl, don't get me started."

You had to really look at her to see she was Jeannette Tomlin. Not that she wasn't pretty. She just seemed older than twenty-six or twenty-seven; there was something broken about her. Living in the *Alms* Apartments was no picnic for sure.

I swallowed before speaking. "I should've introduced myself and gotten your permission to see him. I haven't been thinking straight lately. But I would like to keep seeing him, if it's okay," I ventured. "I'd like to help."

She cocked her brow as if suddenly remembering she was pissed with me for bringing trouble to the door. "You said you went to Mac-Dowell?"

"Four years." *Of hell.*

She squinted and tilted her head to the side, blatantly staring at me. Slowly her features relaxed, and her eyes widened as it began to dawn on her. And then: *"Mudface?"*

I winced visibly. "It's Francine."

Her eyes brightened. "Yeah, but we used to call you Mudface."

True. If I was a witch in elementary school and junior high, I became Mudface or Mudface Witch in high school, thanks to Mom's downward spiral. She was experiencing her first bouts of agoraphobia and severe depression at the time, and I didn't know what the hell was going on. She was anxious and refused to leave the house; I had to convince her to do simple things like take a bath or get out of bed. By the time I finally convinced her to see a doctor I was so stressed from having to look after her, I woke up one morning to find half my face had slid in on itself in a lifeless mass, my cheek sloping toward my neck. I looked like a freak.

Mom tried her best to calm me. She told me it was Bell's palsy, and given time and rest, I'd be okay. She suggested I see the nurse as soon as I arrived at school.

"School?" I shot back. "I'm not going to school!" Was she kidding? My mouth sagged, my words slurred. "First of all, we don't have a nurse.

Second of all, look at my face! I'm not going to school like this. What if I'm dying?" I needed to see a doctor, I told her. If she cared about me, she'd drive me to the emergency room.

She looked both guilt-stricken and fearful, but she relented and said she'd take me. We were near the door when she paused. She was going to back out. I could tell.

"Mom, you can do this. I need you to come with me."

"Please, Francine. I can't. I'm so sorry, baby. Please don't hate me. Call your aunt Liane."

"I don't want Aunt Liane; I want you to take me. You're my mother, not her."

"I can't, okay? It's my anxiety. I can't help."

In the end, Aunt Liane, who still lived in San Leandro at the time, took me inside the emergency room, cursing my mother something good for being selfish.

Mom was right, though. Bell's palsy, a waltzy-sounding name for a terrible condition brought on by stress and with no cure; the only thing I could do was wait it out and try to relax. Mom let me skip school for a few days, but by day four, she said I had to go back, Frankenstein face or not.

On the day of my return, a girl cornered me in the hall. "Your face is messed up because it's God's way of punishing you for being a witch." Classmates posted on my Facebook account that I was diseased. Someone posted a picture of their dog next to my photo and people remarked that the dog was better looking. There were so many posts I deleted the account. A group of boys started calling me Mudface and the name stuck.

Jeannette continued staring, a slow nod of recognition. "Mudface… after all these years."

"It's Francine."

She gave me a once-over, noting my clothes again. "Look at you, girl. All professional and shit."

Still ruffled from hearing my old moniker, I glanced from the apartment complex where she lived to the homeless encampment. *And look at you*, I thought defensively.

"So Davie has been going to your house?"

"It all happened by chance."

"Or not. Everything happens for a reason. I mean, you're here, right? It's got to mean something." She chucked her thumb toward the spot where Davie had been having his outburst. "You know he's on the spectrum. We're trying to teach him how to behave. He doesn't act up around you, does he?"

"He's been fine."

"How long has he been going to your house?"

"About a month?" I wasn't sure. Two weeks? A month? I'd lost track of time since Mom's passing.

"I will say he's been better lately." She paused, then shook her head at me. "I remember the time I was walking with Rasheed to class and he just up and tripped you out of nowhere. You remember that?"

Hardly. I was always getting tripped in the halls. "Rasheed?"

"Yeah, Rasheed. He had those orange highlights in his hair. You remember Rasheed."

Nope. I didn't know why she'd be under the impression that I actually interacted with people in high school.

"I heard somebody put some dog shit on your porch once, too. Was that true?"

"Yes," I murmured. *Can we change the damn subject?*

"So how you been since school?" She surprised me by resting her backside against my car, as if in no rush to return to the Alms or her life. "You look like you're doing all right."

"I've been okay."

I rested against the car along with her. It was so weird standing next to her. Jeannette Tomlin was leaning against my car. *Jeannette Tomlin was Davie's foster mother.*

"Do you have any kids?"

I made a face. "Oh, hell no."

"I have a son," she said.

Shit. "Yes, that's right. Congratulations!"

"I had my boy sophomore year. I don't think you were at MacDowell by then."

I shook my head.

She paused. "Do you really work at Peeps or was Davie confused?"

"I work as an assistant; it's not that impressive. I don't code or anything."

"Sounds impressive to me." She narrowed those hazel eyes. "Are you *sure* Davie's not bothering you?"

"I'm sure. We get along."

"For now." Growing silent, she crossed her legs and surveyed the homeless encampment, not uttering a word for what felt like several minutes. She gave off a lonely vibe. I knew loneliness firsthand and imagined it clawing at her as it did with me.

I tried again: "So, I'd like to keep seeing Davie if it's okay with you."

"I guess," she muttered. "Do you remember Ceci? Ceci Morales?"

I shook my head. Again, there was the mistake of thinking I spoke to people in high school.

"You have to remember Ceci. I used to hang out with her. We both ended up at continuation school together. Anyway, her and her husband live in Modesto, but they're coming to dinner on Sunday. You want to come?"

"To dinner?"

Her expression said, *What else would I be inviting you to?* "Yes, dinner. I know she'd want to see you. Besides, don't you think we should get to know each other if you want to start spending time with Davie? Although how long that's going to last once he starts acting up, I don't know." She rested her hand on her hip and glanced down at her feet. "Tell you the truth, I could use all the help I can get. Fostering was my husband's idea but he doesn't do jack shit." She let out a small hollow laugh. "Girl, I need help with everything lately. I have had such a bad day. So what do you think?"

"Sure. I really would like to help with Davie. And you can trust me. I'll give you all my information so you can vet me."

She pulled back. "You don't talk like anybody who went to Mac-Dowell."

I stiffened. *Oreo. Mudface. Bougie*—all my old names were circling.

She pushed herself off the car. "Anyway, I'm sorry for how I treated you. I was rude. And Davie—I know he can't help it, but he's difficult. I'm trying, though."

"I lost my mother a few weeks ago," I admitted. "I get it. Life, I mean. It's hard."

"Davie was telling the truth about your mother?"

"I get the feeling Davie doesn't lie."

"True. Sorry for your loss."

"Thanks."

"So dinner? Sunday? That way my husband can meet you, too."

"Sounds good." I gave her my phone so she could put in her number. I saw she was now Jeannette Philips.

She asked me to bring a dessert, and we said goodbye. I still couldn't get over it. *Jeannette was Davie's foster mother.*

As I watched her walk away, she began to morph from weary present-day Jeannette to the Jeannette of old: Light brown hair plaited in two braids, swinging down her back. Her short skirts and low-cut tops. The girl sitting in the principal's office for the umpteenth time. The girl cursing one person or another. All that glorious attitude. She was amazing.

With my eyes still on Jeannette's back, I couldn't help but feel Mom was pulling strings from wherever she'd gone to—maybe somewhere with Dad—helping me, helping Davie. How else to explain what was happening? How else to explain that Jeannette was Davie's foster mother? I never believed in Mom's mumbo jumbo. I actually never believed in God, not a God who would allow so much suffering, anyway. But I did believe in an afterlife. I couldn't accept that we just died and nothing became of us.

I got in my car feeling slightly stunned and wondering what universe I'd fallen into. I then whispered a thank-you to Mom and drove off.

CHAPTER THIRTEEN

Maybe I was overcompensating, but I brought a bouquet of flowers, cake, and wine for dinner with Jeannette and her family. I went to a wine store and had someone help me choose the wine, and for the cake I went to Scratch Bakery, my and Mom's favorite.

I was nervous as I climbed the stairs to Jeannette's apartment and wished I'd taken just a tiny nibble of TAKE THESE FOR GOOD TIME. Davie stood at the top of the steps staring into his tablet and wearing headphones. His hair looked like someone had started to tackle one side of his head, then given up, leaving the other side to run wild. He wore his Mr. Science T-shirt, mismatched socks, and a pair of shoes usually paired with a suit and not jeans. I relaxed a little when I saw him. "Hey."

He kept his eyes on his tablet. I could hear *Finding Dory* playing. He raised his foot. "I have new shoes. They're for special occasions. They're called oxfords. Bill Clinton went to college at Oxford and Yale. His mother was abused. Why do you have flowers?"

"You're supposed to bring something when someone invites you to dinner."

I moved closer to the door but Davie blocked me. "I'm not ready."

"I'm not either but let's try to stay positive."

He hummed in response, then clicked to a video of Mr. Science, who wore a bee suit with black leggings and a bowl-shaped hat with antennae. He reminded me of Mom and her costumes, except Mr. Science was damn annoying. He danced until a billowy plume of smoke covered him from head to toe and he fell to the floor and pretended to choke and die.

"What the . . . ?"

"Mr. Science says that forty percent of bee colonies have died. Without bees we're going to run out of certain foods. I emailed Mr. Science once and he emailed back. He's my friend."

He's depressing is what he is.

I asked Davie to help me with the flowers, a hint that it was time to join everyone.

"Mmmmm," he hummed. Without warning he abruptly closed his tablet and went inside.

Okay. I braced myself and followed. As soon as I stepped into the apartment, a woman I didn't recognize wrapped her arms around me, awkwardly positioning her body around the cake and wine I carried. "Mudface! Oh my God! Look at you all grown up. Do you remember me? I was telling Jeannette we had math together." She was heavyset with a short haircut that framed her face and deep brown eyes. Her blouse was low enough that I saw the tops of two faces and the names Myra and Anthony tattooed on her chest. Holy shit that must have hurt.

She drew her face closer, as if that would help me remember who the hell she was. "I'm Ceci! We had Mr. Sumner together. You remember me!"

While I didn't remember Ceci, I did remember Mr. Sumner, who'd assign mindless handouts for classwork. "Oh yeah," I said, trying to play it off like I recognized her. "Ceci."

Jeannette pulled her away. "Give her space." She smiled and said,

"Glad you could make it, Mudface." She winked playfully, then introduced me to her husband, Tucker, who was tall and bulky.

I made a point of saying my name. "It's Francine." He extended his hand, but my hands were full.

"Help her," Jeannette said through a tight smile.

"Yeah, yeah, let me help you. Welcome to our casa." He took the cake, then pointed to a kid on the couch who sat next to Davie playing a video game. The TV took up most of the wall—a battle taking place, sounds of gunshots ricocheting through the apartment. "That's our boy, Sterling. Sterling, say hello to Francine."

Sterling kept his eyes on his avatar, currently wielding a machine gun and firing at several men. "Hey." Except that Sterling was several shades lighter, he looked exactly like Tucker—high forehead, dimples; you knew his smile would charm.

"Not 'hey,'" Jeannette said to Sterling. "Say hello like you have some manners."

"Hi," he mumbled.

"Hey!" I blurted. Flustered by my mistake, I shifted on my feet. "Hi."

I met Ceci's husband next. "Name's Alejandro, but I go by Huevo. Mucho gusto." True to his moniker, Huevo's head was egg shaped, and he had a round chest and round belly with skinny arms and legs.

"You must be confused by all us Mexicans in the house," Ceci said. "Tucker lived with me back in the day."

"Whoa, hold on," Tucker interjected. "We weren't *living together*. She was dating Huevo. I just needed a place to crash. I was supposed to be staying in this group home out in Alameda. Long story I won't bore you with."

"He's like a little brother to me," Ceci said, grinning. "A pinche pendejo little brother, but él es familia."

Tucker responded in fluent Spanish and they laughed together.

I caught Jeannette staring at me. "Is that for us?" She gestured toward the wine.

"Yes, it's a pinot." I started to give her the bottle, but Ceci intercepted it.

"Montau . . . ," she read from the label—or tried to. "Mon . . . Is this *French*?"

Jeannette looked at the label along with Ceci. "Mudface has gone bougie."

I felt my face grow hot. Back to high school I went. Oreo Mudface. Mudface Witch.

Davie said for no discernible reason: "Francine Stevenson is having dinner with us. Francine Stevenson works at Peeps. At Peeps the world is your friend!"

Tucker lifted the cake box. "Wine *and* cake; this is no joke."

"And flowers." I handed the bouquet to Jeannette. "These are for you."

She inhaled the fragrance from the lilies and peonies, her face lighting up. "I can't remember the last time we had fresh flowers in the house."

"Last time was never," said Tucker.

She gave him the bouquet and he took everything to the kitchen, which was long and narrow, barely large enough for the small table and chairs at one end. "Do we have something to put these in?" He lifted the flowers. "Do we even *own* a vase?"

"We must have one somewhere. Just put them in a plastic cup." Jeannette smiled at me, rather bashfully I thought. "Thank you."

Davie said, "Bees pollinate flowers and they're dying. Insects are losing their habitats." He said to Sterling: "Ling Ling, do you know what *habitat* means?"

Jeannette: "Don't quiz him like that, Davie."

"It means where they live. The bees are losing where they live."

"We talked about this." Jeannette tilted her head, a warning. "You should talk about nice things."

Davie hummed for several seconds, as if deciding on how to respond. When he went back to watching Sterling play the video game, I dropped my shoulders in relief.

Whatever was cooking smelled good. I hadn't eaten much since I was nervous about what I was bringing and what I should wear—I'd settled on jeans and a blazer, which I regretted when I saw how casually everyone else had dressed—and what I would talk about and how I could get in Jeannette's good graces so that I could keep seeing Davie, and on and on and on.

It was a team effort moving furniture so we could all fit in the living room. After we moved the two armchairs and recliner, we brought in the kitchen chairs. Huevo helped bring folding chairs from one of the closets. We then pushed a card table and the kitchen table together. Tucker put paper tablecloths over the makeshift table. Jeannette placed the bouquet of flowers, which had been divided into three red plastic cups, down the center.

We served ourselves buffet style in the kitchen after the table was set—chopped chicken and beef tongue for making tacos. *Yeah, tongue.* As in a cow's tongue. Huevo's family owned a Mexican produce and meat market and whenever he and Ceci visited, they'd provide the meat. Tongue, though. Really? But Jeannette and Ceci swore I'd like it, so I made my taco along with everyone else, hoping I wouldn't puke on the spot.

I was starving by the time we sat down to eat and dug my fork into my salad. When Tucker cleared his throat, I realized everyone was staring at me.

"Shall we pray?" Huevo said.

I closed my wide-open mouth and returned my fork to my plate. *Oops.*

Jeannette told Davie to take off his headphones and mute his iPad. When he ignored her and kept watching *Finding Dory*, she tilted her head while simultaneously raising her brows at Tucker. Getting the point, he said, "Li'l Man, take off those headphones and close your eyes for thirty seconds."

Davie continued watching the movie.

"He can hear us, all right," Jeannette explained. "Those headphones keep him calm. He's just choosing to ignore us right now, which is *not* polite." She raised her voice: "Davie, I know you can hear me."

He ignored her. We all waited to see what would happen next, a growing tension in the air.

Sterling nudged Davie with his elbow. "Take off the headphones. We gotta pray."

As if God had spoken to him from on high, Davie took off the headphones, muted the tablet, and bowed his head without a complaint. *What do you know.*

"Thanks, baby," Jeannette said to Sterling.

I bowed my head, thinking of how Mom would roll her eyes at the suggestion that anyone would pray to, as she put it, a monotheistic, patriarchal God.

I took the opportunity to look around the apartment while Huevo rhapsodized about the love of family and Christ. There were two family portraits on the walls, a couple of kitschy African prints in cheap gold frames, a water stain in one corner of the ceiling, and a shredded hole in the screen door that opened to a small balcony. I wondered what Jeannette and Tucker did for work. I let my gaze fall on her, her eyes closed, head bowed. I thought of a blouse she'd worn to school one day. It had cut-out shoulders and tied at the waist high above her navel.

Jeannette had sauntered by me wearing that blouse, smelling of perfume and laughing with her friends, the sun honeying her skin, her long hair a tawny gold. I remembered wanting to kiss each shoulder, to fall to my knees and kiss her belly button and worship her thighs in her short skirt.

"Amen," said Huevo.

I cleared my throat. "Amen."

Davie put his headphones back on and proceeded to arrange the food on his plate in tidy circles.

Ceci asked if I remembered Bryan somebody or other. "He was in Mr. Sumner's class. He used to come in late all the time."

How should I put this so that she and Jeannette would get it? Let me see… *I do not remember Bryan or Rasheed or anyone from high school. High school was hell and all I wanted was out.*

"Oh yeah," I said dreamily. "*Bryan.* Right."

"You know he's a cop now," said Jeannette.

"Scares me to think of Bryan carrying a gun," Ceci said. "And his little brother, Bernard, is at San Quentin for armed robbery."

"A cop and a criminal," Tucker said lightly. Grinning, he took a large bite of his taco.

I glanced down at the tongue on my own plate, half of it sticking out from the tortilla like a dead rodent. I wiggled my own tongue in my mouth.

Jeannette caught me staring in disgust. "Don't be afraid. Try it."

"It don't bite," added Ceci. She opened her mouth and stuck out her tongue. "Yum!" She and Jeannette laughed.

Huevo shook his head, feigning annoyance. "I can't take you anywhere."

I took a small bite of the taco and then another. It was good.

"What did we tell you?" said Ceci. "Muy rico, que sí?"

I nodded with my mouth full of cow's tongue.

Davie chewed in rapid bites. "Mr. Science says when cows burp they produce methane gas. It's not when cows fart that causes the problems, it's when they burp."

Sterling puffed his cheeks, then let out a loud burp and laughed.

"Sterling," said Jeannette sharply.

"Excuse me." He showed Davie what he was watching on his phone.

"Interesting," said Davie, clearly uninterested.

"It's *funny*," Sterling said, correcting him. He wore a Golden State Warriors jersey and silver chain. I looked from him to Jeannette and tried to imagine raising a twelve-year-old. Oh, hell no.

Jeannette, misreading my thoughts, remarked, "I usually don't let him have his phone at the table."

Davie adjusted his headphones. "I can have my iPad at the table and I can eat whenever I want. There's no lock on the fridge."

Tucker bit into his taco and grinned. "That's right, Li'l Man. You're a part of this family and our food is your food."

I thought of Jeannette telling me how he'd wet the bed and now—he could eat whatever he wanted? No lock on the fridge? My heart sank thinking of what he'd been through. I recalled what he'd told me about foster homes and the need to make himself disappear. I wondered if Jeannette and Tucker had discussed his bruise, and if I should bring it up later.

At any rate, I have to say, the dinner conversation was mind-numbingly boring. Sports mostly. Why were people so obsessed with sports? Maybe I *was* bougie. All that money going to people who could dunk a ball or whatever when our schools and cities were in shambles made no sense.

The conversation did take a turn, though, when Jeannette brought up *The Real Housewives of Atlanta*. Now, *that* was something I could get behind. Mom and I loved all things *Real Housewives*. The wine and beer also helped. I don't drink much and the booze went straight to my head. By the end of the meal, I was inspired to thank everyone, Jeannette in particular. I dabbed at the corners of my mouth with my napkin. "I appreciate you inviting me tonight. This has been nice."

That's when Sterling stared up from his phone as if he'd just realized I was there at all. "You sound like a white girl."

"Stop being rude," Jeannette chided.

"I'm not being rude. I'm just saying the truth." He regarded me offhandedly, as if he were the adult and I were the child. "She sounds like a white girl."

He reminded me of the boys who'd bullied me to be honest, and I felt myself shrinking. What was I supposed to say?

Davie filled the awkward silence. "Francine Stevenson works at Peeps."

"I'm just a secretary and an assistant," I muttered.

Jeannette studied me briefly. "Did you go to college?"

"UC Berkeley."

"Damn," said Huevo. "No wonder you sound white."

Everyone laughed.

Jeannette pointed at Sterling. "See there, baby? Francine went to MacDowell High and she graduated from UC Berkeley. If you work hard and get your grades up, you can do anything. You can go to any college you want."

Davie raised his finger high in the air, eyes on his tablet. "Ha!"

Ceci took a pull from her beer. "I went to Laney College for two years after I left continuation school. I was doing good, too. I had my baby by then, but I still got all As and Bs. I just needed a few more credits before I was ready to transfer. But then my father got sick and I had to help my family." She grew suddenly wistful. "I was doing really good, though. All As and Bs."

"You could always go back," I said.

She looked at me like I was crazy. "It is way too late for that."

"I hated school," Tucker said, dousing a taco with hot sauce. "If it wasn't for Nette forcing me to go to class, I doubt I would've graduated. She threatened to break up with my ass if I dropped out."

"Somebody had to help you." Jeannette's tone had no humor whatsoever. "I damn sure wasn't going to have my baby's daddy be a high school dropout. The problem is I still have to help you."

Tucker clenched his jaw, clearly annoyed by her comment, but said nothing. I found myself wondering what their marriage was like considering they'd started their family so young.

"President Harding gambled all of the White House china away," Davie said, staring at his tablet. "*China* means 'dishes,' not the country." He tilted his head toward Tucker. "He gambled—"

Tucker quickly cut him off: "Chill, Li'l Man. It's not the time."

And here is where Davie carefully closed his iPad and things took a sharp turn toward Shitsville. He took off his headphones, rose from his seat, and walked to the front of our makeshift table. "I would like to make an announcement. I would like to announce that I am moving in with Francine Stevenson. I will be leaving with her tonight."

All eyes turned to me, but I had absolutely no idea what was going on.

"What did you tell him?" Jeannette asked.

"Nothing." I looked at Davie. "What are you talking about?"

He stared off toward the kitchen. "I want to say that I'm going to live with Francine Stevenson. I will be leaving with her tonight. It's settled."

Tucker said, "Li'l Man, you live with us. We don't want you to leave."

"Siéntate," said Huevo.

"What's this about?" Jeannette asked me, confused.

"I have no idea. I swear."

Jeannette told Davie to sit down, that he wasn't going anywhere, adding, "And you're definitely not moving in with Francine."

He began to pace back and forth. "Slaves started building the White House in 1792."

"Uh-oh," Sterling muttered.

"The slaves lived in the basement after it was built, but I'm going to live with Francine Stevenson."

"Davie," I said. "You live here."

"Yeah, Li'l Man," Tucker said. "You live with us. You're not going anywhere."

Davie's pacing grew faster and faster. Sure enough, he opened his mouth, and—"AAAAEEEEEE!!!!"

Tucker said, "No screaming in the house. You know better."

"Counselor Hayes says I can scream if I want to! AAAAEEEEE!" With that, he started running around the table, looping through the kitchen, disappearing down the hall only to return seconds later. Every so often—"AAAAEEEEE!"

"Please sit down," I pleaded.

Ceci stood and began collecting plates from the table. "I think I'll help with the cake. Huevo?"

"Sure." Huevo followed her into the kitchen, just missing Davie as he shot past.

"You better sit your ass down," Jeannette warned.

Tucker tried to catch him when he made a second pass around the table. Sterling ignored the mayhem altogether and continued staring into his phone.

Davie let out a final scream—"AAAAEEEE!" and darted straight down the hall. Seconds later we heard a door slam.

Jeannette threw her head back in surrender, then gave Tucker a scolding look that said he needed to do something—or else.

"Everybody keep eating," he said. "Be right back."

Jeannette narrowed her hazel eyes at me. "You can't pretend with him, he doesn't know if you're telling the truth or not."

"I didn't tell him anything. I never said a word about him moving in with me."

She pursed her lips in a way that said that she didn't believe me for a second.

Tucker returned. "He's locked himself in the bathroom. He says he won't come out unless he can live with Francine."

Jeannette threw her napkin on the table. "I just wanted one night without him acting out."

I rose from my seat, thinking, hoping, that I could help. "I'll go talk to him."

Tucker pointed the way. "Second door on your right."

CHAPTER FOURTEEN

There's enough DNA in a human's body to stretch all the way to the sun six hundred times and back! That's a lot of stretching!"

I sat on the edge of the bathtub while Mr. Science's annoying voice shredded my nerves. For the last fifteen minutes or so, Davie had been watching him on his tablet while pacing back and forth from the sink to the door.

"I'm not old enough to be a parent. Not really." I thought I'd try a new tactic, having told him countless times Jeannette and Tucker were his foster parents and he'd have to stay with them.

"That's ridiculous. You're old enough. Miss Jeannette had Ling Ling when she was fifteen."

"Ling Ling?"

He made a U-turn at the sink. "Sterling!"

"*Right*." I tapped my finger against the tub and tried again: "But the thing is, I haven't *lived*. I've been taking care of my mom."

Mr. Science's voice filled the bathroom: "The human genome has three billion based pairs of DNA." A drum kit started to play as he rapped over a bass guitar: "Ge-ge-ge-genome. Ge-ge-ge-genome."

"Could you turn that down?"

"I refuse. Mr. Science is my friend. Unlike some people!"

"Just because you can't live with me doesn't mean we aren't friends. I care about you."

"Mmmmm."

"I do, Davie. But you can't live with me. I'm not a good role model. I need to get my own act together."

"But I wouldn't be in your way. I could spend my time at school and the library. I do not like it here."

I rested my elbows on my knees and grew silent. I knew everyone was in the other room talking about me: invite Mudface to dinner and expect chaos. "Ge-ge-ge-genome!" Mr. Science rapped. "Ge-ge-ge-genome!" Everything was ruined and Mr. Science could go fuck himself. "Would you turn that off, please?"

He closed his tablet, and picked up a toothbrush from a cup on the sink and started dry-brushing his teeth.

"What are you doing?"

He continued brushing, his teeth clenched. "I am trying not to scream."

I knew his effort meant something. But… "That is your toothbrush, isn't it?"

"Of course it is."

A knock at the door. "Everything okay in there?" Tucker.

Davie and I spoke in unison: "No," he said. "We're fine," I said cheerily.

Tucker poked his head inside. "We're going to start the dessert without you, Li'l Man. Why don't you come out now? You've been in here long enough."

"I don't want dessert. I want to live with Francine."

"Give us another minute?" I asked.

"Okay, but that cake you brought sure looks good. We're going to start eating it soon. Just sayin'."

He left and Davie continued pacing and brushing his teeth. I wished I could hug him like Mom would hug me. Forget the new-agey platitudes, it was always her hugs that did the trick when I was upset. Davie hated to be touched, though, so there was nothing I could do except tell him the truth. "Can I see your iPad?"

He handed it over without a word. I patted the empty space next to me on the side of the tub. "Would you stop for a second and sit with me?"

He continued brushing his teeth but sat down. I went to my Peeps Box, basically a knockoff of Dropbox, and pulled up pictures I'd taken of Mom: Mom on the couch, unkempt, staring into nothing. Mom in bed, eyes vacant. I'd taken several pictures of her when she was depressed, most taken before Alfonse started sending his pills. I'd shown them to her once when I was trying to convince her to return to her doctor.

Davie brushed his molars, staring. "What's wrong with her?"

"She's depressed, and it was my responsibility to take care of her when she wasn't feeling well. I worried about her all the time. I know I'm an adult, but I've spent most of my life looking after my mom and now I'm alone. I don't even know who I am or what I want. And I'm scared all the time. But you're helping me to feel better." It was true. I was glad I hadn't committed suicide, grateful he was in my life. "And now that we're friends, life will be a little easier for both of us because we'll always have each other's backs. But we have to try to face what we've been dealt. That's what my mom would say. When she was feeling her best she did have good advice. She'd say our challenges are our lessons and we have to face them no matter what they are."

Davie stopped brushing his teeth. "Mmmmm."

I could hear the chatter coming from the living room. Davie didn't seem to mind at all that we were making everyone wait. I realized I shouldn't care either. It was Davie who needed my attention, not a group of people I barely knew. I said, "That brain of yours is going to help take you wherever you want to go in life. Right now, though, you have to live with Jeannette and Tucker; and maybe sometimes you don't like it here, but it's what you have to deal with. Like I have to deal with losing my mom. It's a miracle that someone I went to school with is your foster mother. I think—I know Mom is trying to help me, and you."

"Your mother is inside a racist Aunt Jemima cookie jar." He stood and looked somewhere above the shower curtain. "A white woman taught Frederick Douglass how to read but then her husband made her stop."

"Right," I said. "*Exactly.*" I hadn't a clue about the connection he was making to what I'd told him, but, hey, he wasn't humming or screaming. "Why do you talk about slavery so much, anyway?"

"Counselor Hayes says I can talk about what I want."

"Yeah, but why slavery?"

"The slaves had it worse than anybody ever."

"So when you think about them you know you don't have it so bad?"

"Mmmmm."

I had to assume that I was right.

"I'm on the spectrum. Counselor Hayes says that means among other things that I'm very smart." He returned his toothbrush. "A genome gives organisms instructions. There are twenty thousand to forty thousand genes in the human body and thirty trillion cells. Ha!"

"You really are exceptionally smart."

"I know." He raised a gallant finger high the air. "Harriet Tubman freed three hundred slaves!" And with that, he opened the bathroom door and walked out.

I took a breath and tried to summon the courage to face everyone in the other room. I was about to leave when Jeannette appeared in the doorway. She studied me coolly, arms crossed.

Shit.

"He can't read social cues so you have to be careful with him. He'll get something into his head and not let it go."

"I swear I didn't say anything about him moving in with me. I'm sorry."

She dropped her arms. "It's okay. He seems better now at least." She caught her reflection in the mirror and stepped inside the bathroom, squeezing beside me so that she could look at herself. She used the tips of her fingers to tug at the skin beneath her eyes. "I look like shit."

"You look nice."

She fussed with her hair. "You don't have to say that."

"You do." Honestly, if I'd had my camera and she were willing I would've snapped a shot, Lorna Simpson style: A quiet moment of Jeannette silently conversing with her reflection. Capture the makeup covering the bags under her eyes and the heavy mascara; the motion of her hands, digging in her light brown hair; her badass, take-no-prisoners stare.

She checked her profile. "I might look like shit now, but remember how I used to look back in the day?"

I felt myself blush.

"Girl, the stories I could tell." She squeezed beside me, our chests almost touching. "Let's get out of here. It is time for cake and something stronger than beer and wine."

◆　◆　◆

A bottle of bourbon went around the table, and the cake I'd brought—a double chocolate cake with dulce de leche—was a hit. It was as if the episode with Davie hadn't happened at all.

Well, at least until we were almost finished eating. He licked chocolate from his fingers with a loud smacking sound. "I can't live with Francine Stevenson because she does not have any idea what she's doing with her life because she always took care of her mother who was depressed and now she has to get her life together."

All eyes were on me in an instant. I searched the living room and kitchen for a crawl space, a bunker, a cave. There was also the front door; I could just run out.

"Don't tell people's business," Jeannette said. "It's not polite."

"Yeah, Li'l Man," said Tucker. "Some things are private." He looked at me from across the table and mouthed, *He can't help it.* He then stretched his arms and said to Davie and Sterling that they should get ready for bed soon; they had school the next day. They put their plates in the kitchen. Before they left, Jeannette told them to thank me for the cake.

Sterling placed his hand on Davie's shoulder and thanked me. I noticed that Davie didn't flinch or yell at him. *What the…?* Why was Sterling allowed to touch him? He gave Davie a nudge. "Say thank you."

"Thank you," Davie repeated robotically before leaving the room.

Jeannette told Sterling to give her a kiss good night. Rising from the table, she wrapped her arms around his waist and kissed the top of his head. "Night, baby."

"Night, Momma."

We cleaned together with a rapper I didn't particularly care for playing in the background. I only knew the *artist*, if you could call her that, because Kelly listened to her. When I told Kelly I thought the singer's lyrics were misogynistic and dumb, she poked fun at my old-school taste and said I needed to come out of the past and move on from singers like Nina Simone and Aretha Franklin. As if that was ever going to happen.

Tucker and Huevo said good night after we cleaned the kitchen. Tucker worked for a vending machine company in Antioch and had a long commute. He started to kiss Jeannette but there was weird energy between them; she turned away before he could reach her lips, his mouth sort of sliding across her cheek. He gave me a hug and told me to come back anytime. "Bring more of that fancy wine," he teased.

Huevo and Ceci were staying the night since Modesto was such a long drive. Tucker and Huevo put sheets and blankets on the floor in Davie and Sterling's room. It was like a regular slumber party. I stood around wishing I could stay, too. It had been far from a perfect night, but I hated to go home to an empty house. Huevo kissed Ceci good night and suddenly the apartment was quiet. I stood in the middle of the living room with nothing to do except say goodbye. "Guess I should get going. Thanks again for everything."

"'Thanks again for everything,'" Jeannette mimicked, pitching her voice squeaky and high, as though I spoke like a white girl from Utah.

Ceci, seeing my reaction, said, "Relax, puta. She's teasing you. Don't leave. Now is when the fun starts."

"It's late," I said—only because I was supposed to.

Jeannette headed to the fridge. "Sit down, bitch. Thirty more minutes won't kill you."

Ceci sat at the small kitchen table. She tilted her head toward one of the empty chairs and gave it a few pats. "Siéntese."

I joined her at the table and we watched Jeannette take a chair and put it in front of the refrigerator. She then climbed up and fumbled blindly until she found what she was looking for: a baggie of weed. She gave it a shake and put it on the kitchen table along with a pipe that looked like something Sherlock Holmes would've used back in the day, with an extra-long stem that curved at the end. Next, she poured three shots of bourbon and placed the remainder of the cake in the center of the table with three forks.

She took a sip of her drink, then picked up the pipe. "You ever smoke weed, bougie?"

I wished she'd stop calling me that. I raised my chin, defensive. "Of course I've smoked weed. My ex-girlfriend smoked all the time."

Jeannette and Ceci stared back with surprise.

Oops.

Ceci gaped like I was a strange, exotic creature newly landed inside the kitchen. "*You're gay?*"

"Ignore her," said Jeannette. "She's being silly."

"But she doesn't act gay," Ceci said, still puzzled.

Jeannette finished filling the pipe. "Would you stop? You sound ignorant."

She handed me the pipe and a lighter. The marijuana wasn't the crunchy stems Kelly typically smoked, it was a lush green and potent.

"Are you dating right now?" Ceci asked.

"I was in a long-term relationship, but we broke up a couple of years ago. I haven't dated seriously since." I toked and fell into a coughing fit.

Jeannette patted my back. "You okay, bougie?"

I hacked out a lung. "I'm fine," I coughed. "It's just been a long time."

I handed Ceci the pipe. She lit up and inhaled for several seconds. "It hasn't been long for me."

Jeannette toked next. She then raised her fork above the cake. "Dig in, y'all."

We ate without plates or manners, stabbing our forks into the cake and moaning with every chocolaty, dulce-de-leche-filled bite. We passed the pipe around and ate and got high, and even the nasty bourbon tasted good.

Soon the cake was gone and we were somehow munching on crack— that is, Circus Animal cookies! A blast from my past! Delights of pink and white sugar with sprinkles on top that you can't stop eating. We talked and laughed at things that would otherwise not have been funny at all without the help of booze and weed. We dissected all the wives of

The Real Housewives of Atlanta, Potomac, Beverly Hills, New York—all the wives. Wives for days.

Jeannette poured another round and she and Ceci told me about Grace Continuation School. After Jeannette had been kicked out of MacDowell for fighting, she was sent to Grace, where more fights ensued; Ceci had truancy issues.

Jeannette passed the bag of cookies to her. "Do you ever think about how things would've been different if we hadn't been sent to continuation high and graduated like everyone else?"

Ceci bit off the head of an elephant-shaped cookie. "Not at all. There's no point. I was really smart, though." She looked at me. "Maybe I will go back to school," she said, referring to my suggestion during dinner. Then to Jeannette: "You know what? We could go back to school together! Let's get our degrees, chica."

Jeannette blew smoke into her face. Ceci opened her hand and pretended to catch it. "I am finished with school. My focus is on Sterling. I want *him* to go to college. Was college hard?" she asked me.

Buzzing on sugar, high on weed, I lapsed into thoughts of sitting in large lecture halls and taking notes, studying with friends at cafés, sex with Kelly. Sex with Kelly had been good. Really really good. "It was the best time of my life," I murmured. I realized my eyes were closing and sat up straight. Keeping my gaze on my shot of bourbon, I added, "It was easier than high school. No one bothered me."

"Yeah," Ceci said. "Everybody picked on your ass. Why'd they call you Mudface anyway?"

I had enough alcohol and weed in my system to not be as triggered as I might've been otherwise. I reminded them of the day I showed up with my destroyed face.

Jeannette nodded slowly. "I remember seeing you. The side of your face was *messed up*. What happened?"

I told them all about my Bell's palsy. I should say Bell's palsy, not *my* Bell's palsy; it wasn't like I owned it. But when I started to explain the name Mudface, I found it difficult to get the words out. The name was a comment on my dark skin: I'm not just dark-skinned, I'm very dark, and the name was as much about my skin tone as about Bell's palsy.

"Half my face was sliding down, and..." I brushed two fingers back and forth across the top of my hand.

"What does that mean?" asked Ceci.

"Her skin," said Jeannette.

"The boys in class would say I'm dark-skinned like mud. My face was drooping, and I'm dark like mud, get it?" I giggled nervously.

"It's not funny," Jeannette remarked.

I pointed at her. "Yeah, but you're light-skinned." I pointed at Ceci. "And you are, too. You don't know anything." I giggled again. The sound of my giggles made me giggle more, my subconscious trying to mask my embarrassment. Plus, I was *hella* high.

Jeannette stared at me, concerned. She then poured a glass of water. "Drink this." She stood over me until I finished most of the glass. "I didn't realize." She sat down, and she and Ceci watched me quietly. "It was just something we called you."

The glass of water sobered me up a bit, but I still couldn't face them and stared at the bag of cookies. "You guys wouldn't get it. Dark skin is considered less-than worldwide. Latin America, Asia... Even Africa. They lighten their skin in Africa!" I giggled. It was like words kept shooting out of my mouth before I had time to stop them. I was ruining the fun. *Shut up already, Francine. Shut up shut up shut up.*

I reached for my shot of bourbon, but Jeannette pushed my glass out of reach. "No more for you."

I thought that I had sobered up, but then my head fell off to the side. Ceci shoved my arm and straightened me up.

"Let me get you some more water," Jeannette said. She spoke in a motherly voice that made me want to weep. I noticed then she had two noses.

Ceci laughed. "You're such a lightweight."

"I'm such a weirdo. I'm sorry."

"For what?" asked Ceci.

"Everything," I moaned.

Jeannette refilled my glass of water and watched me take a sip. "Don't apologize. We started it."

Ceci said, "What you said is true. My mom and my tías were always monitoring how long me and my sisters stayed out in the sun. You know who's to blame for all of this?"

Jeannette sighed and shook her head. "Here we go. Go on and tell her."

Ceci gave the table another tap. "Christopher Columbus."

"She blames Christopher Columbus for everything," said Jeannette.

"Hell yeah I do. I blame him and his three ships. Pinche pendejo messed it up for everybody—except white people. There's no telling what things would be like today if he would've kept his pasty ass in Spain."

I giggled. "She has a point."

"If not for Christopher Columbus, I could be in Mexico right now being an Aztec queen. With all these strong Aztec men massaging my feet."

I laughed, and then Ceci joined in and then Jeannette.

I knew, later, after I sobered up, I'd be kicking myself a thousand times for opening my big mouth about my skin color, and all of my whining. Right then, though? To be honest, it felt good to laugh—high or not. Smiling, I gazed from Jeannette to Ceci, picked up the Sherlock Holmes pipe, and took another hit.

CHAPTER FIFTEEN

A warm mass pressed down on my stomach and chest as I stared into an unfamiliar ceiling; I heard the sound of cooing followed by a loud snort. After my eyes adjusted to the dark room, I turned my head and stared into a foot with bright pink toenails.

I slowly sat up, realizing I was on Jeannette's couch. Ceci slept on the other end with her leg resting on top of me. Her head was thrown over the armrest, her mouth open like she was a baby bird waiting for a worm. She cooed and snorted. I eased her foot up and off my shoulder, placed it on the back of the couch, then picked up a blanket off the floor and covered her with it.

"Somebody awake in there?" Jeannette—from the balcony.

I draped a second blanket over my shoulders. My head pounding, I walked over and peered at her from behind the screen. She sat at a small table in sweats and a jacket. The bottle of bourbon was open.

"What time is it?"

She checked her phone. "Almost one o'clock." She held up the bourbon and gave the bottle a jiggle. "Want some?"

"No thanks. I already feel like I'm going to puke."

"My superpower is that I can drink anyone under the table." She patted the empty chair next to her. "Keep me company for a minute?"

The balcony allowed just enough space for two people, overlooking an alley with trash everywhere and an abandoned couch someone had set on fire.

"Don't look down," Jeannette warned. "If you don't look down, it's nice out here."

I inhaled the cool night air and let it penetrate my hangover. The moon illuminated a cloud-covered sky. "I can't believe I fell asleep."

"Your ass got seriously drunk. You're funny when you're high, though." She stretched her legs beneath the table. "I've had bad insomnia lately. I haven't had a good night's sleep since forever."

"Have you thought of taking anything? Ambien?" I thought of Alfonse's TAKE THESE FOR GOOD SLEEP, but the last thing I needed to do was start peddling pills.

"You're lucky you work at Peeps," she responded, changing the subject entirely. "I hate my job." She worked at Home Insurance in Berkeley, customer service.

"You guys make my job out to be more than what it is. I'm really just a glorified maid." *Hear that, Aunt Liane? I can admit it now.* I considered telling her about cleaning up Hayden's vomit, but I imagined her calling me crazy for doing something so low.

"But I bet you make good money," she added. "And I bet your boss doesn't harass you."

"Your boss harasses you? Like sexually?"

She gave me a look. "What other kind of harassment is there?"

She stared up at the sky. She was so pretty, even now that she was older. I could only imagine what she had to put up with as a girl—from boys, from men twice her age, and now her boss.

Watching her, I recalled the time Wesley Morris groped her at school. I was sitting in the bleachers out by the football field, reading and eating lunch by myself—nothing new there. Jeannette was supposed to be in PE but she hadn't dressed, so she stood with the other students taking an F for the day. Based on the yelling that broke out, Wesley had walked by and groped her ass. I looked up from my book and saw her wielding a pocketknife in Wesley's face, cursing him something good. The blade was no more than three or four inches, but still, it was a knife, and she looked ready to use it. The PE teacher had his eye on students running laps and missed the entire incident. But let me tell you, seeing the shock in Wesley's eyes when Jeannette aimed that blade at his face was priceless. I hated Wesley and was sure he'd been responsible for putting a dead mouse in my backpack when I was in eighth grade. I literally burst into applause when he ran off. A couple of girls sitting on the front bleachers turned but, seeing it was me who was applauding the show, rolled their eyes dismissively and turned back around.

Jeannette hid the pocketknife in her jacket and yelled at the PE teacher that Wesley had touched her ass, but he only shrugged off her complaint, then told her to sit down on the bench and said, "Close your trap." Close your trap, he'd said. As if she were at fault.

She picked up her glass of bourbon. "What I hate more than my boss standing all close to me and giving me these long hugs is when he calls me out my name. He calls me *hazel eyes* when no one's around, like it's okay for him not to use my name. I can't stand him or his nasty breath. Or his fucking fat fingers all over me." She cringed visibly.

"You should tell someone. You should sue and get him fired."

"Bougie bougie bougie. Girl, I don't know *what* to make of you. Who's going to believe me over him? I could end up getting fired, and then what am I supposed to do? Go back to working fast food? Oh, hell no. I'd rather put up with his fat ass. Besides, I can handle him."

"What about telling Tucker?"

"You're funny. Yeah, I'll tell Tucker and he'll kick his ass and end up in jail. Good idea."

I considered suggesting she find another job or go back to school, but I knew how that would land. "Do you remember Wesley Morris?" I asked.

She drank from her glass, thinking.

"You pulled a knife on him in PE."

"I did?"

"You don't remember?"

She shook her head. "I remember the knife I used to carry."

"How did you get a knife into the school, anyway?"

"I hid it behind a bush until that one metal detector that was always breaking went out again. Then I put it in my sock and walked on into school like it was nothing. I kept it in my locker after that so I could keep it on me during the day."

Smart move. I thought of Aunt Liane's suggestion that I carry a knife to school. But unlike Jeannette, I wasn't a fighter. I considered asking how many times she'd been sent to the principal's office.

The sound of her voice broke into my thoughts. "How'd your mother die?"

"Heart attack."

"My mom died from Alzheimer's."

"Alzheimer's? How old was she?"

"*Old*. She had me late." She laughed lightly. "I was a *big* mistake. She hated me."

I couldn't imagine a mother hating her child. "Don't say that."

"No, she hated me. I hated her, too."

She drank from her glass. She didn't seem drunk at all, considering. Mostly it seemed like she just wanted someone to talk to. It was easy talking to her, too, I have to say. Maybe it was the hour. Everything quiet. Most people in Oakland and beyond tucked into their beds, fast asleep. Maybe we were both too tired to put up walls. Whatever the case, I was grateful for it. Someone to talk to.

"Were you and your mother close?" she asked.

"Very. Kind of dysfunctionally close."

"What about your dad?"

"He died when I was nine."

"My dad died when I was nine, too."

We shared morbid smiles at the coincidence. She reached for her phone, scrolled to a picture. A man held a three- or four-year-old Jeannette in his lap, beaming with fatherly pride. The man in the photo was dark-skinned and looked nothing like her—no hazel eyes or light brown hair.

"This was taken before he got sick. He had MS, then died of a stroke. He's not my biological dad. My bio dad... I don't know where he is, and I don't care. This man here is my real dad as far as I'm concerned."

So that explained the difference in appearance. I asked to see her phone, went to a video of Mom answering questions about astrology. She was on a string of good days at the time we'd made the video and wore a suit and fedora. "She was like a counselor and psychic, numerologist, tarot reader. She had all kinds of jobs."

"She was a hustler is what she was," Jeannette said, impressed. She looked from Mom to me. "You have her smile and you have her eyes."

I appreciated hearing that.

The video came to an end; she put down her phone. "Did she make any money?"

She was exceptional at making money. I thought of her savings account; her life insurance policy; our joint savings account, which we planned to use for travel. "She did. She made a good living, actually, but she also liked to say that money was nothing except energy."

Jeannette laughed. "I need me some energy then. I wish it was that easy."

"Let me show you a picture of my father." I went back inside, tiptoeing past a sleeping Ceci, and found my phone.

I showed Jeannette a picture of my father kneeling down next to me, our faces cheek to cheek. "I was six when this was taken."

"That means you had three more years. Between you and me, my husband gets on my last nerve. Don't even get me started. But he is a good father to Sterling, and I'm glad I can give my son a stable two-parent home." She took in a breath, slowly exhaled. "Sterling means the world to me. He's my everything. I worry, though, because he's not doing all that well in school. I wish to God some of Davie's smarts would rub off on him. That boy has issues, but he is damn smart."

"He sure is."

"He's a lot, though." She shook her head slightly as if recounting all she'd endured since taking care of Davie. "It was something to have to go from fostering Mabel to Davie. I still think about that little girl. She was just beginning to talk. But she had family in Richmond and some cousin decided to take her. We must've got Davie maybe four days later. He used to hide food everywhere when he first got here. His previous family was *fucked up*. He won't talk about it, but we don't think they fed him enough. Otherwise, why was he wetting the bed and hiding food? You know what I mean?"

My heart sank. *Poor Davie.* "Did you ever ask him about the bruise on his arm?"

"He won't tell me much of anything, but I saw it. I hate to say this, but he's not like other boys; he's going to have to get used to being picked on."

As someone who was "picked on," I had to disagree. "But the kids trying to take his tablet weren't just picking on him, they were trying to beat him up. And a bruise is serious."

"I told Sterling to keep an eye on him. Kids won't bother him if they know Sterling is looking out for him. Try not to worry. You know how kids are."

Yeah, I do, I thought. *I do know how kids are.*

She gave me a strange look, as if caught off guard. "I like talking to you, bougie."

"I like talking to you, too." Except—I stole some courage: "Would you mind not calling me bougie?"

"Do you want me to call you Mudface?" Seeing my reaction, she grinned. "I'm just teasing you. Lighten up, girl. I like you." She took a swig of bourbon, looked at me from over the glass momentarily, thinking. "We should hang out."

Now it was my turn to be surprised. She wanted to hang out with me, which also meant I'd be able to see Davie. I tried to keep my tone as even as possible to hide my excitement. "That would be great."

"'That would be great,'" she mimicked in her white-girl-from-Utah voice.

When I made a face, clearly expressing my annoyance, she bumped her shoulder to mine. "*I'm kidding.* You're going to have to learn to take a joke. How about next weekend? We could do something with the boys."

"Sounds like fun. What about the Oakland Museum?"

"*The museum?*" she repeated, as if I'd suggested outer space. "And you don't want me to call you bougie."

I tensed. Museums weren't bougie. Were they? "My mom would take me to museums when I was Davie's age," I told her. "She liked the quiet and I learned to like the art."

"You weren't bored? I think a museum would bore Sterling to death."

"They have exhibits for kids and—I don't know, art gives you a new way of seeing things. It's the opposite of boring."

I pulled up work by artists like Kehinde Wiley, who created historical-looking portraits of everyday African Americans, and Glenn Ligon, who worked with text and word images. The photographer Carrie Mae Weems, best known for her *Kitchen Table Series*. I was talking way too much. *Way too much.* But it was like some trapdoor inside my mouth had been opened. I didn't shut up until I noticed how quiet Jeannette had become. She wasn't expecting a PBS series. Flustered, I quickly put down my phone. "Anyway… Never mind. We can go to the movies. Or whatever. We don't have to go to a museum."

"No, let's do the museum. I like that you know about art. Do you paint or something?"

"Photography. Kind of. It's just a hobby." I could've easily clicked to one of my own pictures, but I wasn't ready for any negative criticism.

"Sterling needs to know about those kind of things and go to different places like museums. He needs to see there's more to life than what goes on around here." She picked up her glass of bourbon and gestured toward the homeless encampment. "I really need him to do better in school." She drank, then held her glass in front of me, offering a sip.

I told her no thanks and she finished it off. I still couldn't believe I was spending time with Jeannette Tomlin, having a heart-to-heart. I considered telling her about Mom, actually. It had taken me months before I told Kelly about her agoraphobia, but I wanted Jeannette to know. I didn't want her thinking the woman she saw in the video was always the happy hustler.

"Can I tell you something?"

"Anything. You have me out here spilling my guts."

But then the screen door opened. Ceci stepped out, her hair a mess on her head. "Shit, mujeres. Don't you bitches ever sleep?" She rubbed her eyes and yawned loudly. "I had the most fucked-up dream." She proceeded to tell us about her dream, in which she gave Christopher Columbus a blow job. Jeannette and I laughed, but with Ceci in the mix, the mood shifted, so when Jeannette eventually asked what I was going to tell her, I said it was nothing and left it at that.

CHAPTER SIXTEEN

left Jeannette's at two in the morning. Once at home I took a four-hour nap, dressed for work, and brewed coffee so strong I may as well have eaten the beans straight from the bag.

At work, I greeted Hayden with an overly caffeinated "Happy Monday!" Hearing about Jeannette's boss helped me to appreciate that, while I had to put up with the occasional puke bomb, at least I didn't have to deal with sexual harassment.

I helped Hayden with her coat and asked about her weekend, even though what I really wanted to do was to tell her about *my* weekend. I wanted to tell anyone about my weekend besides my ghost of a mother.

I followed Hayden into her office, hung her coat inside her closet. She said something about Maddie and something something and something about something else, then sat behind her desk and opened her computer. "And you?"

Finally! "I had dinner with an old high school classmate who I haven't seen in years. We happened to run into each other and she invited me to dinner."

"Hmmm."

I assumed the "Hmmm" was about whatever she was staring at on her computer. I stepped closer and cleared my throat. Was she listening? I listened to her all the time. Granted, I was paid to, but still.

My high school friend just happens to be Davie's foster mother. Can you believe? That reminds me, I haven't told you about Davie, have I? Where do I start?

Of course I said none of this. I just stood there watching her type. Without looking my way, she handed me her high-tech travel mug. I managed not to show my disappointment. "Espresso or cappuccino?"

"Double espresso. And get Sundeep on the line when you get back."

"Will do."

"Thanks, Francine."

Sure. Whatever.

I left for the cafeteria to rinse out her mug and get her coffee. But wouldn't you know? The FUN Committee was waiting in line at the café. *Shit.* I would've let the elevator doors close and headed straight back upstairs and waited them out if not for the Jessicas catching sight of me.

"Hey, Francine." White Jessica.

"Hi." *You hypocrite. I heard what you said about me.*

Bethany, her attention on her phone: "Hey."

Asian Jessica: "Have a nice weekend?"

I kept it short and sweet. "Yep."

I knew I shouldn't care, but it stung that I hadn't been invited to the women's retreat. Wanting to avoid them, I excused myself, went to the kitchen area, and rinsed out Hayden's mug. They were still in line when I finished, so I went to the bathroom and hid in a stall to kill time. I just wasn't in the mood to pretend I liked them.

Sitting on the toilet, I wondered how Jeannette would've behaved around the Jessicas and Bethany. I thought of the day she was kicked out of MacDowell for good, how she fought the security guard on the lawn, clawing at his face and cursing him, how she drew her pocket-knife. I remembered watching her in awe and wishing I could fight off all of my haters with the same fury.

I took out my phone and made a few chess moves in a game I had going with a player called ChessPie. When I figured enough time had passed, I went back out and ordered Hayden's coffee.

I'd just returned to my desk when my phone buzzed. I assumed it was yet another text from Aunt Liane. I have to say I didn't miss her at all. She hadn't called me in over a week, and I was glad she was getting the point that I wasn't going to talk to her until I was ready—which at the rate we were going would be never. I picked up my phone expecting to see an all-caps message telling me to contact her, but it was Jeannette.

How are you?

I quickly texted her back: Hanging in there.

I had fun last night. I'm counting
the days til Saturday. Can't wait.

I had fun, too!!!!!!!!!

Okay. Way too many exclamation points, but I'd already hit send. It didn't matter at least. She followed with another text about arriving to work late, which began a thread that lasted into the evening and the rest of the week. We texted while watching *The Real Housewives of Atlanta* and a movie on Netflix we hated.

The following week, she called out of the blue, sometime after eleven. I was in Mom's bedroom getting ready to go to sleep. My initial thought was something had happened to Davie or she was going to cancel, but she said she just wanted to talk. Was I busy? Had she called too late? No and no.

We FaceTimed and I could see her out on the balcony, drinking bourbon. She told me more about her mother's battle with Alzheimer's and the difficulty of looking after her, while her brother, Jordan, who was eighteen years older, was off living his suburban dream life in Atlanta with his family.

It was the perfect time to tell her about Mom.

"Agora what?"

"Agoraphobia. She'd get into these moods and wouldn't leave the house. She would be fine, then out of nowhere would get depressed or have anxiety." I told her more about our codependency, too, then apologized for oversharing.

"Don't apologize. My mother was…" She let her voice trail off, picked up her drink. "She was a nightmare. You don't even want to get me started."

I glanced at Mom's small altar in the corner of her bedroom. It was floor-level with a handmade wooden angel and two crystals on top. I closed my eyes briefly and thanked her for helping me meet Jeannette. She had to have a hand in it, especially since we were getting along so well.

I took a big leap and showed her a few of Mom's gourds and the large altar in the den. I left out creepier things like Hello Mr. Fox and the rattlesnake tails. I also made sure not to include any of the mess I'd made while walking through the house.

"I won't lie," she said as I crawled back into bed. "Some of your mother's stuff freaks me out, but the house is nice. You're lucky. I would do anything to be able to move out of this shithole apartment."

The following night we talked some more about our childhoods and even came up with a plan for me to start helping with Davie. He'd be allowed to visit twice a week if he wanted. *Yes!*

On Saturday, I arrived at the museum thirty minutes early and bought tickets for everyone. I was excited to be a part of a group for a change. I mean, except for online friends and Mom, I was usually by myself.

Jeannette was surprised I'd paid for the tickets, a little miffed, truthfully, but I told her that since the museum was my idea, I wanted to treat everyone. She seemed fine with that and relaxed, mentioning she'd pay for the next outing, which made me smile: there would be another outing.

I wanted to give Davie a big hug, yet, as per his rule, I kept my distance. He wore his shiny new oxfords and a polo shirt neatly tucked into pants. It looked like his hair had been trimmed.

He read from his iPad with his earbuds in his ears. "The Oakland Museum was built in 1969."

"He's excited about being here." Jeannette wore a blouse and low heels, as if she'd thought she needed to dress up. I, meanwhile, wore jeans and a pair of Converse. She smiled at Davie. "He was on his best behavior this morning. Isn't that right, Davie?"

"I had to be on my best behavior at the barbershop and I had to be on my best behavior this morning or I would not have been allowed to come to the museum. Crispus Attucks escaped slavery and was the first person killed in the Revolutionary War."

"But no slavery talk," she said. "You promised." She nudged Sterling. "Say hello to Francine."

"Are you excited about seeing the exhibits today?" My voice practically squeaked. I hadn't meant to sound like Mary fucking Poppins.

He shrugged, stared at his phone. "Not really."

"*Sterling,*" Jeannette admonished.

"I'm supposed to lie? If I had my way I would've stayed home." He looked toward the entrance like he'd been sentenced to a day in the gulags. He wore expensive tricolored high-tops and his hair had been cut into a fade with arrows shooting toward his ears, each ear studded with a fake diamond.

Jeannette told him to put his phone away. "You're going to like this," she said, her voice tinged with doubt.

He slid his phone into his back pocket, glancing at me with enough hatred to make me momentarily look away. "It's good to take a break from your phone," I said to him. "And you'll like the sneaker exhibit. They might have shoes like the ones you're wearing now."

"I doubt it." He shot darts of spite my way. "Museums are for white people."

"Sterling," said Jeannette. "Stop being foolish."

He narrowed his eyes at me just the same, looking like a mean version of his father. I swear I wanted to snatch his phone and throw it into the street. *You will not ruin this day, you spoiled brat. Your mother is worried sick about you throwing your life away. Straighten up and act right.*

Davie read from his tablet. "There are three hundred sneakers in the sneakers exhibit."

"Davie has his iPad," Sterling said to Jeannette. "Why can't I have my phone?"

"That's different and you know it."

"I wanna go home," he said, pouting. "This is boring."

"We're not even inside yet." Jeannette traced her thumb along the back of his neck and straightened his collar. "I'll tell you what. If you're not having a good time in an hour you can take out your phone. Deal?"

"Deal."

Oh brother. He was playing her. *He's playing you, Jeannette!*

Sure enough, he lasted about twenty minutes before he started to complain he was bored. Jeannette caved and told him he could take out his phone. He put in his earbuds and walked to an empty bench, moving his lips as he silently rapped along to music only he could hear.

Davie, though, liked the museum as much as I thought he would. He'd pace the length of a room once or twice, then stop and study whatever painting or sculpture caught his attention. He'd look up the history of the piece or the artist on his tablet and fall into a rabbit hole of history and art. I was really starting to love that kid.

Jeannette seemed fairly interested in the first exhibits, but it was Lloyd Mosier's work that truly captured her attention. Mosier was a mixed-race Afro-Jamaican, raised in the Bay Area during the seventies. I watched how Jeannette slowed and stared at his paintings, tilting her head one way, then the other, lost in thought. At one point, she planted herself a few inches from Mosier's ironically titled *Safety*: A doomed boat rocked beneath black clouds in the center of a fiery orange-red sea. A barely visible figure raised his arms at the bow of the boat, appearing as though he was prepared to jump into the flames.

"Why would he call this *Safety*?" she asked.

"I don't know. The guy is safe on the boat?"

"But he's not safe. I think he *wants* safety." She pulled her head back so she could appraise the entire painting. "As far as I can tell, the person who painted this knows what it's like to feel everything is against you and all you want is something to make you feel safe."

I observed the painting, thinking Mosier would probably agree. She moved closer and gazed at his brushstrokes, some as thin as a strand of hair, others piled on thick and giving the red and orange flames a 3D feel. "I used to draw when I was little. My dad would buy me paper and watercolors. I could sit and paint for hours. I forgot about that."

I liked imagining little-girl Jeannette lost in her artwork. "You could always start again. You could take a class."

"In what?"

"Art. They have classes for everything. Drawing, painting. I've been thinking about taking a photography class."

This was only somewhat true. I'd thought about taking a class after I graduated from college, but every time I considered signing up, I felt nauseous. It was one thing sharing pictures online with people I'd never meet and another to share my photos in a classroom while having to listen to a bunch of strangers say negative things to my face. Then again, life was short—*right, Mom?* And who was I to suggest Jeannette take a class if I was afraid to do the same? So yeah... A photography class. Why the hell not?

Excited now, I said to Jeannette, "We could take a class at the same time and support each other. You could take painting and I'll take photography. It'll be fun."

She looked at me in a way that I was becoming increasingly familiar with. "Bougie bougie bougie, if I hadn't seen you with my own eyes at MacDowell back in the day, I wouldn't believe you went there."

"What's that supposed to mean?"

"No one I know or have ever known has taken an art class."

"And so...?"

"*And so* even if I had time to take a class it wouldn't be in art. I can't make money off of art." She tapped the side of her head, as in, *Think about it.*

"It was just a suggestion. I didn't mean to upset you."

"I'm not upset. I'm just saying."

I stared down at my feet a beat. It was exhausting making new friends—adult friends anyway. I decided to join Davie, who was looking at Mosier's self-portrait. I was sure Mosier based the painting on Van Gogh's *Self Portrait with Pipe* since he had the exact same pose, except instead of a pipe he was smoking a fat doobie. The despondency and sadness in his expression reminded me of Mom during her difficult days. Depression was such a bitch. But I recognized, staring at Mosier's despondent eyes, that Mom had been doing her best with me. Sadly, though, I'd spent so much time bitching and moaning about what she couldn't do, I'd lost my chance to properly thank her for all she'd done. But I would never see her again. That particular thought kept hitting me hard. *I would never see my mother again.*

Two teenage boys entered the exhibit, interrupting my thoughts, one black, one white—Ebony and Ivory—but they looked exactly the same otherwise: same height, same big heads and beefy football-player bodies. They wore letterman jackets with insignias from the private school they attended—Bishop Royce Preparatory, my dream school when I was their age, a school most people could not afford in their wildest dreams. I had to assume they'd been forced to visit the museum since all they were doing was goofing off.

Jeannette and I looked at each other and shook our heads. *Private school pricks.* Bishop Royce Preparatory and MacDowell High were worlds apart.

"No playing in the museum," Davie said under his breath. "The museum is like the library."

The guard, remembering his job, finally told them to quiet down and they left.

Jeannette walked over. "Idiots." She snapped several photos of the paintings, then took a picture of Davie and Sterling.

Sterling put his arm around Davie and smiled—dimples and full lips like Tucker. Davie, on the other hand, remained serious, as though posing for a mug shot. Jeannette slid her phone back into her purse and said it was time for the sneaker exhibit.

"Finally," Sterling groaned.

Davie walked ahead, his finger in the air. "The sneaker exhibit has sneakers from 1876 to today."

I followed everyone into the gallery. Oh my God. It was so boring. I mean, it was *so* boring. Who cared about a bunch of tennis shoes? Well, Sterling did, I suppose. He took selfies and photos of the shoes and talked animatedly with Jeannette.

I pretended to be interested for a while but then decided to give up and join Davie, who was as bored as I was and watched Mr. Science on his tablet with his earbuds in his ears. I was crossing the room when Ebony and Ivory entered, still goofing off like the idiots they were. Ebony threw an imaginary football to Ivory. Ivory jumped and pretended to catch the ball, but he bumped right into me. I stumbled backward, Ivory stumbling along with me, his body pressing against mine—his chest suddenly on my body, his hand on my arm. My ankle strained as I pushed him off, his breath reeking of alcohol. I looked away, sweat beading on my forehead, my heart racing. I felt embarrassed by my body's response, but I had no control over my visceral reaction, the disgust at being touched by a stranger.

Ivory sauntered off as if he hadn't nearly knocked me over at all, as if I weren't worth an apology.

"You okay?" Jeannette was suddenly at my side.

I circled my foot, making sure my ankle wasn't sprained. "Yeah, I'm fine."

"Hey," she yelled at Ivory, her voice reverberating against the museum walls.

People in the exhibit turned and stared.

"I'm talking to you!"

There was no security guard around. Ebony and Ivory were looking at a pair of tennis shoes from the thirties. Jeannette went over and tapped Ivory on his shoulder. When he ignored her she shoved him from behind. *She shoved the private school prick!* Shoved him hard enough he took a step forward. "I'm talking to you."

He turned and faced her. You could tell he was buzzed by the way he swayed and stared at her blankly.

"You just knocked my friend over. You need to apologize."

He and Ebony looked at each other like they had no idea what was going on. Drunk private school pricks.

Davie cried, "You cannot play in the museum! The museum is like the library, assholes. You have to be quiet."

People whispered as they observed the disruption. A guy in the corner of the room took out his phone and began filming.

Sterling looked at Jeannette, then shook his head at Ebony and Ivory in a way that said, *You all don't even know.*

"It's okay," I said, wanting to disappear. "I'm fine."

"It is *not* okay," said Jeannette. She glared at the private school pricks. "You need to apologize. How the hell were you raised to think you can bump into my friend and not say anything? You know you were being disrespectful. Tell her you're sorry."

Jeannette was back to her old high school self—tough and pissed off, not willing to put up with anyone's mess. Ebony and Ivory slunk over to me, heads bowed. They dared not defy her.

Ivory, completely red-faced, mumbled an apology. Ebony apologized, too. "We were just playing," Ivory said to me.

I told them it was okay. I just wanted the moment to be over with and for people to stop staring.

"Get out of here," Jeannette said. They slunk away. She seemed to notice the silence in the room, people staring. She shot a look at the guy filming the incident. "Turn that damn thing off." He quickly turned off his phone. Jeannette placed her arm around me. "Are you sure you're okay?"

"I'm fine." My heart continued to race. I could still feel Ivory's body pushing into me. But Jeannette's protective arm helped me feel better. Who knew what my life would have been like if Jeannette and I had been friends in high school?

She searched my face. "What? I will not apologize for making a scene. Those fuckers deserved it."

"No, it's not that. Just…" I paused. *Just what? Thank you for coming to my defense*, I wanted to say. *Thank you for putting that boy in his place. No one has ever done anything like that for me. Not even my own mother.* But I couldn't form the words and was left with a feeble, "Thanks, I'm fine." Which was not nearly enough to express my gratitude for how she'd taken up for me and not what I'd meant to say at all.

CHAPTER SEVENTEEN

Davie complained he was hungry after we left the museum by way of telling us that Frederick Douglass didn't have enough to eat as a child. There was an Ethiopian restaurant nearby, so I suggested we go there for lunch. I was the only one of us who'd eaten Ethiopian before, but luckily everyone enjoyed it and we scooped up curries with injera bread as bluesy Ethiopian music played in the background. It was a nice meal, and I was feeling good, still replaying how Jeannette had come to my defense with the high school pricks. What a sight! Jeannette Tomlin defending Francine Stevenson. You never know how life is going to change.

She insisted on paying for lunch since I'd paid for the museum tickets. Thing is, when she gave her credit card to the waitress it was declined.

"Decline, incline, be kind! Ha!" Davie cried. He looked to Sterling as though he'd made a funny joke but Sterling only shook his head.

I reached for my purse. "I'll pay, it's not a problem."

Jeannette fumbled through her wallet. "I gave her the wrong card. You bought the museum tickets. Don't worry about it. We're not trying to freeload."

"Freeload!" said Davie. "Loads for free."

Jeannette handed the waitress a second card. I noticed her exhale audibly when the receipt for the bill scrolled from the register.

Sterling and Davie began discussing the latest superhero movie. I hated anything to do with superhero movies, but wanting to get on Sterling's good side, I lied and told him I thought Superman was very cool.

"Superman is very cool?" he repeated. He looked at me as if I was hopeless.

I tried a different tack. "It looked like you had fun today. We should go to SFMOMA next. I bet they'll have an exhibit you'll like."

He appealed to Jeannette for help. "I'm not going to another museum. Don't make me."

Jeannette played with her necklace, a cubic zirconia dangling on a gold chain, the same shape and size as the studs Sterling wore. "All of this is good for you. How many of your friends have had Ethiopian food or gone to a museum? You get to tell everybody about what you did today."

Sterling rolled his eyes and returned to whatever he was watching on his phone.

Davie, then: "Ethiopia is the birthplace of coffee. It's very interesting."

I pointed out a bookstore on our way back to the museum parking lot. I didn't want the day to end; plus, who doesn't love a good bookstore?

"Bookstores are almost obsolete," said Davie. "Ling Ling, do you know what *obsolete* means?"

"Don't quiz him like that," Jeannette said. "It's rude."

Sterling scrolled through his phone. "Doesn't bother me none."

"It should bother you."

"Why?"

Jeannette widened her eyes. *"Because it should."*

I smiled at Sterling. Dang it, I was going to win him over if it killed me. "Tell you what, I'll buy you and Davie two books each, whatever books you want."

"Any book?"

Finally, I'd piqued his interest. "Any book."

Jeannette raised a hand. "Hold on a second. I don't think that's a good idea. You've done enough. You paid for the museum."

"And you paid for lunch," I said lightly. "It's not a big deal."

"They're fine with getting books from the library."

Davie pointed at her. "But you never go to the library." Then he pointed at Sterling. "And Ling Ling never goes to the library either. I'm the only one who goes to the library. Ha!"

"I've been to the library before," Sterling remarked. "Our teacher forced us to go when I was in fourth grade. Haven't been back since." He cupped his hand over his mouth and laughed.

Jeannette played with her necklace, sending the zirconia from one side of the chain to the other.

I had the distinct feeling I'd done something wrong. "If it's a problem that I get them books, we can skip it."

She smiled at Sterling and Davie. "Maybe another time."

Sterling gestured toward the bookstore. "You're not going to let her buy us some books. Why not?"

"Because it's time to go home."

"Just let her buy us some books. Why do you always have to have a problem with everything? Even when it's something good."

"Lower your voice," said Jeannette. "It's my decision and I say it's time to go home."

"I could buy you a book, too," I told her.

She shot me a look that said, *Are you fucking kidding me?* Then she spoke slowly as though I might be hard of hearing: "No, thank you."

Davie began pacing two steps left, two steps right, as if music had started playing. "I would like to have a book. Books are very interesting."

Jeannette frowned. "I said no. It's time for us to get out of here."

"Thomas Jefferson owed a lot of money when he died. He was in debt. Do you know how to spell *debt*, Ling Ling? *Debt* has a silent B."

"Stop it, Davie," Jeannette cautioned.

"He doesn't mean anything," Sterling said. He glanced at me. "All she wants to do is buy us some damn books. You act like she wants to buy us crack."

Davie shot his finger in the air. "Crack! Ha!"

Jeannette rested her hand on her hip and looked from Davie to Sterling. "When I say it's time to leave, it's time to leave. Now say thank you to Francine and let's go."

She was so upset, but I wasn't exactly sure what I'd done. Someone needed to write a beginner's manual for people like me on how to make friends IRL.

Davie paced outright, walking to a parking meter and back again. "Thomas Jefferson was in debt. He owed everyone money so he sold all his slaves when he died instead of freeing them."

"Calm down," warned Jeannette. "Stop with the pacing right now."

He did what he was told at least and joined us. "Mmmmm."

"I'm really sorry," I said, not knowing exactly what I was apologizing for. "I didn't mean anything."

"We know you didn't," she said tersely.

Davie hummed and fidgeted anxiously.

Sterling touched his shoulder lightly. "It's okay, Davie. Let's just go."

We walked back to the museum parking lot in silence. I was trying to think where and how I'd blown it. I'd gone from the high of having Jeannette come to my defense with the private school pricks to the low of having her hate me.

When we reached the parking lot, she gave Sterling her keys and told him and Davie to wait in the car. She wanted to speak to me in private.

Shit.

She waited until they were out of earshot before facing me. "What exactly are you trying to prove?"

Her question threw me. "I'm not trying to prove anything."

"We're not your charity case."

"*What?*"

"Offering to buy everyone books, trying to pay for lunch, paying for the museum."

"I was trying to be nice. I didn't mean anything."

She tilted her head off to one side. "You know what? Whatever this is"—she waved two fingers between us—"it's not going to work."

She started to walk away. I stood frozen for moment. *What the hell?* I then rushed to catch up with her. "Hold up. I didn't mean anything. I swear."

She kept walking.

"I swear on my mother!" That caught her attention. She stopped and studied my face to see if I was lying. "I swear, Jeannette. I was only trying to be nice. I was having a good time."

She tugged at her necklace, growing silent, thinking. At last, she said, "I need to tell you something."

"You can tell me anything."

She lowered her gaze. "But it's embarrassing."

"You don't have to be embarrassed around me. Ever."

She stared at the pavement until she was ready to speak, her voice at a near whisper. "I was saving to move into another apartment so Sterling can switch schools before high school starts. I want him to go to Temescal high because it's way better than MacDowell. Way better. You know how it is at MacDowell. And school is his way out. The apartment I found wasn't great but it was in the right area. I saved most of the deposit money by myself, but Tucker had this idea that he wanted to help. He didn't tell me, but he went to Reno to gamble thinking he would double our savings, but he lost it all. I swear I was going to kill him. I still think I might do it."

I recalled the tension between Jeannette and Tucker at the dinner party, then remembered Davie mentioning something about gambling when I'd invited him into the house the first time. *The foster father gambled their money away and now the foster mother isn't talking to him.*

Jeannette glanced toward her car, frustrated. "We're back to zero. Which isn't anything new because we're always at zero. We have so much credit card debt it's not even funny. I feel like the guy on the boat in that painting. Like I'm drowning in a fire." She shot me a look. "And don't judge me either. I swear to God—"

"I'm not judging you. I'm the last person to judge anyone. You said your older brother has money—what about asking him for help?"

"I'd rather die than borrow money from him again." She folded her arms over her chest and clicked her tongue. "Some people get everything they want in life. It's like those boys in the museum. They get to go to a private school and they get to live in a nice house and they get to act up and no one says a fucking thing. Can you imagine Sterling acting up like that inside a museum? Somebody would've called the cops on him."

I touched her arm. "Everything is going to be okay."

"I shouldn't have gone off inside the museum like I did. I know I embarrassed you."

"You didn't embarrass me. I liked how you helped me."

"You're not judging me, are you?"

"I'm *not* judging you. I'm glad you told me what's going on. I want to help."

"I don't want your help, Francine. I'm not a damn charity case."

"I didn't say you were. But we're friends now and friends help each other." I could feel my excitement growing. I could help her and I wanted to. "My mother had her issues, but like I told you, she was good with money. She had savings accounts—*plural*—life insurance, and no debt. She was like a samurai warrior when it came to money."

"Good for you and your mother."

"Jeannette, all the money my mother saved is going unused. She never got to travel or do anything she wanted. Let me give you the deposit money." I meant it. I was ready to give her the deposit and first month's rent, if she'd let me.

She shook her head vigorously. "No way. I would never let you do that. Tucker would never let you do that. And to be honest, even if we were able to move into the place I was saving up for, I didn't know how we were going to make rent every month. It was more like a pipe dream, but it was *my* pipe dream. And it's still fucked up that he lost all our money." She paused and regarded me curiously. "Why do you always have me spilling my guts? It's like you have a secret power that makes me tell you everything. I haven't even told Ceci about what Tucker did."

The selfish part of me liked that she hadn't said anything to Ceci. I thought of another way to help—aside from paying for the deposit. I mean, I was good with helping people—Hayden and Mom, anyway.

"I want to keep doing things with you and Davie—and Sterling," I quickly added. "I want to go to SFMOMA. I want to go to the movies and whatever else we want to do. And I can afford to pay. So why don't you save up again and work on your debt or whatever and I'll treat when we go out."

She stared down at her feet. "I don't know."

"What's the point of Mom saving all that money if I don't use it? And you want to get out more. You had fun today, right?"

"But I can't let you pay for everything. I'm not a damn freeloader."

"So help when you can. Otherwise, don't worry about it. It's like my mom said, 'Money is nothing but energy.'"

"Are you sure? You're already going to start helping me with Davie."

I was more than sure. She had no idea how alone and lonely I felt—what it meant for me to be able to see Davie and the possibility of continuing to hang out with her. I couldn't have given a shit about the money. "It can't just be a coincidence you're Davie's foster mother. And we get along. Let me do this."

A horn tooted. Sterling from the car: "What's taking so long?"

"I'm coming! Give me a second!" Jeannette smiled at me, shook her head. "Bougie bougie bougie. We'll pay you back. Every penny."

"Fine."

We hugged, her hair brushing against my cheek. Her smile. "Thank you," she whispered next to my ear. She started to walk off but then rushed back.

"Please don't tell me you've changed your mind."

Excited, she took my hand and briefly entwined her fingers with mine. "Let's skip work on Monday."

Of all the ideas. Had I heard her correctly? "Skip work?"

"Yeah. I need a break. You know how much I hate my job. We could spend the day relaxing. I'm going to call in sick anyway, but it would be more fun with someone else."

"I don't know. I just started back since my mom passed."

"That's perfect, though. Your boss knows you're having a hard time. She won't care. It's just a day."

But I wasn't someone who skipped work.

"Never mind."

Not wanting to disappoint her, I said quickly, "No, I want to. Can we skip on Tuesday, though? I want to get my boss's schedule in order."

"You're such a goody-goody. Are you sure?"

I realized I was being foolish. I mean, go to work or hang out with my former high school crush Jeannette Tomlin? What was I thinking? Of course I wanted to skip work. Hell yeah. Badass Francine skipping work! "I'm sure."

She raised her pinkie, gave it a wiggle. "Pinkie swear."

I hooked my pinkie with hers and we giggled. It felt like we were girls again—back to the days before our fathers died. Back to the days when I had friends and no worries. That is, long before Mom came to my school and read depressing fortunes and the kids started calling me the witch's daughter and saying I had cooties.

Jeannette tugged at my pinkie. "I'm glad we're friends."

God, those words. Honestly? I was jumping up and down inside. I played it cool, though. "I'm glad we're friends, too."

CHAPTER EIGHTEEN

'd never thought about skipping work, but I imagined you'd do more than sit around smoking pot and watching courtroom reality shows, which is what we did for most of the morning.

Jeannette, stretched out on the couch, smoked and watched TV. I took a couple of hits to fit in while struggling not to fall into a bad mood since I'd been expecting... oh, I don't know... not sitting around Jeannette's apartment getting high all day, that's for damn sure. I tried not to judge her, but she was a mother, and we weren't in high school anymore—not that I smoked pot in high school, but I'm just saying.

When I hinted that maybe it was a little much smoking pot in the middle of the day, she argued people with money popped Xanax and Ativan and no one judged them.

It was dark inside, all the curtains drawn. Everything was neat and tidy except the coffee table, which was littered with our snacks and Jeannette's smoking paraphernalia.

She blew a plume of smoke into the ceiling, one leg up on the side of the couch, her feet bare. "There's nothing wrong with smoking weed. It's legal and it's natural. I just need to check the fuck out sometimes so I can keep my sanity. You wouldn't understand."

I wasn't so sure. Mom took Alfonse's drugs to keep her "sanity" when really the drugs were only a Band-Aid solution. I mean, after you come down from the high, you're still faced with yourself.

I considered saying as much but kept my mouth shut. I was already playing the role of her therapist that morning: sitting in the recliner across from her, nodding my head as she went on about her problems—most of them dealing with Tucker. *But get this.* Apparently they hadn't had sex in eight months. *Eight months!* I thought one point of marriage was regular sex. Hell, I thought cis men were always horny. Not Tucker apparently. Jeannette said he had issues from growing up in foster care, but he never wanted to talk about whatever happened. When I asked if they'd considered counseling, she rolled her eyes. Divorce wasn't an option either. She wanted Sterling to have a father figure in the home; plus, he and Tucker were close. She also got into more about her mother and "bougie" brother, Jordan, whom her mother always favored.

In turn, I told her about Mom and Aunt Liane. Her advice regarding my aunt: "Just because someone is family doesn't mean you have to talk to them. I hardly ever talk to Jordan. I can't stand his bougie ass."

I was grateful Jeannette and I were growing closer, but after nearly three hours of court shows, I was going stir-crazy. As strange as it was to watch Civil War documentaries and Pixar cartoons with a ten-year-old on the spectrum, I preferred hanging out with Davie for all Jeannette and I were doing. A commercial came on and I checked the time. It was almost noon; one more second and I was going to go insane.

"Let's go on a walk."

Jeannette responded to my suggestion by swinging her bare foot up and down, placing the crook of her arm over her eyes. "Girl, you are so bougie. You're just like my brother."

"Why is walking bougie? And I'm not sure I like you comparing me to your brother."

"I'm just teasing you. Don't worry, you are nothing like my stuck-up brother."

"Lots of people take walks." I shot my gaze at her bong. "It's better than sitting around smoking weed all day."

Hearing my tone, she mimicked me in her white-girl-from-Utah voice: "'Everybody takes walks. It's better than sitting around smoking weed.'"

I started to say, *I don't sound like that.* But did I?

She heaved herself up from the couch with a huff. She wore a pink velour sweat suit with the word *Juicy* covering her chest. She stretched and patted her belly. "I won't lie, I could use the exercise. You're not getting me to walk around here, though."

"We can go to the marina or . . ." I paused. I knew exactly where I wanted to take her. "I know where we can go."

She tilted back a bag of Doritos, draining the remains into her mouth. "This is why I like hanging out with you. You're getting me to do things I wouldn't usually do. I like it."

She smiled, all white shiny teeth, full lips. Those hazel eyes. She was high, of course, but her smile reminded me of the time I saw her walking down the hall in MacDowell High laughing loudly, looking like a celebrity—or a snack—her arm linked around Kobe's. I'd learned more about the Tucker-Kobe triangle by then. She and Tucker met when they were sophomores at a dance at Oakland Tech, where Tucker was going to school. Jeannette became pregnant with Sterling the same year, but they were young, and their relationship remained on again/off again. They were broken up when she met Kobe. She was a senior and had been dating Kobe for about three months. Her seventeen-year-old self was "in love" and thought Kobe was "the one," so when she found out a girl named Ashley was sleeping with him, too, she beat her up in the school parking lot. There'd been enough fights by then that the principal kicked her out of MacDowell for good. She was so angry about the expulsion, one of the security guards had to drag her off campus as she clawed and kicked. I watched the scene with everyone else in my math class, our teacher yelling, "Go back to your seats! Everyone sit down!" I remember how sexy she looked. Fierce. Now here I was, hanging out with her, making her smile. Unreal.

We hopped into my I-on, Jeannette immediately commenting it was "weird" and something a white person would drive. I didn't bother responding. But I did think of Davie and how excited he was that I owned an I-on. *It's like sitting inside a shoe.*

We drove to the Lake Merritt gardens, a place Mom and I liked to visit before her agoraphobia took over. It was late January and overcast, the flowers and plants popping with color beneath the gray sky. I tried not to think about her too much as Jeannette and I strolled past the leafy hollyhocks and chrysanthemums, the bonsai trees with their arthritic trunks. *Ooh, baby, look at those lilies. Aren't they pretty?*

Jeannette asked about Kelly as we made our way through the cacti garden. I told her about our breakup, mentioning I'd hooked up with women I'd met online but nothing had come from it. My focus was always on Mom and trying to help her get better.

We watched a fat goose take off with a squawk and fly low over a pond we were passing. "What did your mother say when you told her you were gay?" she asked.

"She told me to respect whoever I love and make sure they respect and love me back."

She snorted. "My mother would've beat me if I ever said I was gay."

"Beat you?"

"Oh hell yeah. She would have beat me, then kicked me out of the house. She was old-timey religious. That woman would recite Bible verses at the same time she was whooping my ass with an extension cord. How messed up is that?"

She'd told me about her mom, but not this. I couldn't imagine my mother ever raising a hand to me, let alone using an extension cord. I stopped walking. "Wait. So are you saying you were abused?"

"I don't know about abuse. Let's just say I was heavily disciplined. But you know how fast I was. I deserved it. I was always getting in trouble."

"But no one deserves to be hit with an extension cord."

She shrugged. "She only did it a couple of times. The first time was when I was fifteen and she found out I was pregnant. Me and Tucker had only had sex like three times and I go and get pregnant—which is the kind of luck I have. The second time she went at me was when I got expelled from MacDowell." I must have been making a face because Jeannette paused and narrowed her eyes slightly. "Stop looking at me like that. She was just trying to help me in her own way. It wasn't that bad."

"It sounds bad. It sounds really bad."

"No, what was bad was when she kicked me out of the house after I was expelled."

"She kicked you out?"

"She sure did. That woman did not play. She'd had it with me by then."

I did the numbers. Jeannette got pregnant with Sterling at fifteen, so he must have been two years old by then. "But you had a baby."

"*And?*"

"So what did you do?"

"I moved in with my brother and his wife. They had a house in Alameda. A really nice house. This was before they moved to Georgia. But he was like my mom and just always on my fucking case. I have to say, Tucker really stepped up. We got back together—for good—and he started working two jobs. I took the first job I could get, which was McDonald's, and when we had enough money we moved into the Palms. First in a studio, then in the apartment where we are now."

We were nearing a second pond when an egret took flight. "It's pretty out here," she murmured. "I really needed this." I watched her follow the bird with her gaze. "But you know what's funny?" she said. "My mom *loved* Sterling. Spoiled him rotten. She wouldn't let me move back in, but she'd babysit while I worked and went to continuation school." She paused a beat. "Those were hard times, girl. Hard times." She stared out at the pond, reliving, I gathered, days of working at McDonald's while going to school, raising a kid. She looked at me. "You know what? I hate my job so damn much I almost would rather be back at Mickey D's if you can believe it. I wish I could quit."

I wanted to take her hand in a sign of support, not so much for her job, but rather, I was thinking of all she'd been through with her mother: being physically abused—I didn't care how she tried to explain it away, it was abuse—getting kicked out of the house with a baby... it was a miracle she'd graduated from high school at all. She really was a badass.

I was vacillating between asking more questions and letting it go when she shrieked and pointed. I followed her gaze and saw a large turtle creeping along the side of a rock.

"It's just a turtle," I laughed.

"I've never seen one in real life before. That thing is nasty."

"It's cute." I took her hand, tried to pull her toward the turtle for a closer look, but she refused to budge. "You've got to be kidding me. Jeannette Tomlin, who tried to beat up a security guard, is afraid of a turtle?"

"It's nasty!" She broke from my grip and ran past the turtle on her tiptoes, flinging her hands, squealing.

"It's just a turtle!" I caught up with her and pushed her lightly. "Scaredy cat."

She pushed me back, grinning. "I'm not scared, bitch."

I gave her another push. "Yes, you are, bitch."

We laughed and continued our walk.

At the car, she said, a small smile on her lips, "You got me out here liking nature. Where to next, bougie?"

"Nowhere, if you keep calling me bougie."

"Lighten up, girl. You're too serious."

I guess she had a point. Why be a downer? Besides, if liking nature was bougie, so be it. "Okay. If you liked the gardens, I know where we can go next."

We drove through downtown Berkeley, heading east on Marin Avenue, then climbing all the way to the top of Grizzly Peak. I thought of Davie again and how much fun he would've had taking on the hills in my I-on. I told myself we would have to take a drive together someday soon.

After a few miles, I turned off the winding, two-lane road and parked in a dirt lot. There were only two other cars and zero people around. Jeannette said, "This is where we get killed, right?"

We walked through a narrow woodsy path that led to a fire trail, a wide dirt road winding its way through the Berkeley hills. Fifteen minutes of walking and we reached a view of the shimmering bay with the Bay Bridge and the Golden Gate Bridge stretching from San Francisco to Marin County. I mean, it was just view—view for days and days.

"Not in all my life," Jeannette said under her breath. "I live... What? Twenty minutes away from here?"

Two white women, giving off a couple vibe, jogged by. I thought of the times Kelly and I walked the trail together, the rare occasion when she'd hold my hand in public.

"How do you know about this place?" asked Jeannette.

Shit. I should've expected her question. I was going to have to either lie or out myself a second time. I chose the latter: "A guy."

"*A guy?* I thought you liked girls."

"I do."

I started walking so I wouldn't have to look at her. She remained quiet, allowing me to gather my thoughts. And boy, did I need to gather my thoughts. I hated thinking about Isaiah, let alone talking about him. I figured, though, Jeannette had told me so much about her past, I should do the same. And I wanted her to know about my life. So—"He was the first and only guy I was with. We met when I was in high school."

"I didn't think you had any friends in high school and here you were dating. Good for you, Mudface."

"I didn't have any friends, and he wasn't in high school. And don't call me Mudface."

She twirled her finger in front of my nose. "Oooh, look at you dating an older man."

"It's not like that." I pulled up a picture of Isaiah on my phone. If there was anything in my life I had the ability to compartmentalize, it was the time I'd spent with him.

She made a face. "He's so old."

"I was fourteen when we met. He was sixteen years older than me."

"Damn. That's some pedophile shit."

I stared at Isaiah on my screen, his pudgy stomach and balding head. Gross. I turned off my phone.

When I'd told Kelly about Isaiah, she helped me understand the extent to which he'd used me. I was ripe for being taken advantage of, after all. I was barely fourteen years old, Mom was giving zero signs she was ever going to leave the house, and this was during the time I was suffering from Bell's palsy, my face an ugly nightmare.

The day we met, I was at the drugstore shopping for Mom and myself when I saw the worst of my junior high school tormentors goofing off with a couple of her friends. The girl was my personal nightmare, but, thank God, she'd transferred to a different high school. She and her lackeys walked through the drugstore talking loudly and acting stupid. There was no way I wanted her to see my stroke-victim face, so I hid in the aisle that sold toothbrushes. I waited until she and her friends got in line to make their purchases. I turned when I felt someone staring.

"You look too old for hide-and-seek." Isaiah.

We struck up a conversation and ended up dating. I honestly thought I was mature enough for someone older. We did talk about books a lot, and it was Isaiah who kept telling me I had to go to college no matter what. But of course he was using me for sex, I was just too naïve to realize it. Mom never knew about the relationship since I lied and said I was hanging out with a friend. So much for her psychic abilities, right?

I told Jeannette all of this without making eye contact. When I finished she asked if I knew Isaiah's address.

"No, why?"

"I want to slash his tires, fucking pedophile."

We made our way to the first lookout bench on the trail and sat down. I was trying to push thoughts of Isaiah away, especially when I realized we'd had our first kiss on the very bench where Jeannette and I were sitting. *Gross.* "I need some serious fucking therapy," I muttered.

"No you don't. What happened to you happens all the time. You're not the first girl who's been taken advantage of by a man."

"Did something happen to you?"

"Nothing I want to talk about." She began bouncing her knee, playing with her zirconia. "Boys can be dogs; men can be dogs. I'll leave it at that."

"Girls, too," I mumbled. But I spoke in a whisper and she hadn't heard me.

We sat in silence—Jeannette bouncing her knee, me trying to forget Isaiah. Then: "I'm trying to raise Sterling to be respectful. I just need to make sure he grows up to be everything he can be." She gripped her knee as if needing physical force to make it stop bouncing. "It's hard raising a black boy. I swear, I worry about him all the time."

I thought of Davie. What was going to happen to him? She was so stressed. Would she and Tucker keep him until he turned eighteen? I felt my stomach tighten.

"Everything will be okay," I said, no doubt trying to convince myself as much as Jeannette.

We stood from the lookout bench. After a few minutes of walking, Jeannette stopped in the middle of the trail. "There's something I've been meaning to tell you. It's about what you told me and Ceci when you came over for dinner. About your skin color? Light skin and dark skin and all that. Remember?"

Of course I remembered my drunken rant on colorism. *So embarrassing.*

She crossed her arms as though upset, but then—"I just wanted to tell you that you're pretty."

I felt my face go hot. "You don't have to say that."

"You are." She licked her thumb, ran it over the baby hairs near my ear. "Your edges need attention, though," she said, grinning.

If I didn't care about wearing makeup, I certainly didn't care about having my edges laid, as it were. But I loved her touch—thoughtful, tender.

"You've got to stop thinking about high school and whatever people thought about you back then. With everybody treating you the way they did. Even that old dog and the way he treated you. You had every reason to drop out of school, but you didn't. You proved everybody wrong. You've got a lot to be proud of."

"Thank you." My blush deepened. I couldn't remember the last time someone was so nice to me.

"Don't thank me. I'm just speaking the truth. Come here." She opened her arms and I moved into her embrace. "Thank you for skipping work with me today."

Her hug, her words—they meant so much, especially with Mom gone. "You have a lot to be proud of, too, Jeannette," I said, my arms still wrapped around her. "You also graduated from high school." I pulled back. "*You* could have easily dropped out, too—especially considering everything *you* went through."

"Ain't that the truth. I worked so hard for my diploma."

We beamed at each other, high up in the Berkeley Hills, the bay below. We then turned and faced the view together—the seagulls, white dots above the choppy water; the San Francisco skyline in the distance. Everything was perfect except for my growling stomach. I was starving, so I offered to buy lunch. "Chicken and waffles?" I asked.

A smile started at the corner of her lips. "Girl, always."

CHAPTER NINETEEN

avie and I started seeing each other twice a week after my day of skipping work with Jeannette, and she stopped worrying about my paying for things. Over the next month or so, we took the boys to the movies, the Lawrence Hall of Science, and the Exploratorium in San Francisco. In late February, I gave her money so she and Tucker could take Sterling to see the Golden State Warriors for his thirteenth birthday. So Tucker wouldn't be suspicious about where the money came from, Jeannette told him she'd been given a bonus at work—when the bonus was me.

With things going so well, I figured it was time I invited her and Sterling over to the house, which was a huge step when you considered Mom's décor. Jeannette wanted to take the boys to an arcade in Alameda so I offered to serve breakfast at the house before we left. Having them over meant I'd finally need to clean since, believe it or not, the place was still a pigsty; Davie and I just sort of habituated to the mess.

I cleaned over a period of three nights. The mold in the fridge alone was a science experiment gone bad. I won't bother telling you about the bathroom. What I couldn't do was get rid of Mom's things. Every time I reached for a gourd filled with chicken feet and crystals, or one of the horseshoes above a door frame, I'd get teary-eyed and weepy. Removing what she considered her sacred objects was like a breach of some sort, an indication I no longer cared about her. I couldn't even take down the stupid disco ball in the living room. When I tried, I began to sob uncontrollably; that tacky ball brought back so many happy memoires of our dance-a-thons and karaoke nights.

By coincidence, or not, after I'd finished cleaning and was tossing the final bag of trash, Aunt Liane sent one of her annoying texts: **Your Uncle & I are driving over there tomorrow if I don't hear from you. I'll bang down the door if I have to.**

That got my attention.

> **Please leave me alone. I'll contact you when I'm ready.**

> **I cannot believe you're behaving like this. After everything we've done for you.**

Big deal, you helped out in the past, I thought. *Now you're going to hold it over my head? No thank you.*

> **I just need some space.**

> **You don't need space you need your family.**

Did I though?

I texted: **You always treated Mom like shit.**

I RAISED YOUR MOTHER FROM
THE TIME SHE WAS A CHILD. I
WAS ALWAYS GOOD TO YOUR
MOTHER.

Next thing I knew the landline rang. If it hadn't been Uncle CJ I would have hung up.

"We... w... want to see you."

"No, Uncle CJ. I need more time."

I could hear Aunt Liane in the background: "Tell her we're coming whether she wants us to or not."

"Tell her no." Just thinking about how Aunt Liane threw Mom's things in a trash bag and her behavior in general made me so anxious, I worried about my Bell's palsy acting up. I touched the side of my face, fearful of weakening muscles, my cheek sliding down to my neck.

"I'll let you know when I'm ready to see you guys. Besides, I'm doing better now. I'm having company over tomorrow. Will you talk to Aunt Liane for me?"

"Okay. I d-don't want you or Liane t-to be upset. Call us when you're ready t-to see us."

I said goodbye. It sucked that I wasn't getting along with my only connection to Mom, but Jeannette was right: just because someone is family doesn't mean you have to talk to them.

After hanging up, I went straight to the kitchen and took a small dose of TAKE THESE FOR GOOD SLEEP. I hadn't taken a pill since I'd started spending time with Davie, but I wanted to forget my exchange with my aunt and uncle. I slept well, too, although even a small dose left me waking up in the bathtub wrapped in Mom's afghan, clutching her favorite crystal.

After getting dressed, I went to Scratch Bakery and bought muffins and scones. I wished I were in a place emotionally where I could throw out all of Mom's weird things, but I just couldn't.

And wouldn't you know? Of course, as soon as Sterling stepped inside the house he had to say something negative. Spoiled brat. "It's hella creepy in here." He stared up at the disco ball. "What's that?"

"It's for disco," piped Davie. "Disco is music with syncopated beats."

I'd shown Jeannette some of the house and Mom's things on Face-Time, but she hadn't seen most of it. Although she tried to hide it, I kept catching her stealing peeks around the living room as if a ghost might jump out at any second.

When we went into the den and Sterling was faced with Mom's mahogany altar, he blurted, "Do you worship the devil?"

Jeannette eyed him, her expression saying, *We talked about this. I told you the house was strange.* "Don't be rude."

"But it's weird in here," Sterling responded.

Davie petted Mom's taxidermied fox. "It's not weird. Corrina Stevenson is on YouTube. She was a psychic. Say hello to Hello Mr. Fox. He's very friendly."

Sterling made a face. "I ain't touching that thing."

I inadvertently broke into my Mary Poppins voice: "Listen, everyone, I bought muffins and scones. Who's hungry?"

"I'm not eating nothing from this house," Sterling said emphatically. "This place is satanic."

Jeannette looked at her son with sheer bafflement. "Sterling, I swear to God, I did not raise you to behave like this. I told you, you were to keep your comments to yourself once we got here. If you don't have anything positive to say, don't say anything at all."

"But it's scary up in here!"

His reaction made me feel outed, like the freak that I was. But I also felt defensive of Mom. "My mother thought her things were sacred. She considered herself a psychic. They helped her."

"Do you know how to spell *psychic*, Ling Ling?" asked Davie.

"Don't quiz him," Jeannette said. Then to me: "You don't have to explain anything." She narrowed her eyes at Sterling. "You need to mind your manners. Francine has been nothing except nice to you—and me. You have no idea."

True. He had no idea I was paying for the arcade that day. I paid for all of our excursions, including the tickets to the basketball game for his fucking thirteenth birthday, fucking spoiled brat.

Sterling's gaze landed on the gourd filled with rattlesnake tails. He contorted his face in disgust. "I'm not eating anything. The food might be poisoned."

That's when Jeannette grabbed his ear and began twisting it.

"Ow!" Sterling tried to push her hand away but she kept twisting, harder and harder, as though turning a knob on a dial and not someone's flesh—her son's flesh.

"Ow! Ow!"

I couldn't believe what I was seeing. *Whoa, whoa. You're hurting him.*

She dragged Sterling toward the couch by the ear, gave him a hard push. I recalled how she'd shoved the private school prick at the museum, except Sterling was her son. He fell forward onto the couch.

Jeannette bent over him, her face inches from his. "If you don't want to eat, don't eat, but you need to stop embarrassing me."

Dejected, Sterling slumped down into the couch, cupping his ear, his bottom lip sticking out.

He was being rude for sure, but the way Jeannette twisted his ear and pushed him was too much. Mom and I never had physical confrontations. We just yelled at each other when we were angry. Or rather, I yelled at her, then she'd shut down. I told myself to let it go, though. I knew better than to judge. How a parent raises their kid is their business.

In a show of solidarity, Davie sat next to Sterling, setting his face in the same closed-off expression.

I felt bad for both of them. "The food is fine, Sterling. I promise. I bought everything from a bakery."

Jeannette crossed her arms, glowering. "He doesn't deserve anything."

"But they're going to need breakfast. I'm sure he didn't mean anything." I looked at Sterling. "Right, Sterling?"

Sterling kept his face frozen in a sad pout.

Jeannette folded her lower lip into her mouth, her expression softening. "Are you ready to behave?"

"Yeah."

"Say you're sorry."

He hung his head low while his eyes wandered up to meet mine. "Sorry."

I offered a small smile. "It's okay."

Jeannette told him to go and eat, and he plodded to the table with Davie walking from behind, copying his every movement.

"I apologize for him," Jeannette said, massaging her neck, rolling her shoulders. "He's been talking back to me all this morning and I've had it."

"Don't you think you were a little harsh?" I ventured.

"I get after him or the police do, or he joins some gang, or God knows what. So no, I do not think I was too harsh." She cut those hazel eyes. "You're not a mother, Francine, so just mind your business."

I took a step back. I mean, she looked pissed enough that she might grab *my* ear and start twisting it.

Seeing the look on my face, she broke eye contact, took a breath. "Sorry. I don't mean to go after you. Sorry," she repeated.

"It's okay." I appreciated the apology. "Really, it's fine."

She swept her gaze over the kitchen and dining room, her expression brightening. "Ignore your mother's things, and this is a really nice place. You're so lucky to have a house, especially in this neighborhood." She peered out through the patio doors. "That garden is so pretty."

"I'm glad you're here." True. It was a big deal to have new people in the house. She had no idea.

We drove to the arcade in the Prius Mom and I had shared. Once there, Jeannette and Sterling played games together as though nothing had happened between them at all. It was Davie who had a hard time. After about an hour, he complained about the noise and lights. I tried to distract him with a game of foosball, but when he started quoting slavery facts, I knew he'd had enough.

I told Jeannette we should probably leave or Davie was going to have a meltdown. She and Sterling were playing a racing game, laughing and enjoying themselves as their cars sped around a track on a large video screen.

I looked over at Davie near the opposite end of the arcade, pacing and muttering to himself. "I think we should leave," I repeated.

Sterling swung off to one side, forcing his car into a sharp turn. "We just got here."

Jeannette maneuvered her car around Sterling's. "Can you take him outside? Let him look at something on his iPad, that'll calm him down." She glanced up at me, her eyes pleading. "Give us just like twenty more minutes? Please?"

She was having fun with her son. I wasn't going to ruin their time together. "Okay. We'll wait for you outside."

Davie and I sat on the entrance steps, the quiet and fresh air doing us both some good. Jeannette was right; he did calm down once he had his iPad and earbuds. After about fifteen minutes of waiting, I asked if he wanted to go back inside. He shook his head. I texted Jeannette we were ready to leave.

> **Just fifteen more minutes.**
> **Pleeeease?**

I told Davie we should wait in the car. He hadn't uttered a word since we'd left the arcade, which wasn't like him. When we were inside the car, I asked what was going on. He wore a puffy jacket with the hood hiding most of his face, refusing to look in my direction, just leaning against the door, humming and watching Mr. Science. I left him alone.

Twenty more minutes of waiting and still no Jeannette or Sterling. "I'm sure they'll be out any second," I said, trying to sound positive.

No response.

"Why aren't you talking to me? Tell me something about Steve Jobs."

"Mmmmm." He closed his iPad, pressed the side of his forehead into the window.

I texted Jeannette: **We're tired of waiting. Where are you?**

> **We'll be out in a minute.**

I watched people exiting the arcade, Davie and I long forgotten. When I thought about it, Jeannette loved to talk about Sterling but Davie seemed like an afterthought—if that. I knew Davie and Tucker were close at least, but what was going on with Jeannette?

I shifted in the car seat, nervous about what I was going to ask. "Davie, do you like Jeannette?"

"Mmmmm."

"Do you like Sterling?"

"Mmmmm. He's very clean. Ling Ling is in the bathroom all the time making sure he looks good. He's dumb, but he's very good at video games."

I balked at the thought of asking if he liked me. I'd be heartbroken if the answer was no or he gave no other response besides humming. "When you come by this Wednesday, we'll do something special. I'll ask Jeannette if you can stay late"—*I have a feeling it won't be a problem*—"and we'll watch *Queen of Katwe*. It's about chess. Or we can finish the puzzle we started. Whatever you want."

He pressed his small body deeper into the side of the car, his chin quivering.

"Davie?"

Sniffling, he hid his face entirely inside the hood of his jacket.

"Are you crying?"

"No, I am not crying. I would not cry here. The best place to go when you need to cry is behind the bleachers at school where no one can see you."

"Have you been crying behind the bleachers?"

"Mmmmm."

He sat with his face hidden.

It was heartbreaking to see him upset. "You know, I'd wait until I was home, then lock myself in my room and cry. I felt so alone. But you're not alone. You have me, okay? You can always talk to me."

He turned, ready to speak, but then Jeannette and Sterling exited the arcade laughing together, running toward the car.

Davie quickly climbed out from the front seat. Jeannette took his place. "Sorry, we lost track of time."

Sterling joined Davie in the back. "That was hella fun. They have a game that's like flying a fighter jet. I had to land it and everything."

I looked at Davie in the rearview mirror. He listened to Sterling with no indication he was upset. Maybe he was feeling better now that we were leaving.

I felt Jeannette staring at me. "Don't be mad, bougie."

I kept my gaze on Davie. "I'm fine. We're okay, right, Davie?"

Davie continued to listen to Sterling talk animatedly about the arcade, paying me no attention.

Sterling smiled. "We'll come back here again when you feel better and then you can fly the jet plane with me."

"Steve Jobs had a private jet worth over eighty-eight million dollars."

Okay, so he was doing better. It was always a good sign when he talked about Steve Jobs.

"Are you sure you're not mad?" asked Jeannette. "We lost track of time."

"It's fine."

My passive-aggressive tone said otherwise. Jeannette didn't notice, though, and for the entire drive back, she and Sterling went on about the fun they'd had.

At the house, Jeannette and I sat on the deck while Davie and Sterling watched TV. I told her about my concern with Davie.

She sipped from her cup of tea. I'd made a pot of Earl Grey and heated one of the scones from the morning. "Every child is going to get in a mood now and then. He's still getting straight As in school. Ten years old and he's doing way better than Sterling."

"How often does he see his counselor?"

"That would be never. Girl, Counselor Hayes is in Arizona. They email sometimes, but that's it."

"Counselor Hayes is in Arizona? I assumed he was in the area. Does Davie see anyone at all?"

"Not right now. His case manager told us to let her know if he's having trouble and left it at that. I swear, I will never forgive her for tricking us. When he first came to our place, she made it out like he was perfectly fine. The foster care system is fucked up."

Her phone buzzed. She began texting whoever had contacted her. "Tucker will be home late. He's going to have dinner with some friends tonight." She finished her text and looked up at me.

"How's he doing? Is he still okay with us hanging out so much?"

"He's better than okay. He's been good about picking up extra hours at work. If he's not working, he's sleeping or watching a game, or he'll go see friends."

She brought her cup to her lips, glancing down at the teapot and scone, then gazing around the yard with a contented look on her face. A patch of sun shone on Mom's orchids and chrysanthemums; the phlox was a deep bluish purple. *Baby, come sit outside with me for a minute. Get some of this glory.*

"It's so peaceful out here," she said, sipping her tea.

"My mom would like hearing you say that. She loved spending time in her garden."

We heard the screen door just then. Davie stepped outside, stared up at the sky. "Slaves were punished with bullwhips and wooden paddles."

"No slavery talk," said Jeannette.

"Are you excited about watching *Queen of Katwe* this Wednesday?" I asked.

Humming, he swayed from side to side as though the deck were a boat lost at sea, then, just as quickly, he abruptly turned on his heel and went back inside.

"Told you," I said. "He's acting strange."

"He's *always* acting strange." She picked up the scone, paused. "Are you tired of watching him? Because if that's the case—"

"No no, I want to."

Relief. Then: "Good. Thank you. It really helps. But you've got to stop worrying about him so much. He's doing fine in school, which is all that matters."

Is it, though?

Still, I guess she had a point. Like she'd said, I wasn't a mother, so what did I know. Deciding to drop it, I filled our cups with more tea, then looked out at Mom's garden along with Jeannette, the sound of the TV in the background and friends finally at the house.

CHAPTER TWENTY

Not to sound like Davie—or rather, Mr. Science—but when I finally started therapy, I learned that the gut is lined with five hundred million neurons. There are roughly one hundred *billion* neurons in the brain, but still, five hundred million in your gut is no joke, and those neurons communicate with the brain. So there truly is something to the saying *Follow your gut*. As Pamela, my therapist, said, the neurons in our gut are constantly communicating with us. The only thing is, our gut, our intuition, is quieter than the mind. The gut whispers its case and leaves it at that. The mind, or the ego, will spin a story and repeat itself with old, worn patterns. The mind talks and talks until the next thing you know, you're ignoring your gut and going down the wrong path yet again. Pamela put it far more eloquently, but you get the point. Anyway, I can look back now and clearly see all the times I talked myself out of what I was feeling. I do want to say, at least when it came to Davie, I was able to turn off my mind for the most part and listen to my gut.

Wednesday, for instance, four days after the arcade, when he didn't show up to the house and ignored my emails, I knew something was up. I texted Jeannette right away, but she responded that he'd probably lost track of time and was still at the library, which clearly indicated she didn't understand Davie at all. He was never late and never lost track of time.

I called her instead of texting. "I'm going to the library to look for him."

"He's only fifteen minutes late. You need to calm down."

"He's thirty minutes late. I'll keep you posted."

Even though the library was a five-minute walk, I drove my car. When the librarian who ran the after-school program told me he wasn't there, I gave her my number in case he showed up.

I sat in my car wondering where I should search next, willing words like *death* and *kidnapping* from my mind. A light drizzle had started. I watched it fall against my windshield while drumming my fingers on the dashboard, second-guessing myself. Was I overreacting? But... no. He'd been cold toward me since the arcade. I then recalled what he'd said about the bleachers and his hiding place. It was worth a shot.

I phoned Jeannette, told her I was heading to the school. At least she sounded worried this time and said to call if he wasn't there.

I drove straight to Grover Junior High and searched the bleachers by the football field. Nothing. One of the doors to the portable classrooms was open. I walked over, light rain falling all around. School officials had promised a new building to replace the bungalows even while I was a student there, but the row of trailers remained, brown and drab, too hot in spring and summer and freezing in winter.

I gave a light knock on the open door and stepped inside. The low ceiling was marked with water stains. Shadows of bug carcasses glowed behind the fluorescent light panels. In other words, nothing had changed. A teacher, white, curly auburn hair, sat at her desk, marking a stack of papers with a red pen. A lone student sat in the back.

The teacher showed no surprise seeing me. "Can I help you?" Even though she was young, early thirties, she had a burned-out look about her. Anyone could tell her days as a teacher in an inner-city school were numbered. I imagined she planned to go into real estate or any number of jobs that wouldn't cause so much personal stress.

I asked about Davie, but she had no idea who he was. The girl in the back piped, "You know who she's talking about, Miss Harris. The smart kid. He was running around the football field today yelling about slavery and shit."

"Language," said Miss Harris.

The girl picked up her phone, glanced at the screen, and wrote an answer on her paper. She wore a long weave better suited for an adult.

I pictured Davie running around the football field, having one of his outbursts. "Did something happen?"

She shrugged. "I got a video of it if you want to see."

No, I did not want to see the video. The image I'd conjured was enough. "Would you delete the footage for me, please?"

"Are you his mother?"

"No."

"Then why do you care?"

"I don't have to be his mother to care."

She blinked. "You sound white. Miss Harris, do you hear her? She sounds like you."

I rolled my eyes, started back to my car. I told myself Davie was okay, while at the same time seeing him in the hospital with a broken arm, thanks to Saggy Pants or some other bully, or seeing a cop shooting him for doing absolutely nothing, his body lying facedown on the asphalt.

I was nearing the girls' bathroom when my hands began shaking. I realized it was the bathroom where the *incident* had occurred. I inhaled through my nose, my stomach clenching. Now was not the time. *You're fine, you're fine*, I told myself. *Keep moving. You're fine.*

I ran back to the parking lot, trying to think of where Davie could be. Inside my car, I closed my eyes and whispered aloud to Mom, "Please tell me where he is."

And then—there's no other way to explain it—for the first time since her death I felt Mom's presence. I mean, I didn't just think about her or conjure a memory; I could feel her inside the car with me. I just knew she was there. "*Mom?*" I opened my eyes, half expecting to see her ghost. The sensation left, though, and she was gone as quickly as she'd appeared. But I was left with a strong feeling about where I might find Davie and sped out of the parking lot.

I shouted a big thank-you to Mom when I saw him sitting on the curb beneath the huge black Pixar sign wearing a ... *was that a helmet?* It was. An old-fashioned bicycle helmet with no bike in sight.

Relieved, I got out of my car and raced toward him. "I've been looking everywhere for you. I was getting ready to call the cops." He said nothing, just stared at the ground in that odd-looking helmet. "Davie, you can't just disappear. You have to stay in contact with Jeannette and Tucker. Or me."

He kept his gaze toward the gutter. "Go away, asshole."

"Why am I an asshole? Talk to me."

He dug his foot into the ground. His socks were mismatched, and the helmet, with two thin strips of green and black running down the center, was way too big.

I thought of the girl who'd taken a video of him having one of his meltdowns. I sighed and joined him on the curb. Yet again, there we were on a curb, a light mist falling. "What's wrong?"

"Sometimes when slaves were punished, the overseer would hang them up in a tree without any clothes."

"That's horrible. But ... what's going on with *you*?"

"Counselor Hayes says I can talk about whatever I want."

"Would you at least tell me what's up with that helmet you're wearing?"

"I went to a thrift store and the man said I could have it for free."

I wasn't surprised. The thing looked like it was made in the fifties. It looked *unsafe*. "Why were you at a thrift store?"

"Because I want a bike, asshole. What is very upsetting, in case you want to know, is I'm ten years old and I don't know how to ride a bike. Luca had a bike."

"Luca?"

"From Pixar!"

Right. *Luca* was one of the cartoons we'd watched together.

"I can't get into Pixar either, even though I know everything about Steve Jobs."

I glanced back to the entrance gate. "I wish I could get you inside. Maybe one day."

"You're not good for anything. You were my friend, but now you don't like me anymore. You didn't even know that I don't know how to ride a bike. You're an asshole friend. You're shipping me off."

"Shipping you off?"

"Slave children were separated from their parents without warning." He stood, started pacing in his helmet and mismatched socks. "The foster mother is always with us now. You were supposed to be my friend. And I don't like arcades; they're loud and there are too many people. People smell funny and they have germs."

I stood and reached for his shoulder.

"Do not touch me!"

I raised my hands apologetically. "Sorry. I forgot."

It was starting to sprinkle fat drops of rain by then. I told him to get in the car so I could take him home. He followed, grumbling all the way. I sent Jeannette a text saying that I'd found him.

A few seconds later: THANK U Where was he?

I decided to lie. I worried Davie would get in trouble if I told her he'd gone to a thrift store and Pixar. I texted that he'd been in the bathroom in the library and I'd missed him. Something told me to go back and check. I'm glad I did!!!!

She replied with a thumbs-up emoji.

"Jeannette is really happy you're okay," I said. "You can't disappear like that ever again."

"The Spanish brought Africans to Jamaica as slaves in the fifteen hundreds."

I told him about the girl who'd said he'd been running around the football field in circles. "Did something happen?"

"I was upset because you're shipping me off. You were supposed to be *my* friend. My friend. Mine fine line sign."

"We can all be friends. It's better that way. And Jeannette and Tucker have been very nice letting us spend so much time together."

"Mmmmm…" He pulled off his helmet, took his iPad from his backpack, and clicked to Mr. Science. In the video he was giving a tour of the Monterey Bay Aquarium and the octopus exhibit. "They are highly intelligent beings! The octopus has three hearts and blue blood!"

Oh God. That voice. Nails on a chalkboard, I swear.

"I have very important information no one knows about," Davie said.

"I'm listening."

Mr. Science's voice boomed, "The Monterey Bay Aquarium has a variety of animals from sea otters to penguins!"

"Can you mute him, please?"

Davie hit mute and the car went silent except for the patter of rain. "My science teacher, Ms. Walters, entered me into a contest for a scholarship for a summer science camp at Stanford University. Teachers have to recommend students for kids like me who can't afford the camp. It's a very expensive camp, but I'll get in and I'll get the scholarship because I'm exceptionally smart."

"That's great, Davie." Jeannette hadn't said anything about a camp. "Do Jeannette and Tucker know?"

"No one knows. I was going to tell you, but I hated the arcade and everyone's always with us."

"You'll have to tell Tucker and Jeannette right away."

"Mmmmm."

"When do you find out if you're accepted?"

"When they send the acceptance letter."

"No, I mean... Never mind."

"I'm going to get in."

"I know you will. Just make sure to tell us when you do."

"I'm exceptionally smart. There's no other ten-year-old smarter than me. I'm going to get in."

"I'm sorry you've been feeling ignored," I said.

He unmuted his tablet in response.

"Octopuses can mimic things from memory. And they can change colors!" Music started to play as Mr. Science danced through the Monterey Bay Aquarium.

An idea came to mind. I was ready to do anything to help Davie feel better. "We should go somewhere you want to go. No more arcades, okay?"

"Mmmmm."

"Would you want to go to the Monterey Bay Aquarium?"

"The Monterey Bay Aquarium would be very interesting. I could see everything in real life that's in *Finding Dory*, and I can learn more things about the ocean."

"Let's do it. But you know, Jeannette and Sterling will want to come with us. We're all friends now."

"Mmmmm."

"We have to keep trying, Davie. The two of us need to meet people and not be so afraid."

"Mmmmm."

I wished I could at least reach over and touch his shoulder or hand, but I needed to respect his no-touch rule. "Davie," I said, "don't ever disappear on me again."

"Mmmmm."

"Davie, promise me."

"Steve Wozniak helped Steve Jobs make the iPhone."

I took this as a yes and left it alone.

Jeannette invited me to stay for dinner after I dropped Davie off, although, I have to say, it was strange being around Tucker. I would think things like, *You haven't had sex in eight months!* Or *You have gambling issues.* It was disconcerting to know a person's secrets when I hardly knew the person at all.

After dinner, when I told Jeannette about my idea of going to Monterey she was all in. Adding, "Where the hell is Monterey anyway?"

And then there was Davie: "Ha!"

◆ ◆ ◆

Hayden's first meeting the next morning was with Barbara Meyers. Barbara was a retired executive from Los Angeles, and she and Hayden had started a foundation that supported women in tech and business. Barbara loved anything from Recchiuti Confections and Miette Patisserie, so along with a dry-cleaning pickup, I had to make a run to the Ferry Building. Hayden mentioned that there would be another person at the meeting so I should buy extra of everything.

Outside of the Ferry Building, I noticed the sun making slanted shadows on the buildings across the street, the sharp lines juxtaposing with the streetlights and trees. I snapped a picture. I was giving more thought to taking an actual photography class. UC Berkeley Extension offered an intermediate class I was interested in, but I couldn't convince myself to sign up and would fill out the enrollment form only to delete it.

I shared the photo I'd taken to my online photography club and got several likes right away. Next, I loaded up on chocolates from Recchiuti and macarons from Miette for Barbara and for whomever she was bringing.

Barbara was already at the office when I returned, sitting next to a rare sighting: a *black woman* inside Hayden's office—a black woman who wasn't me, or the janitor, or the woman who ran the café—and not only was she black, but she was young, roughly my age. Was she Barbara's assistant? I hated to equate black womanhood with assistant, but there you go.

I placed the pastries on my desk and carried Hayden's dry cleaning to her office. I moved slowly in hopes of catching snippets of conversation.

Barbara offered her condolences as I was heading back to my desk. I thanked her, then Hayden introduced me to the young woman. "This is Wendy Bartlett. She was awarded our founder's prize. We'll be backing her business venture for young girls."

Wendy looked like every black female romantic lead in every movie and TV show ad infinitum—that is to say, light-skinned with "good hair." She smiled warmly and gave a little wave.

"Congratulations." I knew it was wrong, but I felt no sisterly "you go, girl" feelings. I felt the opposite—embarrassed she'd seen me putting away Hayden's dry cleaning, my confidence dissolving further as Hayden told me about Wendy's project that would help inner-city girls thrive in tech.

"You deserve the award," Hayden said to Wendy.

Wendy smiled. "I can't thank you enough. The money is going to make a real difference."

I saw Wendy's entire life flash before my eyes: two parents, good schools, *cheerleading! Class president! Homecoming queen!* I could've choked on my envy.

Hayden cleared her throat. "Francine? The gifts?"

Everyone was staring at me. *Right.* I returned to my desk and retrieved the chocolates and macarons. I then served coffee and pastries. Back at my computer, I stole glances at Wendy. She sat up straight and looked Hayden and Barbara in the eye. And then there was Hayden, nodding and smiling with... *was that respect?* Was that... *admiration?* Dang.

I pulled up Wendy's social media and scrolled through her world: the chic LA apartment, the friends.

When I saw her leaving Hayden's office and walking toward me—*shit*—I quickly navigated out of Peeps to work emails.

"Restroom?"

I pointed in the direction of the bathroom. "Congratulations on the award."

"Thank you so much. This is just the start for me." She lowered her voice. "In five more years I want Techie Girls in at least three more cities, including here in San Francisco. We have to get a stronger foothold in tech and business, you know what I'm saying?" She made tiny fists and wiggled them in the air. "Girl, I'm so excited."

I smiled politely, wanting her to get out of my face. "Bathroom's that way."

I watched her head down the hall, thinking of what Aunt Liane might say: *You could be doing so much more with your life.*

I bolted straight up, went to UC Berkeley Extension's website, and enrolled in the photography class I'd been on the fence about. Instead of backing out, I submitted my payment and clicked send before I could change my mind. A photography class was nowhere near as impressive as a nonprofit for girls, but it was a start.

That evening I went home and edited recent photos I'd taken. It felt good to focus on my pictures, the hours slipping away. Afterward I checked in with Jeannette about Monterey. We decided to spend the night instead of driving out for the day. I booked a double suite at the most expensive hotel in town because I wanted to splurge—because I deserved it and because fuck the FUN Committee. I could go away for the weekend, too, bitches, and I'd do it in style.

I asked Jeannette if she wanted to invite Tucker, but he was going to Reno to gamble, promising to play no more than two hundred dollars. Jeannette said she didn't have a problem with his gambling such a small amount since he'd been working so hard.

Before bed, I sat at Mom's altar, lit the candles and incense. I opened my laptop and watched several of her videos. Next, I went to her website and read messages from her followers: *Rest in power. I'll miss you.* That kind of thing.

I picked up her purple amethyst and thanked her for helping me find Davie and for helping me to meet Jeannette. I looked from the Medusa to Aunt Jemima. "I'm feeling better, Mom. I'm going to start taking photography. I'm no Wendy fucking Bartlett, but I'm trying."

CHAPTER TWENTY-ONE

had zero regrets about the money I spent on L'Auberge, the hotel where we stayed while visiting Monterey. There was a private hot tub adjacent to our suite, a fireplace, bay windows with a view of the ocean, and a sauna-shower, something neither Jeannette nor I knew existed. For the boys, I paid extra for use of a gaming console.

Tired from dealing with Friday night traffic, we ordered pizza and watched a movie. Afterward, Jeannette and I soaked in the hot tub. The boys shared the room with the game console and played long past any reasonable bedtime. After soaking, Jeannette and I watched an hour of trash TV, then took the room closest to the sauna shower. When I said I'd sleep on the daybed, she told me to stop being ridiculous; I paid for everything so I should take the king-sized bed.

Before the boys went to sleep, she called Tucker so he could say good night. She told him about the double suite and our plans. There were no I-love-yous before they hung up, I noticed. They truly lived separate lives.

Later, after showering and checking on Davie and Sterling to make sure they were asleep, she joined me in the bed, taking out her Sherlock Holmes pipe and a bag of weed. When she asked if I wanted any, I told her no, disappointed that she needed to bring weed in the first place, like being in Monterey in an expensive hotel wasn't enough.

She took a long drag, managing to speak as smoke filled her lungs: "I knew being rich would feel good. I can't thank you enough for paying for all of this."

I remained tight-lipped. I tried not to judge how often she drank and smoked. She had a lot going on in her life, after all. We sat close together in bed, our shoulders brushing now and then, her soapy, clean smell mingling with the pungent odor from the weed. I thought momentarily of how good she'd looked in her bathing suit earlier, then quickly kicked the thought from my brain. *She's married. She's your friend.* I scooted away so our shoulders wouldn't touch. Surely I was getting a contact high.

We went to Cannery Row the next day, visited several shops and a few galleries. The Monterey Bay Aquarium itself was filled with more sea life than any of us knew existed, everything from leopard sharks to octopus, to all kinds of underwater creatures. It was great seeing Davie so happy. Jeannette even made an effort to spend time with him. Seeing how she was trying, I figured I should do the same with Sterling. I walked over as he was taking pictures of the sea urchins. "Having fun?"

"Yeah, the sharks were cool."

An awkward silence fell between us.

"How's school?" Not the best question. From what Jeannette had told me, his grades were plummeting when they were already low.

"It's all right. I don't care about school, though. I wanna be a rapper."

I pretended Jeannette hadn't mentioned this. "Oh yeah? A rapper, huh. Why don't you drop me some of your rhymes." I started dancing eighties hip-hop style.

He looked me up and down like I was making a fool of myself, which I was. I had no rhythm and gave up.

"You're going to need school in case you don't make it as a rapper. School is important."

"I know that."

"Well I'm here to help you if you ever want tutoring or anything."

"Thanks, *Francine*." He said my name with a hard smirk, then turned his attention back to the urchins as though I weren't there. I swear he saw straight to my inner Mudface. He was never going to like me.

Then, for no reason that I could tell, on the other side of the room, Davie raised his voice and began recounting the story of *Finding Dory*, reciting memorized lines, loud and without inflection. Jeannette was on him in a second—grabbing him by the arm, shushing him. "I do not like to be touched!" he yelled.

I recalled how she'd twisted Sterling's ear and rushed over. I stood next to Davie and gently removed her hand from his arm. "Easy."

She cast her gaze off to the side, exhaled. She seemed over the sea life after only an hour—although I wasn't sure what she was expecting, it was called the Monterey Bay *Aquarium*.

Appearing regretful for her behavior, she lowered her face to Davie's and spoke in a gentle tone: "You can't shout in places like this, okay? We have to practice our manners."

Davie turned his attention toward the kelp forest, his eyes darting back and forth. "Mmmmm."

"Go look at the fish with Sterling and talk about *Finding Dory* in a quiet voice."

"Ling Ling isn't looking at fish, he's looking at sea urchins. Sea urchins are not fish."

"Okay, go look at the urchins or whatever."

When he left I said, "Nette, he was having fun. You didn't have to get on him like that."

"I know. I'm sorry, okay? But he needs to learn to behave in public."

"He was fine."

"You say that now because he's only ten, but what if he's shouting in some public place when he's older? That behavior can get him killed."

She had a point, sadly. "But you don't have to be so rough."

Sterling walked up with Davie in tow.

"I don't want to leave yet," said Davie.

When Jeannette looked to Sterling for a translation, he said, "I wanna leave. I'm bored."

Davie, finger in the air: "The Monterey Bay Aquarium is not boring. It's very interesting. I do not want to leave."

"But I do," Sterling whined. "I'm bored."

"We'll leave soon," Jeannette said.

"We cannot leave." Davie's tone was a threat: *Try to make me leave and I will explode.*

"He's right," I said. "We can't leave now. There's so much more to see. And don't make me bring up how long we waited for you while we were at the arcade."

Jeannette blinked, nodding slowly. She looked at Sterling. "She's got a point. Besides, this is good for you." She linked her arm in his. "Why don't we take a break, baby." She pointed at an empty bench in front of the kelp forest. "Let's go sit over there."

"Good idea," I said. "Davie and I will check out another exhibit and meet you back here."

Jeannette, already staring at her phone: "Don't take too long."

Seriously? I wanted to scream. It would have been nice if we could find an activity we all liked for once. I'd never have thrown money in her face, but, damn, the tickets were expensive and the aquarium was *not* boring.

"Come on," I said to Davie, thinking: *We are going to take all the fucking time we want.*

Dinner at the hotel restaurant didn't go over well either. Jeannette kept fidgeting in her seat. She was worried we weren't dressed appropriately, which was crazy, we were dressed just fine.

Sterling tried to read from the menu out loud. "What is aru . . . go. Aru . . . go?"

I took a sip from my water. "*Arugula*. It's like a type of lettuce."

"What's po . . . leeenta?"

"It's kind of like Cream of Wheat. Or grits."

"Then why don't they call it grits?" Jeannette said.

Sterling closed his menu and took out his phone. "That's what I'm sayin'."

Davie had his iPad and watched Mr. Science wearing his earbuds, which Jeannette allowed. She continued to scan the menu. "I don't recognize any of this food. And we should be more dressed up."

The restaurant was expensive but not Michelin starred or anything. "It's not that nice. We're fine."

"'It's not that nice,'" Jeannette mimicked.

She and Sterling exchanged looks.

They were both officially on my nerves. I needed new friends! I needed friends like Wendy Bartlett! I couldn't rely on Jeannette to be everything. Maybe we were spending too much time together. I needed to start dating, too. How had I gotten sidetracked from that?

Jeannette surveyed the restaurant. "You do notice we're the only black people up in here."

"I don't care. I'm black and I'm hungry. They have pizza on the menu. Anyone want pizza?"

"I'd rather have pizza than seafood," Davie quipped. "Ha!"

"What about pizza funghi with prosciutto?"

"The what with the what?" said Sterling. "How do you know about all of this weird food?"

"My job, I guess. Work lunches with my boss."

Jeannette grabbed her purse. "Go ahead and order. I'll be right back." She abruptly rose from the table and off she went.

The boys stared at their devices. The waitress came and I ordered for the table. When our drinks and appetizers were served, and still no Jeannette, I told the boys to stay put and went to look for her. I made a useless search of the bathroom, checked to see if she'd returned to our table, then headed outside.

The hotel was a few miles from the commercial area, atop a hill that overlooked the bay. When an older white couple approaching the entrance gave me an accusatory glare, I knew something was up besides general racism and walked along the short plankway on the side of the restaurant, where I found Jeannette smoking from her pipe. *Terrific.*

She blew smoke from the corner of her mouth when she saw me. "Want some?"

"Davie and Sterling are inside the restaurant and you're out here smoking pot? Why did you have to bring weed in the first place?"

"'Smoking pot'?" she mimicked. "I'm not doing anything wrong."

"What's going on?"

"Nothing." She remained closed off. Moody AF.

I was fed up and hungry. "Fine. Stay in your mood. Our appetizers are here and I'm going to eat." I turned to leave.

"Wait." She put the pipe in a baggie, returned it to her purse. She stared at the lapping water in the distance. The night sky was as dark as the bay. "I just feel out of place in there. We're the only black people."

"Who cares? We have a room and we deserve to be here like anyone else."

"I know. I just get down sometimes. Seeing everything today makes me feel less-than. It's the thought of what I don't have and what I don't know that pisses me off. I've never heard of half the food on the menu. I'm giving Sterling a shit childhood." She brought her hand to her necklace, twisting the zirconia, her gaze on the bay. "I had a shitty day at work yesterday, too. I've been trying to forget about it, but it's been putting me in a mood."

"You *should* forget about it. You're here now; that's what matters."

"Yeah," she mumbled. "I'm sorry I'm such a moody bitch. I'm sorry for how I was acting at the aquarium, too. It's like my mom always told me, I can't help but fuck up everything. Are you mad at me?" she asked weakly.

"Yes."

"Are you still my friend?"

I smiled and reached out my hand to lead her back inside. "Always."

+ + +

After dinner we watched TV while the boys played video games until they were too tired to focus. Tucker called from Reno to say good night just as they were heading to bed.

Jeannette and I got into the hot tub soon after. The sky was clear, and there were so many stars it was as if I were seeing the night sky for the first time ever. "Sky for the one percent," Jeannette commented.

Tiny bottles of alcohol from the minibar lined her side of the hot tub. Hypocrite that I was, I'd had a couple of hits of her pot. She created ripples by running her arms back and forth through the water. Like with Mom, I was keenly attuned to her moods, the highs and lows, ups and downs—my codependent superpower.

"It's so beautiful here," she murmured. "I wish I never had to leave, and I wish to God I didn't have to go to work on Monday."

I thought of what she'd mentioned earlier at the restaurant—her shitty day. "What happened?"

She climbed out of the tub so I got out, too. We dried off then sat on the edge of the tub with our feet in the water. I waited while she wrapped a towel around her shoulders, her mouth contorting as if she were reliving whatever happened. "My boss cornered me in his office. He's so fucking nasty. He started pushing his body up against me. He wasn't even doing it for all that long but I still felt trapped. Now I keep having these memories." She paused, lowered her voice. "Not from yesterday but from before."

"Before?"

She stared down into the hot tub as she made tiny circles in the water with her feet. "Yeah, before."

I felt a sense of inevitable dread. I knew the statistics. So many of us were statistics. "I'm here for you, Jeannette. You're not alone."

She rolled her eyes.

"I mean it. You're not alone. I wasn't just bullied. I mean, something happened with me, too."

"Yeah, I know. You and that pedophile. I hate that dog."

"No, not him. Did you ever know a girl named Stefani Haywood?"

"Stefani Haywood... No."

"I didn't think so. I went to junior high with her."

"Why do you ask?"

I noticed my hands were already clammy just from saying Stefani's name out loud. I balled my fingers into fists, stretched them. "She used to beat me up all the time back in junior high. She . . ." I stopped. My hands were trembling now, the memory of the bathroom where she trapped me keeping me from speaking further.

"She what?"

I looked at Jeannette, raised my brows, forcing her to get it. *You know.*

She stared back, puzzled. "But Stefani's a girl."

"Still happened."

"What do you mean? What did she do?"

I put on the hotel robe, crossed my legs. I hadn't even told Kelly about what happened with Stefani that day in the bathroom. I definitely hadn't told Mom. I found myself explaining to Jeannette what happened, though, every detail—how Stefani had already given me a black eye by the time of the incident, how she'd bully me in front of her friends, steal my lunch money.

That particular day I had a hall pass to use the restroom. As soon as I saw her inside, the only person there, I tried to turn and leave, but she ran over and blocked the exit door, her breath hot on my face. "You didn't even use the bathroom yet, stupid."

I wasn't sure if I should try to use the restroom or leave. She made the decision for me. She flung me around, pushed me so hard I fell backward and almost landed on my ass. She then took me by both arms and slammed me against the wall. She was twice as big as me and fully developed. There was no fighting back. I braced myself for whatever she planned next—a punch, a slap, both. But that day, Stefani Haywood did the strangest thing. She locked her eyes with mine and said, "Everybody knows you like girls," and then she pressed her lips against mine. My very first kiss. Her lips on my lips, warm and soft. But when she began groping my chest, I felt uncomfortable and tried to remove her hand, which only angered her. She fought me off, then grabbed at my small chest so hard pain shot through my body. I struggled when she reached down into my pants, her fingers making their way to my underwear. "Stop," I said. But she was moving fast. She unzipped my pants and forced herself on me, using her fingers, splitting me open. I started to cry from the pain but she covered my mouth. My insides burned—her fingers digging, her nails cutting against my flesh. She only stopped when I started crying uncontrollably, then she pushed me away as though I were useless. "You're so fucking ugly." And she left me like that, alone and crying.

I realized Jeannette was tightening the robe I wore around my shoulders. I was shivering, my teeth chattering loudly. I pulled my feet from the water and crossed my arms over my chest while trying to forget the feeling of Stefani's hands on my body.

"I'm so sorry," she whispered, holding me. "Did you ever tell anyone about what happened? Did you tell your mother?"

I shook my head. "My mother would have freaked out and she was already bad off."

"I'm glad you told me." She pressed her cheek next to mine while holding me. My life was so messed up. So much of what happened to me felt trapped inside my body, a darkness keeping me hostage. I vowed to get therapy. I wasn't going to let Stefani or anyone else ruin my life.

Jeannette and I were quiet until she pulled away. She brought her knees into her chest and hid her face. "I'm sorry for what happened to you, Francine," she whispered. She began taking short jerky breaths then, clutching her stomach like she might throw up.

"Are you going to be sick?"

She shot to her feet and darted back inside. I followed as she rushed past the room where the boys slept and ran straight to the bathroom, closing the door behind her.

I knocked softly. "Are you sick? What's wrong?" When I heard the sound of something banging against the floor, I slowly opened the door. I found her in the corner of the bathroom between the tub and toilet. The trash can was on its side, the bottle of hand soap on the floor.

I recognized the look in her eyes, wild and fearful, her breathing erratic. "I think you're having a panic attack."

She nodded as she struggled to inhale.

"It's going to be all right."

I sat next to her, instructing her to breathe, to count along with me, in the same way I helped Mom when she suffered from an attack. I took her hand and we started counting our breaths together.

When her breathing slowed to its normal rhythm, she asked about Sterling. "Do you think he heard me?"

"You weren't loud."

I went to check on the boys anyway. It was almost midnight by then and they were asleep in their beds. I went back to the bathroom, where Jeannette was splashing water on her face. "Has this happened before?"

"After my mother's funeral. A few other times." She reached for a towel and started drying her face. "I'll be all right."

"I wish you would talk to someone."

"I talk to you. Let's just forget about it. I was upset from listening to you tell me what happened with that girl who hurt you."

She brushed past me—already back to her strong, independent self. She went into the bedroom, put on her sweats and T-shirt. I got dressed, too, and followed her into the suite's living room.

"It's not good that you're having panic attacks. My mom had them. They're a sign something's wrong."

"No shit. And I'm not your mom."

"I'm not saying you are."

She went outside and returned with the pot she'd been smoking. She lit the bowl.

"You smoke and you drink too much, Nette."

"Imagine how I'd be if I didn't smoke or drink. And thank you for not lecturing me." She sat on the couch, lit her pipe, and took a long hard pull.

I added a few logs to the fire, then sat on the opposite end of the couch. I wished she'd trust me enough to talk to me, but I chose not to say anything.

We both sat and watched the fire pop and snap. After a moment, she took another hit from her pipe and said, "You are the nicest person I ever met, and you deserve only good things."

I had no idea what she was talking about. "What does it matter if I'm nice if my best friend won't talk to me?"

She arched her brow. "Best friend?"

When I clicked my tongue, she kicked me lightly with her foot. "You're really cute when you're mad."

"Shut up."

"You're really cute... period."

I looked at her, curious, but she avoided eye contact—just nestled her feet up against my thighs.

She toked and blew smoke from the corner of her mouth. "I bet you've never been kissed."

I stared from her toes pressing into my leg up to her face. "What are you even talking about? I was with Kelly for almost three years. You are high and you're drunk."

She tilted her head. "What I mean to say is, I bet you've never been kissed like what you deserve."

"You're not making any sense. Stop talking."

She put the pipe on the side table. "Nope. I refuse. I'm going to say what needs to be said. You're beautiful, Francine. You're really good to me, and I *like* you. Can't you tell that I like you?"

Whaaaat? I'd had my quick moment of lust the night before, but this was coming out of nowhere. It was coming from the nether regions of outer space. *She liked me?* She'd given no indication she liked me. Half the time I seemed to get on her nerves.

Before I could make sense of what she was telling me, she climbed up on all fours and started toward me like a slow-moving cat, a sly smile crossing her face.

"What are you doing?" I retreated, stopping only when I felt my back pressing against the armrest. "You're out of your mind right now. You just had a panic attack."

She moved closer. "I like you, Francine. Don't you know that? Why do you think I act so crazy?"

I swallowed, my throat suddenly parched. "You're straight."

"Not when it comes to you." She grinned.

I rolled my eyes. Did I want to kiss her? Hell yeah. But I would never want to ruin our friendship. Plus, she was straight. Wasn't she? She was definitely married. I stopped her from moving closer by holding her at the shoulders. "You're drunk."

"No, I'm not. You deserve someone who makes you feel good, someone who treats you well. You deserve someone who makes you feel special."

She took my right hand and stretched it behind my head, took my left hand and did the same, holding me like that with my hands stretching back behind me, my chest rising up. "Don't play with me. You're not funny."

"I'm not playing."

She lowered her face just short of touching my nose; her breath, smelling of weed and alcohol, warmed my mouth. I arched up further, my body taking over, an ache of desire running through my bones. I wanted nothing more than her lips against mine. And then it was happening. Our mouths opening, tongues searching and folding and licking. My body shuddered forcefully. Embarrassed, I looked away. But then Jeannette touched my chin with the tip of her finger and gently cupped my face, bringing me back. She peered into my eyes. "You are beautiful."

There was the crackle of the fire, the shadows across her face. The miracle of Jeannette wanting me and calling me beautiful. I relaxed and wrapped my hand around the back of her head, brought her in for more. We kissed until we were out of breath. And then, panting, her face flushed and hovering above mine, Jeannette Tomlin stood up and took my hand, and led me to the bedroom.

CHAPTER TWENTY-TWO

What I go back to, probably more often than I should, is those hours after our first kiss when I had complete reign over Jeannette's body, those hours before the sun rose. If I wanted her light-brown nipple in my mouth, one nipple and then the other, or if I wanted to trace my finger down that particular line that ran from her belly button to her pelvic bone, or bury my nose in her pubic hair and take in as much as I could, I did. And, miracle of miracles, Jeannette was right there with me, reassuring the insecure parts of me, not with her words but with her lips on my mouth, her hands reaching for my body, always meeting me kiss for kiss, touch for touch.

Just before dawn, she gazed into my eyes as if wanting to hold the memory of my face forever. Both of us silent, both of us wanting to hold on to the moment. The light in the room was beginning to brighten, the sun robbing us of our time together: the boys would be up soon.

I asked her how long she'd known.

"Known what?"

"That you"—I gulped, nervous about her response—"*liked me*?" She poked her finger into the center of my dimpled chin and wiggled it around. I pushed her hand away. "I'm trying to be serious."

"I don't know," she said, moving herself further up on her elbow. "It just hit me, or maybe it's been happening since I met you."

"But you do"—gulp—"*like me*? This isn't just about you being queer-curious or something? Because I'm not into straight girls who—"

She ran her hand over my face, gingerly closing my eyes and lips. "Shhhh . . . Stop questioning everything. I like you. What's even more important is I feel safe with you. I never feel safe with people."

The look in her eyes said she was telling the truth. I rose up and kissed her. "Is this it, though?"

She knew what I meant. "No. Hell no. We'll figure it out."

"But what about Tuck—"

"Shhhh." She brought her finger to my lips. "You worry too much. We'll figure it out. Let's just be together before the boys wake up."

She slid the flat of her hand down my stomach, her fingers moving between my thighs, easily sliding inside of me.

Damn it if I didn't feel all the feels those weeks after Monterey. I won't lie, it wasn't as romantic as you'd want a new relationship to be. She was married, after all, and responsible for two kids, but Jeannette was serious when she said she wanted to be with me. We stole time together as often as we could, including playing hooky from work again. When I asked what she wanted to do, she said, those hazel eyes brightening, "Let's go to Great America!" I mean, imagine: roller coasters during the workweek. And I hadn't been to Great America since both my parents were alive.

We went on every single roller coaster, ate junk food, laughed, and had the best time, all before having to head back to Oakland so she could be home before Tucker and the boys. I will never forget holding her hand high up on the RailBlazer right before the first drop, the sight of her hair shooting straight up, our screams mingling in the air.

What can I say? I loved everything about Jeannette. I loved her lips—specifically her juicy lower lip. I loved inhaling the smell of her scalp—scents of coconut and argan oils. I loved looking down and seeing my hand rest on the side of her naked hip, my skin dark against hers. Skin Jeannette loved.

After Monterey we moved with astonishing ease from friendship to full-on sexual relationship. Excuse my language, but we fucked anywhere and everywhere we could without being caught. We were a hot mess and bought our time together by spinning lies. Jeannette would tell Tucker she was getting her nails done or going to the store—staying late at work was a favorite—and we'd let our bodies have at it. Was she bi? Bi-curious? Heteroflexible? When I pressed her to define herself, something I wouldn't do today, she said, "I don't care what I am. I just know that I think about you all the time and have never felt like this." Those were her exact words.

She started coming over to do laundry, which was a perfect excuse since it saved her money and gave us time together. We'd watch TV with Sterling and Davie, and if they stayed long enough we'd eat takeout. All the while, Jeannette and I would steal looks at each other. We'd often sneak off to the bathroom or the garage, where the washer and dryer were kept, and steal a kiss, or whisper something sweet to each other, then head back to the den, Davie and Sterling none the wiser.

Once, while she and the boys were at the house, she offered to finally "do my edges," which she said were driving her crazy. We went into the bathroom while Davie and Sterling played video games. I'd bought an Xbox for the house by then, which miraculously earned a smile from Sterling.

I sat on the toilet and she used a comb not much bigger than a thumb along with a pomade that promised to "bless" type 4C hair. She knelt in front of me as she slicked back my edges. I, meanwhile, stared at her cleavage, her zirconia touching the tip of my nose every so often. When she finished, she cupped the back of my neck and pressed her breasts into my face, rested her chin on the crown of my head. I took the zirconia in my mouth and closed my eyes. "No one will ever care about you the way I care about you," I heard her say.

I pulled her into my lap, and she smiled and regarded her hairstyling skills. "Much better. See?"

She gave me the hand mirror. I stared at our faces staring back at me, her cheek resting on my shoulder. She'd slicked my edges into s-shaped patterns and swirls. I thanked her, then put the mirror on the sink and kissed her. I only stopped when I heard the sound of the video game Davie and Sterling were playing in the other room. I looked into her eyes, raised my brows. She understood and locked the bathroom door. We quickly unzipped our pants. As usual we only had a few minutes before Davie or Sterling became suspicious. I got down on my knees and grabbed her ass from behind, pulling her to me, yanking down her underwear. We had to be quick.

I feel guilty about it now, of course, but Davie had been right to call me out for wanting to "send him away" the day I'd found him at Pixar. Not that exact day, but definitely after Monterey. I wanted to send everyone away after Monterey. I wanted Sterling to go away and Tucker, too. I wanted Jeannette Tomlin all to myself without having to sneak into the bathroom all the time or tell so many lies. I mean, I never would've guessed it. Jeannette Tomlin, who I thought was straight, Jeannette Tomlin, the girl everyone wanted in high school, wanted me. I was tempted to take photos of the two of us kissing and post them on all social media platforms, tagging all of our old classmates. *I'm sleeping with Jeannette Tomlin, bitches! Fuck you!*

Looking back, I can't blame myself for how hard and fast I fell for Jeannette. I'd had a crush on her in high school and now she was my best friend, my only friend; our love for each other was ten-plus years in the making. It felt like fate to fall seamlessly and effortlessly in love with her.

But then there was my therapist, Pamela, who practically choked on that word—*fate*. When I started seeing her, she pumped the brakes on our love story by suggesting what Jeannette and I were doing was trauma bonding. I'd never heard the phrase before, but after our session and from what I saw on the web, my sad, codependent ass ticked off every single characteristic.

Before Pamela, I fought hard to ignore any problems, like Jeannette's drinking and smoking. She was always stressed about something, too, and could be moody AF. Even so, it was easy to go about my merry way pretending all was well. *Husband? What husband?* Jeannette made herself comfortable in fairyland right along with me. We began envisioning our future: she'd leave Tucker, she and the boys would move in with me, and we'd finally be together—happily ever after.

Yeah, fairyland was a magical place until Pamela came along with her truth bombs. I'd started therapy three days after returning from Monterey. I chose Pamela not so much because of her credentials but rather because her smile and short Afro reminded me of Mom. Let me tell you, though, she was a no-bullshit therapist. Every session, she'd pick up her trusty hammer and tap tap tap until I started to see crevices and fissures in my love story with Jeannette. Thanks to her direct approach, the assigned readings, and the journal prompts, I slowly began to acknowledge the five hundred million neurons in my gut sending off warning flares.

All too soon, I became increasingly impatient with the secrets and lies Jeannette and I were spinning. I wanted to hold Jeannette's hand out in the open and not have to worry about time constraints or Tucker or the boys finding out. I also wanted to tell Davie Jeannette and I were together so he'd know he had a family and would never have to worry about getting "shipped off."

I mean, I wanted truth for once. I'd spent most of life with secrets— no one coming to the house, no one knowing what I had to deal with at home with Mom. My secret relationship with Kelly. In the end, having an affair, or whatever, began stressing me out. I started having nightmares, too, the kind where I'd wake up in a sweat. In one dream, I was searching for Mom at Drunk Grandpa's house. A party was taking place and everyone was smoking pot from Sherlock Holmes pipes. I saw Mom sitting on a couch with a doll as if she were a little girl in a grown woman's body, then she disappeared. Aunt Liane was dancing with some guy whose back was turned. Where was Uncle CJ? When I asked if she knew where Mom went, she snapped at me—*The hell I know where she is. I'm not her damn mother. I'm just a teenager. I wanna have fun.* Her dance partner turned. *Isaiah.* Blech! I continued to search the house, eventually finding Mom in the attic, holding her doll, her thumb in her mouth. When I tried to convince her to leave with me, she screamed over and over, *Stay away from me! I don't know you!*

I woke up with the sound of her voice in my ears. It was laughable how literal the dream was. Mom not recognizing me surely had to do with my behavior—sleeping with a married woman and recklessly spending her money.

And… yeah… about that. Mom's money. Along with everything else, I'd paid off two of Jeannette's credit cards after Monterey, secret cards Tucker knew nothing about, to the tune of—*wait for it*—two thousand eight hundred dollars.

If recklessly spending Mom's money and having nightmares wasn't enough to clue me in—and it wasn't—Davie began acting strange when we were alone together. Even though Jeannette and I were extra careful, it was like he was picking up on something. He stopped talking to me as much, and whenever I asked what he was thinking, he'd drop a slavery fact. Jeannette said he was misbehaving at home, too. More tantrums and whatnot.

I initially told Pamela she was flat-out wrong about us trauma bonding or whatever, and while my brain continued spinning expert tales that everything was just fine, *my gut*? Those five hundred million neurons? They were like… they were like a unified Greek chorus. They were like, *Francine Stevenson, what the fuck are you doing?!*

The stress pushed me to start arguing with Jeannette about telling Tucker the truth. She wouldn't have to move out right away, but she should at least tell him we were seeing each other; it was the right thing to do.

I was repeating this exact argument the first night of my photography class. It was mid-April by then. I was excited about attending but nervous. Jeannette's timing couldn't have been worse, though. She showed up at the house completely unannounced not long before I had to head out. Apparently she'd told Tucker I had a cold and she was dropping off cough medicine. The lie was beyond lame, but I figured he believed her lies because they barely communicated in the first place.

The class started at seven. I needed to change out of my work clothes, then drive to Berkeley and find parking. She watched me get dressed from the doorway. "Don't leave," she begged.

"I told you I had class tonight."

"No, you didn't."

"Yes, I did." I'd definitely told her.

"Can't you be a little late? It's not like it's a real class."

That got my attention. "It's real to me. Can't you be a little more supportive? And we wouldn't have to sneak around if you'd tell Tucker the truth. Kelly never told anyone about me because I was her lie. Now I'm your lie."

202 • Renee Swindle

I started putting on my shoes, a pair of Converse. I had chosen a T-shirt that said *Art Whore* but figured it was too on the nose and changed into a plain blue T-shirt and jeans. I swear it felt like the first day of school and I was a kid and wanted to make a good impression. I hoped I could make a friend, too. My world with Jeannette was becoming too insular.

She crossed the room, bumping my right shoulder rather hard as she moved to the bed. "Fine, bougie. Whatever. Go to your class, even though I took the time to sneak out of the house." She sat with her back against the headboard, her mouth in a pout.

I was going to comment on how hard she'd bumped into me, but from her expression, the way she started to speak, then chose not to, I knew something was up. "What's wrong?"

"Nothing."

I'd learned it was my role to play mind reader and figure out whatever was bothering her. "Just tell me."

"Everything is wrong."

Well, that's nothing new, I thought. But then she blinked several times, tears glistening in her eyes.

I softened in an instant, a part of me thinking she was about to break up with me. I always worried she was going to break up with me. "What is it?"

"I'm too embarrassed to tell you."

I moved to the edge of the bed, placed my hand on her thigh. "Don't do that. We tell each other everything. Talk to me."

She grabbed a throw pillow and hid her face. "Sterling was suspended," she said, her voice muffled.

"What did he do?"

She dropped the pillow in an instant, eyes blazing. "Why do you have to assume he did something?"

She was right, actually. I quickly backpedaled: "Sorry, that came out wrong. What happened?"

"I thought you had to go to class," she said, tight-lipped. "'Cause I don't want to make you *late*."

"I'm sorry. I didn't know Sterling had been suspended. Why didn't you tell me?"

"Why should I? You don't even like Sterling."

"That's not true. I love Sterling." All I could do was hope that I sounded even remotely believable. I took her hand. Sterling's suspension was more important than my class. I'd have to be late. "What happened?"

She took a long, bracing breath. "Some girl said he groped her chest. But it wasn't his fault. These girls are fast these days. She was flirting with *him*. He showed me the texts she was sending him, so I know he's not lying. But the girl said he touched her without consent, which is bullshit. I showed the principal the texts, but I'm not good at talking to principals, they make me nervous. He wouldn't listen to me. And the principal at Grover is white, which only makes it worse. Tucker had to work; otherwise I would've sent him to talk to him."

I remembered the time I saw Jeannette at MacDowell, sitting in the principal's office, looking sullen while he berated her. Who knows why she was there. Another fight, or maybe she'd gone off on yet another teacher. I was in the office and the door was cracked just enough that I could see her profile and overhear Principal Lathem saying, *You're going to end up in prison or on the streets if you don't get your act together.*

"So the principal believes this girl over my son," she continued. "Nothing happens to that girl, but my son gets suspended."

"When did all this happen?"

"A couple of days ago."

"*Days?* Why didn't you tell me?"

"Because, like I said, it's embarrassing. And look how you assumed it was Sterling's fault. Everybody at Grover always thinks he's up to no good." She looked at me. Teary again, she wiped at the corners of her eyes. "The principal showed me this video, too, but Sterling said the tape didn't get everything that happened. He said the girl tried to touch his privates first so he touched her right back. But the tape only caught him touching her. So the video makes it look like everything is his fault. I tried to tell the principal what Sterling told me, but he kept looking at me like I was a bad mother and wouldn't listen to anything I had to say. He just went on about school policy and some other bullshit that had nothing to do with anything."

Honestly? I didn't trust Sterling's story for a second. I also recalled the time Jeannette pulled a knife on Wesley Morris for groping her, yet she seemed to lack any sympathy for the girl Sterling had groped. But damn if I was going to say anything. Keeping the peace with Jeannette meant keeping my mouth shut.

"Sterling is already getting Ds and Fs," she murmured, "now this. Everything is so fucked."

I reached up and massaged her shoulders. "We can turn things around, Nette. You guys will move in with me and we can get Sterling tutoring and—" I almost said *therapy* but knew that wouldn't go over well. "And things will work out."

She closed her eyes and clasped her hands in front of her chin like someone in prayer.

"What is it?"

"After I left the principal's office, I had another one of those panic attacks." She stared at her hands in her lap. "No one saw me, thank God. I was in my car in the parking lot. I swear I thought I was going to die."

I thought of finding her in the bathroom in Monterey, terrified and short of breath. "Nette, you can't go on like this."

"I know."

I glanced at the clock on the nightstand. "We should talk. I'll call you later tonight."

"Can you please just not go?" She looked so helpless. I also knew it was difficult for her to ask.

Still... "I've been waiting for this class for weeks."

"If things were the other way around and you were in my position, I would stay with you."

"But we can talk tonight."

"When you love somebody, you're supposed to be there for them. I went out of my way to come over here and tell you what happened, and you can't even stay with me for a few minutes when I need you."

"If you'd talk to Tucker we wouldn't have to sneak around to begin with."

She distorted her face and mimicked me, her voice nasal: "'If you'd talk to Tucker we wouldn't have to sneak around to begin with.'"

I pulled away. She knew how much I hated it when she mimicked me like that.

"Sorry," she mumbled. Then, more like a whimper: "I'm scared, Francine. He was *suspended*. He's going to turn out like me—or worse."

I pulled her into my lap. She was right. She needed me. When she nestled her head into the crook of my neck, I kissed her near the temple, then on the forehead. "There's nothing wrong with you, Nette. And you're not alone in this. I'm always here for you."

I found myself glancing at the clock again. I was going to be so late I might as well skip class altogether. But I told myself to let it go and cradled her in my arms.

CHAPTER TWENTY-THREE

was nearly an hour late to class. I was proud of myself for not backing out, but still—*I was an hour late.* The teacher was already mid lecture and showing slides, the classroom pitch dark. I immediately tripped over a chair someone was sitting in—*Excuse me, sorry*—then my hand landed on another person's desk and I knocked their legal pad to the floor. *Excuse me, sorry.* Someone in the front of the room shushed me. It was like a slapstick comedy without the humor.

Rick Blum, the teacher, hearing the commotion, paused. I pulled out an empty chair and slunk down in my seat. He cleared his throat and continued his talk—an overview of important photographers of the last century. I was way late, but as far as I could tell, he'd only included one female, Dorothea Lange, which was fine, but there were so many others, and he'd mentioned no photographers of color.

When he turned on the lights, I thought of Mom: his thick mustache and curly brown hair made him look like he belonged onstage singing the disco music she loved; all he needed was polyester pants and a shirt unbuttoned to his navel.

There were about fifteen students, from older folks to people my age. My eyes gravitated to a brown-skinned woman sitting up front, the only person of color in the room besides me. Even from behind I could tell she was butch. But there was also something about her... Something about her squat, muscular body... the 1950s crew cut... My thoughts slowed to a halt. *It couldn't be.* But then she raised her hand and before Rick could call on her, sure enough—"Yo, I noticed you didn't mention Rinko Kawauchi or Shirin Neshat during your talk." As soon as I heard that old-school *yo*, my hunch was confirmed: it was Kenji, the woman I'd gone out with. Cue the horror music.

Rick fell into mansplaining as he tried to cover the fact that Kenji was right to call him out for not including more than one female photographer. "Neshat's work is intriguing. I know it well." Blah blah. His face reddening, he checked the clock. "Let's take a break, everyone. Be back in fifteen."

Kenji shook her head and grabbed her bag. Our eyes locked momentarily, but either she didn't recognize me or she was pretending not to, and she darted from the room. *Fine with me.*

During the second half of class, Rick showed us techniques we could use for close-ups. Kenji was the type of student who'd raise their hand first and aim to answer all the questions. I officially hated her as much that night as I had on our date—or whatever you'd call it. She was so annoying. I will say, it did feel good to be inside a classroom again. I enjoyed learning, always had, and I was especially happy to be learning techniques to help my photography.

After class, I waited until Kenji left to introduce myself to Rick and apologize for being late. My phone buzzed as I exited the room: a text from Jeannette asking when I'd be home so we could talk. I sighed loudly. I wanted to go home and go to bed, not talk about Sterling and his issues.

I was about to get in my car and text her back when I heard, "Yo! I know you."

Shit. *Kenji.* She walked up to me. Her crew cut was shorter around the sides with a dollop of shiny black hair crowning her head. "What's your name again? We went out, remember?"

"I remember." *Wish I could forget, though.*

"If you remember me, why didn't you say hello when you saw me in class?"

Why didn't you *say hello?* God, she annoyed me.

She pointed, nodding slowly as though remembering something about me. "Yo, did you and the sneater get married?" She started laughing, cupping her hand around her mouth, making a scene.

I rolled my eyes.

"I'm just messin' with you. What's your name again?"

"Francine."

"Right. I'm Kenji. It's good to see you. So I guess you were serious when you said you were into photography. This class is no joke." Before I could agree, she said, "You wanna get some doughnuts?"

I raised my brows. "Doughnuts? It's late."

"So? I know a place. We can eat doughnuts and deconstruct the fuck out of Rick's shitty, sexist, racist lecture."

"So true. I mean he can't even include Gordon Parks?"

"Yo, exactly! Not even Carrie Mae Weems? What's up with that? So you wanna grab a doughnut, some soup?"

"*Soup?*"

"My cousin owns a doughnut shop nearby. He makes a mean samlor korko. It's a Cambodian soup."

I tried to repeat what she'd said. "Samlor kor…"

"Samlor korko. Just come with me. I can convince you that *Star Wars* is way better than *Star Trek.*"

"But it's not," I said. But then I smiled.

The next thing you know I was following Kenji Bou to her cousin's doughnut shop: V's Doughnuts—open until midnight! Buy two coffees, get the third cup free!

Kenji's cousin Vithu was about ten years older, with the same build as Kenji and a balding head. He led us down a long hall past the kitchen to a back room with a table and chairs and a small statue of a Buddha with an offering of tangerines and lit incense. On the walls were two posters of Tupac Shakur as if he was right up there with the Buddha as far as Vithu was concerned. We sat on stripped seats from a minivan. It was kind of surreal. I mean, who would've thought I'd end up in a back room of a doughnut shop eating soup with Kenji that night? But, *yo*, Vithu's soup, made with fresh pumpkin, lemongrass, and shiitake mushrooms, was delicious.

"Yo," Kenji had said after introducing me to Vithu. "We don't know *fuck* about Cambodia. Me and Vithu grew up in Richmond."

"But we know how to cook Cambodian food and doughnuts," Vithu said before heading back to the front to manage his store.

Kenji and Vithu's grandfather moved to the States as a refugee. He worked for a relative who owned a doughnut shop, which led to their grandfather buying his own shop. Kenji explained that it was the same situation for other Cambodians, due to Pol Pot's atrocities and the Cambodian refugee crises. Now Cambodians owned up to 90 percent of independent doughnut shops across the country, a fact I planned to pass on to Davie.

Kenji and I shared some of our photos while eating soup. I liked her work a lot. Mostly black and white photos that captured contemporary life for Asian Americans, in the vein of Michel Kameni's work.

Kenji mentioned her parents initially refused to accept her as gay. They came around after she stopped talking to them for two years. And, like me, Kenji had also met someone. In true lesbian fashion she and her girlfriend were already living together. I could only hope the same for Jeannette and me.

Eve, her girlfriend, was working on her PhD in sociology. Kenji showed me a few pictures of her after we'd moved on from soup to doughnuts. Eve was black with a pierced septum and a pierced nostril. There was also a birthmark the size of a newborn's fist on the left side of her forehead, which you could tell she gave no fucks about, since while she could've grown bangs or styled her hair to cover it, she chose instead to go bald, the fine hairs on her head dyed yellow. She was gorgeous. "You go, Kenji," I said. "Score."

"Yo, she's the one who scored." She winked and put her phone away.

"How did you meet?"

"At the farmer's market."

"Of course you did. That is *so* Berkeley."

She chewed her doughnut in large bites. She still ate too quickly—powdered sugar covered her upper lip; a pink sprinkle was glued to the side of her mouth. She licked her fingers. "I saw her checking out the figs."

"No," I laughed.

"Oh yeah." She grinned. "I was like, *Yo, I will do anything to get that girl.* I hate to drop clichés, but she's as beautiful on the inside as the outside." Her grin turned into a shy smile. "She supports me and makes me feel safe. I've never felt like this."

"I'm happy for you."

"Had your chance," she teased.

I told Kenji all about meeting Davie, which led to telling her about Jeannette. I went back and forth on whether or not I should tell her Jeannette was married, then figured it might be good to hear someone else's perspective. "There's something else I need to tell you about Jeannette."

Kenji paused, doughnut in hand. "She's a Republican."

"What? No."

"She's in prison."

"No, she's not in prison."

"Then what is it?"

"She's married."

"What? Speak up, I can't hear you."

"SHE'S MARRIED."

"Married like polyamorous married or *married* married?"

"Married *married*. To a man."

"*To a man?!*"

"It's complicated." I could no longer look her in the eye, so I picked up my phone while also trying not to show alarm at the number of texts Jeannette had sent. I put the phone down right away. "Things will work out," I found myself saying. "We care about each other. I shouldn't have said anything in the first place. I'm fine."

Kenji stared up at the Buddha statue with alarm, as if at any moment I might be sent to Buddhist hell, if there was such a place. "That's bad karma. You are so lying to yourself, if you think you're fine. Yo, you are not fine. If you were fine you wouldn't be dating a married woman."

I was left with nothing to do except stare at the mic she'd dropped in the middle of the table.

We said goodbye in front of the doughnut shop. Rick had assigned the class to see the Wexler exhibit at the Berkeley Art Museum and take pictures inspired by his style. We decided to go together that Saturday.

I read Jeannette's texts in my car. The first text started with a concerned Where r u? R u okay?, then she went from the more pissed-off Where R U? if it was davie you would've responded right away (true) to the even more pissed-off ur being a bitch Text me back!

I assumed she was drunk by the time she'd sent the last text and forgave her for calling me a bitch. She was stressed, after all. There was Sterling's suspension and having yet another panic attack. It was a lot. These are the things I told myself, anyway. I wasn't in the mood to argue.

I texted her after driving home and changing into my PJs:

> Sorry! I know someone in class.
> We went out for doughnuts after.
> I'm home now. Xoxox!!

We FaceTimed a few seconds later. I was right: she was on the balcony drinking. She wore an extra-large hoodie I had to assume was Tucker's. Was she ever going to leave him?

"You should have texted me sooner instead of letting me worry. I never would've left you hanging like that."

I considered mentioning I would never call her a bitch but reminded myself it was the alcohol in her, the stress. "Sorry."

"You don't have to apologize for everything, Francine."

"Sorry."

She paused, regrouping: "How was your class?"

I told her about Rick and what we'd learned, about Kenji and eating doughnuts and soup. "She's actually not like what I thought. We had fun."

"Was she flirting with you?"

"She has a girlfriend."

"That doesn't matter."

My smaller self kind of liked that she was jealous. Maybe she'd understand on some level what I had to put up with knowing she was sharing her bed with Tucker, no matter that they weren't having sex—thank goodness.

She pulled her zirconia from inside his hoodie, swung it on the chain. "You said you'd talk with me after your class, but you left me hanging."

"I lost track of time. I'm sorry." I could've defended myself, but between flight and fight? I chose flight. I was tired; plus she was clearly buzzed. "You want to talk tomorrow?" I let the words *when you're sober* hang between us.

She lowered her voice to a whisper. "You keep saying I should move in with you but look how you act. Sterling was *suspended*. This is important. Do you even care about me?" She looked genuinely worried.

"Of course I do." I started to tell her that I was there for her *and* Sterling, but she suddenly turned abruptly toward her apartment. I heard Tucker's voice. *Shit.*

Bad karma. Very bad karma.

Their voices were muffled so I couldn't make out what they were saying. Then I heard: "Yeah, she's feeling better. Yeah…"

Right. The lie she'd told him about my having a cold. "I'll ask her now." She appeared back on-screen. "We're going to Modesto to see Ceci and Huevo this Saturday. We're planning to stay the night, but Davie doesn't want to go. He has a fit any time I bring it up. Can you watch him for us?"

An entire weekend with Davie? Absolutely. We needed it, too. My stomach dropped just thinking about how I'd been ignoring him, how quiet he was becoming around me. I could use the weekend to get back into his good graces. I was already picturing us watching Pixar cartoons and documentaries together.

I told her about the assignment to visit the Berkeley museum; she could bring him by afterward.

"She can watch him," she said to Tucker.

"Thanks, Francine!" I heard Tucker say from somewhere inside the apartment. "We owe you. And we appreciate you!" My stomach tightened. Bad karma.

I heard more mumbling, then Davie's voice, but I couldn't make out what he was saying, nor could I see anything on the screen except Jeannette's hand.

"No, not right now," I heard her say. "Because I said so. Get your water and go back to bed. *No, Davie.* She doesn't want to talk to you right now. Hurry up."

I tried to get Jeannette's attention. "Does he want to talk to me? Jeannette?" Silence. Then I heard Tucker tell her good night. Davie said something, but I couldn't make it out.

After a moment, Jeannette returned. "Sorry about that."

"Is Davie there? Does he want to talk to me?"

"He went back to bed."

"I never said I didn't want to talk to him, Nette. I wish you wouldn't have told him that."

"It's after eleven. He needs to be in bed."

She rolled her shoulders back, took a hit from her Sherlock Holmes pipe. I knew she never smoked in front of Davie or Sterling, she'd wait until they were in bed or lock herself in the bathroom, but still, she smoked so much. Also, if she was moody around me, surely she was temperamental around Davie. I guess I was starting to wonder, really wonder, what the hell went on at their house when I wasn't around.

She thanked me again for agreeing to look after Davie. With that out of the way, she brought up what was really on her mind. "I'm still trying to think of what I can do to get the suspension off Sterling's record. I was thinking Tucker could try to talk some sense into the principal. Or maybe you can help me write a letter? Would you do that for me?"

What about the fact that Sterling shouldn't have been groping girls in the first place? What about that? I bit down on my lower lip. What if it *wasn't* his fault? "Sure," I said, "whatever I can do to help."

She started replaying her visit with the principal, describing again his dismissive behavior, her worries about her son, and on and on. I'd had such a good time at class and with Kenji and now my mood was plummeting.

A throbbing pain started at the back of my neck. Nodding my head now and then, muttering the occasional word of support, I discreetly walked to the bathroom, opened the medicine cabinet, and peered at the row of Alfonse's beautiful pills. They were so tempting. I thought again that I had no right to judge Jeannette for drinking and smoking pot. I knew what it was like to need to disassociate. Even so, I gathered strength and tossed the pills into the outside bin for pickup the next day. They were too tempting and I didn't trust myself. I went back inside and swallowed a couple of Advils, then wandered into the den and sat at Mom's altar as Jeannette droned on. I mindlessly picked up Aunt Jemima, feeling nothing inside. Feeling like I was losing my mom, her spirit anyway. The dream I'd had came sharply into focus: Mom, a terrified little girl, not recognizing me.

Jeannette said something about the principal possibly being racist. "Uh-huh," I mumbled. "Could be."

I absently divided Mom's tarot deck and stacked it together again. I turned over the top card and stared at an image of a dead man, facedown in his own blood, skewered by ten swords spiked into his back. *Seriously?*

"You okay?"

I glanced at Jeannette on-screen.

"Are you even listening? What are you doing?"

"Nothing. I'm listening. Go on. I'm here for you."

The pot and booze settling her nerves, she smiled softly. "Thank you for being my friend, B." She'd started calling me "B" sometimes, not for *bougie* but for *boo*. Her boo. "Sorry to talk so much. I feel better now. Thank you." She inhaled deeply, licking her lower lip the way I liked. "I don't know what I'd do without you."

See? That right there. My heart melted—just mush somewhere on the floor.

She checked over her shoulder to make sure she was alone, then brought two fingers to her lips and blew me a kiss. *Love you*, she mouthed.

I brought my fingers to my lips, whispered, "I love you, too."

We said good night. I put my phone down next to the tarot card with the skewered dead guy. I had to wonder what it meant, but then— *whatever*—I turned the card over, facedown. As Mom knew, I didn't believe in all that new age, mumbo jumbo crap anyway. Fuck the tarot.

CHAPTER TWENTY-FOUR

Rick assigned the class to shoot photos based on the word *contrast* as part of our portfolio. "See what comes up," he'd told us. I'd stay up for all hours into the night, high not on Alfonse's pills but on my art. His assignment sparked one idea after another. I bought crisp new white sheets, then set up my tripod and took a self-portrait of my naked body against all that white. Using an editing technique Rick had taught us, I faded my skin until it appeared ghostly pale. Next, I blurred and duplicated the image, darkening each take until my skin appeared as black as ink—with the final touch, the shock of my eyes and teeth, brightened to a neon white, the viewer left with several rows of my body, gradations from white to dark. I based the title of the image on a skin-whitening product sold in India, changing the words to make a point: *Go from White and Fair to Dark and Beautiful in Less Than One Week!*

In another image, I printed a photo of my face and poured bleach over it until my skin looked puckered and discolored. I then took a second shot and edited the two images so that one half of my face was normal and the other half disfigured—a side-by-side before and after. I placed the image beneath a caption from an ad I'd found online advertising bleaching cream from the early 1900s. The old-timey caption read, *Throw off the chains that have held you in poverty! Bleach your dark skin!* No exaggeration. That was the exact caption.

I wanted my photos to say, in so many words . . . fuck colorism. I mean, the entire world seemed to buy into the adage "Light is right." I'd even found ads advertising whitening creams for vaginas. Vaginas!

At any rate, I couldn't remember the last time I had given something my all. I was proud of my photos. We were going to have to share our work at some point and I was ready. Even if Rick turned out to be a lousy teacher for the rest of the course, I owed him for that one-word assignment.

I showed Kenji my pictures that Saturday at a café before seeing the Wexler exhibit. Jeannette and Tucker would be dropping Davie off later in the day.

Kenji scrolled through the images, pausing on the photo in which I created gradations of my naked body going from white to obsidian. "What speed did you use for the aperture?"

"One point two."

She nodded and continued to scroll. "I doubt if Rick will get everything your photos convey, but I do. These photos are good, Francine." She eyed the self-portrait in which I'd bleached and destroyed my skin. "Really good. And they're important. You should put a portfolio together."

"Stop."

"I'm serious. You're talented. Have you ever thought about going to art school?"

Kenji worked as a grant writer. Her goal was to start her own nonprofit helping third- and fourth-generation Cambodian kids discover art and photography. She was almost finished with her grant proposal. Kenji wanted to pursue both her dreams: photography and starting an arts program.

I tapped my finger against my mug of coffee. I'd never told anyone what I was about to tell Kenji, not even Mom. "I sometimes think about becoming a photographer. But what if something goes wrong, like, what if I fail?"

"Fuck the what-ifs. What if you succeed, yo? Apply to art school and see what happens."

"You think?" I'd shown some of my photos to Jeannette, my online community, and Mom of course, but it meant something that someone as talented as Kenji liked my work. "You're not just trying to be nice, are you?"

She studied me for a moment as if I were a stranger, as if seeing me for the first time. "You know what you need, Francine?"

"No, but I have a feeling you're going to tell me."

"You need some fucking self-esteem. You gotta claim what you want, yo. Don't be embarrassed about what you want in life or who you are."

She had a point, of course. *What did I want?* I did like photography, and working on Rick's assignment had been more fun and more engaging than anything I could remember doing in a long time. Why was I so afraid?

I thought about Kenji's advice as we walked through the Wexler exhibit. Wexler was a photographer from the fifties known for extreme close-ups. After viewing his work, we went to the sculpture garden to take pictures in his style. Kenji took close-ups of my elbow, the photos so close up, my elbow looked like an unknown body part or a tiny knee. I, in turn, took photos of Kenji's cropped hair so the hairs shooting from her scalp resembled alien terrain.

We were putting our cameras away when her phone chimed. "Eve is back from the farmer's market. Want to meet her? She picked up a quiche."

"Sure." But *hold up*—"Did you tell her about Jeannette?"

"Of course I did. I tell Eve everything."

"I wish you hadn't. It's kind of private."

"Yo, it wouldn't be private if she wasn't married."

Another mic drop. Damn, she was harsh.

"Don't worry," she said. "Eve thinks everyone is basically good. She's nothing like me in that way."

She wasn't exaggerating. If Kenji was brash and outspoken, Eve was chill and gave me a long hug when we met as though we'd known each other for years. While I would have tried to hide a birthmark on my forehead, she was as bald as in the pictures I'd seen, the fine hairs on her shaven head dyed a neon yellowish green.

Their apartment was homey and comfortable; the décor blended so well you would've thought they'd been living together for years. And Kenji was like a happy kid around Eve. They'd touch each other sweetly for no reason. Everything with those two was "babe" this and "baby" that.

I felt comfortable enough to show them a couple of Mom's videos. Eve said, "I can't believe that's your mom. I love her. I'm going to watch more of these." I knew Mom would have liked her, too.

She told me about her dissertation on equity issues, specifically the problems of growth mindset and how meritocracy in education put the onus on kids to succeed. Listening to her made me think of Davie and Sterling and all the other kids trapped in poor schools. She had a point. If kids could graduate based on effort and determination, half of my classmates would've gone to college, but we were all fighting structural issues like segregated school systems. I felt a pang of guilt for not supporting Sterling more. Jeannette had every right to be worried about his future.

Although Eve knew about Jeannette, most of her questions centered on Davie—probably due to her dissertation. I told them about his obsessions, about the science camp and the day he went missing and I found him at Pixar wearing the bicycle helmet. More guilt. There was a chance I could lose my connection with him for good if I kept focusing on Jeannette. I loved him, too, and needed to make sure he knew it. I was excited to see him later for our sleepover. Our weekend together would be our reboot.

"I hope I can meet him one day," said Eve. "And Jeannette, too. We should have you over for dinner or go out on a double date."

Kenji pretended to choke on a piece of quiche she was chewing, coughing loudly, theatrically pounding her chest.

Eve rolled her eyes. "Pay her no attention. If you and Jeannette love each other, things will work out."

Kenji took Eve's hand in hers, kissed it. "Told you she was nicer than me."

I realized how envious I felt of their relationship as I drove home. They represented all that I wanted for Jeannette and me—a homey vibe, lots of love.

◆ ◆ ◆

Jeannette arrived with Davie right on time. They stood on the porch while Tucker and Sterling waited in his truck. Tucker called out, "Thanks for keeping Li'l Man, Francine. We appreciate you." He waved, then said something to Sterling, who chucked his chin my way dismissively.

Davie brushed past me wearing his backpack and headed down the hall.

Jeannette called after him, "Say hello."

"Hello," Davie yelled from inside the house.

Jeannette glanced back at Tucker. He and Sterling were occupied on their phones. "Did you have fun at the museum?"

"Yeah. I met Kenji's girlfriend afterward. They invited us to dinner."

"Dinner? Do they know about Tucker?"

"Of course not." Oh my God, the lies, the lies.

She moved closer. "I miss you," she whispered, choosing not to comment on Kenji and Eve's invite. Then again, her husband was only a few yards away.

"I miss you, too." She had her hair up in two small buns twisted above her ears. She looked adorable. I glanced over her shoulder at Tucker. "We really need to figure something out. We can't go on like this. It's not right."

"I know. Everything is shit right now, but I'll try to see you soon. Will you help me write that letter to the principal? I need to get the suspension off Sterling's record."

"Yeah, sure."

With her back to Tucker, she puckered her lips, blew me a kiss, then started back to the truck. I waved goodbye, my Mary Poppins voice taking over: "Drive safe! Have fun!" Sterling looked up from his phone and shook his head with a smirk.

I narrowed my eyes. *I'm trying to help you with your suspension, jerk.* I was going to have to do some serious work on figuring out how to love that kid.

I watched them drive off, then went to join Davie. I found him pacing in front of the dining table with an odd look on his face. Shit.

"What's wrong?"

He wore his Mr. Science T-shirt. His hair had grown back and needed a major trim or cut. "You've been an asshole. You have not been a good friend."

"You're right. As a matter of fact, I was thinking—"

"But," he interjected, his finger high in the air, "I'm going to forgive you because I have very important news. It's very very important."

"Is it what you wanted to tell me the other night when I was talking to Jeannette? Listen, I never said I didn't want to talk to you. It was late."

"I was going to tell you that you weren't my friend, but that's in the past. It's finished. It's finito! Right now I have very important news." He stopped pacing, pulled back his lips, and exposed his small teeth. He looked frightening to be honest.

"What's wrong?"

He pulled his lips back further.

"What are you doing?"

"*I'm smiling*," he said through gritted teeth.

His so-called smile was freaking me out. "You call that a smile?"

He nodded, teeth bared. "I have good news!"

Wearing his strange smile, he started performing this odd dance, moving his waist from side to side and shooting his finger into the air, up and down. I realized he was "disco dancing."

"So tell me."

"I got into science camp!" he exclaimed. "I got a scholarship for needy kids. Ha! I'm very needy! Ha!"

I was so excited I forgot about his no-touch rule and went in for a big hug. He jumped back. "Sorry," I said, raising my hands. "I forgot. No touching. I'm just really happy for you."

He raised his index finger. "There's one more thing. You will never guess in a million years. A million light-years times two."

"Let me think. You're going to camp… You won a full scholarship… What else could it be? Steve Jobs has risen from the dead?"

"Ha!" He bared his teeth, *smiling*. "Mr. Science is the guest speaker at the camp! I'm going to meet Mr. Science in person!" He pointed his finger into the air. "Mr. Science emailed me once and we are very good friends! I'm going to shake his hand. He can touch me because he's clean and smart and he's Mr. Science."

I couldn't believe it. I was so happy for him. I wished that he were okay with hugs. Mom always gave the best hugs. Instead, I shot my arms in the air. "I'm so happy for you! I'm so proud of you."

He went to Mom's altar, picked up the Aunt Jemima cookie jar, and held it at eye level. "Hello, Corrina Stevenson, it's me, Davie. I'm going to science camp. I'm going to meet Mr. Science. I sent him an email once when I was nine and he wrote me back. The camp is at Stanford." He then knelt down and shared his news with Hello Mr. Fox.

I realized, watching him, neither Jeannette nor Tucker had mentioned the camp. They would have said something if they'd known, right? "Do Jeannette and Tucker know you were accepted to the camp?"

"I'm not allowed to bring trouble to the door."

"This is good news. It's not trouble."

"Sterling was suspended for touching a girl. You're not supposed to touch people, especially girls. Counselor Hayes told me that no one should ever touch me unless I said they could touch me. Sterling has all Ds and Fs on his progress report. He's very good at video games, but he's dumb. I'm going to summer camp and got all As on my progress report. I'll get in trouble if I brag. I'm not supposed to hurt Sterling's feelings."

"But this is good news. Sterling is going to be happy for you and we want to celebrate. Were Jeannette and Tucker notified?"

He rocked from side to side and stared into space. "Mmmmm."

I found my phone and messaged Jeannette, asking if she knew about Davie's news.

She called a few minutes later. She hadn't read her emails yet and they had no clue he'd been accepted. She sounded excited, though, and asked to talk to Davie. I put her on speaker and she and Tucker congratulated him.

After I hung up, Davie, appearing doubtful of their enthusiasm, hummed and rocked on his feet. "It's fine, Davie. Really. They're happy for you and so am I. What should we do to celebrate?" I snapped my fingers, giving him zero time to respond. "Davie!" I shouted.

"Francine Stevenson!" he shouted back.

"You know what? Let's get you a bike! I'll get one, too. We can go bike riding!"

"Mmmmm." He frowned.

"Now what?"

"I told you already. I'm ten and I don't know how to ride a bike. And you said my helmet wasn't safe. What if I fall? What if I fall and my skull breaks open and my brain falls out and I can't go to science camp because I'm dead?"

"You're not going to fall. I'll be right next to you." I remembered my dad teaching me to ride a bike—running alongside of me as I wobbled and tried to gain balance, clapping his hands when I got the hang of it. *That's my baby girl!* "My father taught me to ride a bike, and I'll teach you. It's just a matter of practice."

"Mmmmm. I'm not very familiar with practice."

"No one gets on a bike and knows how to ride without practice. It'll be fun, I promise."

He looked off to one side, suspicious. "Okay, but just don't let me die. I want to go to science camp and meet Mr. Science."

"I promise I won't let you die. Cross my heart."

"You can't cross your heart, it's inside your chest."

Oh… my God. I loved this kid so much.

"Davie?"

"Mmmmm."

"You know I love you, right? You do know that. I love you a lot and I'm always here for you."

"Steve Jobs and Steve Wozniak were best friends. Steve and Steve!"

"That's right. We're just like Steve and Steve. You can always count on me, okay?"

Gazing high above my head, he pulled his lips back. There it was again, the baring of teeth, his weird, beautiful smile.

✦ ✦ ✦

I used Mom's money to buy our bicycles. Her accounts were fine, but if I planned to go to art school, which was starting to feel like something I might consider, I'd have to watch my spending.

We drove Mom's car to the bike store to buy bikes and have her car fitted with a bicycle rack. Next, we drove to an empty parking lot behind an office building in Emeryville so Davie would have plenty of room to practice. But he had no sense of balance and after several wobbly attempts and one near fall, he shouted, "George Washington owned three hundred seventeen slaves by the time he died. Asshole!" He took off his helmet and kicked the bike as if it had offended him.

"Davie, it's okay," I said.

"No it's not. I'm ten and I can't ride a bike."

I had to think before he spiraled into full meltdown. The solution was simple really. I picked up his bike and helmet. "Let's go back to the store and get you some training wheels."

"Mmmmm."

"I had to use training wheels."

"No you didn't. Your dad taught you to ride a bike."

"Before he taught me I had training wheels. Everyone starts with training wheels. I bet you Steve Jobs started with training wheels."

He looked at me dubiously, then pointed his finger in the air at the mention of Steve Jobs. "Steve Jobs said the computer is like the bicycle of the mind. Ha!"

"It's going to be okay," I said. "We'll get you training wheels and you'll be riding your bike in no time."

Again, the finger high in the air. "I'm ten and I need training wheels."

I assumed he thought it was a good thing. His professorial finger was usually positive anyway.

So we headed back to the bike store and had training wheels put on. Then we drove to the parking lot yet again. After I picked a spot to place the bike, Davie knelt down and gave each metal stabilizer a firm shake. He tapped the training wheels with his foot and finally climbed on. I held the seat from behind, even though I didn't need to.

"Luca had to learn to ride a bike," he said, referring to the Pixar cartoon.

"That's right. And in the end he won the triathlon."

"Luca fell in a lake, but I won't fall into a lake because we're in a parking lot." He rose up on the pedals, prepared to push off.

"Ready?"

He gripped the handlebars. "Ready."

I gave the bike a push and he was off.

"Ha!"

Later, for dinner, we ate sandwiches from Ike's and watched *Brave*. By the time we said good night—he slept in my room, I slept in Mom's room—I knew we were right back on track. I loved having him around, and I was recognizing more and more that Jeannette and I needed to last so I could have Davie with me, too. I mean, I knew this, but it was starting to hit me—I never wanted to lose Davie.

The next morning, he read and reread the schedule for camp. He had to write a bio introducing himself to other campers. We discussed what he could write after riding our bikes to Lois the Pie Queen for breakfast. "I'm going to tell them I know everything about slavery," he remarked.

"I'm not so sure that's the way to go. What about telling your new friends something about Steve Jobs?"

"Steve Jobs gave his last speech at Stanford. I can write about that."

"Absolutely."

"And I know how to ride a bike now. And I know everything about Pixar."

"That's right. And you'll make lots of new friends."

He raised his fork in the air. "Ha!"

We spent the day riding our bikes around the neighborhood. Afterward we played chess on the deck, then ate dinner while watching *Finding Dory*. I couldn't wait for the day when he and Jeannette moved in permanently—Sterling, too. I mean, I was sure I would learn to love him given enough time.

Later that evening, I was surprised when Tucker, and not Jeannette, met me at the door to pick up Davie. She gave an apologetic shrug from the truck, where she waited with Sterling, which meant I was left to greet Tucker and his bulky six-foot-two frame alone. *Nope. I am not sleeping with your wife. Everything is fine here.*

He congratulated Davie about getting into camp. They gave imaginary high-fives to each other—raising their hands but not touching.

"I have a bike and I'm going to meet Mr. Science. I know how to ride it without falling because it has training wheels. I'm ten and I have training wheels on my bike. They're for balance."

"A bike?" said Tucker curiously.

"I hope it's okay," I said. "I wanted to get him something to celebrate his acceptance into camp. I'll keep it here for when he visits."

"It's cool. Sterling used to like riding bikes till he got into playing video games and riding his bike stopped real quick." He told Davie to wait in the truck. When Davie started to leave, he reminded him to say thank you.

"Thank you, Francine Stevenson," he said. "Steve and Steve. And Stevenson. Ha!"

I smiled. Tucker and I watched him walk off.

Looking sheepish, Tucker turned back to me. "We'll pay you for the bike."

"No, it's a gift."

He scratched the back of his neck, briefly avoiding eye contact. "We're keeping a tab of every cent we owe you."

I thought of Jeannette's secret credit cards that I'd paid off. He had no clue.

I could hardly meet his gaze. "It's fine. You all have helped me, too. I mean, you and Jeannette have been good friends to me. Before I met Jeannette, I…" *I love your wife. I am madly in love with your wife.* "I… She … ," I stammered. "Anyway." I folded my lips together. *Shut up, Francine. Shut up!*

"It's all good." Tucker grinned. "We're happy we met you, too." He let out a low whistle as he took in the house. "This is a nice place. What year is it?"

"Nineteen thirties, I think."

"If you ever need any help with maintenance, you let me know. You're practically family to us."

"I feel the same." My guilt showed up in the form of a dull ache creeping across my upper back and neck. I couldn't say goodbye quickly enough.

Jeannette texted within the hour. Apparently Davie wouldn't be quiet about getting into camp or the bike.

Jeannette: **You bought him a bike? Why would you do that? He won't stop bragging about it.**

Shit. Could I get a fucking break?

I wanted to celebrate the fact that he got into camp, I texted. **Tucker doesn't have a problem with it.**

You should've asked first. You're not his foster mother. How is a

new bike supposed to make
Sterling feel?

I'm sorry. I could get Sterling a
bike too. All of us.

You don't get it. You shouldn't be
showing favors. It's not fair that
you gave him a bike. I wish you
would talk to me before you do
things like that.

We were back to the day at the bookstore when I'd pissed her off by offering to buy books for everyone. I texted a lengthy apology, but she didn't reply. I stared at my phone while massaging my neck and upper back. I was so tense. It was a good thing I'd thrown Alfonse's pills away; I lacked any willpower in the moment.

I went to the couch, continuing to massage my shoulders, feeling like shit. The inner-child work Pamela and I were doing came to mind. She was helping me recognize coping mechanisms I'd developed when I was younger, like hiding from everything and everyone in the name of helping Mom.

I could hear her calm, meditative voice: *This isn't about Jeannette. It's about you. What does the little girl in you want to do? How can you take care of her right now?*

An answer came in an instant, and thirty minutes later I wasn't thinking about Jeannette at all; I was riding my bike around the Emeryville marina while listening to Donna Summer, my way of trying to feel close to Mom again, the little girl in me pumping her fists in the air, pigtails flying.

CHAPTER TWENTY-FIVE

learned so much from my time with Pamela, Goddess bless her, as Mom would say. Most of all I learned that therapy is fucking hard. Even now, every Tuesday night, I sit across from her having to prepare to face my demons, which can be exhausting. Initially, she was big on pushing me to feel all of my feelings. Her motto: there is no such thing as a bad feeling—*all* feelings were welcome. So-called bad feelings, or what she called difficult feelings, were pointing you to places that needed healing and nothing more. The key was to stay with the emotion without numbing out so you could learn from it and take care. Mom sort of—*kind of*—spouted the same advice in her videos, but the difference was Mom's advice was closer to toxic positivity: once someone felt emotional pain, the cure was to squash the feeling with positive thoughts—and, in her case, illegal drugs. Pamela, on the other hand, would pull her glasses down her long nose and say, "Go on," meaning, *Get out of your head and tell me about the hurt you're feeling.* "Don't abandon yourself," she'd say, as if it were easy to do such a thing, to turn around and move *toward* the fear, toward the shame, instead of bolting in the opposite direction. I'd sometimes leave her office with red eyes and a puffy nose from all the crying and *feeling.* Her early feedback, in so many words, was that I might have unconsciously started a shitstorm with Jeannette as a way to avoid mourning the loss of my mother and the residual impact of our highly dysfunctional relationship.

Another thing we worked on was my need to start taking responsibility. Any time I tried to defend myself by blaming Jeannette, Pamela wouldn't have it. She'd look at me over her glasses and say, "And what's your responsibility in all of this?" She'd say, "I'm not here with Jeannette. I'm interested in you and your choices." At the time I wanted to save Jeannette, save her from her marriage, her job; help her heal from her past—the physical abuse at the hands of her mother, the assaults— every trauma, major and minor, that made her angry and afraid. Therapy, though, helped me see that my intentions were a joke. How the hell was I supposed to save Jeannette when I couldn't save myself? I needed to process my own grief, my own pain—all the bullying I endured when I was younger, having to look after Mom, what happened with Stefani. I had to stop trying to skirt around my own traumas and move *through* them, as Pamela would say. "Not around but through," another motto of hers.

Anyway, I was lucky Pamela and I were already working together when I needed her most. Because it was around this time—Davie's announcement about camp—that things went to shit so fast I still can't get my head around it.

Everything seemed fine at first. Sure, Jeannette was pissed about the bike I'd bought for Davie, but things fell right back into place. Davie came over on Wednesday and we watched *My Octopus Teacher*, a documentary about a friendship between an octopus and a scuba diver. Off and on he'd repeat the itinerary for camp. "We have breakfast from eight a.m. to eight thirty, then it's class time. A hike at noon. Dinner starts at six o'clock. Mr. Science is going to give a talk and presentation on Saturday at seven p.m." Having to listen to him go on about camp was a lot, but I would've chosen having to listen to him talk about camp over slavery any day.

Saturday, a week after I bought our bikes, Jeannette brought Davie and Sterling along while she did her laundry, and we spent the afternoon together at the house. Sunday I had dinner at her place. Tucker made barbecue on a small grill on their balcony, while I acted as if everything were perfectly fine and Jeannette and I weren't sleeping together behind his back. I heard Pamela's voice telling me to follow my feelings and see where they led. They led to an overwhelming feeling of guilt, that's where.

You could tell, though, that Tucker truly had no clue. Matter of fact, he was overly gracious—asking if I wanted seconds and loading me up with leftovers. Jeannette was also extra. She'd made macaroni and cheese and baked a cake and went on about what a good friend I was. You would've thought it was my birthday. I felt loved, except it was all so twisted. I mean, Jeannette and I had been making out in the garage just the day before.

The next morning, after the hearty dinner at her place, Jeannette texted me while I was at work. She needed to talk and wanted to come by the house later. Tucker knew she was going to stop by, which meant we wouldn't have to worry about her having to rush home.

That night, knowing we had time, we made out on the couch for several minutes. I was about to pull off her top when she placed her hands between us. "Wait." Strands of her hair stuck out in all directions, both of us panting. I stared at her eyes and lips. I mean, despite everything I wanted her all the time.

"We need to talk." She straightened her hair and pulled down her shirt. I, meanwhile, needed a cold shower. I waited to catch my breath before rolling off her.

She asked to see my laptop, then told me to move to the end of the couch so I couldn't see what she was pulling up. She was nervous, I noticed, which made me nervous.

After finding what she wanted, she clasped her hands in her lap and pulled back her shoulders as though she'd practiced what she was about to say.

"So me and Tucker were talking. With Davie going to camp we thought it would be a good idea if Sterling went to camp, too."

She turned the laptop. I stared at a website advertising a summer camp for teens: *Lake Pines Summer Camp, Inspiring Tomorrow's Leaders Today!* I scanned the page: *Rigorous engagement... academic programs for middle and high school students from around the globe... Diversity... Inspiring curriculum...*

"You don't have to say anything now. I want you to think about it first."

"Think about what?" I was so lost.

"Sterling going to camp."

"*With Davie?*"

"No, not with Davie." She pointed to the screen. "At Lake Pines." She took a deep breath. "I know I'm asking a lot, but something like this could change everything for Sterling. We never thought about sending him to camp before, but now with Davie going, we think it would be a good idea. Sterling would be with teachers who know how to teach for once, and he'll be around kids who want to learn. He needs that. And they have horseback riding and kayaking."

I wondered if she was high. "You really see Sterling kayaking?"

"I don't know. But he could go to this camp and find something he loves to do outside of video games. Tucker and I will pay you back, I swear."

I heard a loud internal tire screech. *Whoa whoa whoa*, I thought. *Somebody pump the brakes.* Was she serious? "You want *me* to pay?"

"Well, yeah. We can't afford it. But I swear we'll pay you back. I know you've done a lot for me already, but this is really important."

She clicked to a new page. I stared at a picture of a bunch of white kids and a lone black girl kayaking down a river.

Things were starting to fall into place—the barbecue from the night before, her and Tucker's overly gracious behavior. "So *that's* why you guys were being so nice last night."

"No," she said flatly, "we were just being nice to be nice."

Sure you were.

She put down the laptop and briefly touched my hand. "We appreciate you. There's nothing wrong with us showing it."

"Why don't you show your appreciation by leaving him?"

"I'm going to, B. It's not like I'm happy with him. I keep telling you that. But I need to take care of Sterling first."

"We can do both. I still plan to write the letter to the principal for you. And in the meantime, you can talk to Tucker."

"Forget about writing a stupid letter. That man isn't going to listen to me. His mind was made up from the beginning, which is another reason why camp is a good idea. Sterling could go this summer and come back inspired about learning. Davie gets to go to camp. Why not my son? This could change the direction of his life. I need for him to do better in school, Francine. He's struggling." Her voice trembled. "I want him to do better than me." She began bouncing her knee, winding her necklace around her finger. "I don't need an answer tonight. I know you need time to think. Look through the website. The camp has everything."

I picked up the laptop, started clicking around to find the cost. "How much is it?"

She paused, hesitant. "Go to 'Services,' then 'Details.' You don't have to give me an answer tonight."

She was quiet while I pulled up the fee. A three-week stay amounted to $6,780. *She is definitely high.*

"I know it seems like a lot."

"Well, yeah. I can't pay that much."

"But you can. Please? You said your mother has like a hundred thousand dollars in her account. And like I said, we'll pay you back."

I wish I hadn't told her the amount. And just because I had it didn't mean I wanted to spend nearly seven thousand dollars so a boy I didn't necessarily like could ride a fucking horse. "I don't know. I'm thinking of going to art school. I'll need money for that."

"Since when do you want to go to art school?"

"I've been thinking about it."

"What are you going to do in art school?"

"What do you think I'm going to do? Photography."

She looked at me as though the idea were beyond ridiculous. *"Photography?"*

"Why not? Life is short. And what I'm doing now is no better." I lowered my gaze, embarrassed. There was a reason I hadn't mentioned art school to her sooner. "It's just a thought."

"I'm not trying to say you're not good or anything, but how are you going to make money doing photography?"

"I don't know. And anyway, I'm in charge of property taxes now, and what if the house needs a major repair? It's not like the money is going to last forever. Davie's going to need to go to college."

She pointed her long, manicured nail in my face. She always had enough money to get her nails done. "What about Sterling going to college? See, you always care about Davie more than Sterling. That boy always gets all the attention, and I know it's fucking Sterling up. Part of me thinks it's time Davie got a new family."

Fear shot through my body. She wouldn't dare. "Don't say that, Nette. Don't even think it. I was going to mention Sterling going to college. You didn't give me a chance." Total lie. "I was just trying to explain that I have to watch what I spend."

She stared at the kids on the computer. "Sterling's not going anywhere if things don't change." She regrouped, her eyes imploring me. "I will pay you back in monthly installments. I'll work overtime. I'll do whatever it takes."

"I don't know." I could hardly hear myself over my gut screaming, *No no no! Don't do it!*

She placed her hand on my knee. "I support whatever you want to do in life. You want to be a photographer or whatever? You should do it. I'm your friend first, and I love you. I will always have your back." She gave my knee a tight squeeze. "Sterling will be yours as much as he's mine soon. We have to shape his life together. What I was thinking was, while he's at camp, I'll talk to Tucker and tell him about us. I'm sick of all this lying, too."

"You are?"

"Of course I am. With Sterling and Davie out of the house and at camp, I'll tell Tucker everything. And we can talk to the boys once they get back. Think about it, Francine. The camp is what Sterling needs and it's what *we* need." She took my hand and kissed my fingers. "You and me till death do us part."

It was difficult to look into her hazel eyes and stand up for myself at the same time. I glanced over at Mom's altar, but it was only a remnant of her by then. She was gone. I no longer felt her presence in the house or my life. My choices, the shitstorm I'd created, had pushed her away.

I looked back at Jeannette. She was all I had left. "You swear you'll tell Tucker while the boys are at camp?"

She raised her right hand, making an oath. "I swear to God."

"Okay. If you swear you'll tell Tucker and we can stop the secrets and be together, I don't mind paying."

"*Really?*" she squealed, and Jeannette was not a squealer. "Are you sure?"

"Yeah, I'm sure."

She was on me in a second—kissing me all over my face. "Thank you, B." She kissed me fully on the lips, her eyes bright and happy, her hands already grabbing at my shirt.

Normally I would've been excited about her coming on to me like this, but she was moving too fast. Or rather, I was too much in my head—thinking about the cost of camp and whether I'd made the right decision. In the end it was terrible sex, specifically the kind of sex where the number 6,780 is flashing through your brain and there's no way you can relax; the kind of sex where you fake your orgasm just so you can make it stop.

I wrote the check before she left. As soon as I gave it to her, though, I started talking out of my ass. I told her I needed to transfer the money from Mom's account—*true*—and for such a large amount the bank would have to clear the deposit—true? I doubted it. But I told her it took three to four business days and she should wait until I heard from the bank before depositing the check. My lie was my escape in case I changed my mind. I needed time to accept what I'd done. Three to four business days, plus the weekend meant she wouldn't be able to cash the check until Monday or Tuesday of the following week. Jesus, our relationship was stressful.

The next morning I found a note from her on the porch. I looked up and down the street as if she might still be around, watching. She must have snuck out of the house so I could find it before work. There were several bills inside the envelope, her handwriting careful and neat.

Dear Francine,

I have never had someone support me like you do. I wonder sometimes what my life would have been like if we had met sooner. I think it would have helped me in life to know what it's like to have the kind of love and friendship you give me.

I wanted to say thank you. Here's something to start the repayment. I want you to know from my heart that it's not just about the money. I love you because of who you are as a person. I love you. I will always love you.

Love always, J

I read and reread the note before counting the money. One hundred dollars. Initially I was moved. I knew how difficult it was for her to express her feelings at times. Even so, as I put the note inside my purse, I wondered what Pamela would have to say about my decision to drop nearly seven thousand dollars for Sterling's camp. I considered not telling her at all. Which said everything.

CHAPTER TWENTY-SIX

Hayden was in true boss mode the day Jeannette left her note on my porch—double the amount of espresso for her, double the tasks for me. Do this, do that. Go here, go there. At one point, I even had to contact Wendy Bartlett, the founder of Techie Girls, on her behalf. Hayden was going to be in LA the following week and wanted to meet for lunch. I finalized a date with Wendy via email, reserving a spot at one of Hayden's favorite LA restaurants. I then took a moment to Insta-stalk her IG. Yep, the girl was still living large: Techie Girls had recently won another award and she'd gone on a trip with her boyfriend to Barbados. I put my phone away before my envy overwhelmed me.

Hayden's busy schedule was beneficial in a way. For starters, it kept my mind off the check I'd written to Jeannette. I was also giving my photography presentation later that night; all the work Hayden assigned helped ease some of my anxiety around standing in front of a bunch of people I didn't know who could rip my pictures to shreds—figuratively, of course, but still.

It was late May and our six-week semester was coming to an end. We were asked to share ten of our best photos with the class based on assignments we'd completed since the start of the semester. I planned to include my colorism photos along with a picture of Jeannette I'd taken while we were in Monterey, which felt like centuries ago. In the photo she stood next to the bay window of our suite staring out at the view, her tracksuit and somber expression contrasting with the wealth of the room. I also planned to include a cropped black-and-white picture in which Davie stared fixedly off-camera, his Steve Jobs T-shirt hanging off his small frame. I had no idea what Rick or my classmates would think.

By the end of the day, Hayden was still going strong, chatting it up with her four o'clock, a Meta exec, who was also a friend. Goodness knows what those two were going on about. Some million-dollar plan for a new business venture? Their last ski trip? Who the hell knew. I kept looking into Hayden's office and tapping my fingers. I couldn't be late to class when it was my turn to present. I was tempted to march right into her office and interrupt them. *Look here, honey, I got a class to get to. Can you wrap this up?*

I had to wait another thirty minutes before she walked her friend to the elevator.

I reached for my jacket when she returned—*hint hint*. "Need anything else?"

Hayden raised those blond brows. "Are we in a rush?"

"Not at all. I just thought I could call it a night... well, unless..."

She gave me a look I couldn't read, then turned on her Fendi heel and headed to her office. "That'll do for today. See you tomorrow."

I said goodbye to her back and was out of there.

Less than three hours later, as if in a dream, I, Francine Stevenson, stood in front of my photography class as they applauded my work, and Rick declared my photos were, and I quote, "provocative" and "exciting." "These images show talent," he said for all to hear.

We weren't allowed to explain or defend our pictures, so I wasn't sure if Rick totally understood the point I was trying to make about the ramifications of colorism, but his praise felt great. He droned on about a photographer I'd never heard of, but I was fine with his mansplaining. I had talent! My photos were provocative and exciting! My face went hot as Rick and the class heaped on the praise. Sure, my online community appreciated my pictures, but there was something different about sharing my work with people in the real world, standing in front of a class and receiving praise from an instructor. For a girl who, for the most part, only knew negative attention, this whole praise thing was brand-spanking-new. I was used to being the butt of the joke, after all, or left out for being weird, à la the FUN Committee. But that night I was feeling some Wendy Bartlett kind of emotions: I was feeling something I could barely recognize—*pride*. I mean, I wasn't sure why pride had such a bad rap. It felt good!

Kenji gave me a hug after class was dismissed. "Yo, you had that cis white man fawning over your pictures."

"I know. Can you believe it?" I was still reeling from everyone's feedback, my body humming with excitement.

"Told you you were talented. We should celebrate. Vithu was by yesterday. He made your favorite soup. We got leftovers. You wanna come over and eat some of that *samlor koooorko*?" She cooed and shook her wide, flat ass without any rhythm whatsoever.

Not that I can talk as a black girl with zero rhythm. But I danced along and cooed right back: "Yeah, girl, let's eat some of that *samlor koooorko*." You would've thought we were referring to something sexual the way we giggled.

I got inside my car, took out my phone to call Jeannette and tell her about the critique. My finger was a millimeter away from the call button when my phone buzzed. It was her. Don't you love that about relationships? Those magical moments when you're thinking of the person and they're thinking of you, too.

"I was just about to call you."

"How did it go?"

"Rick said my pictures were 'exciting' and 'provocative' and I have talent."

"That's great, B." She whispered so softly I could barely hear her: "I wish I could give you a kiss. I'm proud of you." Whispering meant that Tucker or Sterling was in earshot. Or Davie. I realized how much I wanted to tell Davie about my critique. I knew he'd be happy for me.

"I wish I could kiss you, too." Why was *I* whispering?

"Maybe I can sneak out tonight."

It was after nine. I wasn't sure how she'd be able to leave the house at such a late hour. "Don't worry about it. I'm heading over to Kenji's. We're going to hang out for a little while."

"Oh," she said, falling silent. I waited for her to say more, but that was it. Just one of those passive-aggressive *oh*s that told you it was your job to decipher where you had gone wrong because goodness knows the other person wasn't going to express what they were feeling.

I assumed the problem was Kenji. So: "I'm just staying for a little while. Eve will be there, too. They have some of the soup I like." I wanted to say, *You're going to some stupid car show with your friends and your fucking husband on Saturday. Why is it you're the only person who gets to have a life? What do you want me to do? Sit around pining for you all the time?*

Jeannette and Tucker were going to a car show with Ceci and Huevo out in Hayward. I knew nothing about car shows but apparently they involved barbecuing or some such thing. She'd invited me, but—no thank you to hanging out with her husband and friends and playing like nothing was going on between us. She swore, by the way, that she hadn't told Ceci we were sleeping together. She wanted to tell Tucker first, which was going to be a lot for him to digest to say the least. *Not only am I leaving you for a woman, I'm leaving you for Francine, our supposed family friend.* Yeah, it was a lot.

Since I wasn't remotely interested in staring at cars all day and barbecuing in a parking lot—what a strange ritual—it was a no-brainer to agree to watch Davie.

I waited for Jeannette to say something, anything besides her passive-aggressive *oh*.

Kenji backed her car out, gave her horn a toot. "I should get going."

"Hold on."

I heard mumbling.

After a few seconds, she whispered, "Tucker came into the kitchen. I had to go out to the balcony." Then, with bite: "You don't have time for me, but you have time for your bougie friends."

"You're seeing Ceci and Huevo this weekend. I deserve a life, too."

A long silence. Finally, her voice soft, childlike: "Are you going to leave me, Francine? Are you going to leave me for Kenji?"

The insecurity in her voice, her question, caught me off guard. I'd assumed the check I'd given her was proof of my love, but obviously it wasn't enough. I realized she felt as vulnerable as I did. Sure, love made you feel secure, but it also opened up levels of vulnerability you didn't know existed. It was like when I was dating Kelly. The closer we became, the more comfortable we were with revealing our fears and weaknesses. Problems began, though, when we started weaponizing our insecurities against each other. I wouldn't let that happen to Jeannette and me. There was no way.

"I'm never leaving you, Nette," I said. "You don't have to worry about that. I will never leave you."

"Promise?"

"Promise."

"It's just . . . you've done so much for me, B. But I don't know what I do for you. You have your therapist now and your bougie friends, and I don't give you anything. You know what I give you? I give you nothing."

She sounded sullen, whiny. Drunk-whiny. I reassured her just the same: "You do a lot for me. You've helped me become more confident, which is huge."

"I don't know. I wish I could do more . . . how you're helping us with the camp. All what you do . . ." Her voice trailed off. Yeah, she was drunk.

I started my car. "I have to go, okay?"

Silence. Then Tucker's voice in the background: "Let me holler at her."

No! I thought. *DO NOT let him holler at me.*

More mumbling and—*shit*—there he was, his voice booming in my ear.

"Francine! I've been wanting to thank you for everything. Sterling is hyped. I'm hyped. You're the best, girl. And you know we'll pay you back."

"It's nothing."

"Oh, it's something, all right. You've been helping Davie *and* Sterling. Ain't no one like you. Ain't no one like Francine."

He sounded drunk, too. What the hell? Were they both high? More important, would they be having sex later?

"You are a saint, Francine. Saint Francine!"

It took everything in me to not blurt out, *I'm no saint, I'm sleeping with your wife.*

I started to back my car out. "I need to get going."

"Fabulous Francine!"

"Uh . . . no."

"Sterling is going to have a great time. Both my boys going to camp! I never got to do anything like that when I was their age. Listen here. Like I said, we'll be paying you back. Every penny we save coming your way."

"It's fine."

"All right. I'll let you finish talking to Nette."

"That's okay. Tell her I said good night."

"You sure? Looks like she wants to—"

"No, it's fine. I have to get going. Bye!"

My phone buzzed as soon as I hung up.

A text from Kenji: Yo, Are you lost?

I'm on my way.

I sped out of the parking lot.

And then...

About an hour or so later...

"Seven thousand dollars? Are you fucking crazy, yo?!"

"It's more like six thousand seven hundred eighty dollars."

Kenji and Eve stared at me with their mouths wide open. I'd waited until we'd finished our soup to tell them about the check. I could still change my mind, thanks to my lie about the time it takes for the bank to make a transfer, and I wanted their advice. I was flip-flopping big-time: a part of me was like *Hell no, it's too expensive*; another part, especially after my conversation with Jeannette, wanted to prove to her once and for all just how much I loved her.

I explained as much to Kenji and Eve.

"She thinks I'm going to leave her."

"That's her problem, yo," Kenji said. "She's got to work that shit out on her own."

"But I can't go back on my word. I want to be there for her. And Sterling needs this." Here, I appealed to Eve: "We both know there are systemic issues that keep black and brown kids down. It's just a fact. This camp could help change the trajectory of his life."

Kenji rolled her eyes. "Oh, so now you're going to blame systemic racism for the fact that your girl is cheating on her husband and taking all of your money? Yo, you need to listen to yourself."

Eve wore oversized hoop earrings, so big and round they touched her shoulders. "How you spend your money reflects how you feel about yourself. You have to think of money as energy."

"You sound like my mom," I grumbled.

"Your mom is right." She stared at me much like Pamela during one of my therapy sessions, like she could see directly into my flip-flopping, self-doubting soul. "You and Jeannette need to communicate with each other. This is all turning toxic."

Kenji slapped her hand on the table. "That's what I've been trying to tell her. This is bad karma. This is really bad karma."

"When you're making a healthy decision," Eve said, "you don't have to convince yourself you're doing the right thing."

"Boom!" said Kenji.

Eve did have a point. I stared into my empty bowl of soup. "But I can't change my mind now. She'll be pissed if I change my mind. It wouldn't be right."

Kenji shot her hands in the air. "It's *your* damn mind, yo. You can change it whenever you want."

"Nette's had a tough life. I want to help her."

"I've had a tough life," Eve said, shrugging.

"I've had a tough life, too," said Kenji. "Why don't you give me seven thousand dollars? I'll take it, too, yo."

I plopped my elbow on the table, rested my hand against my cheek.

They didn't understand. I'd traced my fingers down the scars on Jeannette's thighs and back where her mother had beaten her. She'd gone through so much. She needed something good for a change.

I fixed my gaze on the lit candles in the center of the table; the smell of spicy samlor korko lingered in the apartment. Their place was always so peaceful. I briefly considered asking if I could spend the night, just curl up on the couch and hide under a blanket—kidding, not kidding. On the other hand, if I played things right, Jeannette and I could also share a quiet home together.

Eve touched my hand. "Her son is not your responsibility."

"He will be one day," I said. "And she's going to pay me back. I know she will."

Kenji said, "Yo, that girl is not paying you back. You know who she reminds me of?" She picked up the bottle of Cambodian beer she was drinking from and held it in front of her lips. "Sneater Jasmine. I hate girls like that. They just use people and shit." She took a swig of beer and tipped the bottle my way. "Yo, you could be doing so much better than her. You have to stop letting people use your insecure ass. You are a talented, up-and-coming photographer."

"Hardly."

"Kenji is right," Eve said. "You're talented. Both of you are. I'd see a Stevenson and Bou show in a heartbeat."

I stared at my two friends, grateful for the potential they saw in me.

Kenji said, "If you're going to take your art seriously, and you should, you're going to need money for art school."

She was right. I imagined myself studying photography at California College of the Arts, or RISD or NYU. I heard Rick's voice: "These images show talent." Not a second later, though, he was drowned out by a fearful Jeannette: *Are you going to leave me?*

The answer was no. I would never leave her.

I mindlessly played with my soup spoon, turning it in my fingers, then letting it drop back into my empty bowl with a clang. "You guys have no idea. She's Jeannette Tomlin. She was like the Beyoncé of our school, and I was a nobody—worse than nobody."

"Yeah, but this isn't high school, yo."

I looked up. "But she *loves* me and I love her. And I need to be there for her; that's what love is."

Eve relaxed into her chair with a shrug. "Then it's settled. I just don't understand why if this is the right decision you seem so miserable."

"Word," said Kenji. She looked at Eve. "You're so smart, babe." Then it was like she was suddenly lost in Eve's big brown eyes. She reached over, touched Eve's chin, leaned in for a kiss. They shared a peck, then tilted their heads in the opposite direction for another peck, then Kenji reached behind Eve's neck and pulled her in for a full-on tongue exchange.

I cleared my throat. Nothing.

"Hello!"

They both turned and faced me, loopy in their love.

"Lucky bastards," I griped.

CHAPTER TWENTY-SEVEN

D avie marched up to the house and disappeared inside without a hello.

Tucker and Jeannette were dropping him off before the car show.

"Fabulous Francine!" Tucker shouted from his truck. "Thanks again for watching him." He smiled his clueless smile. He always seemed so happy. For the first time I considered he could be having an affair, too, for all Jeannette and I knew. Then again . . . *Nah.* He was too nice. He wouldn't have the capability to lie and sneak around. I thought about what I knew of his childhood—foster care and group homes—and wondered how much pain his smile masked.

Jeannette leaned forward in the front seat and waved. She wore more makeup than I preferred, a low-cut blouse. She turned to Sterling, who sat in the back. "Say hello to Francine."

Sterling looked up from his phone. He was decked out in a 49ers cap and jersey, his swag off the charts. "Hey."

"Not 'hey,'" Jeannette said.

"*Helloooo,*" he said, drawing out the word sarcastically.

Jeannette playfully tugged at his hat. "Boy, you and your attitude."

He pretended to be annoyed but clearly liked the attention, spoiled brat that he was.

Jeannette and Tucker decided they weren't going to tell him where the loan for camp was coming from. Jeannette told him she'd applied for scholarship money instead.

"You excited about camp?" I asked. "Horseback riding and kayaking! Wow! You're going to have so much fun!"

He shook his head at my Mary Poppins ways. "Yeah, it'll be all right."

"Don't pay him any attention," remarked Jeannette. "He's just acting foolish."

"He's going to have a great time!" said Tucker. "I'd go with him if I could." He laughed and revved the engine of the truck. "Tell Li'l Man we said goodbye. You guys stay out of trouble."

"Thank you for *everything*, Francine," Jeannette said. The look on her face was so dreamy, so filled with gratitude, I caught myself waiting for her to blow a kiss.

I watched them drive off while massaging the ever-tightening muscles making a home between my shoulder blades and upper back. I hadn't slept well the night before due to yet another dream where I searched for Mom at one of Drunk Grandpa's parties—the house filled with sweaty people, the air thick with the smell of pot. I found Aunt Liane slow-dancing again with my pedophile ex-boyfriend, Isaiah. He winked and drew her closer. *How ya been, girl?* I ignored him and asked Aunt Liane if she'd seen Mom. *Oh, now you wanna talk to me*, she said. *You go for weeks ignoring my calls and now all of a sudden you want to talk. You're as messed up as my sister—keeping her ashes in a cookie jar. Get out of my face.* She went back to dancing with Isaiah. I headed up to the attic, where I found Mom scared and cowering like last time. I ran to her, but then Stefani Haywood came out of nowhere. She grabbed me by the ear and began twisting it so hard it felt like she might tear it off. "Ow ow ow." I dropped to my knees. She punched me, then tried to shove her hand down my pants. When I screamed she began choking me.

I woke up holding my hand to my throat and trying to catch my breath. The dream was so terrifying I went straight to the bathroom to check my face and make sure my Bell's palsy hadn't returned. I was fine, but needless to say, I didn't get much sleep afterward. Giving Jeannette the money for Sterling's camp was causing all kinds of stress. I mean, Eve had a point: If I was making the right decision, why was I so miserable? Why was I having nightmares? If I was making the right decision, shouldn't I have been sleeping peacefully and dreaming of hot sex?

I gazed at the spot where Mom had taken her last breath and died, fighting back tears.

Tucker's truck was long gone. "I would like to finish this game, please!" Davie.

I pulled myself together and headed inside. He sat at the dining table, where we'd started a game of chess during his last visit. Only a few more moves and the game would be over.

He stared intently at the board with his elbows propped on the table, his chin resting on his balled fists. "I've been waiting."

"Do you want a snack?"

"Crackers and juice."

"'Please'?"

"Please."

I went to the kitchen. "How was school yesterday?"

"Everybody's an idiot."

I made his snack and sat across from him, took my turn.

Rubbing his hands together maniacally, he moved his knight to B6 in no time. "Yes!" he whispered.

I saw now that my king was royally screwed. Dang it, he was good. "You trapped me."

"Checkmate!" He shot a triumphant finger in the air. "Ha! I'm exceptionally smart. I'm going to play chess at camp and win all the games."

"Try not to gloat."

He opened his tablet and pulled up a video of Magnus Carlsen, his latest obsession. I sat, watching him watch Magnus. He was such a world unto himself. I felt oddly welcomed into his world and forever trapped outside of it, too.

He sipped his juice, eyes on his tablet. "Magnus Carlsen was the youngest player in history to be ranked number one in chess. I'm considering playing him one day. I think I can win."

"You *think* you can win? I don't know if I've ever heard you hedge about anything."

He pinched his nose. "Hedge? What's that?" He typed, then read from his tablet: "'Hedge: to equivocate, fudge, quibble.' Quibble quibble." He clicked to a new page and turned his iPad so I could see the screen: the science camp's schedule. He checked the site daily, as though camp might be canceled without warning. "Breakfast starts at eight a.m."

"What do you think about Sterling going to camp?" I ventured. "He seems excited."

"My camp is better. The kids are all exceptionally smart like me, and I'm meeting Mr. Science."

"Do you think Sterling will like camp?"

"Ha!"

"What's that supposed to mean?"

"Ling Ling doesn't want to go to camp."

"What do you mean he doesn't want to go to camp?"

"I mean," he said slowly, as if I were the most obtuse person he'd ever met, "Ling Ling... does not... want to go... to camp."

"Okay, okay, I get it. Did he tell you that?"

"Ling Ling was suspended from school. He touched a girl without permission. The British enslaved hundreds of thousands of Africans and took them to Jamaica and made them work in sugar plantations."

Talk of slavery? Never a good sign. Time to redirect. "What do you say we go for a bike ride?"

"Yes!"

We rode around the neighborhood, followed by lunch at Can't Fail Café, which was across the street from Pixar. I guess you could say it was a Pixar kind of day, because afterward Davie asked if we could watch *Coco*. I'd never seen it and had no idea all the family stuff would keep me on the verge of tears. By the end of the movie, I even questioned if I should call Aunt Liane and Uncle CJ and beg them to be a part of my life again. My eyes blurred with tears as the credits rolled. What was up with Pixar and their sad movies?

Davie said flatly, "You should cry where no one can see you."

I pulled my feet up onto the couch, brushed at an escaped tear. "I'm sorry. I'm actually very happy for Hector."

"Then you shouldn't cry."

"I'm not crying. Not really." I wiped at another tear. Between the nightmare I'd had and the movie, I was a wreck. "It's okay to cry, you know."

"You should cry where no one can see you."

"Do you still cry sometimes? Behind the bleachers at school?"

"Mmmmm."

"Do you?"

"One in three people in Kentucky owned a minimum of four slaves."

I muted the TV. If I couldn't get my own shit together, I at least wanted to know Davie was doing better. And I was curious. "Do you like Jeannette?" This wasn't the first time I had asked but it couldn't hurt to try again.

"Sojourner Truth was bought and sold four times. They sold her son away. He was five. I know everything about slavery."

I pressed, gently: "Do you like living with Jeannette and Tucker?"

"Counselor Hayes says I can talk to him about whatever I want. I can talk about how much I hate it there. He says everyone is doing the best they can, but that's the dumbest thing I've ever heard."

My heart sank. "You *hate* it there?"

"Mmmmm. I would like to talk about something else in five seconds. One thousand one... one thousand two..."

"Okay. I understand." Davie would be living with me permanently if I played things right with Jeannette. "Things will get better. I promise."

He stared just above my head. "Ha!"

He asked if we could watch *Queen of Katwe*, which we'd seen at least three times by then. "Sure."

I pulled up the movie. Davie watched the screen intently as if he'd never seen it before. The thought landed hard as we sat together: Things needed to work with Jeannette so I could keep Davie in my life. I was ready to put up with all of the stress and nightmares to make it work, because I loved her, yes, but I loved Davie in a way I hadn't loved anyone else before. I couldn't imagine Davie being sent to another family or a group home like Tucker endured; just the thought of losing contact with him sickened me to the core. If Jeannette and I were going to work, Kenji and Eve were right, communication was key. I couldn't be afraid of my own girlfriend.

The dream from the night before came bubbling up. Stefani twisting my ear. I suddenly remembered how Jeannette had twisted Sterling's ear the first time they'd come to the house. I sat straight up on the couch. I was so stupid. Why hadn't I made the connection? That shit was not okay, and I had let it slide. I'd let so many things slide—like my own feelings. And you know what? I didn't want to pay all that money for a camp Sterling had no interest in.

Yeah, we needed to talk. Like Pamela had told me more than once, I was good at pointing my finger, but I was doing a poor job of expressing myself, which wasn't fair to Jeannette. How was she supposed to know what I was feeling if I never spoke up?

I grabbed my phone and texted:

> Hey! Hope you're having fun! I was thinking we need to have a conversation about our relationship. I'd like to make some changes.

Delete delete delete.

> Hey, so I've been thinking about the check. Can we talk? I don't think I want to give you the money. Let's come up with a new plan.

Delete delete delete.

I put my phone down. Fuuuuuck. I had zero courage.

I watched *Queen of Katwe* a beat, then went to Mom's altar and picked up the Aunt Jemima cookie jar, carried it back to the couch, and sat with it in my lap. Davie paid no attention.

I cradled Aunt Jemima. I really missed my mom. I wanted to eat her food and hear her voice. Even with all the fights and our weird-ass life together, I would've given anything for a hug.

Holding "Mom" close to my chest, I stared at Davie's profile, wondering about his mother, if they looked alike, her personality.

"Davie?" I said. "What was your mother's name?"

"Ida B. Wells."

"I'm serious. Do you remember?"

"Ida B. Wells."

"What else do you remember about your mom besides that she liked Pixar movies?"

"Mmmmm." His eyes darkened. I waited for a slavery fact, but he paused the movie and reached for his tablet. He then showed me an advertisement of Mr. Science at Stanford's science camp. "Mr. Science is going to give a talk and a presentation. I'm going to sit in the front row."

I got the hint and put the Aunt Jemima cookie jar on the coffee table. Still… Just one more question. "Davie?"

"Mmmmm."

"Will you miss me while you're away at camp? Because I'm going to miss you." My voice caught in my throat. I missed him all the time, truthfully. "I'm going to miss you a lot while you're away."

He frowned deeply, tilted his head to the right, then the left. "Mmmmm, that's a dumb question."

"Why is it a dumb question?"

He glanced my way, almost meeting my gaze. "Because I always miss you."

Don't you dare cry, I thought. *Do not cry.* "I always miss you, too, Davie. All the time. And I promise, I *promise* things will work out."

He continued looking somewhere near my eyes, his expression growing doubtful. "Ha!"

CHAPTER TWENTY-EIGHT

The next day, a typical Monday, I led the third applicant of the morning into Hayden's office. The woman was straight out of the 1920s with her short black bob, vintage dress, and Mary Janes—you half expected her to break into the Charleston. Hayden had been approached by a publishing house and would be writing a book—part memoir, part advice—on how to become a strong female leader. She was hiring a cowriter to help organize the contents and stories.

I glanced up from my desk and saw Flapper Girl bouncing her head in agreement to whatever Hayden was saying. Poor thing was not going to get the job; Hayden wasn't one for nervous energy or sycophants.

Sure enough, the interview concluded within fifteen minutes. Hayden stopped short at the edge of her office and told the woman she'd be in touch.

"Thank you for everything," Flapper Girl said cheerfully. "I think you're amazing." She made it as far as my desk, then turned around, walked straight back to Hayden, and gave her a hug.

Hayden froze, her arms rigid at her sides, blinking nervously. "That's enough," she said stiffly. But Flapper Girl held on until Hayden had to grip her by the arms and push her off.

Flapper Girl, though, missing the memo, was all like, *You are going to accept my hug whether you want to or not,* and lunged at Hayden again. "I have to tell you how much I appreciate you in case I never see you again. Thank you so much for all you do!"

The only evidence that Hayden was flustered was the single strand of blond hair falling out of place. She moved out of Flapper Girl's embrace and coolly tucked the rogue strand behind her ear. "I appreciate your kind words. We'll be in touch."

Flapper Girl started to leave, waving wildly to Hayden. "Thank you! Bye!" Then me: "Bye! Thank you!"

"Bye!" I said, matching her enthusiasm.

When she disappeared behind the elevator doors, Hayden raised her brows, as in, *What was that?,* and we laughed together.

"How did she pass the interview at the agency?" Hayden asked.

"I have no idea."

My cell buzzed. A text from Jeannette asking if the money had been cleared in my account: I want to cash it this week.

I sighed. I needed to talk to her. After speaking with Kenji and Eve, spending time with Davie on Saturday, and just listening to my gut for once, I had decided I wasn't going to give her the money for Sterling's camp. My plan was to wait until Tuesday to tell her since I'd be seeing Pamela, then if she went off on me, which I had a strong feeling she would, I'd at least be seeing my therapist within hours to get support.

"Everything okay?"

I returned my phone to my desk. *No, Hayden, everything is not okay. Apparently I'm afraid to talk to my girlfriend about a silly little check and it's driving me fucking crazy. I thought the way she could go off on people was sexy, but now I'm thinking she's going to go off on me.*

"It's nothing." I tried to ease the throbbing pain at the base of my skull by rolling my shoulders back. "I'm fine."

"You sure?"

Looking briefly into Hayden's cool blue eyes, I considered shedding my perfectly composed work persona and falling into her arms. *Where do you get your confidence from? And can you loan some to me, please? Just a little?*

I glanced down at Jeannette's text again, turned off my phone. "Yeah, I'm fine."

"What time is the next interview?"

"You have an hour."

She walked back to her office, taking her confidence right along with her. The thought that she might write about *me* in her memoir came to mind. But then, what the hell would she say? I was certainly no example of female leadership. I recalled how impressed she was with Wendy Bartlett. Wendy would be included in her book for sure—her and her non-profit for inner-city girls and her grant money. I wanted to be a part of *that* group, a group of women like Hayden and Wendy and Kenji and Eve. Women like Aunt Liane even, when she wasn't driving me crazy. Women who could say *hell no* without the need for explanation. Women who followed their gut and communicated with their partners without fear or dread. Women who refused to date married people in the first place.

I picked up my phone. *Fuck this.* I didn't want to give Jeannette the money. Why wait one more day to tell her.

> Nette, I'm sorry, but I've changed my mind. I'm not going to transfer the money. Let's think of a different camp for Sterling.

There. That wasn't so bad.

I hit send before I could chicken out, then turned off the phone. I didn't check my messages again until my lunch break. That's when I saw Jeannette had sent a barrage of texts berating me for breaking my promise. **You say you care about Sterling but you don't. You don't care about me or Sterling.** That kind of thing.

I sent another text in response: **Let's find another camp.**

She called seconds later. I grabbed my phone and walked toward the elevator to distance myself from Hayden.

"Did your therapist tell you to do this?"

"No, therapy doesn't work like that. I still want to help. Let's just find a cheaper camp."

"You're always telling me it's your mother's money and you don't care. So what happened? You wouldn't suggest a cheaper camp if it was for Davie. You do everything for that boy." She was practically shouting.

"Where are you? Are you at work?"

"Yeah, I'm in the parking lot." She paused a beat. "Sterling has been excited, and now you go and do this to him. I swear, *I can't with you.* I keep telling you it's about more than a stupid camp. He is failing school, and I can't get him to care about anything that matters." She drew a sharp breath. "You and me are supposed to be together. I'm supposed to be moving in with you, and you go and break a promise like this? You had me out here thinking things were going to change, but you're like everybody else." Her voice dropping, she sounded now as if she was on the verge of tears. "I swear I just wanted one good thing for my son. You know what'll happen if I don't turn things around for him. You know what happened to half the boys we went to school with." She was crying now.

I glanced over at Hayden's desk to make sure she wasn't watching, then whispered into my phone: "Nette, don't cry. I'm still here for you."

"No, you're not," she sniffled. "I thought you were my friend, but really you're just a stuck-up bitch. I knew it, too, and I still trusted you."

"*Jeannette*," I murmured, stung by her words.

"Nobody has ever been there for me. I try to do better, then something always happens. I try to climb the fucking ladder to success or whatever the fuck and life keeps knocking me back down. I feel like I'm trapped out here. And what hurts is that you know this about me."

"I'm not saying I don't want to help. There are other camps."

Silence.

"*Hello?*"

"Never mind," she said at last. "I don't need your help. I should've known better than to trust you in the first place. Always trying to act better than. You know what? People put you down back in the day for a reason. You were weird back then and you're weird now, you and your weird-ass house."

I knew she was upset and tried to not take what she'd said personally.

A throbbing, hot pain was making its way down my neck to my upper back. Taking a deep breath, trying to relax, I kneaded my shoulder. "Can we talk later? I'm sure we can figure something out."

"No, I don't want to talk." Her voice was tight, low. "You stay away from me. And you can forget about seeing Davie again, you hear? You and your bougie ass. Forget you." She hung up.

I remembered where I was and checked again to see if Hayden was watching. She was on the phone with her back turned.

I kneaded the burning spot between my shoulder blades and circled my head in an attempt to relax, but the muscles in my neck only stiffened. I considered calling Jeannette back, but then my jaw began to throb and a woozy numbness started spreading along the side of my face. I touched my cheek and felt absolutely nothing.

No, I thought. *No. Please no.*

I rushed to the bathroom and looked at my reflection in the mirror. Mudface stared back: my left eyelid drooped as though I were giving a lazy, eternal wink; the left side of my mouth sloped downward. My Bell's palsy had returned.

Barricading myself behind one of the stalls, I quickly locked the door, then sat on the toilet and bawled. I sobbed and sobbed. Jeannette was right. I wasn't a good friend or partner. I was weird. And now I'd lost her, and Davie, too.

I don't know how long I sat on that toilet crying, but I was prepared to stay hidden until my face was normal again, all day if needed, weeks.

At some point I heard Hayden's voice and bolted upright. "Francine?"

Shit.

"I know you're in there, I can see your shoes."

I pulled my feet back.

"What's going on? Are you sick?"

I shook my head as if she could see me, then stared at the tips of her Jimmy Choos beneath the stall.

"What is it?"

My eyes fixed on the floor, I slowly unlocked the door and stepped out. She touched my chin ever so lightly. "It's called Bell's palsy." I'd lost movement on the left side of my face and my words were thick, sluggish, as if my mouth were filled with cotton.

I waited for her to recoil or show some sign of horror, but she made no reaction. She gestured at the wadded-up toilet paper in my hand. When I gave it to her, she carefully dotted at my tear-streaked face, as if I were a child, as if I were her daughter, Maddi. "Come with me," she said, tossing the toilet paper.

I followed her past my desk and straight to her office, where she pointed at her couch. "Lie down." She grabbed the throw and placed it over me. Next, she closed the drapes that separated her office from mine. "What can I do?"

"Ibuprofen." My mouth moved like I'd been to the dentist and given too much Novocain; my head pounded. "There's nothing else. I have to wait it out."

She left and returned with water and two ibuprofens, watching closely as I swallowed the capsules.

"Has this happened before?"

"When I was in high school. It's caused by stress."

She walked to her desk. I hid under the throw as she typed into her computer. When my desk phone rang, I thought of the messages I should have been taking.

After a bit of time, Hayden claimed a spot next to me on the couch. "I looked up Bell's palsy. We need to get your stress levels down right away. I booked a driver who'll take you to my acupuncturist."

"I can't let you do that."

"Yes, you can. She's incredible. She'll give you a full treatment." She placed the back of her hand against my forehead, checking for a fever. "Can you tell me what's so stressful? Is this about your mother? Or is it me?" she asked. "Am I *that* bad?"

"It's not you," I sniffled. "It's personal stuff."

"Okay," she said. "You're staying put until the car arrives."

I lay on the couch, my mind spinning. I couldn't help but replay the sad sequence of events that made up my life. Since my father's passing, my mother was the only person in the world who had loved me, and she was gone.

After ten minutes or so Hayden announced the arrival of the driver. But I stayed on my side with my eyes closed. I didn't want to leave. I wanted to die.

"Francine? The car is here."

I peeked from behind the throw and slowly sat up. "I don't want to go outside," I confided. "I don't want anyone to see me."

Hayden sat next to me. "Don't be silly. Who cares what people think?

I will never understand why people care about what other people think. It's your life, not theirs. Who cares what people think about *your* life?"

She clamped her hand on mine. Despite everything going on, my brain hyperfocused on one thing: Hayden holding my hand. It was a bit surreal. I studied the bluish veins beneath her pale skin, until she squeezed my hand and I met her gaze. I couldn't believe how kind she was being.

"I'll walk outside with you. And if anyone so much as looks your way—" She drew her finger across her throat and winked.

But then... *Hold up.*

Have you ever seen the movie *Ghost*? I swear at that moment, as I was staring into Hayden's eyes... I don't know how to describe it, except to say Hayden disappeared and I suddenly felt Mom had taken her place. Mom was there with me and I was staring into *her* eyes. It was like in *Ghost* when Demi Moore gazed at Whoopi Goldberg but saw Patrick Swayze. Then I heard her voice in my head as if she were sitting right in front of me: *Baby, hold your head up. You've got nothing to be ashamed of.*

"You're back," I whispered.

Hayden looked at me curiously. "Are you okay?"

I nodded. And just like that, the supernatural moment or whatever you'd call it was over. But the point is I knew Mom was with me again. Maybe she had never left, I don't know, but what I'd heard stayed with me.

Hayden tightened her hand around mine. "Francine?"

I didn't budge. I was too busy repeating Mom's words to myself. *Baby, hold your head up. You've got nothing to be ashamed of.*

Hearing Mom's voice flipped a switch. Suddenly Pamela's advice started to hit home. She'd often say: *People's feelings are not your responsibility.* She'd say, *Other people's shame is not yours to carry.*

She was right. And Mom was right, too. It wasn't my fault Jeannette felt attacked. And all that bullying I'd put up with for my dark skin, for my Bell's palsy, for the way I talked, the way I dressed—*for just being*—all of it was not my fault, not my shame to carry. I'd done nothing wrong the day Stefani Haywood assaulted me in the bathroom, and I hadn't deserved to be used by Isaiah or bullied by anyone. Not my shame to carry.

Hold your head up, baby. You've got nothing to be ashamed of.

I closed my eyes and thanked Mom for showing up for me. I didn't care if I'd concocted her voice in my head and imagined it all. So what? I felt better. You know what I'll own? Sleeping with a married woman in the first place. That was my responsibility, my mistake. Otherwise, Mom was right. Sure, I was a codependent, insecure mess at times, but I hadn't intentionally set out to hurt anyone. I didn't go around bullying people or sexually assaulting them—*I'm talking to you, Stefani Haywood*—and yet here I was carrying all the stress and shame of other people's actions. But their shame and dysfunction was not mine to carry. It was bullshit when you got down to it.

Hayden rose from the couch, gave my hand a light shake. "We should go. The car is waiting."

I touched the side of my face. "You don't have to come with me. I can go by myself."

"You sure?"

I'd made so many mistakes, but I was basically a good person. "I'll be okay. Thank you."

She helped me to my feet. I collected my things and left the office. I made my way into the elevator and downstairs to the lobby repeating Mom's words: *Hold your head up, baby. You've got nothing to be ashamed of.*

I ignored the stares as I walked through the lobby. I was near the entrance when—wouldn't you know it? *Why me?!* The FUN Committee stepped inside just as I was about to exit. My first reaction was to try to hide my ruined face. But no. *Not my shame to carry. Plus, my photography instructor thinks my work is provocative and exciting and my friends think I have talent*—so there.

The Jessicas and Bethany openly gawked when they saw me.

I stared right back, looking from White Jessica to Asian Jessica to Bethany.

"Are you okay?" the Jessicas said in unison.

I looked at them again, one at a time. I was surprised when I saw the concern in their faces, like they honestly cared.

"Do you need a doctor?" Bethany asked.

"Do you want me to call 911?" said Asian Jessica.

Without my anxiety and self-doubt clouding my every thought, I could see they wanted to help, which made me think briefly—except for the silly retreat, maybe they'd been trying to be friendly all along. Maybe I'd only been seeing them through the lens of my insecurities. Mom always said no one behaves just one way. Then again, they might have been faking their concern like mean girls are known to do.

At any rate, I kept eye contact as I spoke, which is the main point— me keeping eye contact even with my destroyed face. I had nothing to be ashamed of. "I'll be okay," I said politely. "Thank you."

I saw the car through the entrance doors and, without giving them another thought, walked out of the building, chin up.

CHAPTER TWENTY-NINE

The following day, avoiding mirrors at all costs, I visited Dr. Zhou, Hayden's acupuncturist, again. I spent another full hour under her care as she poked needles into my face and lined my back with weird sucking cups. Basically she told me my chi was fucked up, which came as absolutely no surprise. Hayden paid for my treatment, plus six more visits. When I was through with that first session, I saw her text saying I should come back to work when I felt better. I still couldn't get over how nice she was being.

Excluding my visit to Dr. Zhou, I spent the day sleeping and watching TV wrapped inside Mom's afghan. I had to reschedule my appointment with Pamela that evening. What would be the point? I could hardly talk without sounding like a drunk.

I ate soup for dinner and drank a cup of tea with the herbs Dr. Zhou had given me. I woke up on the couch sometime before nine, surprised I'd fallen asleep. It took me a few seconds to realize the doorbell was ringing. *Jeannette.* I hadn't heard from her since our call the day before and figured she'd finally come to her senses and was ready to have an adult conversation. But it was Davie. He pushed past me, lugging a heavy trash bag from behind with his backpack strapped to his shoulder.

I checked outside expecting to see Jeannette, but the street was empty. "What are you doing here?"

He stopped short in the hallway. "I am running away!" He continued toward the den, dragging the trash bag. "Underground Railroad! Harriet Tubman, Frederick Douglass." I followed from behind as he shouted a litany of names. "Henry Brown, Robert Smalls!"

"You can't walk here in the middle of the night all alone. Where's Jeannette?"

He put the trash bag in front of the TV and took off his backpack, letting it drop to the floor with a heavy thud. "I'm very very upset right now!"

"I get that."

He stared at me directly for a split second before shifting his gaze somewhere near my ear. He pinched his nose, squinted. "What happened to your face?"

"It's called Bell's palsy. I had it when I was a teenager. It came back." My words were no longer slurring as much, I noticed, thanks to Dr. Zhou.

"Is it contagious?"

"No, it's from stress. Now will you tell me what's going on?"

"The asshole foster parent is not letting me go to camp. She won't sign the permission slip and she says I can't go! She's an asshole and I hope she gets a disease and dies."

Damn. What a shitty move. Jeannette could hate me all she wanted and never speak to me again, but not letting Davie go to camp was flat-out wrong. I realized my hands were balled into fists and stretched my fingers. I needed to stay calm. "I'll talk to her. You're going to camp, Davie. Don't worry."

"She's an asshole." His mouth trembled, his eyes welling with tears, and then he was full-on sobbing. Since we'd met, I'd never once seen him cry—not like this. I wanted to comfort him, but when I moved closer, he stepped out of reach.

"Do not touch me!" he sobbed. "I do not like to be touched! Everybody's an asshole!"

"Don't cry, Davie. It'll be okay."

"Counselor Hayes says I can be upset if I want to be, and I am very very upset!"

I grabbed my phone. "Let's call Counselor Hayes right now. This is an emergency. I'm sure he'll want to talk to you."

He shot his gaze toward the ceiling, choking back tears. "Counselor Hayes is dead, you idiot."

"*What?*"

"He's dead, idiot!" He started pacing back and forth, wiping snot and tears from his face with the sleeve of his sweatshirt. "He was old and he died because he was old. He can still be my friend, though. He said so before he retired. He said I was special and I could talk to him whenever I wanted. Mr. Science and Counselor Hayes are my friends, but not you. You're an asshole."

I felt like an asshole, that's for sure. Counselor Hayes was dead? Jeannette had said he lived in Arizona.

"I'm so sorry. I didn't know. Why did you make me think he was alive?"

He stopped pacing. "Why did you make me think you weren't an asshole?"

He threw his head back, as though prepared to scream, but appearing to change his mind, he picked up Hello Mr. Fox and stared into its beady eyes. "Underground Railroad. William Still helped six hundred forty-nine slaves to freedom."

"Don't shut me out," I said. "I'll help you go to camp. I promise."

He returned Hello Mr. Fox to the floor, used the back of his hand to wipe his face dry. He then picked up his backpack. "No thanks. I'm leaving now. I am running away."

"Where are you going to go at this hour?"

"I will figure it out! I am very smart. You should've let me live with you. Now I hate you and I have to find a place to sleep."

"I'm so sorry about Counselor Hayes. Things will get better, though." My words were failing me. Would things get better? "Let me call Jeannette and find out what's going on."

"What's going on is she's not letting me go to camp. It's all I ever wanted."

"Let me talk to her. Why don't you sit down?"

"I don't want to sit down. You were supposed to be my friend, but you like the asshole better and you were going to forget about me." He let his backpack fall from his arm and wearily lowered his head as though he might start crying again. "Everybody's an idiot."

I grabbed Mom's purple amethyst from her altar. I needed to prove to him he could trust me and I was truly on his side. I held the gem in front of him. "This was Mom's favorite crystal. She'd hold it whenever she wanted positive energy. I want you to have it."

He ignored me, rocking on his feet, eyes shifting back and forth across the ceiling.

I moved closer, gesturing for him to take the crystal. "Davie, I promise I'll always do my best to be there for you."

"Mmmmm."

"I just need you to give me a chance. I love you. I swear on my mother's grave."

He took a step back, casting his gaze from the ceiling to somewhere near my chin. "Your mother's not in a grave, she's in a racist cookie jar."

"Right." I went to the coffee table and placed my hand on Aunt Jemima as if giving an oath. "I swear on my mother I will do my best to always be there for you."

"You always say that but you don't mean it." He frowned and stretched out his hand. "I'll take the crystal," he said, wiggling his fingers. "For now."

I gave him the amethyst, which was almost as large as his hand. He started to put it in the trash bag but changed his mind.

"What's with the trash bag anyway?"

"It's what they give you in foster care for your stuff. Foster care where no one cares."

"A trash bag? Unbelievable. I'll tell you what, I'll make you some of your favorite peppermint tea and you can run away tomorrow."

He stared at Mom's crystal in his hand, felt the weight of it. "Counselor Hayes and Corrina Stevenson are with each other all the time now. They're with my mom and my dad and Frederick Douglass. When Frederick Douglass got older, he tried to teach other slaves to read, but a mob made him stop. A mob is a group of people intending harm."

He unzipped his backpack and put the crystal inside, started to pace rapidly, talking about slavery—sometimes making sense, sometimes not. I let him talk it out and went to make tea.

Fucking Jeannette. I swear I could feel any love for her draining away with every second Davie paced and muttered to himself. Her resentment and anger had crossed the line. She was Jeannette Tomlin from high school, all right, a mean bully, a shitstorm I'd let into my life. *How could she do this to him?* I touched the side of my face, reminding myself to stay calm so I could heal.

Davie was willing to sit with me on the couch by the time I made tea. I thought about how he had walked from the Alms all alone with his backpack and that awful trash bag. When I asked how he left without anyone noticing, he told me Sterling was playing video games and Tucker and Jeannette were yelling in their bedroom, so he snuck out.

"No one has called here yet, haven't you noticed?" he said.

"Yeah, I noticed." I picked up my phone so I could tell Jeannette and Tucker he was at my place. Davie was watching TV while he drank his tea. It was when he took off his jacket and picked up the remote that I saw on the inside of his arm a bruise in the shape of two fingers.

I put down my phone. "What is that?"

He saw I was staring at the bruise and scrambled to put his jacket back on.

"Too late. What happened?"

"Frederick Douglass was—"

"What happened, Davie? Who's hurting you? Did those boys do this to you?"

"Mmmmm."

I thought of Jeannette grabbing Sterling by his ear. Her temper. Her fights in school. Even the way she pushed the prep school boy in the museum was less romantic now. I was such an idiot. The girl was a bully.

I had to ask, even though it scared me to: "Davie, is Jeannette hurting you? You can tell me."

He squeezed his eyes shut and rocked from left to right. "Mmmmm…"

"Davie, please. I want to help."

"Mmmmm."

The doorbell rang. We both froze. I gave Davie a look. "Stay put."

I went to the door and checked through the peephole. It was Jeannette. She wore jeans and a hoodie, her head held too low for me to see her face. As soon as I opened the door, I was hit by the smell of alcohol on her breath. I couldn't believe she'd show up drunk. What was wrong with her?

I glanced at her car parked in front of the house. "You drove here drunk?" I said in disbelief.

As if needing to focus, she leaned in close, her nose inches from mine. "What's wrong with your face?"

"I have Bell's palsy again. You're not the only one who's been stressed."

I was surprised when her gaze grew suddenly gentle, tender. She reached toward my cheek as though she cared for me and we weren't on the verge of breaking up or already broken up or whatever we were doing. But I wanted nothing to do with her sympathy and brushed her hand away.

"So it's like that?"

I shrugged. "You started it."

She glanced out toward the street when a car drove past, the porch light casting a shadow across her face, her hazel eyes less pretty now. When she turned back to me, any tenderness was replaced with anger. "Where's Davie? Tell him to come on."

I stayed put, blocking the door. "You're not taking him anywhere. You're not fit to drive."

"And you're not his foster mother so mind your business."

"I don't know why you're acting like this. I said we could discuss Sterling going to another camp. It's not like I don't want to help."

"I don't want your help. You know what I realized about you? You've been looking down on me and mine this whole time. I'm not your damn charity case, bitch."

"You need to stop calling me a bitch." Due to my condition, *bitch* sounded more like *bit*.

Maybe it was hearing my garbled speech, but her expression softened. She kicked her foot against the porch like a child might. "I wouldn't have to call you anything if you'd stop looking down on me. You and my brother looking down on me. Everybody always judging me and taking advantage. Using me like I'm nothing. I thought you'd be different."

"Using you? How did I use you?"

"You got me to sleep with you, didn't you?" Her eyelids fell to half-mast as though she was about to doze off.

Hopeless. This was all hopeless. We weren't going to get anywhere. She was too drunk. I stepped out onto the porch, closing the door behind me. A helicopter trekked through the dark sky. I watched it briefly while trying to gather my thoughts. "Davie has another bruise on his arm."

"And?"

"Did you hurt him?"

"See there," she said, waving her finger in front of me. "You do judge me. I have never raised my hand to a child in my life."

"Yeah, right," I muttered, thinking of the time she twisted Sterling's ear.

"I have never touched that boy."

I searched her eyes and face for the truth. She stared right back until her head bobbed forward and she stretched her hands out to each side as if the porch were moving and she needed to regain control.

I sighed loudly. I'd have to bring up the bruise later when she was sober. I said instead, "Why didn't you ever say anything about Counselor Hayes?"

"Who?"

"Counselor Hayes. *He's dead.*"

"What do you mean he's dead?"

"Davie told me he died."

"That's not true; he emails him all the time."

"He's emailing a ghost. Counselor Hayes is dead, and you didn't know a thing about it."

"I guess I know now. It doesn't matter anyway. I'm finished with Davie and you. Tell him to come on so we can go."

"You're not taking him anywhere. You're too drunk to drive."

She bit down on the inside of her lip, stared at her feet. "I hate you right now," she said quietly. "It hurts, how you treat Sterling. We have no future because of how you do me and my son."

I knew she was hurt. I was, too. "We should talk when you're sober." I gestured toward the door. "Come inside and I'll make you some coffee."

"I don't want any coffee." She kept her gaze on her feet. "I want you, Francine. That's what all of this is about. You hurt me."

"Nette, I didn't mean to—"

Before I knew what she was doing, she pulled me in, holding me close, the smell of alcohol wafting from her body. But it was no time for hugs. "Get off me, Jeannette." She held on tighter, pressing her body into mine, as though she hadn't heard me.

I tried to wiggle my way out of her embrace but she was stronger. "What are you doing?"

"You only want me for one thing," she slurred.

I thought of Stefani Haywood as I struggled against her, my brain going straight to panic mode. "Let me go! Stop it, Jeannette!"

She was drunk at least, and after a few more seconds of wrestling, I was able to twist out of her hold. I shoved her hard with both hands and she fell backward, a tightrope walker waving her arms in the air before regaining her footing. "Take your drunk ass home."

The tone of my voice gave her pause; she stared with her mouth slack as though seeing me in a different light. I guess she was finally realizing I was finished with her bullshit, finished trying to placate or kiss up. I was over trying to please anyone except Davie.

"I'm not going anywhere without Davie. Get him out here so we can leave."

I stretched my arm across the door. There was no way I was letting her inside. "I won't. And he's going to camp."

She made a sharp guttural sound, then, eyes filled with hatred, she pushed me aside in one motion and opened the door. She marched right into the house, yelling for Davie. I rushed past her and straight into the den.

Davie was on his feet, panic set in his eyes.

"It's going to be okay," I told him.

Jeannette called from inside the hall. "Davie, get your shit. Let's go home."

"Don't make me," he whispered.

"Go to my bedroom and lock the door."

He stared toward the hallway, unsure.

"Now, Davie. Go."

He ran off just before Jeannette staggered into the den. "Where is he?"

"Leave or let me make you coffee, your choice. It's just a check, Jeannette. Why are you acting like this?"

"Because you're a liar and a bitch." She started toward my bedroom. "Where is he?"

I caught hold of her wrist. She seemed to notice I was grabbing her and stared down at my hand before meeting my gaze.

"You better take your damn hand off me."

I knew the hard look in her eyes; bullies always wore the same expression before they'd beat me up. Stefani Haywood certainly had. I let go right away and stepped back. But it was too late, I had crossed the ambiguous threshold that pushed a bully over the top.

I tried my best not to show any fear. "You should go home."

"'You should go home,'" she mimicked.

She lunged, catching me by my hair, jerking my head off to one side, my scalp burning as though it had been set aflame. I fell backward, landing in the corner of Mom's altar, the sharp edge of the wood stabbing my lower back. She came at me, fists flying. I swung at her with everything I had, but I was trying to fight Jeannette Tomlin and she was drunk and pissed. She pushed me back against Mom's altar, sending Mom's tarot cards and crystals, her statues and candles, to the floor. *We are fighting on my mother's altar—I am getting beat up in my own home.* I froze from the sheer shock of it. Jeannette held me down by my wrists and watched me curiously, wondering, I guessed, why I wasn't fighting back. I remained stiff and immobile. I was a good person, I thought. I deserved respect just like everyone else. *Baby, hold your head up. You've got nothing to be ashamed of.* Thinking of Mom's words, I closed my eyes, gathered as much spit in my mouth as I could, and hurled it into her face.

There was a flicker of surprise as she wiped the spittle off her cheek. She stared at my spit in the palm of her hand, wiped it on her sweatshirt, then balled her hand into a fist, the blow landing directly in my eye.

I shot up my arm and blocked a second blow, but she returned by punching me hard in my nose; pain shot in all directions across my face, my eyes watering in an instant. I became her punching bag, years of frustration and heartache landing on my face with every punch. I tried to defend myself without any success. I had sense enough to think of Davie in the other room, at least, and refused to scream as she went at me, blow after blow.

She was only brought back to sanity by the sound of the doorbell.

Her breaths were labored as she stood over me, asking with her eyes if I had something to do with whoever was at the door.

I caught sight of Davie out of the corner of my eye.

Jeannette heard his footsteps and moved away from me. "Get back here." But he kept running toward the living room. She straightened up, fussed with her hair, then pulled her zirconia from inside her shirt as if some fake diamond were going to make her presentable.

I moved at half her speed. My right eye throbbed, my left eye drooped. Snot trickled down to my mouth. When I wiped it away, I saw that it was blood.

I looked over at her, but she ignored me, her attention on the sound of approaching footsteps, the heavy sounds of a man's footfalls. Had Davie called the cops?

I grabbed a wad of tissues from the coffee table and held them against my nose.

Davie walked into the den first, followed by Tucker.

When they both stared at my wrecked face, I averted my eyes, but then realized what I was doing and raised my head. I had absolutely nothing to be ashamed of. I had done nothing wrong.

I gazed over at Jeannette again and our eyes met. *Look what you did to me.* She quickly turned away. "What are you doing here?" she asked Tucker.

Davie held up the cordless phone from Mom's office. "I called him."

She frowned at him, then said to Tucker: "None of this is what you're thinking."

"Yes it is," I said, dabbing at the last spots of blood under my nose.

Tucker said to Jeannette, "Apologize to Francine."

"Hell no. You don't even know what happened."

Tucker furrowed his brow, raised his deep voice. "Apologize so we can get out of here." I'd never seen him angry before, didn't know he had it in him.

Jeannette pursed her lips as if ready to defend herself but, thinking better of it, cast her gaze off to the side of my face as Davie might have, the haze of booze appearing to lift long enough for a moment of clarity. "I'm sorry."

"Mmmmm," Davie hummed, his tone dubious. I'd forgotten he was there and told him to go back to my room.

"But—"

"Now, please."

"But—"

"Now, Davie."

Tucker didn't speak until he heard the door close. He looked at Jeannette as though embarrassed by the sight of her—rightly so. "Wait in the truck for me."

"You're not even going to—"

"Get in the damn truck, Nette."

She stared at him a beat, but then her entire body seemed to deflate. Twisting her zirconia between her fingers, she dared not look at either me or Tucker and left without a word—her head low, shoulders hunched, much like the day she'd been kicked out of MacDowell.

"I apologize for her," Tucker said when she was gone. He stared at me momentarily: "Your face . . ." By the way he let his voice trail off I assumed he meant the Bell's palsy and not any bruises Jeannette had left.

"It's nothing." Thinking of Kenji, I added, "It's just my karma." I was no saint after all. I'd had choices from the start and I had chosen to sleep with his wife.

He took off his baseball cap. "Try not to blame her. It's the alcohol. She had a bad night, you know. She just got out of control."

"I don't care about any of that. Davie has a bruise on his arm. Does she hit him?"

"No, never."

"Somebody hurt him again and he won't tell me who. You said you'd look after him. I don't trust Jeannette to do it."

"Yeah, I will. I promise. I just want to explain, though. We're sorry. I know she's sorry. We really do appreciate you." He scratched nervously at the back of his neck. "Look here, if we could talk about a different plan…"

Was he serious? "Are you serious? Look what she did to me."

He nodded. "Yeah. Yeah…I understand. We'll make things right with you. She means well. She's a good person."

"Ha!" Davie cried from somewhere in the hallway.

I glanced toward the hall but couldn't see him. "Davie, go into my bedroom and stay there."

"Mmmmm."

I waited until I heard the door close.

Tucker looked at me, contrite. "You won't call the police, will you? She was upset about Sterling not being able to go to camp and had too much to drink. Like I said, she can get like that sometimes, but I swear she means well. And look here, I'll make her go back to anger management if I have to."

"Anger management?" I repeated. "Since when did she have anger management?"

"She didn't tell you? She had to go last year. Look at this." He stepped closer, pointed to a thin scar running across the bridge of his nose. He smiled shyly. "I won't lie. I was gambling and lost too much money. She got fucked up. Next thing I know she was cursing me somethin' good. She picked up this mug and—bam. Got me right here." He rubbed his nose. "Someone heard us yelling and called the cops. When they showed up, I was bleeding and my nose was swollen up. She got a citation to show up in court. The judge was a sister, though, and told her if she went to anger management, she'd let her off with a warning."

I managed to shift my stiff facial muscles into a frown.

He swallowed visibly, cleared his throat. "Anyway, that's Nette for you. What are you gonna do?" He shook his head softly, as if her abuse were a cute incident, a funny anecdote he'd tell his grandkids one day.

Jeannette had never mentioned anger management classes. What else had she been hiding? I was such a fool. Did he and Jeannette really live like celibate roommates?

He wrung his hat in his hands. "I know I have some nerve asking, but would you do me a solid and look after Davie tonight? And maybe tomorrow night? See that he gets to school and just let him stay with you. I think he kind of pushes Nette's buttons."

"That's not his fault."

"I know, but would you? She needs a day or two to get it together."

"Yeah, of course."

"And you won't call the police, right? 'Cause Sterling needs his mother and—"

"I'm not going to call the police."

"Thank you. Thank you," he repeated, relieved. He called for Davie to come out and explained he'd be staying with me for a few days.

"I'm staying indefinitely," Davie said. "*Indefinitely* means I am not leaving. I'm either staying or running away. Those are the two options."

"No, Li'l Man, you're going to stay here for a couple of days, then you're coming home. We want you with us."

"Slaves in Virginia would get their ears cut off if they robbed someone. They would get sixty lashes for—"

Tucker interrupted him, mid-slavery fact. "I see you have your things," he said, gesturing toward the trash bag, "but you call if you need something."

"Mmmmm."

I told Davie I'd be right back, then led Tucker outside. I glimpsed

Jeannette slouching in the front seat of his truck, her hoodie over her head.

"I'll come back and get her car," he said.

"She needs help."

"You gotta understand. Nette loses control sometimes, but she has a good heart. You of all people know that. She cares about you, Francine. I swear to God, she's never had a friend like you. She just loses it sometimes."

And she's cheating on you and she beat me up and I'm finished with this shit. I glanced at Jeannette, leaning against the passenger door, her face hidden behind her hoodie. I was done. "Good night." I turned and went inside, locking the door behind me.

I went back to the den, where Davie paced anxiously in front of the TV.

"We should talk," I said, not wanting to talk at all. "I'm sorry you had to see all of that."

"In 1741 there was a revolt and many slaves were burned at the stake. You have a black eye and Bell's palsy. Bell's palsy is caused by stress."

"Yeah, I know. I must look like crap."

"I looked it up on Corrina Stevenson's computer. It's a paralysis on the side of the face. Some people's lips go up like a half a smile. Some people's lips droop down like half a frown. Some people get dry eyes or some people get runny eyes."

I sat down on the couch. Both of my eyes pulsated with pain. My back hurt, too. Drool trickled down the deadened side of my mouth. I didn't feel it until it reached my chin, and I wiped it with my finger.

Mom's altar was a disaster. Her Medusa was on the floor surrounded by her candles and crystals. Black-eyed peas were scattered everywhere. Hello Mr. Fox lay on his side, staring at the chaos with his beady, dead eyes.

Davie stood over me for a moment. Then he walked into the kitchen, pushed a chair close to the refrigerator, climbed up, and opened the freezer.

He returned with a bag of frozen blueberries. "Here."

"What's that?"

"It's for your black eye. You're supposed to put something frozen on your black eye."

I took the bag of blueberries, sighing at the thought of all he'd seen in his ten short years. I pressed the bag against my swollen eye. "Sit down with me. Let's not talk. We'll talk about what happened tomorrow."

Instead of sitting, he started picking up Mom's things and putting them on her altar—the crystals and tarot cards, the numerology chart. He picked up Hello Mr. Fox, patting him gently on the head. When he couldn't lift the Medusa, I got off the couch and helped him, and together we put everything back in its place.

Afterward we sat on the couch and stared at Mom's altar. Davie held Mom's purple crystal in his lap. "Now?" he asked.

The neurons in my gut were firing; I knew exactly what he meant. I'd thought Mom had wanted me to meet Jeannette so we could be together, but she'd wanted me to meet Davie. Just Davie. She'd been trying to help the two of us find each other all along.

Feeling her presence, I looked up at the altar, felt her say, *Baby, be happy*. With that, I pushed my doubts aside and found my laptop. I wanted Davie with me. I loved him and we belonged together.

I placed my laptop on my knees so he could see the screen. I typed *foster-to-adopt* into the search engine and we stared at our future together.

CHAPTER THIRTY

woke up early the next morning in Mom's bed. By "early," I mean really early, three a.m. early. I put on my robe and walked down the hall, pausing in front of my bedroom, where Davie slept. I stood in the doorway and watched him sleeping, the light from the hall illuminating his profile. I was willing to do anything to protect him. I was like those women you hear about whose lives are going nowhere, but as soon as they find out they're pregnant, they do a big-ass one-eighty: they stop drinking or doing drugs, or they sneak out with a packed suitcase in the middle of the night, finally leaving the abusive partner behind. They're willing to do anything for their unborn child. Not that I was pregnant, of course, but I was sort of with child. I had Davie to look out for now, and nothing was going to stand between us, and I mean nothing—not his case manager, the foster care agency, or any judge granting adoption. Hell, if Jeannette and Tucker were allowed to foster him, I most certainly could.

I headed to the den, picked up my laptop from the coffee table, and carried it to Mom's altar. Once the candles were lit and incense burning, I closed my eyes and asked for her help, then opened my laptop and sent Jeannette an email.

Jeannette—

Davie is going to science camp or I will report you to social services
and the police. If Davie even hints that you've abused him, I will
report you to social services and the police. Don't ever come near
me again or I will call the police.

—F

I took a picture of my bruised eye and fat lip and sent it with the
email.

I then texted Aunt Liane and Uncle CJ. I mean, it was time to face
them. If I was going to foster, and eventually adopt, Davie, I would need
their help. I figured if I practiced my boundaries with Aunt Liane, we'd
be okay. They were family, my only family. And in the end, it's like they
say: not forgiving someone is poison for you, not the other person. As I
was learning from Pamela, most of us were acting on unresolved childhood wounds, anyway. It doesn't excuse poor behavior, but it sure as hell
explains it.

Next, I requested information for foster care and set up an appointment to meet with a case manager. I then found Tucker on Peeps and
messaged him about my plan to keep Davie. Davie would stay with me
until I was approved to foster. At that point, Jeannette and Tucker
would tell their case manager they could no longer look after him, and
then I'd request him. It wasn't completely ethical, but I was not going to
give him back. I couldn't have given a shit whether Tucker agreed with
my plan or not. I still didn't trust that Jeannette hadn't hurt Davie. My
bruised eye was proof she was capable of abuse. And if either of them
tried to take him, I would report Jeannette to the police. I said so in my

message to Tucker. To be honest, I felt better by the time Davie woke up. I was proud of myself for facing my shit head-on.

I told Davie he could skip school and stay home with me for the day, especially considering the night we'd had, but he said they were dissecting worms in his science class and he didn't want to miss out. I asked more than once if he was sure, but he clearly wanted to go.

While he ate breakfast, I looked up some autism basics, something I'd been meaning to do since I met him. Turns out I was ableist in many ways. Autism is not something to be fixed with drugs, for instance. I mean, there was no "fixing" Davie. He was who he was, and I loved him for it. I also learned girls and women are less likely to be diagnosed. And data on African Americans was sorely lacking, which led to adults and children being misdiagnosed or ignored.

Some characteristics of autism included difficulty making friends, anxiousness in social settings, sensitivity to loud noises. It all sounded very familiar, in more ways than one. A small part of me wondered if it was something to bring up to Pamela.

I closed the laptop, telling myself I'd put my own evaluation on hold, at least for the time being.

I glanced at Davie, who was eating his cereal and watching *The Incredibles* on his tablet. I planned to ask Pamela if she could help me find a therapist for him. I never knew what he was thinking or feeling. He'd been through so much. Then again, when I dropped him off at school that morning, he climbed out of the car and, staring somewhere between my eyebrows, said, "Francine Stevenson to the rescue! Ha!" Then he pulled back his lips and smiled his odd smile. "Francine Stevenson drives an electric I-on. It's turbocharged!" And he strode off to class, as if we hadn't had a horrible night together at all, his hulking backpack bouncing against his back with every step.

I watched him enter the school building, smiling my own weird smile—half smile, half smirk, due to the lack of movement on the left side of my face. As Davie disappeared inside the same junior high school I'd gone to, I saw my eleven-, twelve-, thirteen-year-old self walking up the steps. And I thought, you know, I'm proud of that girl, enduring all the bullshit through the day, then going home to her mother not knowing what to expect. She didn't drop out of school, didn't get hooked on drugs or alcohol, or get pregnant—no thanks to pedophile Isaiah—and she graduated from college, too. I had a long way to go, but that eleven-, twelve-, thirteen-year-old girl had brought me here to this moment. She was a survivor. *Thanks, Francine.*

Aunt Liane responded to my text by calling as I was leaving my appointment with Dr. Zhou. She acted as though no time had passed at all, with no mention of our falling-out. She had been keeping busy—on the move with Uncle CJ visiting one of his cousins in Texas, then a business trip to a hair show in Florida. I initially played along and acted like our fight never happened, too, but then I began to wonder what ignoring the big fat elephant in the room got us except for more fat elephants and more built-up resentment.

So I did what I didn't want to do: I swallowed my pride and apologized for kicking her out of the house and giving her the silent treatment for so long. Aunt Liane, to her credit, didn't push it. "It's okay. I know you were upset." I waited for her to apologize for trying to throw away Mom's things but got nothing. It wasn't going to happen, so I decided to let it go. I told her about my photography class and my thoughts about going back to school, which made her happy since she always hated that I worked as "someone's maid." It was nice to chitchat as we tentatively made our way back to each other. I mean, she was being so nice! We were getting along!

Things were going so well, I decided to tell her about Jeannette and

Davie, leaving out all the traumatic events, of course, but telling her how much I loved Davie and my plans to eventually adopt.

Sure enough, that's when the real Aunt Liane made her presence known. "Adopt a kid? Have you lost your damn mind? The last thing on earth you need is a kid. That is the most foolish thing I have ever heard of. You don't know how to live your own damn life, how are you going to raise a kid? You and your mother living the way you were and now you act like you know how to mother somebody? You are acting like you have absolutely no sense. Your mother would be rolling in her grave right now if she *had* a grave in the first place and wasn't inside a damn cookie jar. I swear, in all my life—"

I hung up.

Fuck her. Fuck family.

So yeah. Davie and I carried on as we were. I took him to school and bought him new clothes. I tried to convince him to get a haircut, but he wasn't having it and started talking about slavery. We also visited Kenji and Eve, who liked Davie right away. Believe it or not, when I told them what happened with Jeannette, Kenji said "I told you so" only once, then dropped it, which was a true miracle, yo.

By the following week my face was nearly back to normal thanks to visits to Dr. Zhou. And since the bruise under my right eye was undetectable with enough makeup, I returned to work.

I enrolled Davie in an after-school program in Emeryville, perfect for those days I had to stay late at work. And surprise surprise... He made a friend! *A friend!* Another ten-year-old named Demar, who was shy and awkward. Davie would come home repeating stories about Demar. Demar this, Demar that. "D and D! Ha!"

We were playing chess one Saturday, roughly three weeks after he moved in with me, when the doorbell rang. Davie and I froze in place. I could tell he was worried it might be Jeannette or Tucker showing up

290 · Renee Swindle

unannounced. I reassured him as best I could and went to see who it was.

After checking through the peephole, I opened the door right away. It was Aunt Liane and Uncle CJ. Seeing them in the flesh after all those months, hearing Uncle CJ—"B… b… baby, we c… came to help. We l… love you." I don't know, hearing those words, seeing them on the porch like that? My eyes welled with tears.

"We… we're so sorry."

"Thank you." I gave him a big hug. "It's good to see you, Uncle CJ."

I looked at Aunt Liane and waited for her to ruin the moment. Her latest weave was jet-black and shoulder length, and her thick fake eyelashes curled upward toward her expertly shaped brows. I wondered briefly if Mom had shown up for her as she had with me, like a ghost whispering in her ear. Had Mom told her, as I would have, that it was okay to let her guard down, to soften up for once?

Either way, I waited, blocking the entrance to the house. There was an invisible sign plastered on the door and my entire being: *No disrespect allowed.* I could no longer put up with her craziness, and *she* owed me an apology, not Uncle CJ.

I tapped my foot, tilted my head to the side, waiting.

Uncle CJ nudged her and she coughed as though something had caught in her throat. "I apologize." Her voice was reedy and several octaves too high, but she'd done it, she'd managed an apology. I half expected fireworks to go off in the sky.

I opened the door further but stopped. "Just one last thing," I said, looking directly at her. "If you say one negative thing about my mother, out you go. If you disrespect me or say anything negative or mean to Davie, out you go."

She pulled back, eyes widening with surprise, as in, *Oh really? You're talking to me like that?* But I gave no shits. On the outside I appeared the same, my face had healed—no evidence of Bell's palsy or bruises—but on the inside it was a different story.

I noticed she started to bring her hand to her hip, but seeing I was prepared to close the door and never see them again if it came to it, she smirked and inhaled sharply. She glanced at Uncle CJ, then said, "Fine with me. I've always just wanted the best for you and my sister. *I loved her,*" she said defensively.

"I know you did."

"Well, can we come inside now or what? You gonna keep us out here forever?"

It was a veritable love fest as far as my aunt and I were concerned. I certainly couldn't hope for any better and stepped aside.

Davie paced in the den in the same way he had on the night he ran away and Jeannette showed up. "Everything is fine," I told him. "I want you to meet my aunt and uncle."

"The mean aunt?" he said, suspicious.

Aunt Liane stifled a smile. "Don't believe everything she says about me. You need to meet a person before you judge them."

Davie hummed thoughtfully. "I'll be eleven in August," he said, apropos of nothing. "Then I'll be in eighth grade. In six weeks and five days I'm going to science camp at Stanford University. I'm going to meet Mr. Science."

"You d… do sound… smart," said Uncle CJ.

Aunt Liane peered at him, her gaze softening. "Eleven years old and starting eighth grade? My my my. Francine told me you were smart. It's nice to meet you."

Davie kept his attention on Uncle CJ, his eyes narrowing. "Why do you talk like that? Why do you use a cane?"

I whispered through clenched teeth, "Try not to be rude."

"I'm not being rude. What's wrong with him?"

"I had a… st… stroke. It's when…"

Davie grabbed his iPad from the coffee table, pulled up an answer before Uncle CJ finished speaking. "It's when your blood can't get to your brain. That's very interesting."

Aunt Liane frowned at Davie. I worried she was going to say something rude or mean. "Child, what is going on with your hair?"

"He's not a fan of getting his hair cut," I explained. "He has to be in the right mood."

When she stepped toward him, Davie stepped back. "I don't like to be touched," he warned.

"No one's going to touch you," Aunt Liane said. "I'm just looking at that hair on your head. I think you should let me give you a trim. You want to look good when you go to camp, don't you?"

"Ha!"

"She knows what she's talking about, Davie," I said. "She's a hairdresser."

He looked at Aunt Liane's weave dubiously.

Uncle CJ raised his cane toward the game of chess set up on the dining room table. "You p… play chess, D… Davie?"

"Francine Stevenson taught me to play and I'm already better than she is. I live here now. We play chess and we ride our bikes. She's not going to ship me off."

"Of course she's not," said Aunt Liane. "From what Francine told me you're going to be a part of our family. Good luck with that." She smiled, though, and I saw Mom's smile—my smile; we all had the same dimpled chin and full lips, after all.

Uncle CJ made his way to the dining room table and sat down. "Let's see what you g… got."

"You know how to play?" Davie asked.

"D… do I know how to play? B… boy, I taught Francine how to play. G… get over here and let me school you."

Davie raised his finger. "Yes!" he cried, always eager for a game of chess. "Magnus Carlsen became a grandmaster when he was thirteen years old. He's very interesting but not as interesting as Steve Jobs. I know everything about Steve Jobs. His best friend was Steve Wozniak. Steve and Steve! My best friend is Demar. D and D!" He sat opposite Uncle CJ. "Don't feel bad when you lose," he said. "Francine Stevenson says losing is how you learn. It's like practice."

Aunt Liane and I watched them set up the board, then she looked over at Mom's altar—the Aunt Jemima cookie jar next to the Medusa. She briefly put her arm over my shoulder, then realized she was being affectionate and withdrew it. But, too late, the deed had been done. I smiled and she offered a quick smile in return. At some point I'd tell her about Jeannette and give her all the tea, and maybe she'd tell me about how she was doing now that Mom was gone, what it was like growing up with her, and all they'd endured in Drunk Grandpa's house. I imagined the two of us sitting out on the deck finally getting to know each other. A girl can hope.

Davie stared at the chessboard. Uncle CJ started to make his first move. "Wait!" he said, holding up his finger. He proceeded to clap his hands two times, then vigorously rub them together. He shot his arms out to the sides, clapped twice again—his pregame ritual.

Uncle CJ glanced over at me. *Is he okay?*

He does this all the time, I mouthed. *He's fine.*

And he was. I realized he hadn't said a single word about slavery since they'd arrived, which was a good sign.

Davie rubbed his hands again, shot his arms out a second time, wiggled his fingers in the air, and clapped twice. "Ready!"

CHAPTER THIRTY-ONE

U ncle CJ and Aunt Liane took Davie out to lunch during my first home inspection to become a foster parent. We had to hide all of Davie's things and clear Mom's altar and offerings to make the house look normal. We'd move everything back after the inspections were completed. For my second interview, Davie stayed with Kenji and Eve. Lots of trickery was involved since no one from the agency was supposed to know he was already living with me.

After my paperwork and home inspections were approved, there was only one last thing to do: meet with Tucker and Jeannette's case manager, Brenda, and formally request that I become Davie's foster parent. Since he'd moved in, Tucker would occasionally send texts asking how Davie was doing, but I'd heard nothing from Jeannette—which was fine with me, I wanted to stay as far away from her as possible. In fact, I messaged Tucker that I did not want to see her at the final meeting. He and Jeannette had already met with Brenda by then and told her they could no longer keep Davie and wanted to recommend me. Terri, my caseworker, had given Brenda my paperwork and letter of request. One last meeting with Brenda, and Davie would be mine.

Uncle CJ and Aunt Liane drove from Fresno the day of the meeting to watch Davie and spend the weekend with us. I left them watching a documentary together on the Reconstruction period. It wasn't the best sign that Davie wanted to watch a documentary on slavery, but I told him everything would work out fine. "Try not to worry," I said before leaving. "Mom is with us." Mentioning Mom seemed to help him feel better.

Once at the agency, I purposely waited in my car until the exact time of the appointment to avoid having to talk to Tucker. I passed the minutes by listening to Nina Simone's *Black Gold*, then pulled up a video I'd taken of Mom in her garden. There was nothing to the video—just Mom tending to her plants—but that's why I liked it. Just a normal day. This was before Alfonse came into the picture with his fucking pills.

I watched her trimming her flowers, the sun shining on her face. "I need your help today, Mom," I whispered.

Tucker pulled up just then. He was parked far enough away to not see me. I sighed in relief when I saw Jeannette was nowhere in sight, thank goodness. I watched him go inside and whispered to Mom, "Here we go."

Brenda's office was as small and cluttered as my caseworker Terri's office. Tucker stood when I entered and we put on our game faces and hugged each other as if we were old pals. He introduced me to Brenda as a close friend of the family. Unlike Terri, who was energetic and bubbly, Brenda appeared burned out by her job, a woman who'd seen far too many kids hurt by the system. She drank from a can of Diet Coke while hunched over my paperwork. She appeared to only half listen to Tucker while he explained why I should be allowed to foster Davie.

When it was my turn to speak, I told her about how I rescued Davie from the bullies the day we met, adding that his foster mother and I had gone to school together. I showed her pictures of Davie and me on our bikes and a picture Kenji took of the two of us playing chess. "We've always gotten along. We're both—" I was going to say *misfits* but thought better of it. "We're both... We understand each other." It didn't seem to matter whether I fumbled with my words or not since Brenda hardly paid attention and rarely looked up from my paperwork. I fought the urge to snap my fingers. *Hello? Are you listening?*

Tucker jumped in as she continued skimming through my file. "Francine and Davie have been close since they met. And you know how Li'l Man is. He's picky about who he spends time with. You can't just send him to someone he doesn't know. He's had enough of going from home to home; it would break him. And I know what that's like."

I leaned forward in my seat and cleared my throat, as in, *Wake up! Are you listening at all?* "I want to do more than just foster Davie," I said, doing my best to stay calm. "I want to adopt him. You saw that in my file, right?"

Brenda sipped from her can of Coke, looking bone-tired and uninterested.

For the first time, I was starting to worry. Maybe I was too young. Maybe they were looking for a two-parent home. "There's no one better suited for Davie than me." I heard the desperation in my voice and took a deep breath. "I know I'm young, but I'm responsible and Davie and I get along. And I'm doing my best to change my life. I didn't have many friends growing up—" *Oh God, don't tell her that.* "But I'm in therapy now..." *What are you saying? Shut up! Shut up!* "But that's not important. What's important is I love Davie very much. And I know he loves me. He hardly ever talks about slavery around me, and he likes to—"

Tucker tapped the side of my arm, indicating I should be quiet. "Brenda, listen here. Francine is better with him than Nette and I ever were or ever will be. Those two belong together. You can't send him to anybody else."

I glanced his way. *Thanks.* "I also have the support from my family, and it's not like—"

Brenda brought her index finger to her lips, literally shushing me. "Ms. Stevenson, do not say another word." She neatly stacked my paperwork and regarded me sternly. "There are four hundred thousand kids in need of homes in this country. At eighteen, kids are kicked out of the system with no resources. Forty to fifty percent become homeless. Don't get me started on our trans and queer youth. And here you are coming into my office *requesting* to foster Davie. I have had trouble placing that boy for years. *Chiiiild,*" she said, dropping decorum, "all I can do is say thank you. I needed some good news today. You have no idea." She shook her head, probably thinking of all she'd seen in just that morning alone. She shuffled a few papers. "I can fit you both in my schedule tomorrow if it works for you."

Tucker and I looked at each other. He seemed as surprised as me. "Sure," he said.

I fell back into my chair, relieved. "Tomorrow would be great."

Brenda shook her hands at the ceiling like she'd suddenly gone to church and found Jesus. "You all have no idea what a week I've had." She rose just enough to reach over her desk and extend her hand. We shook, beaming at each other.

Tucker and I reviewed the final plan in the parking lot. Brenda would pick Davie up from his apartment the following day since we had to make it look like he'd been living there, which meant I would need to drop Davie off a couple of hours before Brenda was scheduled to arrive. Davie would have to pretend he'd been living with Tucker and Jeannette all along, then Brenda would pick him up and bring him to my house, right back home.

"I'm glad everything worked out," Tucker said, digging his hands into his front pockets. "We never should've had Davie in the first place, tell you the truth. I just want to help kids because I know what it's like growing up in the system. Davie was probably a little too much for us, though." He scratched at the back of his neck. "Anyway, Jeannette misses you. She hasn't been the same since you guys had your argument. She's been kind of depressed."

Oh my God. "It wasn't an *argument*; she beat me up."

"She didn't mean it, though. She learned her lesson this time. You should see her. She has me worried, Francine. Can you talk to her?"

"She needs to talk to a therapist or go to AA—or both." I ended the conversation by walking away. "Thanks again for helping me out. I'll see you tomorrow."

"All right," I heard him say from behind. "See you tomorrow."

Davie, Aunt Liane, and Uncle CJ and I went to Fentons Creamery to celebrate. Later, while Davie lay in bed, I reminded him he'd only have to stay with Jeannette and Tucker for two hours at the most before Brenda picked him up the next day. I sat next to him and asked if he was nervous about returning to Jeannette and Tucker's.

"George Washington got his first enslaved person when he was eleven." Kenji and Eve had taught him to say *enslaved person* instead of *slave*, a reminder that those in bondage were not "slaves" at their core.

"Remember you'll only be there for a couple hours tops. Ask Sterling if he'll play a video game with you."

"Can Ling Ling come see my room after we paint it and change the furniture?"

"I don't think so. But don't worry, you'll make new friends at camp and your new school." I was enrolling him in a charter with small class sizes in the fall. I pulled up the book he liked me to read to him, a biography of Frederick Douglass. I paused. Since he was moving out permanently, I thought of trying to ask him one more time. "Are you sure Jeannette never hurt you?"

"Ida B. Wells started the anti-lynching campaign after her friend was lynched for opening his own store."

"But do you want to tell me anything else? Did she ever hurt you? Physically?"

"Mmmmm…"

"Okay. I get it." Pamela had helped me find him a therapist. They'd start meeting after he returned from camp. Davie needed a professional to talk to. "Just remember our secret for tomorrow."

"Do not tell Miss Brenda I've been living with you. Do not. It's the Underground Railroad."

"Good. You'll be fine. Just one more day and then no more secrets. Ever."

"Uncle CJ says he's going to teach me to drive when I turn sixteen, but I'm going to ask him to teach me when I'm fifteen because I'll need my permit first."

"Whoa, whoa, slow down. Let's stay ten for a while."

"I'll be eleven in six weeks, five days. I'll be in eighth grade. Demar will be in sixth grade, but he can still be my friend. He's very good at puzzles."

For his birthday that August, I'd asked Hayden if she knew of anyone who could get us a tour of Pixar. She contacted Brad, our CEO. Turned out he knew someone who knew someone and he'd get back to me. Fingers crossed.

Aunt Liane made pancakes for breakfast the next morning, but I was too nervous to eat and stuck with coffee. We said goodbye, and Davie and I drove to the Alms one last time. The homeless encampment had taken over the entire empty lot since the last time we were there— more tents and makeshift living quarters. A few men sat in mismatched chairs, chatting. A woman riffled through a pile of clothes. She held a T-shirt against her chest, then decided against it and tossed it back.

I lagged behind Davie as he walked through the broken entry gate. I was growing increasingly anxious about seeing Jeannette and had to focus on staying calm. Davie continued up the stairs with his backpack strapped over his shoulder. I carried his trash bag with his things inside.

We needed to do better by kids in foster care. Trash bags? Really?

I knocked on the door, my thoughts returning to the first time I'd met Jeannette. "This is it," I said to Davie. "I'll see you soon and then it's just the two of us."

"I know," Davie said. "Underground Railroad. I can almost beat Uncle CJ at chess. He's going to teach me to drive."

Sterling opened the door. "Hey," he said to Davie.

Davie said, "I'm not supposed to tell Miss Brenda that I don't live here. I'm here for a minimum of two hours and then I leave. I won't see you anymore. And you can't see my new room. I'm going to go to a new school."

Sterling placed his hand on his shoulder and smiled. "I'll beat you in a game of Mortal Kombat one last time."

"Ha!"

Sterling glanced up at me, dismissive and cold. I couldn't blame him. I had swooped in and taken his foster brother and pissed off his mom with promises of paying for his camp.

"It's so great to see you!" I blurted. "How have you been? Is everything good?" It sucked how I reverted right back to my Mary Poppins voice.

"I'm good," he said. "Bye."

He proceeded to close the door in my face. *Brat.* "Wait." I handed over Davie's trash bag. He and Davie disappeared inside without saying goodbye.

"See you soon," I called to Davie.

Tucker pulled the door back, reprimanding Sterling for not inviting me inside.

"Ask her if she wants to stay for breakfast. There's plenty." *Jeannette.* My stomach clenched at the sound of her voice.

"She makes some mean French toast," said Tucker.

Jeannette again: "Tell her it's a goodbye breakfast for Davie. She can't leave."

Tucker grinned. "Hear that? Come on, you gotta stay."

Of course I knew there'd be a chance I'd see Jeannette, but I certainly hadn't expected an invite to breakfast. I swear they lived on Planet Denial. It was unbelievable.

"Davie and I already ate. Thanks, though. Goodbye."

"Cooking is her way of apologizing," Tucker said under his breath. "Just come inside and say hello. She's not asking for much. Like I told you, she hasn't been the same."

For a split second I thought of yelling in his face: *You do not want me over for breakfast, fool. Jeannette and I were sleeping together! She beat me up!* "Text me when Davie and Brenda leave."

I took the stairs two at a time and darted past the graffitied fountain in the same way I had when Jeannette and I first met and Davie had his outburst. I was crossing the street when I heard footsteps from behind and Jeannette calling after me. "Francine, wait up."

I sucked in a sharp breath and walked faster. Shit. *Shit.* I reached my car door, ready to speed off.

"Francine, I know you hear me."

I turned and waited as she approached. Her hair was down and framing her face. She wore jeans and a blouse with patterned flowers, slingback sandals with kitten heels. She'd dressed up for me or Brenda or both.

"I have something for you." She shielded her eyes from the sun with one hand; even the thick layer of makeup couldn't cover the dark circles under her eyes. She held up a business-sized envelope. "This is for you."

I stared.

"It's a letter I wrote you. I wanted to explain everything."

"There's nothing to explain."

"Yes, there is." She tugged at her zirconia, her outstretched hand holding the envelope. "You can read it later. Please?"

I recalled the card she'd given me. *I love you because of who you are as a person. I love you. I will always love you.* I feared whatever she'd written in that letter might draw me back into our shitstorm. Pitiful as it sounds, I could already feel the pull of attraction. Her lips, her eyes. I was pathetic.

She wiggled the envelope, her wrist limp. "Take it. I wanted to explain."

"Let's forget it."

She stepped forward, ready to shove the letter in my hand. "*Take it.*"

I moved out of reach. "I'm not reading that letter."

"Francine, please?"

"No."

She dropped her gaze, tucked the envelope in the back pocket of her jeans. "Fine. I wish you would read it, though. I stayed up all night writing it. I was trying to explain."

"There's nothing to explain. You assaulted me."

"And I'm sorry. I was drunk." She looked away, her eyes landing on a pigeon pecking at the ground. "I freaked out while I was at work that day and had a panic attack. I went home and started drinking."

"You had a panic attack?"

"I was in my boss's office and I just started freaking out and crying. It was embarrassing as shit."

"Was he trying to touch you? Is that what started it?"

"No. It was after you changed your mind about everything. I started feeling like my life was being choked out of me. My boss was all right about it, though. He let me go home early, and that's when I started drinking. I don't know why I made everything about that fucking camp. I should've talked to you. I'm just not good at talking sometimes. All day I could feel everything coming in on me and my life going to shit." She regarded me closely, her eyes pooling with tears. "And now it has. Everything has gone to shit. I hate my life."

My heart banged inside my chest. *Look at her. She's so broken. Do something! She needs you!*

"I'm so sorry, Francine. If I could go back in time, I swear, I never would've laid a hand on you. You know that, don't you?" She pressed her eyes shut as if making a fervent wish. "I swear … I swear … ," she whispered, shaking her head. "I didn't mean to hurt you."

Goose bumps formed on my arms. *She's sorry*, I thought. *She's learned her lesson.* I realized how much I missed her, too.

I needed to get the hell out of there. "I should leave."

She nodded, then reached into her back pocket for the letter and tried to hand it to me. "Please? Take it with you. You can read it at home. It tells you everything. All I've been through in life. Why I mess up sometimes."

"That's okay," I said.

She twisted the edge of the envelope, tucked it in her jeans. "I swear I never meant to go off on you."

"But you did."

"*I was drunk.* Can we meet and talk somewhere? Are you seriously going to be like this? I know I'm fucked up, okay? Everything just comes down on me when I'm angry. I'm sorry." Her chin quivered. Tears now, spilling down her cheeks.

"Jeannette." Despite everything, I hated to see her cry. "Jeannette. Don't cry."

Her tears flowing, she pressed the tips of her fingers over her eyes as if she could make herself stop crying.

Damn. This was not going as planned. I'd imagined not having to see her at all or cursing her out. Not this. I forgot everything Pamela and I had discussed about boundaries or whatever. "Come here," I whispered.

I took her in my arms and held her as she sobbed. All too soon, I was kissing the side of her face, kissing her just above her ear, light and quick. When I felt her relax, I closed my eyes and nuzzled my nose in her hair, inhaled the scent of coconut and argan. Where would we be now if I'd paid for Sterling's camp? Why hadn't I paid? I'd purposely destroyed our relationship. *Why did I ruin everything?*

She looked at me and I ran my thumbs over her cheeks, wiping her tears from her face. She closed her eyes and hugged me, her arms tightening around my waist.

She said something into my chest, her breath warm against my shirt.

"What did you say?" I asked.

She pulled back and peered into my eyes. "I said I don't want to lose you."

I placed my hands on either side of her face and stared at her lips, her mouth.

I felt dizzy.

I touched the tip of her chin and drew her mouth to mine, pressing my lips into hers. The slick feel of lip gloss, strawberry flavor. I licked my lips and kissed her again, my thoughts hurtling forward toward our future as I felt her tongue slide deep into my mouth: We'd tell our children about how we'd met, our brief breakup and how we got back together again. For good. First, we needed couple's counseling. She'd finally go to therapy and deal with her panic attacks and anger issues. We'd tell

Tucker about our love. We'd sit across from him holding hands and tell him we wanted him to find happiness, too.

Jeannette wrapped her hands around the back of my neck. Our kiss deepening, my thoughts moved from our future to the present: Aunt Liane and Uncle CJ at home waiting for me. Sunday we were going to celebrate Davie's officially moving in—Aunt Liane, Uncle CJ, Kenji, Eve. I was throwing a party at the house with my friends and Davie. Davie was moving in with me permanently. I was going to be his mother.

Jeannette and Sterling would be moving into the house, of course, which meant I would need to sit down with Davie and tell him . . . tell him . . . *Jeannette was moving in.* But how could I tell him that? I mean, what kind of fuckery would that be? *Hey, Davie, the woman who might have—probably did—hurt you, and definitely hurt me, is moving in with us. I will now model to you what it's like to go backward in life, what it's like not to go for what you deserve, to not like yourself enough to move on, to settle into dysfunction because that's what you know. Sound like a plan?*

My breathing slowed. Jeannette's tongue felt cold and slippery with spittle now. My endorphins draining from my body, the kiss shifted from longing and desire to a final goodbye, punctuated when a man yelled at us from across the street, "Hot damn!"

I pulled away. "I should go."

"Don't, let's talk." Studying my face, she traced her fingers across my forehead and along the side of my cheek, the tip of her finger landing in the center of my dimpled chin, her touch taking me back to Monterey, to all of our moments together. "I miss you," she said, her voice filled with longing and regret.

"I can't, Jeannette. I'm done with this. I have to think about Davie now."

It was as though hearing his name hardened something inside of her, those hazel eyes darkening. "Which is what you wanted. You always put him first."

She stuck out her foot and placed her hand on her hip, daring me to disagree, as if purposely wanting to pick a fight, as if an argument would be better than nothing.

But I could see through her actions now and wanted nothing to do with the games and dysfunction. Kissing her was a mistake, but you know what? It wasn't like I had to live in my mistakes. I opened the car door and started to get inside. "Bye, Jeannette."

She grabbed my arm. When I turned, she took hold of my hand and shoved the letter at me. "No. I told you I don't want it. And take your fucking hand off my arm."

She appeared surprised by my tone, that I dared stand up to her. She drew her lips into a thin line, held the envelope directly in front of me, and began shredding the letter into tiny fragments while searching my face for a reaction.

As if. I watched pieces of the letter fall from her hands like leaves. Pamela told me it takes two people to create drama. I wanted peace. For me. For Davie.

"This is it," she said as if making a threat. "You won't be seeing me ever again."

I almost laughed. We were a spectacular crash and burn, Jeannette and I. But then again, it had all led to Davie. So there was that. "Bye, Jeannette. Have a nice life."

She cut her eyes at me at first, then faced me, resigned. Wrapping her arms around her waist, she stared at the torn letter on the ground, her voice barely audible. "Bye, Francine."

I got into my car and drove off. I didn't bother looking into the rear-view mirror to see if she was watching. I kept my gaze straight ahead.

CHAPTER THIRTY-TWO

T hat movie had absolutely no plot."

   "Yo, that movie changed people's lives. Plot is beside the point."

"That movie was boring as hell and you know it."

Kenji and Aunt Liane were arguing about a movie I hadn't seen. They'd discovered they liked bantering and went at it over any given topic.

"It's called art," said Kenji.

"It's called boring if you ask me."

"It won an Oscar, yo!"

Aunt Liane raised her brow at Kenji. "Don't nobody care about no Oscars."

We were sitting on the deck, eating pizza. I'd let Davie choose whatever he wanted for dinner. He asked for strawberry ice cream for our main course and pizza for dessert. Fine by me; it was his official move-in day.

We ate beneath the trellis lights. In Mom's honor I played her favorite disco songs. Davie and I made a bouquet using flowers from her garden and put them in the center of the table next to the Aunt Jemima cookie jar.

While Davie was away at camp, Kenji and I planned to visit SFMOMA and work on an art project together. I was also going to fly to LA and visit the Los Angeles County Museum of Art, or LACMA for short, which would mark my first time on a plane. According to Pamela, it was high time I started getting out more and getting to know myself. I'd stay for a week, fly back, then visit Davie at camp, where I'd have a chance to meet Mr. Science. *God help me.* I still found that man annoying as hell.

I thought of Jeannette while we ate our pizza. Arizmendi's pizza was her favorite. I wondered about the letter she'd written and if I'd made a mistake by not reading it. Then I told myself to stop. *Just stop, Francine. Look around. Stay present.*

So I took a deep breath, inhaling through my nose, exhaling through my mouth. Eve was talking with Uncle CJ and filling his glass with iced tea. Kenji and Aunt Liane were laughing now. Who knew those two would get along so well? Then Aunt Liane asked Davie if he wanted another slice of pizza. He raised a finger high in the air and told her yes. Kenji and Eve were coming by tomorrow to help paint his room and assemble the bookshelves I'd bought for him.

Another breath and I imagined Mom sitting with us. And my dad, too. And Davie's parents and Counselor Hayes. I have no idea what happens after death, but I had a feeling they were with us. I knew Mom was proud. I glanced at the bouquet of flowers on the table, the lilies and zinnias from her garden. That's when Davie met my eyes from across the table. He pulled back his lips and bared his teeth, his own sweet smile. I smiled right back.

ACKNOWLEDGMENTS

Special thanks to my agent, BJ Robbins, who has been with me from the beginning.

Lashanda Anakwah is the editor of my dreams. Thank you, Lashanda, for your insightful observations and invaluable feedback. Your belief in this story has meant the world. Huge thanks as well to Phoebe Robinson and the entire Tiny Reparations team. Thank you!

Kelly Allgaier, Emily Morganti, Eric Pfeiffer, and Molly Thomas read countless crappy drafts and miraculously did not kick me out of the writing group. You all are the best.

Thanks to Deborah Santana for reading an early draft and for your support; Don Weise also read an early draft and gave thoughtful feedback.

Allie Larkin and Regina Marler, knowing you both are only a text away means so much. Thank you for your kindness and friendship.

Joanne "Joa" Meiyi Chan, thank you for dreaming along with me. Here's to many more.

Thanks to Susan Carpendale for walks and tea dates; and Natalie Harris-Spencer for email exchanges and support. #OBWS

Acknowledgments

Thanks to Not Just Books—the book club of all book clubs! With a special thanks to Crystal Charleston for always checking in.

My academic son, Ricardo Lopez, who overcomes every hurdle with his signature humor and determination. You inspire me in ways you'll never know.

I'm deeply grateful to liz gonzález for all our talks over the years and her sisterly friendship.

Finally, I'd like to thank my parents for their support and encouragement.

ABOUT THE AUTHOR

Renee Swindle earned her BA from UC Irvine and her MFA in creative writing from San Diego State University. She lives in Oakland, California.